THROUGH THE DOOR

A Door to Door Paranormal Mystery

T.L. Brown

Copyright © 2021 Tracy Brown-Simmons

All rights reserved.

The characters and events portrayed in this book are fictitious. Any similarity to real persons, living or dead, business establishments, events, or locales is coincidental and not intended by the author.

No part of this book may be reproduced, or stored in a retrieval system, or transmitted in any form or by any means, electronic, mechanical, photocopying, recording, or otherwise, without express written permission of the publisher.

ISBN: 978-1-7359290-5-7

First Edition: May 2021

Book Cover Design by ebooklaunch.com
Created / printed in the United States of America

PRAISE FOR SERIES

Door to Door, by T.L. Brown

Lovable characters, intriguing mystery and a fresh approach to the cozy genre!
- Brook Peterson, author of A History of Murder (Jericho Falls Cozy Mystery Series)

With a novel premise, engaging characters, and a wholly original world, T.L. Brown's first-in-series will draw you through her magical doors - and refuse to let you go...
- Book review site Jill-Elizabeth.com

Through the Door, by T.L. Brown

T.L. Brown throws us right into the thick of things from the opening pages. With her characteristic wit and humor, we find ourselves right back in the world of doors and magical objects and people who are definitely not all that they seem...
- Book review site Jill-Elizabeth.com

BOOKS IN THIS SERIES

Door to Door (Book One)
Through the Door (Book Two)
Doors Wide Open (Book Three)
 - *Coming in 2021!*

*for all of the friends
who say yes! to the journey…
especially when the going gets tough*

CONTENTS

Title Page
Copyright
Praise for Series
Books In This Series
Dedication

CHAPTER 1	1
CHAPTER 2	17
CHAPTER 3	36
CHAPTER 4	53
CHAPTER 5	73
CHAPTER 6	92
CHAPTER 7	117
CHAPTER 8	140
CHAPTER 9	164
CHAPTER 10	190
CHAPTER 11	209
CHAPTER 12	229

CHAPTER 13	248
CHAPTER 14	268
CHAPTER 15	286
CHAPTER 16	309
CHAPTER 17	324
CHAPTER 18	342
CHAPTER 19	359
CHAPTER 20	378
CHAPTER 21	393
CHAPTER 22	413
EPILOGUE	421
Acknowledgements	425
Find T.L. Brown Online	427
Books In This Series	429
About The Author	433

CHAPTER 1

After several weeks of slipping, sliding, and crashing to my knees, I was getting better at staying on my feet during door travel. I'd start by sending out my energy as a kind of feeling to find a door that was receptive to it. Once I discovered which door could serve as a portal, I could sense its power zipping up from the bottom in thick rivers before hitting the top of the doorframe and zooming down the sides. The handle vibrated with the invitation – *c'mon in Emily, this is the right door.*

Sometimes the doors rattled; other times they buzzed or hummed. But they all threw off the vibration I sought when looking to move from where I was to where I needed to be. The 'right' door was easy to find. My heightened awareness dialed in quickly. Actual door travel was never hard for me. Even destination accuracy was improving after a rocky start.

But the arrival? Brutal.

As the first and only child of the late Salesman Daniel Swift – that's Salesman with a capital 'S' – I inherited this unique ability to travel from place-to-place simply by stepping through a door. The discovery came after a series of unplanned travels took me to unexpected destinations. Some were fairly tame, like ending up in my bathroom instead of the pantry. Others were more frightening, taking me from my hometown in Upstate New York, to a back alley in a strange world called the Empire. As I learned about my legacy, I began to understand it wasn't just about finding the 'right' door. Much responsibility came with my new role.

As a Salesman, I'm part of a network of travelers who transport magical and mundane items from those who sell them, to those who buy or barter for them. As the daughter of Daniel Swift, I'm also responsible for protecting the Empire against the Fringe – a terrorist group of rogue Salesmen seeking absolute power. Their violence is notorious. They assassinated my father when I was thirteen.

I learned all of this in the weeks following my thirtieth birthday. Now, several months later with a disgraced Justice of the Salesman Court awaiting trial, I find myself spending my free time learning more about the Empire and my role as a Salesman. I've also been assigned a mentor, one Josephine Carter, who is trying to help me get a grip on my door traveling energy while pressing the rules and regulations of door travel into my brain.

My name is Emily Swift and I'm a Salesman. It's springtime and this is where my story picks up.

❊ ❊ ❊

"What I need you to do is raise your energy to find the right door, direct the energy to move into a tunnel of power, but then reign it back before you arrive so that you're not shooting through the door to the other side. You need to recognize when to center and still the power so you arrive as if stepping into a room, not blasting in like a S.W.A.T. team." Jo punctuated the description of what I needed to do with a series of gestures. Put a baton in her hand and from a distance you'd think she was directing a symphony.

"I understand what you're saying," I replied. "But it's over so fast. I touch the doorknob and BAM! I'm through it to the other side. I'm not trying to rush."

Jo cocked her head to the side. "I understand what you're describing. What I'm telling you is that you can control the energy. Raise, channel, direct, pull back."

"Maybe I should try to pull back before I channel it."

"Maybe. And maybe you'll end up taking a wrong turn." She raised her eyebrows.

I blew out a breath in response. "I've gotten much better. Plus, I think the issue is less about pulling back too early and more about... I don't know. Just getting shoved through the wrong door when arriving."

Jo shook her head. "No, it's not." She stood and began to pack up her paperwork, sliding documents into a folder before putting it into her briefcase. She snapped it shut and looked up at me with a smile. "But you will get there. I have no doubt. You need to keep studying. Continue to practice raising and lowering the energy when you are calm, when you are meditating. Harness it."

I rolled my eyes. "Harness it. It's a beast."

"I get it, Emily," Jo said. "And, I suspect you have a significantly high level of energy designed for door travel. That's why you were traveling before you even knew you could. Your excitement, your fear – all of that fueled the power Salesmen need." She paused, pushing a ginger lock of hair behind her ear. "But excuses are not going to cut it. Dedication to study and practice will move you toward mastery. Without it, the Court will never approve you for door travel by yourself. You don't want me following you around forever, do you?"

"I know," I sighed. "I'm just frustrated."

"You'll get beyond that," she said. "Friday we're heading to a local flower shop to introduce you to the owners, Gertrude and Bernard Bloom. Nothing to pick up or deliver, but *Petaling* provides the magical community with some of the more hard-to-find plants they use. Lovely people. They've been anxious to meet you. They knew your father."

"Really?" I hadn't met any local vendors who were a part of my father's network. This was news to me. I told Jo.

"Then this will be a nice treat for you both. We'll meet here at Blackstone's at nine in the morning and travel straight to their shop."

Rene Blackstone lived in a wealthy part of Kincaid. He was a Record Keeper who helped log history for the Empire, as well as cataloged the items Salesmen carry. He was the Warden of the North Door which led to Matar, a city in the Empire. Jo and I met twice weekly in his library as part of my training. Blackstone was not a Salesman but served as my first resource for gathering information about my father – and my future. He'd also been attacked when the Fringe invaded his home last December. His housekeeper, Elsa, was killed.

Blackstone was instrumental in having Jo assigned as my mentor. He knew the Empire desired a firm hand to teach me, but he also knew I'd do better with a tough-but-fair Salesman who could guide me. Enter Jo.

She was at the top of her class when she entered the Salesman ranks. An accomplished lawyer, Jo lived in New York City with her husband and teenage daughter. She had a fast mind and a sharp eye. She pulled no punches and didn't shy away from providing criticism if she believed it was necessary. She was also kind.

During this mentorship, Jo and I traveled together once or twice a week. While I was prohibited from traveling by myself until the Empire approved me, I was allowed to travel with a Senior Salesman. At first, we started with simple departures and destinations. She'd take my hand and we'd practice going from Blackstone's library to my kitchen at home. Even with Jo's control it was a jarring experience for both of us. My travel energy was wild. The first time we traveled I think I nearly dislocated her shoulder. The second time she was prepared, but we always arrived as if riding the offspring of a bullet train and a roller coaster. We both looked shell-shocked when we were on the other side of the 'right' door.

After the back and forth between Blackstone's house and my home, I graduated to traveling from Blackstone's library to my best friend Tara's bookstore in downtown Kincaid. Our destination was the storage room of *Pages & Pens*. Jo encouraged me to travel by myself first; her plan was to follow me. After I ripped through the universe and ended up in the breakroom of a wine shop a block away, I found myself explaining to a confused employee that I was just looking for the bathroom.

It was the best I could come up with in the moment.

Undaunted, Jo was not about to give up on me traveling by myself. We weren't going to go back to partner travel. We set up a series of departures and destinations as practice. Personally, I think Jo was worried she'd end up with a torn rotator cuff. She was not eager to return to hand-holding.

With practice, I was getting more accurate traveling in front of Jo. When intending to door travel from home to my friend Anne's apartment, my wrong turn only dumped me in Anne's bedroom instead of coming in through her front door. At least I tumbled onto a pile of laundry when I arrived. But the clothing must have reacted to the residual energy from my door travel. I walked into the living room pulling off Anne's socks and underclothes as the static cling... well, *clung*. Jo was standing in Anne's living room, hands on hips. Anne laughed when she saw me. Jo did not. She shook her head and told me I had to work on my focus.

Which brings us back to today's training session at Blackwell's. Jo picked up a dark blazer and slipped it on over her fit frame. I wondered if she'd come from a lawyerly meeting that morning. She was dressed sharp in a black pencil skirt and a light taupe blouse with capped sleeves. The top showed off the defined triceps in her arms. No underarm wattle for Jo. I watched as she picked up her top hat, a demure piece with a short stack and a cream-colored ribbon that wrapped around it, brought together with a flat, rectangular bow sitting on the right side. She pointed her hat at me.

"And remember to bring your hat."

"Will do," I said. Salesmen received an official top hat permitting door travel when recognized by the Salesman Court. I'd received mine at the end of last year, a stylish design with a purple feather and a pink bow. It was incredibly feminine. While I didn't typically seek out such frilly items, I'd seen it in an antique store while traveling through the Empire. It brought back both good and sad memories.

"Wonderful. I'm off then. Review the section on regulations surrounding the transport of horticultural items, with an emphasis on the magical. Remember, you will be transporting mundane plants as well, but even those require an understanding of what is allowed and what is not, as well as what governing body you might need to contact prior to delivery." She put her hat on her head and adjusted it. "If you need anything between now and Friday, send me a message."

"Okay, thanks." I walked her to the door leading out of Blackstone's library. Jo gave me a side hug before switching her briefcase to her left hand.

"Great. Well, I'm off then." With that, Jo put her hand on the doorknob, glanced back at me with a raised eyebrow as she opened the door, and gracefully stepped on through. The door closed behind her with the softest *Click!*

I sighed. As tempted as I was to look, I didn't. I knew Jo had traveled from Upstate to Downstate in a blink of an eye. She was probably back in her apartment or maybe she'd returned to her office. She always made it look effortless.

When I door traveled, my sense was I resembled a cartoon character being pulled through a tornado with hair flying and lips flapping.

Blackstone indicated he'd be out for the morning, so I picked up my bag and snagged my coat as I exited the library by the same door. I did not door travel but walked into the room just outside the library which housed the various monitors providing a watchful eye over the house. And yet, I never saw anyone in the room keeping an eye on the screens. I mentioned this to Blackstone. He offered a vague explanation about how the Empire wasn't able to staff the various doors leading directly into it like it had in the past. I was surprised in light of recent events proving that the Fringe, though deeper underground than years prior, were still active in their quest for absolute power.

I made my way through Blackstone's house to

the outside. The sun was shining but the air was still cold. A curved driveway led up to the big brick house. My old Subaru was parked close. I hopped inside and headed for home.

❊ ❊ ❊

When I first sat down with Jo and started to go over the nuts and bolts of door travel, I learned that the 'right' door was not necessarily a door leading to one specific place at all times. No, the 'right' door was simply the door you could more strongly tune into and travel through. If there were five doors on a wall, any door might take me to my favorite restaurant. It depended on which door I could connect with the best in the moment. I could go through door three and travel to Buffalo. I could use the same door and travel to Anne's new café in downtown Kincaid. Door travel wasn't without limitations, however. Salesmen weren't allowed to door travel into restricted places. In other words, visiting the White House without permission was a big no-no.

What Jo and I didn't talk about is how I started door traveling before I even knew such a thing existed. This is where the natural talent kicked in. Not exactly a diamond in the rough, but there might be a speck of something sparkly inside me. Recent events certainly pointed in that direction.

While I was finding out about a whole new world called the Empire, I was chased – yet thwarted capture – by the Fringe; connected to a murder case involving Blackstone's former housekeeper; held at gunpoint by a power-hungry justice; and recovered a hidden magical gemstone called the Crimson Stone.

I also met Templeton, a Salesman with exceptional abilities and questionable motives. He knew about me before I even knew he existed. He visited me in both dreams and public spaces before I finally caught up to him and drew a line in the sand.

My father had written in his travel journal – also known as The Book, capital 'T,' capital 'B' – that he wondered if Templeton was a friend or not. Despite our last encounter and Templeton's role in helping me stop the bad guys, the jury was still out.

I hadn't heard from him in over four months. This was probably a good thing. I did wonder what he was up to, though. Prior to my turning thirty, no one in the Empire had seen him in years. Templeton was powerful and there were rumors of an affiliation with the Fringe when my father was alive many years ago. Some believe he was on the train right before my father was killed in the explosion.

Many were surprised when he resurfaced. His

actions sometimes worked against me. Templeton sought the same magical gemstone as I did and it was a race between the Fringe, Templeton, and me to find it. The Fringe almost got it, Templeton had it, and I walked away with it. Well, a piece of it.

I didn't ask Blackstone if he knew of Templeton's whereabouts these days and he offered no updates. I didn't ask Anne, owner of a destroyed café in Matar, if she'd heard anything new. I didn't reach out to Templeton through dreamwork. I didn't want to encourage him to start playing cat and mouse in my head again.

But I did wonder where he disappeared to after we parted ways.

❉ ❉ ❉

"How'd it go today?" Jack inquired as he set the table.

I finished putting the cat food into the bowls on the counter. "You know, the Empire looms large, I need to focus on controlling my energy, it's a huge responsibility, blah blah blah."

"It's what you need to do so you can door travel by yourself, right? Learn how to do it without causing trouble, don't break any rules?"

"Yeah," I answered. William, my big boy and the largest of the three Furious Furballs, wound his way around my ankles adding a loud meow to hurry me along. I balanced the three bowls in my hands as I stepped over him to set his bowl down in the dining room. Mystery would be fed in the living room, away from William so he could eat in peace. Mischief required her dinner upstairs. She would be waiting. Anyone with house cats understands this type of human behavior.

The Furballs fed, I returned to the kitchen. Jack set a big bowl of mashed potatoes on the table by the meatloaf. We were going old-school tonight. We even had canned peas.

"Friday we're going to travel together to a florist here in Kincaid," I told him. "There are several local businesses using Salesmen to deliver some of their products. *Petaling* is one of them."

"Special products?" Jack raised an eyebrow.

I put my finger to the tip of my nose. "But we won't be transporting anything on Friday. That'll come later."

"This is just a meet and greet, then?"

"Yup."

"Good." My boyfriend was trying hard to be supportive. He was balancing encouragement and worry – a result of the danger I found myself thrust into after receiving The Book on my last birthday. We didn't tiptoe around the subject, but Jack was in no hurry for me to dive fully into the role of a Salesman. I promised him once I passed the exam, I'd pick and choose what work I took on for the Empire. At least I hoped I'd be able to do that.

"Tomorrow morning I'll work at Anne's. In the afternoon it's back to work for *Swift Services*." I'd run my own copywriting business for over five years. I was modestly successful, but I took on a part-time gig working for Anne. She recently moved to Kincaid and opened a café called *The Daily Brew Too*.

"Still wishing you could just step through the door and walk into *Brew Too* without Jo?" Jack grinned.

"You know it," I said. I reached for the bottle of wine sitting on the table. I smiled. "Hopefully soon."

※ ※ ※

It would be so much easier if I could door travel back and forth between home and Anne's café. New York weather was up to its old tricks and the temps took another nasty dive into the low thirties after sending about four inches of wintry mix our way overnight. Welcome to spring. I piled on the layers before heading out: thick sweater, pea coat, scarf, knitted gloves, a matching knit hat, and boots lined with sheep's wool.

My Subaru took pity on me during the drive downtown to the more eclectic part of Kincaid, the heater blasting a lukewarm stream of air at my face. It was after seven and traffic was heavy with commuters. I kept a wary eye on my rearview mirror. The roads were slick enough to turn my tailgater into a back seat passenger.

As I drove, I thought about how the past few months had turned my world on its ear. I still wasn't sure what to do with all I knew. People rushing by on the sidewalk couldn't begin to imagine what was happening all around them, right under their noses – mysterious people; strange places that don't exist on any map they've ever seen; magical items being traded, bought and sold, and stolen.

Then again, I wondered, what secrets do they keep to themselves?

I drove past the grocery store and under the train trestle, taking the same shortcut everyone else knew. As the road curved and swept up to meet one of the main arteries running through the city, the weather band in my car radio screeched out static, jarring me from my musings. The silence that followed was interrupted by the weather band's mechanical voice.

"This is the NOAA Radio Weather station. The time is now seven-fifteen. Emily Swift, the Fringe is watching you."

My first instinct was to slam on the brakes – which I did. I slid in the road slop and lost control of the car for a moment. The SUV behind me turned the wheel hard and bounced into the curb before jerking back onto the road. The two vehicles behind him cranked the wheel and edged into the oncoming lane before swinging back into ours. My foot zoomed back to the gas pedal and I kept moving. Traffic rebounded and everyone got back on track as my heart stayed lodged in my throat.

What in the hell was that?

I glanced in my rearview mirror at the jerk behind me. He was now hanging back. That'll teach him to tailgate.

CHAPTER 2

"Wait, it said what? Are you sure?" Anne Lace offered her customer a smile as she handed over his coffee and vanilla sugar cookie. "Thanks. Good to see you, Adam!" Anne had an uncanny knack for remembering people's names from the first time they came into her café.

"It said 'Emily Swift, the Fringe is watching you.' I'm telling you, Anne, I did not imagine it." I was still a bit unnerved by the experience.

"I believe you. This sounds like something you should tell Blackstone about right away," Anne said.

"Tell Blackstone about what?" Tara came into the café and leaned against the counter. She was buried under a layer of orange knit. Her soft, brown eyes grew wide. "Ooh, what trouble are you getting into now?"

"No trouble," I said. "But I swear, when I was driving this morning the weather band in my radio made this horrible noise before saying my name and telling me the Fringe is watching me."

Tara grimaced. "That doesn't sound good."

"That's my point." I wiped the counter with a damp rag. "I don't know what to think. I don't know if it's a warning *from* them or a warning *about* them."

"It could be either," Anne nodded.

"Did you tell Jack yet?" Tara asked.

"No. Things finally settled down. I'd hate to rock the boat right now." I finished wiping the same clean spot on the counter before tossing the rag into a bucket underneath it.

Anne took my hand and gave me a kind smile. "Emily, things are not going to return to the way they were. Jack will have to accept that. And he will."

"He will," Tara echoed.

"Listen," Anne continued. "Call Blackstone. In fact, go now. Go out to Northgate and find out what you can. You're not going to do yourself any good waiting here until the end of your shift."

I nodded. She was right. "Yeah, I need to do this."

I removed my apron and walked to the back room where I hung it up on a peg. I grabbed my winter wear and headed back out to the counter.

"If Jack calls…" I began as I wrapped my scarf around my neck.

"You're with a customer and you'll call him back," Anne finished.

Perfect.

✽ ✽ ✽

The drive to Blackstone's was less eventful

than the morning commute. The temperature moved the mercury up a bit and the plows pushed the slush to the sides of the road. Ah, springtime in New York.

I left the weather band off. I didn't want to invite any more messages from my radio. The Book was home in the special wooden box Tara had gifted me, so there was no digging through the pages to see if I could find an answer – or at least a clue. It led me on some crazy chases and the words my father wrote were often cryptic, but in the end, it guided me to where I needed to go. After talking to Blackstone, I would hurry back home to look through it.

Blackstone's house at 1221 Northgate Way was quiet when I arrived. I drove through the always open gates and up the driveway. I parked in my usual spot and walked up to the front door. Ringing the bell, I waited.

His latest housekeeper, Patricia Pickelsimer, opened the door a few moments later. Patricia was hired after Elsa, Blackstone's former housekeeper, was killed by the Fringe.

"Emily," Patricia frowned, a vertical line appearing between her brows. "I thought we weren't expecting you until Friday."

"That's right," I said. "I'm not here to meet with Jo. I'm actually hoping to catch up with Mr. Blackstone. I had a strange experience this morning and I think I need to talk to him. It's important."

Patricia didn't move. She lingered in the doorway.

"Would now be a good time?" I asked.

She stepped to the side and motioned for me to come in. "Please wait here," she said as she disappeared from the foyer.

Granted, this was only the second housekeeper of Blackstone's I'd met, but Patricia was just as odd as Elsa had been – may her soul rest in peace. I wondered if Blackstone noted the same.

A few minutes later, he appeared. He hesitated for a moment when he saw me, then smiled. "Emily. Good to see you. Let's go to the sitting room. Patricia will bring some coffee unless you would like something else?"

"No, coffee is fine," I said. I handed Patricia my coat and scarf. Okay, something was off. I never set foot into Blackstone's sitting room. I always conducted Salesman business in his library downstairs.

The sitting room was comfortable with a small fireplace. It had been lit earlier, but now the fire was dying out. I took a seat at the end of the sofa. Blackstone sat across from me in a leather chair. It would've been cozy with a stronger fire.

"So, Emily," he began, "what brings you here? I know you're meeting Jo on Friday."

"I am. But something happened this morning and I didn't want to wait to talk to you about it." I stopped as Patricia returned and set down a tray with two filled coffee cups, a small carafe of cream, and a bowl with sugar cubes. There was a small plate of homemade peanut butter cookies. I picked one up before adding cream to my coffee.

"Thank you, Patricia," Blackstone said. He turned back to me as the housekeeper made her exit. "What happened?"

"This morning on my drive downtown to Anne's café, my car's weather band made a strange noise and then the mechanical NOAA voice said my name. It also said the Fringe is watching me."

Blackstone's eyebrows lifted as he added a cube of sugar to his coffee. "What exactly did this voice say?"

"That's it. It said: 'Emily Swift, the Fringe is watching you.' Then it stopped. Nothing more." I didn't like the way Blackstone was looking at me.

"Are you sure you didn't imagine something? Your mind was wandering, and the radio said something else?"

Something was definitely up. Blackstone wasn't one to question me or strange events. In fact, when I first met him and told him about the weird things that were popping up in my life, he was unfazed. He expected those extraordinary situations. It was me who had to learn to believe.

"I am sure," I stated. "I know what I heard."

"Then this is very troubling." He tapped his index finger against a bearded chin. "I've been made aware of some other activity."

Now we were getting somewhere. "What kind of activity?"

"The Salesman Court admits they've noted unapproved door travel," he answered.

"Which means?"

"Door travel with unregistered top hats."

A Salesman's top hat is registered with the Empire. It must be approved. I like to think of it as a car's license plate. If you have one and the registration is up to date, you are free to travel. If you don't have one, you can still drive the car, but it's likely you'll get caught by the authorities.

It's the same with a missing top hat during door travel. This is one way the Empire regulates its Salesmen. Although I have an approved top hat, you might say I've got a learner's permit right now. I'm still not sanctioned to travel without a Senior Salesman. If I do, somewhere in the Empire bells and whistles go off. Or so I'm told.

The top hat is more than just a license. It's also a conduit allowing you to more easily tap into the energy to door travel. It was explained to me this way: Picture a Salesman who used a door to travel to a particular place. If I need to go to that same place through that same door, I should be able to do so more easily because a trail's already been blazed. For some Salesmen who aren't as adept, this ends up being very helpful. For others, it's a nice addition, but not always necessary. It's like sprinkles on your ice cream.

"Do they know who's doing it? What doors? Where are they going?"

Blackstone held up a hand. "They don't know for certain who is traveling or why. They do know what doors have been used, but so far no door has been used more than once."

"But where are these Salesmen going?"

"There's been a significant amount of unauthorized door travel to Kincaid," he told me. "I was notified because I'm the Warden of the North Door and you know…" He waved his hand. "Because of last year's attack."

The attack that left Elsa dead, Blackstone unconscious, and an important book of fairytales missing. That book has never been recovered.

"When did you find this out?" I asked. Why didn't he tell me this right away?

"This morning." Blackstone looked down into his coffee cup. I could see he was holding back.

"Mr. Blackstone," I said. "What are you not telling me?"

He sighed and set his cup on the tray before sitting back and gazing at me. "Justice Beverly Spell came here before you arrived, Emily. Unless she's left – and she might have by now – she's reviewing some documents in the library downstairs. I received word late last night she would be visiting. She was here first thing this morning."

So that's why I was directed to the sitting room instead of the library. "She didn't want anyone to know she was here," I said.

Blackstone nodded. "She preferred the visit be kept quiet, Emily. She has valid concerns. For you and for the pieces of the Crimson Stone that are, shall we say, 'missing.'"

I averted my eyes. Blackstone knew as well as I did that not one of the three pieces of the Crimson Stone was missing. Spell had a piece, a man called Rabbit took a piece, and I kept the third. The intent was to keep the pieces separate from each other so they couldn't be united into the powerful magical gemstone sought by the Fringe. This was my decision. Although I made sure the trusted Justice was given a piece to protect, I knew she was unhappy I didn't hand over the entire Crimson Stone to the Empire.

The truth was the Fringe had infiltrated the Empire's highest body of ranking officials. I couldn't risk it falling into the wrong hands.

"She is also concerned for your safety," he emphasized. "You were targeted before. There is no guarantee the Fringe will let loose ends go."

"I understand," I said. "But it's been quiet since

we got the Stone back. There really hasn't been a lot of activity, at least not any I've heard about. Has there been?"

"Not until now," he said. "I think we should continue to operate as we have, of course. Jo reports you're doing well. She told me she's almost ready to recommend you for review. Once that finish line is crossed, you'll be able to travel without Jo and that will make a big difference for you. And yet, it doesn't remove the danger of the Fringe. You'll always have to be vigilant."

"It's not like I went looking for trouble the first time," I reminded him.

At this he smiled. "That's one perspective." He stood. "I really should get back to Justice Spell if she's still here. I'll let you know if I learn of anything else."

I joined him in walking to the door. Patricia stood in the foyer, my winter wear in hand. Blackstone held my coat for me as I slipped it back on. I thanked him.

"Emily, I'll tell Justice Spell about your experience with the weather band radio message. I don't know what to make of it, but if anything like that happens again, please let me know right away, day or night."

"I will," I said. Pausing before I left, I turned to Blackstone. "You know, when I mentioned this to Anne at the café, we talked about whether it was a warning from the Fringe or about the

Fringe. The message said the Fringe was watching me, not 'hey Emily, it's the Fringe and we're watching you.'"

"You might be splitting hairs there," he said. "But you do have a point. Maybe the warning is from a friend. Someone who can manipulate communication channels to deliver a message."

"Right. Maybe someone with magical abilities." I cringed a bit on the inside. Just this past December, Templeton sent me a text message in response to a note I'd written by hand in my father's journal. Don't even go there, I told myself.

"I believe we're thinking of the same person," he replied. "Let's not get ahead of ourselves. Keep in touch from now until Friday. I'll talk to you after you travel with Jo."

I nodded as I left.

I really needed to go home and check The Book. There had to be an answer – or at least one of its riddles to solve.

❊ ❊ ❊

The Book. My father's travel journal. My connection to my Dad. Seventeen years had passed since his death. I was only thirteen when he died – when he was killed. Until a few months ago, we thought the train wreck was an accident. After learning a bomb had been placed on the train with my father as the target, the dull sadness I'd carried for almost two decades resurfaced as a sharp stab to my heart. An accident was tragic; an assassination was evil.

I sat in my small home office and traced my finger over the faded, blue cover with the gold-embossed 'S.' Originally, I'd thought it stood for Swift, our last name. I came to realize it stood for Salesman. And my father, as a Salesman, stood for the Empire.

When I was confronted with something out of the ordinary, or even at a crossroads of sorts, I came to The Book. Now I was back. I opened it and began to page through.

I smoothed the old pages as I browsed past hand-drawn maps highlighting places like Matar and Vue. I reread some of the lines that became so important as I turned thirty and crossed the threshold into the Salesman world. My gaze fell upon a familiar note:

If a Rabbit has no tale, can he still tell a story?

I smiled. I wondered what Rabbit was doing now. The last time I'd seen him, he'd left with a piece of the Crimson Stone in his pocket. Getting a message to him would be difficult. Rabbits were so hard to find unless they wanted to be found. I also knew that Rabbit probably already knew about the Fringe's latest activity. His network was extensive, and he traded in information. And sandwiches.

The pages in The Book seemed to never end. Often when I flipped through, even in the earlier pages of The Book, I'd find a passage I couldn't remember seeing before. Some just seemed to be lists of items my father carried. Many of them, I'd learned, were magical objects.

Salesmen, for all their talents, cannot actually handle magical items. They transport them cautiously, wrapped in protective packaging depending upon the size and shape. This is common. What is not common is the ability for a Salesman to hold or use them. That's me. I can hold and use a magical object.

And so can John Templeton.

In fact, before me, he was the only Salesman in known history to be able to do so. He became powerful. When my father was still alive, Templeton entered the Salesman trade at nineteen. His talent for door traveling fast-tracked him into the ranks. My father took Templeton under his wing, recognizing the vulnerability of such a gifted young person entering the chaos of the Empire. But Templeton proved he belonged to no one. Not the Empire, and even though some wondered, not the Fringe either.

The Book revealed my father didn't know if Templeton was a friend or not. Still, I never found a passage warning me away from him.

My avoidance of Templeton was my own decision.

As I turned through some of the pages in the middle of the book, I noticed a word written in a heavy hand:

COMMUNICATION

Under the heading I read:

News will travel
Through many mediums
Sent by both
Friend and foe
Learning the difference
Makes all the difference.

And there you have it. My father's clear advice and direction. I sighed. Well, I didn't have an answer, but I had a place to start. Sort of.

I looked at the clock. I'd have time to visit Tara at *Pages & Pens*. I'd run back downtown and show her the passage. I'd also fill her in on what I'd learned at Blackstone's. Tara had a great mind for solving problems.

❊ ❊ ❊

It was a little after three when I walked into the bookstore. Tara's assistant, Marley, was staffing the counter and chatting with a customer. He waved as I walked by.

I pointed to the back and mouthed: *Is she back there?*

He nodded.

The bookstore specialized in rare and hard-to-find books. Tara managed the store for the owner who moved to Florida. She'd been running *Pages & Pens* successfully for years. She was an expert in her field.

Tara was on the phone taking a note when I entered the back room. The brightly lit space housed tables for book examination and packing special orders. A hutch was set-up for coffee and tea. A box of cupcakes topped with green frosting sat on the counter. They were dotted with colorful flower-shaped sprinkles, most likely to celebrate spring. Marley liked to bake seasonally.

I grabbed a cupcake and poured myself a passable cup of coffee before settling in on the couch. In a way, this space was Tara's living room. She probably spent more time here than she did in her apartment. She lived books.

"Thanks again, Matt," Tara spoke into her phone. "I appreciate the follow-up. What?" Her eyebrows drew together as she listened. Then, a sly smile slid across her face. "Sure, I might be free. Why don't I look at my calendar and we'll see when you're in town? I'll let you know. Okay, sounds good. Bye."

I dropped my head back and looked up. I don't know how she kept track of them all. Tara Parker-Jones was a petite, soft-featured woman approaching her thirtieth birthday. She was also a little vixen. Men could not escape her charm when she turned it on. They were bewitched by wide innocent eyes and baby-soft hair. One too many thought he could be her knight in shining armor. I knew better. She'd eat them for breakfast.

"Date night?" I spoke to the ceiling.

"Maybe. Matt's nice. Wears a suit well," she said. "But this is just casual. I'm pretty much considering it a business dinner." She shrugged. "So, what's going on? Did you talk to Blackstone?"

"I did," I answered, shifting my position so I was facing Tara. She sat down on the other end of the couch, pulling her legs up and curling into the corner. She balanced a cup of tea on her knee. I continued. "It was a weird visit. I found out some disturbing news while I was there."

"Not good."

"No, definitely not. Turns out Blackstone had a visitor this morning. Beverly Spell was there. She told him they're seeing a lot of suspicious door travel in the Empire. Some of it is spilling into Kincaid." I sipped my coffee. "I know it's the Fringe. Today's weather band radio message has to be connected."

"I'd bet on that," Tara said. "What was Blackstone's take?"

"I wasn't sure he believed me at first, but I think he was preoccupied. He told me to keep him informed if anything else happens. He said he'd do the same." I tapped the rim of the coffee cup with my finger. "But a part of me wonders how much he's going to share with me. Just a gut feeling. I think he's holding back."

"It wouldn't be the first time."

"True. Anyhow, I've been going through The Book." I put my coffee cup to the side and grabbed my bag. I'd brought The Book with me to show Tara. I pulled it out and used the tiny hat pin that served as the key to its lock and opened it. I paged through until I found the message under the heading COMMUNICATION. "Here."

Tara set her tea down on the coffee table before taking The Book. She read aloud:

"**COMMUNICATION**
News will travel
Through many mediums
Sent by both
Friend and foe
Learning the difference
Makes all the difference."

She shook her head. "Daniel Swift and his mysterious messages strike again."

"I wonder, though, if this is related to this morning's weather band message?" I replied.

"If that's true, this circles back to the question if the message was a warning about the Fringe, or a threat from the Fringe saying they're coming for you," she said.

"Exactly. It's easy to get fooled, but I'm still leaning toward a message from 'a friend.' But why tell me this way? That part doesn't make sense," I said.

"Well, if we go on the assumption it's someone trying to warn you to be careful, maybe they're in danger too. Maybe they don't have any other way to get a message to you."

"That's a good point," I said. A lightbulb went off. "Someone who deals in information and has a knack for hacking into networks and stuff."

"Yeah, but hacking into the radio?"

"Just go with it," I said. I knew exactly who might be able to break in and deliver a warning to me without magic. "Tara, maybe it was from Rabbit!"

"Ooh, maybe it was!" Tara turned a few pages. "Is there anything else? Anything new about Rabbit in The Book?"

If anyone other than Tara started going through my father's book – *my book* – I would pitch a fit. Well, Jack would be okay, but that's about it. Tara, I trusted completely. She was a part of my new world, even if it was only tangentially.

"Nope. Nothing new as of yet. But now I'm wondering if I should be reaching out to him."

"Can you send him a message? Use the Empire service?" she asked.

There was a number I could call, and a service in the Empire would deliver a message for me. But Rabbit had no real address. None of the Rabbits did. You couldn't just message a Rabbit.

Unless you were a Rabbit. They have an awesome network.

"Not an option. But I'll see what I can find out. Maybe Anne will have an idea," I said.

"You could always door travel to a last known address." Tara tried to be helpful.

"I could door travel if I had the go ahead from the Empire. I'm still working with Jo," I told her. "Maybe in a couple of weeks I'll be allowed to travel freely. But I don't think I'll find Rabbit in Anwat. I'm sure he's moved on."

Tara passed The Book back to me. "Well, I wish I could be of more help."

"Sometimes it's just good to sit with a friend," I said. I pulled out my phone and looked at the time. "I'd better get going. I'll let you know what I find out."

"Hey, if you need some company for a little trip…" Tara began.

I held up my hand. "No. We're not going to the Empire. It's definitely not a good time and I need to get a handle on everything first."

"Fine. Party pooper." Tara followed me out of the back room. "But if you change your mind…"

"Again, no," I said. Tara was persistent when she wanted something. Personally, I wouldn't be that eager to jump into someone else's mess. But that's Tara. She's always willing to join in. I also suspected she was itching for an adventure.

Marley's customer left and he returned to setting up a new display in the front window. He worked close to the door.

"Working at *Brew Too* tomorrow?" Tara asked as I pulled on my coat.

"No, I have to focus on some client work for *Swift Services*. I don't want to give that up." I buttoned my coat. "And I'll probably want to do some more research to figure out if the message I received has anything to do with the Fringe activity."

Tara nodded as she looked around her store evaluating its current state before her gaze shifted toward the front and Marley's work.

I concentrated on pulling on my gloves as the India bells on the door tinkled, announcing a new customer. Tara's eyes widened as she looked past me. A pretty little smile appeared on her lips.

"Well, hello," she cooed.

Curious, I turned to see who caused such a reaction. This 'customer' was the last person I expected to see crossing the threshold.

Templeton.

CHAPTER 3

"Seriously?" I asked.

Templeton stood just inside the door brushing a couple of wet snowflakes from his coat. He stopped for a beat; his eyes fixated on his sleeve. As if making a supreme effort, he looked up and scowled.

"Ms. Swift," he acknowledged, removing his top hat.

"What in the hell are you doing here?" I hiked my shoulder bag up higher and frowned. Months had passed since I'd seen Templeton. I'd heard nothing since he delivered my, well, my own top hat. Oh, how it grated on me. He made sure I got the top hat I wanted. I should be gracious. I should say thank you. I should even acknowledge how he jumped between me and a gun. Instead, I heard myself say, "I'd ask to what do we owe the pleasure, but there is none."

"Speak for yourself," said Tara as she slid past me and sauntered toward Templeton. She extended her hand. "Welcome to *Pages & Pens*. I'm Tara –"

"Parker-Jones," Templeton finished for her. He smiled. *Templeton actually smiled!* "It's nice to meet you, Ms. Parker-Jones. Your reputation in the rare and priceless books community precedes you. I've been meaning to come by and introduce myself."

"I'll forgive you for taking so long," Tara flirted.

"No! No, no, no," I interrupted as I walked between the two with my hands out. I turned to Tara. "Stop. This is Templeton."

"Yes, Emily, I know." She looked up and over my head. I am not tall. Templeton is.

"Marley?" I called, still glaring at my friend. "Don't you want to show Tara the display you're working on? Like right now?"

Marley was still at the front window watching the exchange. He finally found his voice. "He just walked in out of nowhere," he said. "There was no one on the sidewalk."

"Okay, show's over." I put my hands on Tara's upper arms and turned her around. "Let's go. Back to work for the busy rare books expert." I marched her toward the back of the store.

Tara craned her neck and called over her shoulder to Templeton. "Stop by on a Friday. If I'm here in the evening, I'll order some Thai food for takeout."

"No!" I pushed her through the door into the back room. "Enough."

"He is much better looking than I remembered," Tara said. She handily slipped from my grasp and tried to peek around me. I closed the door.

"Tara, that's Templeton!"

"I know," she said grinning. "I've decided I like him."

"No, you don't! No, *we* don't! We don't like him!" I waved my hands frantically. Wait a minute, what was Templeton doing here? I paused and took a breath. "Listen, Templeton is not to be trusted. There's no playing steamy 'temptress Tara' here."

Tara rolled her eyes at me, but then smiled. "I know. I just like to have fun."

"Well, he's not fun."

"Okay, I got it, I'll stop. Go. But if I walk out there in five minutes and he's still there, I'm giving him my phone number and telling him to use it." She lifted her chin. Then she winked.

Good grief. "Just stay here," I begged.

I spun around and returned to the retail space. Templeton had wandered farther into the store and was flipping through a not-so-rare book on the history of Kincaid. Marley sat behind the counter staring at him.

Templeton looked up when he heard the door. He must've been expecting Tara because he was still wearing that smile. He looked sort of handsome – in an arrogant jerk sort of way. It was unsettling. When he realized it was only me, the smile disappeared and the scowl returned. Much better.

"Don't tell me you ordered your friend to stay in the back. Oh, Emily, don't like Ms. Parker-

Jones sharing the limelight?" He tsked, then paused. "Wait, are you jealous?"

"You wish." I looked at Marley before addressing Templeton again. "Let's step... Um, outside."

"Or we could travel somewhere?" He suggested, his pale blue eyes narrowing. He took a verbal swipe at me. "Oh, that's right. Your babysitter isn't here. You're not fully approved by the Empire."

"Not fully approved yet," I corrected. I walked to the front and opened the door. "Meet you outside."

❋ ❋ ❋

I stood there for barely a minute with my back to the store. Templeton walked out of *Pages & Pens*, standing to the side behind me. I watched the cars driving past.

"What are you really doing here, Templeton?" I asked.

"Maybe I'm just checking up on you, see how you're faring these days," he mocked.

"No, you're not." I turned to face him. I wasn't afraid of Templeton anymore and I was annoyed. He calmly pulled on a pair of leather gloves. The friendliness he presented to Tara was long gone. I studied his face, the sharp angles, the thin nose. He had reduced the length of his sideburns – an improvement. Dark hair was still cut short. His lips pulled into a thin line. His chilly gaze met mine and I heard the rushing sound of wind fill my ears. A familiar sense of falling made me sway on my feet. I inhaled sharply and shook myself out of it. "Knock it off. You're here for a reason."

"I am."

"And?"

"Have you talked to your mother lately?"

"My mother?" I asked. I took a hard look at his expression. He revealed nothing, but I felt fear bloom in my chest. "What are you talking about? Wait, Templeton, what's going on? Is something wrong?"

When was the last time I spoke to my mother? Three days ago, a week? I started to frantically search for my phone. "What's going on?" I repeated, my voice raising. A couple passing by slowed and gave us a strange look. They eyed Templeton's top hat.

Templeton spotted the attention and reached out. He pulled me aside by my coat sleeve. "Stop it," he hissed. "You're making a scene. Listen to me."

I jerked my arm free. Ignoring Templeton, I called my mother. It started to ring.

"Answer, answer," I chanted. "Answer the phone, Mom."

"Hello! This is Lydia. I'm out and about, off and away, and sharing inspiration. Leave your name at the beep. Ta-tah!" My mother's voicemail greeting, though cheery, was not what I wanted to hear.

"Mom, it's me," I said. I looked down at the sidewalk. Marley had salted the pavement heavily and it would stain my boots. "Listen, I need you to call me immediately when you get this message. No waiting, got it? Call me." I ended the connection. Taking a deep breath, I looked up at Templeton. He watched me closely.

"Emily," he said, his voice low. "I'm not here to suggest that something happened to your mother. Stop jumping to conclusions. I'm here to talk to you about the unusual travel activity the Empire picked up. My guess is you're aware of it by now."

"Of course," I said. Templeton didn't need to know I'd just found out, or that if I hadn't gone to Blackstone's today, I'd probably still be in the dark at this point.

"With Kincaid being one of the destinations of this travel, that puts a certain piece of Stone at risk. Don't be fooled by the quiet left behind when the Fringe disappeared after Petrovich's arrest. They still want the Crimson Stone. They know you found it and kept Petrovich from taking it."

"How would they know that?" I began. "It's not like we announced it."

"If you think their reach no longer extends

into the Empire's top offices just because Petrovich lost power, you're foolish."

"I have no delusions, Templeton," I said.

Templeton's eyes wandered over the scenery behind me. I recognized his behavior. He was getting ready to leave.

I snapped my fingers in front of his face. He didn't flinch but sent me a hateful look. "Hey, not so fast. We're not done here."

"We are," he said. "But I want to be very clear with you, Emily. The Fringe will not stop until they get the Stone, and they will not leave you or your family unharmed. I would keep in closer contact with your mother."

"Even if they did take a piece of the Stone from me – if I still even have it – they can do nothing without Spell's piece or Rabbit's. I would think Spell has her piece under Empire lock and key, so that'll be impossible to get. And good luck finding a Rabbit who doesn't want to be found."

The air between us was cold and sharp, undisturbed until one of Kincaid's vicious wind gusts pummeled us out of nowhere. Templeton snorted and adjusted the front of his dress coat.

"Come to your senses, Emily. Give me your piece of the Stone and I'll protect it. You know I can." I watched as his attention moved to the door leading into a gift shop near *Pages & Pens*. He would be leaving.

"Not going to happen, Templeton," I said.

He shook his head and brushed by me on the way to the door. I felt a chill scurry down my spine upon contact. Templeton tends to do that to people. Well, at least to me. He placed his hand on the doorknob. He paused but didn't turn around. His words still reached my ears.

"You lack experience, Emily. You won't win this war with the Fringe even though you took the first battle. For all his talent and power, the mighty Daniel Swift still lost in the end." With that, he was through the door and gone.

Sudden tears stung my eyes. How dare he?

❖ ❖ ❖

"Mom? It's me again. Hey, I know you must've gotten my other messages by now. Can you call me? Please?" I left yet another voicemail for my mother.

After the Templeton encounter, I drove straight home. I didn't even go back into *Pages & Pens* to tell Tara about the exchange on the sidewalk. I was too upset.

Templeton's words cut into me. Although my Dad was more successful than many of the other Salesmen fighting the Fringe, he was still unable to defeat them. If my father, a revered and powerful Salesman could be defeated, what could inexperienced Emily Swift do? I wasn't even allowed to door travel by myself!

But I could handle magical items. Holding the Crimson Stone and stopping Petrovich proved my ability. And yet, that was all I knew about it.

Anne planned to find someone who'd be willing to talk to me about magical abilities I might have. With everything keeping us both busy in the past few months, nothing ever came of it. Maybe this was the time to see if there was someone I could learn from. I needed to follow up with her.

I sat on the end of my couch, The Book balanced on the wide arm. Mystery was dozing next to me, and William had settled in on the back of the couch, his jowly face squished between his front paws. William, like my boyfriend Jack, could sleep like the dead. I touched the top of Mystery's head and he opened his eyes, mouthing a meow up at me. The three of us were settled in and if my brain wasn't twisted in such turmoil, we would've made a lovely picture.

Jack texted me earlier. He was bogged down in a departmental meeting and wouldn't be home until after seven. He taught English at the local community college. While he loved his work, he hated the politics of higher education. His absence left me time to look through The Book to see what else I could learn.

I reread the passage under COMMUNICATION. Okay, so I'd keep my eye on what was coming from a friend and what was not. Got it. I turned several pages and looked at the hand-drawn map my father created so many years ago. Matar, Anwat, and Vue. These were now known to me. My fingertip glided over the map, tracing an imaginary trail – my recent journey – from Matar, to Anwat, skipping the Port of North, and landing in Vue. My eyes travelled back up the page to the Walled Zone. My father had drawn little points, little inverted V's overlapping one another. The sketch seemed to indicate mountains.

The Walled Zone was northwest of Matar and I'd yet to travel into the unknown territory. My father left a note southeast of Matar questioning if Rabbit might be there with a hidden cluster. A cluster was another way of describing a colony of Rabbits. I wondered if that might be a place to look for mine?

I turned pages past records of items my father once transported, random numbers, and other mysterious notes. A favorite was an odd statement in brackets:

<a door jam needs no jelly>

I had no idea what that meant, but it always made me smile.

A few pages later, I noted a new message, one I'd not yet seen:

Don't miss
The loudest Whis-

...per.

Hmm. That was interesting. Duly noted. I felt like it could be connected to the other COMMUNICATION message. I peeked at the clock sitting on the mantle. Jack would be home soon. I decided to turn on the oven to reheat some leftover meatloaf. Gently moving Mystery to the side, I climbed off the couch and went into the kitchen. Putting a pan into the oven, I set the temperature and called dinner done. I'd microwave a veggie to go with it.

A hidden cluster of Rabbits, I thought as I tapped the stovetop. I don't suppose the Empire might be able to deliver a message? Oh, what the hell. I decided to call.

I learned about this unusual relay service when my mother had The Book delivered to me for my last birthday. She called it her 'discreet delivery service.' I now understood it to be a part of the Salesman network. I could call it now and maybe a Salesman could deliver a message to the cluster. It was a long shot – an awfully long shot – but what did I have to lose?

My mother shared the number she'd used, and I'd put it into my phone. I called it now.

"Hello. May I help you?" The voice was sharp, as if the words were outlined in crisp edges.

"I hope so," I said. "I'd like to get a message to someone, um, located sort of between Matar and Anwat."

"Do you have an address?"

"Well, that's just it. I'm not really sure of the actual address."

"Is this to be sent to a business or a residence?"

"Residence. Definitely." I hoped that was correct.

"Very good. What information can you provide? We can look up the address."

"Great. That would be great. Um…" I faltered. "Well, I have a note that says it's a hidden cluster of Rabbits."

"Rabbits?"

"Yes. It's sort of to the southeast of Matar."

"Rabbits," the voice said again.

"Yeah, I don't suppose any of that is helpful."

"It is not. Rabbits are not easily found, even by our superior service."

"Okay, well, I wasn't sure, but I thought I'd give it a try," I said.

"Very good. Will that be all?"

"Yes, I guess so." I sighed.

"Very good. Have a nice day." And the voice was gone.

Well, that was a bust.

❊ ❊ ❊

At quarter to eight, I decided to perch on the arm of Jack's Morris chair and watch for his car. An occasional vehicle drove by, lights flashing against the window through the dark. Jack was not one to run late. After the day I'd had, I could not help but feel worried. I breathed a sigh of relief when I saw his car pull into the driveway. I returned to the kitchen to pull the meatloaf from the oven. A few minutes later, Jack came into the house. He stopped at the refrigerator long enough to retrieve a jar of Spanish olives and pull a bottle of gin from the freezer. Walking past me to the dining room, he swiped a glass from the buffet and poured himself a martini. Two olives plunked into the liquid. He didn't even bother to hover the vermouth bottle over the glass.

"Rough meeting?" I teased.

Jack turned to face me. His expression made my heart drop. He shook his head no.

"Jack, what's wrong?" I crossed the room and put my hand on his arm. "What happened?"

"Someone tailgated me from the college all the way home tonight. They stayed right on my bumper the whole time, even on the inner loop. I'd speed up, so would they. I'd slow down so they'd pass, but no. Right on my tail." He took a swig of his drink.

"Okay," I nodded. "That's pretty jerky. But you're home now." I didn't like this.

"They got off the exit right behind me. I decided to drive all the way around a block to test. They followed me. I drove in the opposite direction of the house. Then I thought, I'll just drive to a police station and pull in. So, I did. They kept going." Another swallow of the martini. "I started to head home, and everything was fine until I turned onto our street. Again, a car right on my backend. They kept going when I turned into the driveway."

"Are you sure it was the same car?" I asked.

"Not a hundred percent, no. But I just know it was." Jack looked at his drink before setting it on the dining room table. William had wandered in and curled his grey tail around his calf. Jack picked him up. William rubbed the top of his head against the five o'clock shadow on my boyfriend's chin before turning his furry face toward me and sending a look of disdain my way.

Now, after the craziness I'd experienced a few months ago, I promised Jack I'd tell him everything. Anything strange that happened to me, I was to let Jack know. This was different. I didn't want to upset him more. And frankly, I was pretty rattled by his story.

"Do you think it was a student since it started at the college?" I asked. It was a fair question. Jack was well-liked, but you never know what got into people.

"I suppose it could be," he answered. "But it doesn't have to be. Anyone could've been parked in that lot."

"Do you think they were waiting for you?" I

worked to keep my voice calm.

"I don't know, Emily." He set William down and picked up his drink. "Is there anything you want to tell me? Anything I should know?"

And there it was.

"No," I answered. That was true. There was nothing I wanted to tell him. Plus, I still didn't have all the facts. Sure, both Blackstone and Templeton revealed there was unauthorized travel coming to Kincaid, and yes, the weather band message was, well, significant, but telling Jack right now was not a good idea. Besides, as scary as the tailgating was, I had no proof it was Fringe-related. Jumping to that conclusion would just make things worse.

"But my mother isn't answering her phone and that's bothering me," I finished.

Jack frowned. "Are you really worried? Is there someone you can call?"

Now that was an idea. "Actually, yes," I said. "Let me look up one of her neighbor's numbers."

I did a quick search online and found a number for her next-door neighbor, Judy. I called and explained I hadn't heard from my mother in the past few days. I wondered if she'd look to see if my Mom was home.

"Hang on, Emily," Judy said into my ear. "Let me look out the window. I can see the driveway from here."

"Thanks," I replied. "Sorry to bother you."

"No bother," Judy said. A moment later she was back. "Nope, no car. I think she's out. The car wouldn't be in the garage because of her latest project."

"Which is?"

"The welding."

"Still with the welding?" I asked.

"Yes, they hauled out a pretty mammoth piece about a week ago. Carried it off on a short trailer," Judy said. My mother, Lydia McKay Swift, was kind of an artist. She dabbled in all sorts of mediums – painting, sculpting, interpretive dance. The welding had been going on for months. "You know what a one-track mind your mother can have when she's in a creative zone. She's probably just caught up in her work right now."

"Sure," I answered. "That's probably why she's not answering her phone. Still, if you see her, will you tell her to call her daughter? I need to catch up with her."

"Will do. No problem."

"Thanks." I ended the call and directed my attention back to Jack. "Her neighbor says she's not at home. No car in the driveway."

"Try her again tomorrow." Jack finished his drink. He looked longingly back at the bar and shook his head. "I'm going to take a shower. I'm done with this day." He stepped closer and kissed my forehead.

"No dinner?" I asked.

"Do I smell leftover meatloaf?"

I nodded.

"Then yes." Jack headed for the stairs and I looked down at William. I swear, he was giving me the eye. I looked up and saw Mystery sitting on the arm of the couch. One paw rested on the cover of The Book. He offered his silent meow.

I sat down at the dining room table. "I know," I told my two boys. "But until I get a better idea of what is going on, I'm not involving Jack."

CHAPTER 4

First thing Thursday morning, I called my mother.

"Okay, Mom," I said into the phone. "I am so mad at you right now! You need to call me or I'm driving in to check on you. Call me A.S.A.P." I hung up. I hesitated. I wasn't done.

Jack stood drinking a cup of coffee, watching me as I punched my mother's number back into my phone.

"And if I drive all the way in and you're home and just too caught up in whatever to answer the phone, I'm going to pitch a fit!" I hung up a second time.

"Such a lovely daughter," Jack commented.

"Look, you know how she is. It puts me in the worst position. She gets flighty and I know I'm going to end up wasting time driving out there today. Then again, if something has happened to her, I'll never forgive myself." I swallowed the last bit of my coffee – and guilt – and followed it with a bite of bagel. On top of my frustration, I was terribly worried.

"I take it you're skipping *Swift Services* work?"

"Yes. I have to. I need to check in on her," I answered.

"Can you take someone with you?" Jack asked.

"Maybe Tara or Anne?"

"It's short notice for both of them. Tara might be able to pull it off though if Marley is working. I'll ask her. When we get to my mother's house, she can be a buffer."

"That's a good idea." He looked at his watch. "And I think I'll go in a little early today to read a few essays before my first class. Beat the rush."

"Still rattled from last night?" I asked.

He shrugged. "A little. Mostly mad. I wish I would've been able to figure out the make and model. But it was too dark, and the lights were right in my back window."

"If it happens again, do the same thing. Drive to a police station. Maybe go in?"

"I'm sure it was a one-off," he said. "Alright, I'm leaving." He rinsed his coffee cup out in the sink and then leaned in to give me a kiss. "Text or call me when you know what you're doing. Let me know what's going on with Lydia."

"I will," I said. I wrapped my arms around his waist and kissed him back. I adored Jack. We'd been together for many years and the thought of him being threatened wasn't one I wanted to entertain. "I love you."

He smiled. "Love you too, Em."

I let him go and he retrieved his coat from the closet. He pulled up the collar, sighing. Jack was not a fan of cold weather. I handed him the soft leather bag holding his laptop. As I watched him leave, I tried to let go of any worrisome thoughts. Right now, I had to focus on nailing down my mother.

I texted Tara, briefly explaining my plans and asked if she wanted to join me on the drive to my mother's house. A few minutes later she texted a *'Yes!'* Her message also said she'd be waiting at *Pages & Pens* with two coffees from *Brew Too.*

I hurried through a shower and blow dry before putting on a pair of jeans and a sweater. The weather outside my window, though slightly warmer than the day before, didn't promise much in the way of a spring day. The world was still filled with cold and damp and dirty slush. I wished for sunshine on the road trip. Maybe it would brighten my outlook.

Mischief watched me brush my hair from her spot on the dresser. She was a pretty little kitty with white fur. She was also a princess. William and Mystery avoided her and her hissy fits. I ran my hand along her back as she purred.

"You understand," I told her. "Right? There's nothing really to tell Jack at this point."

Mischief turned and head-butted my hand. She purred louder, licked my finger, then bit me.

"Exactly," I answered.

❋ ❋ ❋

I didn't even have to text Tara when I arrived

at *Pages & Pens*. She was on her phone watching out the window. I double-parked and put on my blinkers. Tara disappeared from the window for a moment, then reappeared as she left her store, carrying a container tray with two coffees.

"Hey," she said as she climbed into the car. I took the coffee tray from her while she tossed her bag into the back and buckled herself in. "Perfect timing. Marley's going on and on about a blind date no-show. I felt bad, but I couldn't listen to it this morning."

"Poor Marley," I said. Tara took a cup of coffee and I placed mine in the car's cupholder.

"Lattes," Tara noted nodding toward my cup. "Anne's not quite up to *The Green Bean's* standards, but I'd feel too guilty buying coffee from them now."

In the past, Tara and I would hit up *The Green Bean* often for awesome lattes and excellent quiche. However, after Anne moved to Kincaid and opened her café, we made the switch.

"I don't know what it was about the *Bean*," I agreed. "But you know, if we ever feel like quiche, we should go. That's not on Anne's menu yet. Then we can get lattes without the guilt."

"We should. Hey, let's bring Anne and the three of us will try to break down the lattes and see if Anne can copy what they do," Tara said.

"I'll let you start that conversation." I navigated through the intersection and headed for the highway. "Maybe, hey Anne, about your lattes. Let's go to your competition and see if you can figure out how to do what they do."

"Funny," Tara said. "But a good business owner learns from her competition. A great business owner learns and does it better."

"Good advice," I replied. I merged into the traffic. Now that the morning commuters were out of the way, it wasn't bad. I checked my rearview mirror. I decided to keep an eye out just in case I was being followed. Nothing seemed unusual.

"So, what's going on? Wait, start with Templeton. What happened yesterday?"

"You mean after my best friend betrayed me?" I ran the windshield wipers when a truck passed me and threw road crud on my car.

"Get over it," Tara laughed. "You know, I never really got to see him up close. I just saw him that one time and he was across the room. Oh! That was at the *Bean*, wasn't it?"

"Yup."

"Anyhow, he's pretty good-looking, don't you think? You know, in an aristocratic throwback sort of way."

"I don't really look at Templeton and consider his looks. I'm wondering what he wants," I said.

"Well? What does he want?"

"Other than to annoy me? He wants the Crimson Stone." After returning from my adventure in the Empire last year I told Tara about everything, including my piece of the Stone.

"So, nothing new then," Tara answered. "Weird for him to show up only for that, though."

"And he also wanted to know if I knew about the strange happenings with the unauthorized door travel. He also thinks – well, knows – it's the Fringe."

"Did you tell him you talked to Blackstone about it?"

"I didn't give him details, but I told him I was aware of the problem."

"What else?" she asked.

"What do you mean?"

"You're gripping the steering wheel like death is on our tail." She leaned over and looked at the speedometer. "You're also pushing seventy-five. I normally wouldn't care so much, but I'd say you're going a tad too fast for conditions."

I backed my foot off the gas pedal and dropped my speed. "I'm sorry."

"That's okay. Things are weird again," Tara said. "What else is going on?"

"Last night Jack was followed by a strange car. I mean really followed. Tailgated, followed in circles. He was a bit shook up about it."

"I would be, too. What happened?"

"He tried to lose them, but they caught up with him again on our street."

"That's scary, Em." Tara shivered with the willies. "And then what?"

"Well, they kept on driving and he pulled into the driveway."

"Do you think it's related to, you know, the Fringe?"

I shook my head. "I don't know. It could be a coincidence. It could be a stupid student, or something totally random."

"What's your Salesmany sense tell you?"

"I don't have 'Salesmany sense.'" I took the exit for the Interstate. I held out my hand for the EZ-PASS. Tara fished it from the glove compartment and held it up against the window.

"I got it," she said.

"Thanks." I slowed down enough for the EZ-PASS lane and the light blinked green. I gunned it to beat the 18-wheeler shifting beside me and zipped back in line. Tara returned the EZPASS to the glovebox.

"What does your gut tell you?"

"It's Fringe-related." I didn't even hesitate. I just knew.

"Does Jack agree?"

"I didn't tell Jack about what Blackstone told me. Or Templeton's visit."

"Ah," Tara answered. "Got it. And when are we telling Jack about what we know?"

I bit my lip and didn't answer. I wasn't ready to tell Jack about what was going on until I had a better understanding.

I could see Tara looking at me out of the corner of my eye. "He's going to start putting two and two together if things like this keep cropping up."

"Maybe. I'm putting off the conversation for now," I said. "One thing at a time and right now it's all about my Mom."

"I love your mother."

"I know you do." And Tara did. In fact, they adored each other. That's one reason for bringing Tara along. She would do anything to help my Mom if she were in trouble.

I hated to think she could be in trouble.

"You still haven't heard from her?" Tara asked. "When was the last time you talked?"

"Please don't make me feel guilty by asking that," I said. "I don't remember. But I've been calling her since Templeton asked me about her yesterday. No answer, no callback."

"What exactly did he say?"

"He asked me when I talked to her last. But it was so like him. The real message was between the words." I eyeballed the car's clock. It was going to take us about two hours to get to my Mom's house, my childhood home.

"He wouldn't have done something?" Tara began.

"No. No, he wouldn't." I shook my head. "He's a jerk, but he wouldn't go after my mother. That's not what he's about."

"I didn't think so," Tara said.

Templeton was a real pain, an arrogant adversary who was only in the game for himself, yes, but he wasn't someone who would hurt an innocent person like my mother. He wasn't the Fringe. I blew out a breath.

"He gets to you, doesn't he?"

"Yes."

"You shouldn't let him. You're better than that."

I glanced over at my dearest friend. "You're right. To hell with him."

"Of course, he might've been warning you to keep an eye on Lydia and that's the real reason for his visit."

"Okay, now's a good time for you to stop," I said.

She laughed. "Sure. Hey, you don't mind if I ask him out, right?"

"Seriously. Stop." I reached for the weather band radio before pulling my hand back. As tempted as I was to check the forecast, I was a little leery of turning it on.

Tara noticed. "Any more messages?"

"None, but I haven't been looking for them either."

"Let's turn it on and see if anything new comes through. I can be your witness."

"Witness for what?"

"That you're not hearing things." She fiddled

with the dial.

"I thought you believed me?"

"I do. It's just better to have proof." The NOAA Radio Station droned out the current weather conditions.

"That reminds me," I began. "I tried to send a message to Rabbit through the Empire service."

"And?"

"I was pretty much laughed at when I told them I was trying to get a message to a Rabbit."

"Well, you tried."

"Yeah. But I'd like to see if I could find him. I'm really starting to think it was from him."

"Another gut feeling?" Tara asked.

"Yes. And I trust Rabbit. I'd like to know what he's heard," I said.

"Maybe Blackstone can help you get in touch."

I doubted it, but I'd still keep looking for a way to connect with my friend, wherever he was. "Hey, how about trying my Mom? Call her from your phone."

"You think that'll make a difference?"

"Probably not. But maybe she'll answer if the call is from someone other than me."

"Sure." Tara pulled her phone from her coat pocket and scrolled for my mother's number. "Let's see what happens."

Tara pressed the connect and waited. A couple of seconds later I could hear my mother's voicemail greeting wisping out from Tara's phone.

"Hi Lydia," Tara spoke into her phone. "It's Tara Parker-Jones. I'm with Emily and we're on our way to your house. We're a bit worried about you. Call me back when you get this message." Tara gave her callback number before hanging up.

"Thanks," I said. "It was worth a shot."

"Worried?" she asked.

"Freaked."

"Me too."

Right then, my own phone started to ring. "Hey, get my phone. It's in my bag. Maybe it's my Mom."

Tara pulled out my phone and looked at the caller ID. "Blackstone," she said.

"Answer it."

"Hello? This is Tara for Emily," she said into the phone. "Yes. Yes, I'm with Emily now. She's driving – we're heading to her mother's. What?"

"What's going on?" I asked, again pulling my eyes away from the road to look at Tara. She pointed back at the Interstate and frowned.

"Hang on, Mr. Blackstone. I'm going to put you on speaker phone." Tara pressed a button and held the phone out in front of her. "Can you hear me?"

"Yes, I can," answered Blackstone from the phone. "Is Emily listening?"

"Right here," I said. I had a bad feeling. "What's wrong?"

"Emily, I have some news about your mother," he said.

My heart skipped a beat. "What about my Mom?"

"We have a bit of a problem."

"Mr. Blackstone," I said, veering off the Interstate at the next exit I saw. I needed to stop driving before I caused an accident. Tara hurriedly put up the EZPASS as I cruised through the toll lane. "What's going on with my mother?"

"Your mother," his voice was strained. He cleared his throat. "Emily, your mother is in the Empire!"

* * *

"What?" I pulled over into the parking lot after the toll booths, putting my Subaru into park. "What do you mean she's 'in the Empire?' How is that possible?"

I looked at Tara. She put her palms up and shrugged.

"Possible?" Blackstone repeated.

"Mr. Blackstone, how did my mother get into the Empire?"

"I don't know. Maybe she drove or took a train."

I drummed my fingers on the wheel, looking out the window. *Oh.* How could I've been so stupid? She never asked any real questions about the Empire when I returned home last year because she already knew about it. I didn't even consider she'd know how to get there. In fact, I didn't know how to get there unless I door traveled. My mother wasn't a Salesman. There was no door traveling for her.

"Has my mother ever visited the Empire before?" I asked. "Gone to any of the cities?"

"I don't know for certain," Blackstone said. "But I would guess she must've at least once or twice. Maybe with your father? Did you ever ask her?"

"Well, no. I assumed she hadn't because when everything was hitting the fan last December, she didn't seem to know much about my father's work," I said.

Tara suddenly pressed the mute button. "Assumed being the key here, Emily. This is Lydia we're talking about. She might very well know more than you think – and then believes that you know!"

Blackstone, unable to hear Tara, kept talking. "I only know she's in the Empire because there was –" he cleared his throat again "– a situation in Anwat."

I pointed to the phone and Tara unmuted it. "I'm afraid to ask."

"Well, apparently there is a musical group, a rock band of some sort. They don't play the kind of music I listen to."

I rolled my hand, motioning for Blackstone to

continue as if he could see me. "And?"

"The band was traveling by bus and leaving a hotel. Your mother was there for some reason, maybe staying at the hotel, I don't know. Anyhow, the group is pretty popular, I guess. They were getting ready to board the bus and somehow your mother was in the mix of fans. As the band members were ushered through, stopping for the occasional photo or whatever, the lead singer ended up talking to your mother!"

"What?" This time I raised my voice. Tara and I looked at each other. She started to smile. I was not at all smiling. "Wait, how do you even know this?"

"There's more. He talked to your mother, and the next thing you know, the band began to set-up an impromptu concert on the sidewalk. Before any authorities could get there, a huge crowd filled the street and they managed to get some sort of electricity access because they started playing. Loudly." Blackstone was quiet for a moment. "Do you know what Death Metal is?"

Tara couldn't hold it in any longer and burst out laughing. "This is classic Lydia."

"Yeah, I know what it is," I answered Blackstone. I closed my eyes. What had she gotten herself into?

"It's very loud." He noted a second time.

"Then what happened?" Tara asked.

"This 'pop-up concert' went on for about 30 minutes before the Empire guards were able to shut it down. There was still a massive amount of people to move from the street," Blackstone said.

"And my mother?" I hated to even ask.

"Last seen getting on the tour bus with, wait a minute, hold on." Blackstone's voice was muffled and I heard him talking. He returned to the conversation. "The group's name is *Rhino Vomit*."

"Pretty," I replied. "And she got on a bus with these people? How do you know?"

"The media blew up with photos of the mess. Lydia was featured in one of them. It showed her getting on the bus and waving. The lead singer was holding her hand."

I took a couple of deep breaths. "So, is she okay?"

"She was smiling in the picture. She looked like she was having fun. The caption read *'Who is the mystery mom traveling with Rhino Vomit?'*" We heard Blackstone sigh. "But there's more."

"More?" Tara and I both spoke at the same time.

"Yes," he answered. "Because this happened in the middle of Anwat – the main travel hub in the region – the mess affected traffic and the city had to use resources to get everything cleared and moving again. Justice Spell is very aware of what happened and that your mother seemed to be the instigator."

"Okay, wait a minute," I replied. "I don't see how my mother caused this or can be blamed."

"I'm not saying she purposely set out to cause the chaos, but she might've served as some sort of catalyst. I wanted to let you know that Spell is not happy. Emily, what worries me the most is now your mother is in the Empire and people know. That means the Fringe knows, too."

His words hit me like a bucket of cold water. "She's in danger?"

"Not immediate, but it would be better if she came home."

"I'll go get her," I said.

"No, you're in the middle of your Salesman training and it cannot be interrupted," he said. "You're not authorized for door travel without a Senior Salesman, Emily. Let the Empire guards find her and safely return her home," he finished.

Before I could reply, Tara interrupted. "Mr. Blackstone, is Lydia not allowed to be in the Empire? Is she breaking some sort of law?"

"Well, no, of course not. She hasn't directly broken any law," he said.

"And is she forbidden from going into the Empire?" Tara asked.

"No," he said.

"Then, I don't see why guards should be sent

after her." Tara looked at me and held up her hand. She continued. "That seems like overkill. It's intimidating."

"It's for her own protection, Tara," he answered. "Right now, there is uncertainty in the Empire. Even in the best of times, someone like Lydia tends to inspire pandemonium."

I thought his choice of words was a bit over the top, but I wasn't going to get into it over the phone. "Mr. Blackstone, Tara and I were actually driving to my mother's house when you called. We're going to turn around and come back. I want to talk more about this. Do you mind if we come over to your house?"

"Of course not, Emily," he said. "I'll be here all day.

❋ ❋ ❋

Tara said 'in for a penny, in for a pound' so she came with me to Blackstone's. I texted Jack a brief message that my mother was out of town and cell phone coverage wasn't great in the area she was traveling. That was all true. In fact, there were no cell towers in the Empire. Even if my mother were traveling with her phone, she wouldn't be getting my messages.

In the meantime, Tara and I would look for answers from Blackstone.

Patricia let us in and guided us downstairs to

Blackstone's library. Tara, a bibliophile moth to the book collector's flame, perused the extensive bookshelves. I waited for the Record Keeper to join us.

"I'm not sure whether to be relieved or more worried," I admitted.

"Lydia will be fine," Tara assured me. "I'm more upset by this attitude we're getting from Blackstone – or maybe even the Empire's leadership – that Lydia shouldn't be allowed in the Empire. That's ridiculous."

While I agreed with Tara on principle, it would be easier to keep my mother safe if she were at home. The Fringe's reach was more extensive in the Empire. "I'm just glad I know where she is."

Before Tara could comment further, Blackstone came through the door. He hesitated, gave us both a feeble smile, and then made his way behind the desk. He sat down and leaned forward.

"I haven't heard anything yet, but I think Justice Spell asked for guards to track down the band's tour bus. It shouldn't be hard to find," he said.

"And then what?"

"Then the guards help your mother return home. If she was on the band's tour bus, I'm guessing she traveled to the Empire by train," Blackstone answered.

Tara snorted. She'd climbed up one of Blackstone's rolling ladders and was perched on a rung about four feet off the ground. She had a book open and refused to look up.

I got the hint. "Mr. Blackstone, why don't we simply send a message to my mother telling her to return home? I agree with Tara on this. It feels heavy-handed. In fact, I don't like it at all."

Blackstone dropped his gaze to his desk for a moment, perhaps deciding on what to say next. He sighed and looked up with tired eyes. "It's just not safe for her to be there."

I understood. It wasn't. "Then I should go get her."

"Emily," he began. "I understand you want to protect her, but that's not a good idea either. Let the Empire do the work. Focus on what you need to do to receive approval. Jo will meet you here in the morning. I strongly advise you to stay the course. This is what you need to do."

I looked up at Tara. She leaned against the ladder, book in hand and lips pressed tightly together. The shake of her head was barely perceptible.

My attention returned to Blackstone. "Okay. I understand. I'll be here tomorrow to work with Jo. Is there anything you want me to do in the meantime?"

Blackstone looked utterly and completely relieved. "No, you don't have to do anything other than what was planned. This is good. Good. You and Jo will visit the owners of *Petaling* in the morning. Who knows? Maybe by the afternoon your mother will be on her way home!"

"Sounds like everything is working out," I gave Blackstone a thin smile. "Alright. Tara? You ready?"

"Very." Tara descended from her perch with a book in hand. She walked over to Blackstone and placed it on his leather desk blotter. She tapped a fingertip on the cover. "This first edition is a fake. Look at the markings seven pages in from the back cover. Not present in the original from the press – which is currently in a private collection of a French ambassador living in New Zealand."

Blackstone frowned as he opened the book to check on Tara's observations.

"Okay," I said to Blackstone. "We'll leave you to it then. I'll see you tomorrow. We'll let ourselves out." Tara and I gathered our coats and left the library. We were silent until we reached the car. Tara was the first to speak.

"I'm going with you to get your Mom," she told me.

"Damn straight."

CHAPTER 5

Tara and I met in college. We hit it off right away and became great friends. She was also the person who introduced me to Jack.

During our years on campus, we hatched a few schemes here and there. Nothing too outrageous and certainly nothing dangerous. But we were no strangers to setting up a plan when tackling an adventure.

"So, this is what I'm thinking," Tara began as we left Blackstone's driveway. "If you travel to Anwat by door, the Empire will likely find out. Plus, I can't go with you that way. I'll have to drive. If we go together by car, we'll have it at our disposal. It'll be easier to catch up with your mother, too."

She was right. There was no way I was sneaking into the Empire under the radar with door travel this time. I might've pulled it off before, but I probably couldn't now. And frankly, sometimes the simplest plan is the best one.

There were two problems with it.

"I'm not disagreeing with you, but aren't you skipping over two big issues?" I asked.

"Such as?"

"Well, one, I don't know how to drive to the Empire, and two, um, hello, Jack?" I jumped on the inner loop and headed toward downtown Kincaid.

"Easy, we're going to ask Anne how to get there," Tara said. "And as for Jack, we're going to tell him you're making a run with Jo into the Empire – this will explain why you aren't available by phone. I doubt he's going to wonder about me, but I'll ask Marley to run the shop Friday and Saturday. I'll tell him I'm being whisked away for a romantic weekend!"

Tara had given some thought to her alibi. She was probably thinking about what she'd like to do for one of her passionate weekend getaways.

"I'm not sure if he's going to buy it," I said. "Leaving on a Friday? Staying overnight? And why would Jo and I be heading into the Empire?"

"It'll work. This is what you're going to say. You're going to tell Jack you've found Lydia, that she is in Anwat, and Jo is going to escort you into the Empire so you can catch up with her. Don't make a big deal about it. Tell him you'll probably spend some time showing your mother around before coming back home. Maybe even spend a couple of nights." Tara sat back in her seat and smiled. She was satisfied with her plan.

"I don't know," I said. "It's going to be a hard sell. Like, how did my mother even get into the Empire?"

"Boy, you are out of practice," she laughed. "Stick as close to the truth as you can. You just don't know. Tell him you're going to either rent a car to return home or take a train like Anne does."

"Well, maybe." The plan was growing on me. The truth was, I didn't have anything better.

"And you can always send him a message once we're there. You know, you caught up with Lydia, spending the night, sightseeing the next day, meeting up with an old friend for dinner – like Rabbit. Impromptu decision to spend another night. Home by Sunday."

"You scare me." I glanced at Tara before getting off the highway and turning onto Main Street.

"You love me," she grinned. "Trust me. This will work. We'll zip in, find Lydia, and be back home before the weekend is over."

❊ ❊ ❊

The first stop was the *Brew Too* so we could talk to Anne about driving into the Empire. Plus, it probably wouldn't hurt to have someone in Kincaid know exactly what we were up to in case something went wrong. The café was quiet, and Anne brought a pot of tea to our table. She sat with us as we enjoyed the fragrant herbal blend. We updated her on the situation with Lydia trekking through the Empire and told her what we intended to do.

Anne wiped her hands on the towel that was

always tucked into her apron. She nodded her head. "Well, it's a plan."

"We need to learn how to drive to the Empire," I said. "Is there a map?"

"I said it's a plan. I didn't say it's a good one," she replied.

"It'll work," Tara protested as she set down her cup. "Why don't you think so?"

"Because there's a little something called a border checkpoint. How is that going to play out? Emily Swift out for a drive?" Anne tilted her head to the side. "I'm not seeing that. If there's been an uptick in Fringe activity, they'll be paying close attention to who is going in and out of the Empire."

Oh.

"What if I'm driving my car?" Tara asked.

"They're going to want to see some sort of ID from both of you," Anne said.

Oh, again.

Tara looked at me. "Plan B?"

"There's a plan B?" I asked.

"The train." Tara turned back to Anne. "You travel to the Empire by train. Can't Emily and I do the same?"

Anne nodded. "That's probably the better idea. In fact, I'll request the tickets for you. There's a train leaving late in the morning that will get you there by two. As a citizen of the Empire, it's not unusual to take the train in and out. I'll put the tickets in my name and list Tara as the second traveler. Then Emily can use my ticket. Having said all that, there is still the possibility they'll want to see some ID once you board the train. While you won't throw any red flags," she looked at Tara before pointing at me, "Emily will."

"We might not be stopped," I said.

"Right, but they spot-check occasionally. I'd be ready for that possibility in light of what you learned about the Fringe this week." Anne waved at a couple of customers as they left the café, calling out a thank you across the café. She turned back to me. "I know you've door traveled from a train before, Emily, but you don't want to make a habit of breaking the Empire's rules."

"Since when are you a big rule follower?" I teased. Anne was no stranger to bending the rules when the situation called for it. I'd also seen her kick some butt when we were on the run last year.

Anne held up her hands. "I'm not telling you to not do this but be smart. Be careful."

"How fast can you get the tickets?" Tara asked.

Anne checked the café's clock. "I can have them here by this evening."

"Good. I'll pick them up in the morning," Tara replied. She looked at me. "Then I'll pick you up when it's time to go. We can leave my car in the long-term parking lot at the train station."

"When I'm done traveling with Jo, I think Blackstone is still expecting me to meet up with him. We're already going to be cutting it close," I said.

Tara shrugged. "Tell him in light of everything, you just want to stay home and wait for Lydia. Or tell him you don't feel well. Make something up. Anything."

I nodded. In fact, Blackstone might prefer I not pepper him with more questions about everything that was happening. He might be relieved if I canceled our plans to talk.

"The train will leave the station at eleven sharp so I'd get there thirty minutes before departure time," Anne told us.

"And we'll know the train how?" I asked before sipping my tea. I still wasn't sure how this worked. How would a train take us from Upstate New York to... the Salesman Empire?

Anne grinned. "By the number on the ticket. Make sure you're on the right car, too. It'll tell you which platform to queue on. At some point during the trip, the train will move over to a side track and unhook the cars destined for the Empire – for Anwat, specifically. Eventually a train from the Empire will come along and pick up the cars and continue the journey."

I rubbed the back of my neck with my hand. It was a lot to wrap my head around. I decided to table any more questions for another day.

"I'd say we're good to go then," said Tara standing. "I'm off. I need to check in on Marley and make sure he's all set for this weekend." She pulled her coat over her shoulders.

"I'll make sure I'm home in time for you to pick me up tomorrow," I told her. "About ten-fifteen?"

"We'll be pushing it, but yeah, I'll beep when I pull up to your house," Tara said. "And Anne, I'll pick up the tickets when I come over for coffee in the morning. Thanks for doing this."

"Yes, thanks so much," I repeated. "I owe you one."

Anne smiled. "I wish I could go on this adventure with you."

"No, let's not call it an adventure," I said. "I've had too many of them. Let's call it an errand."

"Adventure, errand, whatever," Tara said. She pulled on her knit hat and waved once before leaving the café. "See you tomorrow!"

I watched my best friend go. I hoped we wouldn't have any 'whatever' to deal with once we were in the Empire. Turning to Anne, I asked her if she knew of a store named *Petaling*. She didn't, so I filled her in on what Jo told me.

"I'm so happy to learn there's someplace local I can shop!" Anne was pleased. She'd been ordering some of her 'special-ty' plants from shops in the Empire. If she had someplace local, she might be able to build a relationship with the owners and both businesses could benefit.

"I'm excited to meet them," I said. "They knew my father."

"Daniel had a broad network," Anne nodded. "And if they carry magical botanicals, that might be a good resource for you, Emily."

"Which reminds me," I said. "I think it got away from us, but did you ever come up with someone who might be willing to talk to me about, well, you know."

Anne's white eyebrows raised a bit. "You can say it, Emily."

"Say what?"

"You can say magical abilities," she said.

"I feel ridiculous," I admitted. "I mean, I know there's something I should know how to do, but I really don't know what it is or how to do it. It's just…" I trailed off. I wasn't sure how to explain what I felt.

"When you held the Crimson Stone, you felt its power, correct? You felt it and understood it. Your instinct allowed you to use it," Anne supplied.

"Yeah, I guess. But I still don't know how," I said.

"Emily, think of it this way. You tap into doors because you're reaching out and feeling for energy. The Crimson Stone holds a lot of energy, too. That power seeks a receptive agent. Someone like you," she said, bringing her hands together and interlocking her fingers. "When its power and your ability come together, then magic can happen. You might not know any spells or have tools of your own to use, but you were able to receive its power and channel it to your desire. In Vue, that meant stopping Petrovich."

"Someone like me," I said.

"Yes."

"And someone like Templeton."

"Yes, and like Templeton." Anne slowly turned her teacup in a circle on the table. "Tara told me this morning he visited her store yesterday while you were there. What happened?"

"Same old Templeton," I said. "Rude, arrogant."

"And?"

"And he wanted to make sure I knew the Fringe was showing up in Kincaid. He says they're looking for the Crimson Stone."

"I'm sure they are," Anne said.

"And of course, he wants my piece of the Stone."

"I'm sure he does." Anne stopped spinning her cup and smiled. "He probably also wanted to check up on you. He knows about Lydia?"

"I think so. He asked me about her, which was odd. I think he knew she was in the Empire when he came into *Pages & Pens*," I said. "He could've told me then."

Anne shrugged before standing and beginning

to pick up our empty cups. "I don't think you want Templeton to be your babysitter."

"I don't need him to be my babysitter," I said, a little miffed at Anne's words.

"I didn't mean it to come off sounding quite like that." She paused. "It's better if you know things without Templeton. Right now, you're at a disadvantage because there are so many new things for you to learn. Plus, your ability to door travel is being limited by the Empire. Templeton knows this. I have a feeling he worries about the impact you'll make on his world once you come more fully into your own. He's able to keep an eye on you because you're not able to do the same in return. But..."

"But what?" I asked, curious.

"But I don't know why..." Anne's voice trailed off again. She gave herself a little shake. "I think Templeton also is a little fascinated by you. I think that's why he behaves as he does."

"Fascinated by me," I repeated. Okay, what kind of herbal blend was Anne putting together when no one was around? "Anne, I don't think so."

"Look, I have a true fondness for Templeton," she began. "But I also believe he's a complete narcissist. And when you take that into consideration, then it makes sense."

"It does?" No, it didn't.

"Yes, it does. Suddenly there's a Salesman in

the Empire who seems to be a little like him – at least in the magical sense. Of course, he'd be interested. You're like him and no one else is," Anne finished.

I rubbed the back of my neck and thought about what she said. Maybe she was right. But, I reminded myself, Templeton liked to play games. I did not. "Maybe. Anyhow, I'm not dealing with him right now. I have enough on my plate."

"You do," she agreed. "But back to your original question. Yes, I've found someone who'd be happy to talk to you about magic and learning how to use your abilities. Her name is Lucie Bellerose. She recently returned from Europe and moved back to Matar."

It was my turn to raise my eyebrows at Anne. "Is she… is she from here or the Empire?"

"She's from Matar. She might be someone to get in contact with when you're looking for Lydia. It's possible she could help you locate your mother more quickly. She would be discreet."

"That would be great," I said. "How do I get in touch with her?"

"I'll write down her address," Anne said. "I'll also send her a message letting her know you'll be in touch soon."

"Thanks," I said, standing. I pulled on my coat. "I should get going. I need to get my thoughts together before Jack comes home tonight. He'd kill me if he knew what was really going on."

"You could tell him the truth," Anne suggested. "Things are a lot different for you now. Jack realizes this."

"Jack isn't so big on different," I said. "Until I actually know what's going on, I'm not going to worry him."

Anne's expression proved she didn't agree, but she let it go. "Let me get a pencil and paper. I'll give you Lucie's address."

* * *

I had so much to do before Jack came home that evening. After stopping off at the bank to withdraw some cash, I hurried home. I threw a bag together for my trip to the Empire, placing it in the back of the closet. I packed The Book inside as well as the cash I would exchange for Empire dollars once I was at the station in Anwat. Anne explained there'd be a counter for handling such transactions. While I didn't like carrying a lot of cash on me, I didn't want to use my credit card and create a paper trail. However, I decided to take a card with me this time around just in case. If there was an emergency, I wanted to have some sort of backup.

Three silent felines watched me from various perches in my bedroom. The weight of their stares made my head hurt.

"Trust me," I told them as I changed into my pajamas. "It's better we keep this a secret. I'll tell him tomorrow after he's left for work. I won't have to look him in the eye then."

Three pairs of cat eyes judged me. I shut out the light and left them upstairs. I could do without the additional guilt.

I was nervous to answer questions about Lydia. I'd already told Jack my mother was out of town with poor phone reception – I just wouldn't be coming clean on how far out of town until tomorrow. I wasn't looking forward to dancing around the topic.

Unlike the previous night, Jack was home on time, and thankfully, had no scary incidents to report. I made us sandwiches while he told me about his day. We took our dinner into the living room.

"Anyhow," Jack said, "enough of me. What's the deal with Lydia?"

I felt myself cringe inside. Well, here we go. "I don't know, Jack. She took off and I guess the reception is bad."

Okay, no lies there, but pretty lame.

"Did she call you?" he asked.

"Um, no. Well, yes. Kind of. It went straight to voicemail." Lie number one.

"She called from a landline then?" Jack frowned.

"I guess. Surprised me too." Lie number two.

Jack studied me. "Well, where is she?"

"I honestly don't know." I was counting that one as the truth. I had no idea exactly where Lydia was.

"Hmm." Jack sat his plate on the coffee table. He fiddled with his napkin, his eyes still on the plate. "Is there anything you're not telling me, Em?" He finally looked up.

"Yes."

"And?"

"Anne found someone to talk to me about my ability to handle magical objects." And she pulls a card from up her sleeve.

Jack leaned back into the couch cushions. "Do you know who it is?"

"I don't know her, but her name is Lucie Bellerose and she lives in Matar." I took a sip of my wine. "I'm thinking of seeing how I can meet her."

"Here or in Matar?"

"In Matar. I guess she recently moved back from Europe. She's probably not up for more traveling. She's not a Salesman, so she can't door travel to me."

"I see." Jack's gaze didn't waver, and I grew even more uncomfortable.

"Anyhow, tomorrow I'm meeting Jo at Blackstone's and we'll be traveling to that florist shop I told you about. *Petaling*."

Jack nodded slowly. "Make sure you're careful."

"Oh, I always am. And Jo's right there with me." I gave him a weak smile. "It'll be fine."

"And then what? After meeting the *Petaling* people?" he asked.

"And then Jo and I go back to Blackstone's house, and then I come home. Easy peasy."

"Hmm. Okay, Emily. You'll let me know how it goes? Text me afterwards?"

It didn't take a genius to see Jack was suspicious. He was, however, not going to push. In a way, he was letting me squirm under the weight of my own guilt. He might not know the what, but he knew there *was* a what.

"I'll definitely let you know how it goes." I grabbed our empty plates and headed for the kitchen.

❖ ❖ ❖

That night, after we went to bed, I listened to Jack's deep breathing beside me. We hadn't said much to each other after dinner. We hand-washed our plates and turned into bed early. I told Jack I wanted to get a good night's sleep so I'd be prepared for tomorrow's door travel. He didn't say much in return but followed me to bed.

I looked at the clock. Eleven. Sleep wasn't coming to me easily. Maybe I needed some warm milk. Or a glass of water. Or maybe another big glass of wine.

I padded downstairs to the kitchen. I decided to go with a glass of water. Warming milk seemed like too much of an effort, and another glass of wine was probably not the best of ideas. Sipping from the glass, I walked through the dark house, a streetlight throwing a narrow beam into the front of the living room.

As I stood a step past the kitchen doorway, a black shape moved through the light. I froze as my heart rate jumped and the hair on the back of my neck pricked up. I set my glass down on the mantle and assured myself the shadow was cast by something outside. But what?

I crept to the front window and peeked around the edge, keeping most of myself hidden. There was nothing out of the ordinary. I reminded myself it was only a bit after eleven. Maybe a neighbor was walking a dog before turning in for the night. Still, for a shadow to move through the room, whatever – or whoever – it was would need to be close to the window.

My eyes scanned what little I could see beyond the streetlight's glow. What hid beyond the limited light remained a secret. I studied the dark corners where porch lights could not touch and watched for movement in the bushes. I concentrated on the back of the big lawn across the street where a group of trees stood. Something could easily find cover there. Much like when I planned to door travel, I allowed myself to feel my way to the back of the yard. I pushed my energy out and through the window, a ribbon of power seeking something that could be hiding, something that could be watching.

"Who is out there?" I whispered. I could sense something. I couldn't see it, but I could feel it. I pushed my energy harder, placing my hand against the cold window and trying to capture a picture of what was there in my mind's eye. A fuzzy image started to take shape against the wall of my brain. It was a person, but the impression I began to see was not what I expected. It was a woman. I closed my eyes to focus on the vision being created. The darkness I peered into was not peeling back. The energy I was sending through the night was weakening as I tried to keep it moving forward. Whoever it was became aware of my presence, my pushing to learn just who was there. I realized this too late as I felt a sharp smack against my energy, manifesting as a stinging slap against the hand I held pressed to my window. I jerked my arm back, my eyes flying open. The streetlight flashed out just as a hand touched my shoulder. I shrieked and spun around, throwing a wild punch that landed nowhere.

"Emily! It's me!" Jack managed to grab both of my wrists and shook me. "Look at me!"

I stilled, the awareness I pushed out of my body snapping back in. It was Jack. My whole body trembled as I realized where I was. Neither of us moved in the darkness.

"I need to sit down," I murmured. Jack guided me to the couch before turning on a lamp. He grabbed an afghan and wrapped it around my shoulders. It was so cold in the room. I lowered my chin to my chest and shivered.

Jack knelt on the floor in front of me, rubbing my arms. "Emily," he said gently. "Emily, look at me. Are you okay?"

I raised my eyes to his and nodded. "You just scared me."

Jack scanned my face, looking for a clue of what happened. He spoke softly. "I was right behind you for a good minute asking what you were doing. I was saying your name, but you weren't responding. It's like you didn't know I was here."

"I didn't hear you," I answered. This was the truth.

Jack turned his head and looked toward the front window. "What were you looking at out there?"

"I don't know. I mean, I couldn't see anything. I just…" My voice trailed off.

"You just what?" he asked.

"I thought something was out there. I was concentrating." The room felt so cold. "Did you turn the heat off?"

"No," Jack answered. "Let's get you back to bed." He stood and held out his hand. I took it and let him lead me back upstairs.

I didn't know what I'd seen but I knew someone had been there – watching me.

CHAPTER 6

I didn't fall asleep easily and I was freezing. Jack pulled me against his body and tried to keep me warm. He held onto me until morning. Eventually, I managed to get a few hours of sleep, but I certainly had better nights. Even though I felt more secure in Jack's arms, I did not feel safe.

Before leaving for work, Jack hovered around me, making breakfast and coffee. Concern was stamped into worry lines in his forehead.

"If you think you might be sick," he began, "maybe you should skip meeting with Jo today. Postpone any door traveling practice." He put his hand against my forehead.

I gently removed it. "Jack, I feel fine. I'm not sick, I'm tired."

"That probably doesn't help with door travel," he replied. He opened a cupboard.

"True, but some days you have to go to work tired." I tried to smile. "It's okay."

"Are you sure? You were really shook-up last night." He transferred his coffee into a to-go mug. "What was going on?"

"I told you, I thought I saw something and…" I hesitated.

"And?"

"And I tried to reach out to it – to them. Or, to

her." I shook my head and took a deep breath. "I had a weird feeling someone was outside. I was concentrating to see if I could find out who it was. I think I was able to use energy like I do with door travel. I was... I was getting the impression a woman was across the street watching our house."

Jack adjusted the lid on the travel mug, watching his fingers as he made sure the opening was closed. He didn't look up. "Talk to Jo about it. Maybe she knows about stuff like this."

I knew Jack was uncomfortable. And I knew he was frustrated he couldn't answer these questions. These new experiences were mine. He was a spectator.

For his safety, I wanted to keep it that way.

I stood and took the coffee from his hands. I set it on the counter before wrapping my arms around his neck. He met my gaze.

"I love you more than anything, Jack. More than anyone. But I can't always give you an answer," I said.

"My fear, Emily, is sometimes you have the answer, but you don't tell me." His hand slid to the back of my head and pulled me to his chest. I laid my cheek against his shirt and his chin rested on the top of my head.

"I know," I said softly. I closed my eyes and thought about my plans to travel to Anwat with Tara. I'd need to make this up to Jack in some way.

※ ※ ※

"If you're ready, Emily, you can start. Relax, breathe deep, and let it out. Listen for the right door and learn which one will take you to *Petaling*," Jo instructed.

I nodded. Today's trip was going to be a tad more difficult because part of successful door travel included tapping into a feeling about your destination. It was easier if you were going home, or to another place that held meaning for you. Still, I was excited to meet the owners since they'd known my father. That was the feeling I was going to use. Jo thought it was a good idea.

I placed my pretty top hat on my head. It was a perfect fit, but if I didn't execute a proper landing, it would tumble off of my head while I fumbled through the universe. I stood in the middle of Blackstone's library. There were several doors that could serve as a portal to *Petaling*. The plan was to step through the florists' front door. I closed my eyes and concentrated on my breathing. In. Out. In. Out again. I rolled my shoulders and tried to relax. I was still fretting over my morning with Jack and what Tara and I planned for later. My focus was fraying a bit at the corners.

I rolled my shoulders again. C'mon, Emily, I

encouraged myself. You want to do this. You're going to meet local people who knew your father. I had no idea what *Petaling* even looked like. With the latest drama, I didn't take the time to drive by the shop's address to get a sneak peek. I let my thoughts wander to my father and wondered what he picked up from the florist. What would they need a Salesman to transport? I pictured colorful flowers, poisonous plants, bulbs, and seeds. Okay, Gertrude and Bernard Bloom, I want to come meet you. I breathed in through my nose. Bloom, I chuckled. A perfect name for a florist.

My eyes flew open. "There!" I pointed to a door at the back of the narrow library. "That's the door I'm using."

The door's hum got louder as I approached it. I didn't bother to look at Jo; I didn't want to break my concentration. I hiked my bag higher up on my left shoulder as the fingers of my right hand reached for the doorknob. I could feel the energy already pulling on me. Once I began to open the door, I'd be jerked inside and thrust through the front door of *Petaling*. I hoped. Well, I didn't hope for the thrusting part, just the accurate destination.

I'd try to do as Jo taught, to pull back on my energy once I was engaged through the door so my entry would be graceful. At least, that was my intention.

The reality was once my fingers brushed the doorknob, the door swung open and I was sucked on through as if a wind tunnel had suddenly formed and I was as light as an autumn leaf. The experience happened so fast – as always – that before I had time to even think to pull back, I found myself shoved into a humid shop full of plants and flowers. I was also shoved into a chubby little woman carrying a plastic watering can.

"Oh!" she startled as we both stumbled together. My arms wrapped around her for support, and we did a little side dance as we both worked to stay on our feet. My hat remained on my head – a miracle – but the watering can flew from her grip and tipped over onto the floor.

"I'm so sorry!" I said as I managed to regain balance and kept us both upright.

"That was quite the experience," she answered, straightening her glasses and peering through the lenses at me. "What was that?"

"That was a new Salesman who's still not exercising discipline during door travel," Jo answered from the doorway. She frowned at the mess on the floor.

I let go of the woman and picked up the watering can. "I can clean this up," I said.

The woman laughed. "This isn't the first spill in the shop. Bernie can take care of it. Bernie!"

A man's balding head poked out from a doorway in the back. "What do you need, Trudy?"

"Bring a mop," she told him. "We have a little spill. And our guests have arrived!"

I set the watering can on a table and wiped my damp hands on the front of my jeans. "I really am very sorry," I said again. "I slammed into you kind of hard. Are you okay?"

"Oh, hon," she said. "I'm absolutely fine. Don't worry about it! I'm thrilled to get to meet you."

"I'm happy to meet you as well," I said, avoiding Jo's glare. I did my best to turn away from my mentor. "I had no idea my father used to come here. I've been looking forward to today."

Bernie appeared with the mop and ran it over the floor. He smiled at me as he swished back and forth. He wore a long rubber apron. "Always something, isn't it?"

"You could say that," I replied.

"Well, now that Emily made her grand entrance," Jo shot me a dark look. "I'd like to formally introduce Emily Swift, Salesman. She will be at your service as soon as she receives full approval from the Empire. Emily, this is Gertrude and Bernard Bloom."

"Call me Trudy," the florist said. She motioned to her husband. "And he prefers Bernie."

"My father was Bernard," he said by way of explanation.

"Trudy and Bernie it is." I smiled. Hmm. *Trudy Bloom*. I giggled. I wondered if... I peeked at Jo.

Another dark look from her stifled me.

"Well, come on over to the counter. Would either of you like something to drink? Coffee or tea?" Trudy asked.

"We're fine," Jo answered for both of us. "But thank you. How is everything going? Is there anything you need from the Empire?"

"All is well," Bernie said. "Valentine's Day was a lovely holiday this year. We partnered with a local chocolatier to deliver special orders of roses and chocolates. As crazy as the Season of Love can be, it was wonderful to bring delight to so many lovebirds."

"Bernie is a true romantic," Trudy said as she put her arm around her husband. "It's all I can do to keep him from dressing up like a cupid!"

That visual was one not to dwell on. As sweet as Bernie seemed to be, I didn't want to picture the older man in his skivvies.

"But I bet Emily is more interested in hearing about her father, right?" Bernie continued. "Although, I do remember him picking up bouquets of flowers to take home to your mother rather frequently. Daniel wasn't afraid of showing his love."

A lump formed in my throat and I had the sudden flash of my father stepping through the front door with a huge bouquet for my mother. Bernie was right. He brought her flowers a lot. I blinked back my tears.

Trudy noted my watery eyes and patted my hand. "It's okay. You miss him."

"I do," I said, using a fingertip to wipe away any stray wetness from the corners of my eyes. "It's nice to hear stories about him, though. He died when I was thirteen, so I didn't get to know him as an adult. I didn't know him as a Salesman. I only knew him as my Dad."

"Well, Emily, he was a good, good man. We liked him very much," Trudy said. Bernie nodded.

"Can I ask what he delivered for you? I'm still learning about what he transported," I said. "Was it only magical items? I mean, magical plants?"

"He carried both mundane and magical items into the Empire," Bernie replied. "We shipped both. And he'd bring us certain items from other places across the world. If we were looking to acquire a particular plant for a customer, Daniel often completed the transaction for us. We could send payment through him as well. It was reliable and swift service."

I grinned. "Actually, that's the name of my copywriting business. *Swift Services*."

"How wonderful!" Trudy laughed as she pushed her glasses up to the top of her head. She rubbed the sides of her nose. "Very clever."

"Can you tell me more about the magical items he delivered? I don't know much about magical plants," I admitted.

"You're supposed to be studying the list I gave you," Jo admonished. "You'll need to understand the regulations surrounding the transport of botanicals."

"Don't fret," Trudy said before I could defend my lack of studying. "In fact, we've been doing this for so long, we're well aware of the Empire's many rules and regulations. You can always ask us if you would like to double-check on something."

Bernie interrupted. "Would you like to see some of our more 'special' plants?"

"I definitely would!" I looked at Jo.

"Go," she said, waving her hand at me. "I'm going to look at the houseplants."

"Back this way." Bernie led me through the door to the large back room. If I thought the retail portion of the shop was filled with the scent of many flowers, I was not prepared for the wave of fragrance washing over me in the back.

"Whoa," I said, stopping short. Trudy ran into me from behind. We shuffled our feet a bit.

"We have to stop meeting like this," she giggled.

"Sorry, it's just…" I gestured into the air.

"All the flowers. Potent, yes?"

"Very."

"You get used to it." Trudy motioned to a table with rows of short plants with dark leaves. A bright light hung above them. "Now these, these are Sleeping Sues. By day, they look like any decorative plant you'd use for ground cover – think of Lamium or even Bishop's Weed. But at night, a thick batch of blooms rise out of the leaves. The purple flowers are protective of whatever they've been planted to guard. If anyone should dare to cross over them, they puff out a little powder. Once inhaled, the intruder is put into a long, deep sleep. Quickly."

She moved on to the next table and I gave the Sleeping Sues a wide berth. "Over here we have tiny Giggle Berry Bushes," Trudy continued. "They're just sprouting. When mature, they'll produce little pink berries that when consumed, will lift the spirits of the person who ate them. It can make them a little silly."

"That doesn't sound so bad," I said.

"They're usually given as good-will gifts," she explained.

Trudy continued her tour, showing me a selection of plants, both fantastic and frightening. She described both types cheerfully. Bernie joined in with equal enthusiasm.

"And look what we got in this week!" He pointed to a swath of bright, yellow flowers. Their fluted blooms pointed in our direction.

"Oh! Daffodils," I said. "I absolutely love Daffodils."

"Ah, ah, ah!" Bernie replied, shaking a finger

at me. "These, my dear, are definitely not Daffodils."

"Really? Wow. They look just like them," I said. "What are they?"

"These are Whispering Flowers," Trudy answered.

I paused. Whispering Flowers. Had I heard of such a thing before? It sounded familiar. "What exactly do they do?"

"Whispering Flowers are used to gather information for their keeper," Trudy said.

"Keeper?" I asked.

"Whoever plants and cares for them. If you whisper your question into their blooms, they'll listen for an answer. Once they hear it, they'll whisper it back to you." Trudy ran her fingertips lightly over the flowers. The trumpets fluttered at her fingertips.

"Really?" This was very cool. "How much do they –"

"No, Emily." Jo appeared at my side, shooting me a warning look. "We're not shopping today."

Bernie laughed. "Tempting, aren't they? We don't often have the plants in stock. We were able to locate some seeds, however. These have done well." He looked at me. "Yet another way they're not like Daffodils. Whispering Flowers are grown from little brown seeds. Daffodils are planted as bulbs. Whispering Flowers also grow to maturity very quickly."

"How quickly?"

"Overnight."

I cocked my head to the side. "That is fast. There's so much I need to learn."

"Come back anytime," he told me. "We're happy to teach you."

"I'd love to," I said. "Actually, my good friend Anne Lace recently moved from Matar. She opened a café here in Kincaid. I think she might be interested in buying some plants from you."

"Bring her with you," Bernie said. He switched his attention to Jo. "I know you're not shopping today, but can I show you this orchid out front?" He touched her elbow and they turned.

"Sure, Bernie." She looked back to me. "Emily, are you ready to go? It's quarter to ten and I need to get back to The City."

Where had the time gone? Tara would be at my house in thirty minutes. We definitely needed to get moving. "I'm ready. We should get going."

I started to follow my mentor. A hand on my arm stopped me. I turned and Trudy stood smiling. She put a finger to her lips.

"Something for you to put into your pocket." Her eyes twinkled as she handed me a tiny, white envelope. It was sealed shut.

I looked at it, then back to Trudy. She winked and wiggled her finger at my coat pocket. I obliged and slipped the mystery packet inside. It was clear she didn't want Jo to know. I would look at it later.

Back at the front of the flower shop, I caught up with Jo. Bernie was wrapping up the orchid. Jo avoided my eyes.

"I thought we weren't shopping." I pointed to the plant.

"Bernie is persuasive," she said. She adjusted her hat and picked up the plant. "Are you ready?"

"I am," I said. I turned back to Trudy. She gave me a hug.

"I'm so glad you came by. Please come back again soon," she said. Bernie followed, giving me a sweet hug. It was rather nice. Fatherly, even.

"I will. I promise." I straightened my top hat and picked up my bag. As I stepped toward Jo, I realized I'd be starting my door travel with an audience. I stopped and looked at the Blooms. Then I looked toward the front of the shop. I wasn't even sure I could travel back to Blackstone's library through the same door.

Jo understood my hesitation. "Emily, let's go for a walk." She nodded to the door.

"Oh, right!" I was relieved. I could leave *Petaling* to find the right door. Waving goodbye to Trudy and Bernie, I stepped outside and began to walk.

I felt so good. The door travel was successful even if my arrival lacked Jo's gracefulness. The Blooms were the nicest people, and I'd go back to visit them when I had more time. Right now, I had a big day ahead of me, but I felt really good about it. I could do this.

The door leading into the corner deli rattled and I automatically turned toward it. I glanced back at Jo before stepping on through.

* * *

I did not tumble into Blackstone's library as expected. Instead, I found myself lurching like a puppet pulled on strings through the front door of his house on Northgate. I also stayed on my feet. I considered it a win. Straightening my top hat, I headed for the basement library. I passed Patricia as I worked my way through the house.

"What are you doing?" she demanded. She stopped abruptly, blocking my path.

I motioned behind me. "Came in through the front door. I was supposed to land in the library."

She still didn't move. "And where are you going now?"

"The library." Maybe I'd buy a book for the housekeeper on improving conversational skills.

"I'm taking Mr. Blackstone's car and running an errand," she stated. She pulled up the hood on the oversized coat she wore.

"Great. Well, have fun. I'm just going to wait for Jo in the library." I edged around Patricia and kept walking. I didn't look back, but I had a feeling she was watching me. Where did Blackstone find these housekeepers?

A moment later, I descended the stairs to the monitor room before crossing to the library door. When I entered, Jo was already there with Blackstone. She sighed and shook her head.

"Hey," I said, lifting a finger. "I came in through the front door and stayed on my feet."

"Were you concentrating on the library?" she asked. Her eyes narrowed. "What were you thinking about?"

"Um, Blackstone's house?"

"Not the library here?" She pointed to the floor.

"Well, no. I was thinking about how great this morning was," I answered truthfully.

Jo smiled suddenly. "Yes, this was a good morning. The Blooms are wonderful people." She turned to Blackstone. "They were happy to meet Emily."

Blackstone nodded. "I'm glad it went well."

"And Emily's traveling is getting better overall." She retrieved her orchid from *Petaling* off a small table. She threw a sideways look to me. "But she still needs to work on arrivals."

"I know," I said, fishing my phone out of my pocket. I looked at the time. It was a couple of minutes before ten. Tara would be at my house soon. I had to go. "Mr. Blackstone, I know we planned to meet today, but I've got to get back home. I, ah, have a plumber coming by in about fifteen minutes."

Blackstone walked back to his desk. "Alright. I don't have much to report to you about, well, you know. The situation with your mother."

Jo looked from Blackstone to me, then back to Blackstone. "Is everything okay?"

"Yes, of course," he answered. "Emily's mother is on a trip and we're just checking in on her."

"I see." It was clear that Jo did not. She turned back to me, shrewd eyes questioning. "If there is anything you need, please let me know, Emily. Anything. I'm available to help."

"I will. Thanks, Jo."

"Good. I'm off then." She studied me for another moment before placing her top hat on her head. Jo gave Blackstone a nod as she prepared to door travel back Downstate. She balanced the orchid in the crook of her arm so she could hold her briefcase. As she left through the library's door, I heard her mutter something about Bernie suckering her into yet another plant.

"If you don't have much of an update on my Mom, I'm off too," I told Blackstone, eager to go. I shuffled my bag to my other shoulder. I'd drive straight home. I'd have only enough time to grab my overnight bag from my closet.

"Emily," Blackstone began. I paused. Oh, no. There *was* something to report. "I wanted to let you know the Empire guards did catch up with the *Rhino Vomit* tour bus."

I held my breath. "And?"

"And she was no longer on the bus," he finished.

"Where did she go? What happened? Is she okay?" My heartrate picked up. My mother's wandering could not be good for my health.

"Apparently, your mother only rode with the band until they reached Matar. After joining them for a 'jam session' at some recording studio, she left with a costume designer named Angelique Lavie to go over some sketches for a musical she's working on. That was the last *Rhino Vomit* saw of your mother. But they told the guards they wrote several new songs on the trip from Anwat to Matar. They also said Lydia had a real talent for Death Metal." Blackstone blinked several times. "The guards located the costume designer later that night. She told them she and Lydia had dinner at a popular restaurant before parting ways. Her story checks out. The hostess saw Lydia getting into a cab by herself."

"And?" I prompted again. I was concerned for my mother. I also wanted to kill her. What was she thinking?

"That's where the Empire guards left off. They're checking with local cab companies to see who might've picked her up and where they dropped her off next. That's all we know as of last night. I haven't had an update yet this morning." Blackstone sighed as he sat down in the chair behind his desk. "I'll keep you posted."

"Thanks," I said. Ugh. Well, I might not be able to catch up with my mother by locating *Rhino Vomit*, but at least I knew she was last seen in Matar. After Tara and I arrived in Anwat, we'd head straight for the next city. "Mr. Blackstone, what was the name of the restaurant?"

He frowned at me before dropping his eyes to a notepad on his desk. He looked back up. "*Zenith*. Why?"

I shrugged. "No reason," I replied. "I'll talk to you later. If I don't answer my phone, leave a message."

"I'll do that," he said, tilting his head to the side. I decided I'd better get out of there before he started asking any more questions. I was paranoid he was becoming suspicious. I smiled and gave a little wave before I rushed out the door. I hustled outside to my Subaru and jumped in. It would be a race to beat Tara to my house.

※ ※ ※

I pulled into my driveway as Tara zipped her red Cooper Mini over to the curb in front of the old colonial Jack and I shared. As I climbed from my vehicle, I held up my index finger and mouthed I'd be right out. She gave me the thumbs up through the windshield.

Once inside, I hurriedly grabbed the bag I

packed the night before. William followed me up the stairs, then down the stairs. He meowed.

"I know," I said. "But tell him it's what I had to do." I put the can of kitty treats on the kitchen's rolling butcher block and scribbled a note: *Please remember to give the Furballs their treats.*

I grabbed my petite top hat and eased it into my shoulder bag. It was pretty full, but the hat always nestled in nicely. I looked around my kitchen. I'd text Jack from the train to tell him I was meeting up with my Mom, that Jo was escorting me into the Empire. I'd tell him once I settled in with my mother, I'd send him a message through the Empire's delivery service. I'd remind him my phone wouldn't work in the Empire, and not to be alarmed if I didn't reply.

"I'll be back real soon," I said to the empty kitchen. William wrapped his tail around my calf. He sent up a second loud meow. I hoped my optimism wasn't misplaced.

❊ ❊ ❊

"We're pushing it," Tara said as she navigated through traffic. The train station was located near downtown Kincaid. The drive should only take about ten minutes, and we hit every red light on the way.

"Yeah, I know," I said. "I was doing my best to hurry. I think Blackstone knows I'm up to something."

"Oh, who cares," Tara replied. "I'm annoyed with him."

"Me, too." I fumbled through my bag and grabbed a small notebook.

"Pencil's in the glove compartment," Tara said as she glanced at my hand. "What are you writing down?"

"Where my mother's been. *Rhino Vomit* isn't an easy name to forget, but I want to make sure I remember the restaurant and the costume designer's name in case I need it." I wrote down *Zenith* and Angelique Lavie. "This Lavie woman might be a place to start in Matar. Maybe Mom told her where she was going."

Tara downshifted and slipped in front of another car turning into the overnight parking lot by the train station. The driver laid on the horn. Tara waved and smiled. Cheeky. She lowered her window and grabbed a ticket from the dispenser at the gate. The bar raised to let us in, and she drove through. It was ten thirty-five.

"Grab the first open space you find," I told her. A minute later we were parked and hoofing it toward the station.

"Here's your ticket," Tara said, pulling it from the large satchel draped across her chest. Tara knew to pack light. She also carried a backpack slung over her shoulder.

"Thanks," I said. I looked at the ticket. "The

train we're supposed to board is number three-oh-nine. Let's look at the departure board inside." The train station in Kincaid was never terribly busy, but being a Friday, there were always people heading to New York City for the weekend. The board indicated our train and the one headed Downstate were one and the same. Boarding would be on platforms C and D. Our tickets indicated the last four cars were available for the 'bearer of the ticket.' The name Anne Lace also appeared on mine.

We queued up on platform C. I looked around, surprised at the number of people on the platforms designated for those traveling to the Empire. That's what I had to assume, right? I caught Tara taking in the crowd as well. We were probably having similar thoughts. Several porters were coming through and assisting those with baggage. A ticket collector moved to the front of our line and started to admit people.

"Let's sit in this car if we can," Tara said. I nodded and we flashed our tickets at the man allowing us to board. He barely even looked at them. Tara tossed me a grin as we worked our way down the aisle. She found two empty seats facing forward near the back. After storing her backpack in the overhead rack, she slipped into the window seat. I paused long enough to pull my father's journal from the travel bag and added it to my large shoulder bag. I moved it under my top hat. My travel bag joined Tara's in the overhead storage.

"So far, so good," I breathed. Now as long as no one decided to check our IDs, we were good to go. I didn't want to alert the Empire – and possibly the Fringe – to my return. The train rumbled to life as we sat and waited. We watched as others got on, most moving past us to one of the cars behind ours. There was quite a stream of travelers. At precisely eleven o'clock, the sound of the engine grew louder, and a shudder rippled through the train as it began to slowly pull out of the station. This was a good sign.

"And here we go!" Tara announced from beside me. She was all smiles.

"You know this isn't a pleasure cruise," I reminded her.

"I know, but I'm excited to finally be going to the Empire." She stood and looked both ways over the seats around us. "We're pretty full up in here."

"I know, I was surprised to see how many people were boarding into these cars."

Tara's gaze remained facing the front of our car. "Huh," she said. She pursed her lips.

"What?" I asked looking up.

"The ticket collector. He's coming through and stopping at each row. He's checking tickets and I think he's asking everyone for ID. I can see people flashing their driver's licenses."

"Are you sure?" I asked. I leaned my head out into the aisle. What Tara reported seemed to be the case. The man was checking IDs. I turned and looked toward the back of the car. I watched as an older man shuffled through a narrow door into the bathroom. There were three more cars behind ours. There had to be a bathroom on each one. Maybe I could hide until the collector passed.

"He's getting closer," Tara noted.

"I'm going to see if I can hide," I said. "I'm heading for a bathroom."

"Go!" my friend ordered. "I'll move into your seat. Take your shoulder bag. Make it look like I'm traveling alone!"

I grabbed my bag and moved swiftly down the aisle, resisting the urge to look back to see if the ticket collector noticed. I slid the car door open and hurried into the vestibule connecting our car to the one behind it. This next car was fairly full of passengers as well. I could see a couple of women standing near the back near the bathroom. I kept going, excusing myself as I scooted by the women. Once again, I passed through a swaying vestibule connecting the cars. No one noticed me as I walked to the back of the third car. There was no line for the bathroom, but the door was locked. Someone had beaten me to it.

I waited. This was not the first time I had to make an escape on a train. Last time, I door traveled to avoid capture. It was not without risk. Door traveling from a train meant essentially passing through a moving target. Not many Salesmen would ever dare it. I didn't have a choice before. I might not have a choice again.

Chewing on my thumbnail, I considered my options. What if I door traveled on the train and stayed on the train? What if I went through a door in one car to return to the first car, homing in on Tara and our seats as a destination? I didn't need to be an experienced Salesman to understand the instability of this kind of travel.

There was another problem, too. I wasn't authorized for door travel without a Senior Salesman. But by the time the Empire found out – if they found out – I could be back home. Plus, I was still on a train in New York, not the Empire. If my door travel was discovered, I could throw myself at the mercy of the Court. I could claim an accidental door travel experience. It wouldn't be the first time I traveled without intending to do so. I'd leave my top hat in my bag.

I made up my mind. I heard the door slide open at the front of the third car. The ticket collector worked fast. I'd need to get a move on.

There was one car left and one more bathroom. I needed it to be the right door. I closed my eyes before exiting. I pictured Tara waiting in our seats in the first car in as much detail as possible, from her clothing to her cheerful attitude.

Tara never backed down from backing me up. I loved her.

I opened my eyes and once more entered a rocking vestibule. I crossed into the fourth train car. The final car. The path to my target was clear. Ignoring the other passengers, I strode down the aisle, my eyes glued to the bathroom door. I pressed out my energy as hard as I could against the door as I approached. I pictured my best friend waiting for me, worrying about me. Anticipating the hum, I reached for the handle and slid the door open.

The fierce power of door travel drew me through.

CHAPTER 7

Note to self: Door traveling from one car to another on a train is not impossible. But the arrival is quite different. I think it's because the doors have to slide open.

Oh, I made it back to Tara in the first car. My landing wasn't pretty. The door to the front of the car where we first boarded slid open with a bang before the universe spat me out onto the aisle floor.

I climbed to my feet, looking up into a crowd of curious eyes. My face burned. No one said anything.

"I tripped," I explained to the spectators as I hiked my bag over my shoulder.

Tara stood up and waved her hand, encouraging me to hurry. Her eyes were wide. As I maneuvered around her to take the window seat, she whispered: "Smooth."

I shot her a dark look. "Let's hope the ticket collector doesn't come back this way."

"Try not to draw any more attention to yourself," she admonished.

We settled into our seats and I pulled my cell phone out of my pocket. I needed to text Jack. There was a missed call and a voicemail from Blackstone. He probably tried to reach me when

I was door traveling.

"Blackstone called," I said.

Tara leaned over and looked at my phone. "What'd he say?"

I signaled to her to wait while I listened to Blackstone's message.

"Hi Emily," the recording began. "I hope you can call me back soon. I have an update on your mother. It's important."

"He says he has an update on my Mom," I said to Tara as I returned the call. Blackstone answered quickly and I asked him what he'd heard.

"It seems like your mother stayed in Matar," he reported. "She was on a late-night talk show last night."

"What?" My voice rose. Tara shushed me and then leaned closer. I tipped the phone so she could listen in.

"Yes, it's called *Good Night, Matar* and it appears Lydia made yet another friend." Blackstone sighed.

"I need more than this," I said into my phone. What now?

"You know how actors make the rounds when they're promoting a new movie?"

"Yes?" I was dreading this one.

"There's a popular actor named Lubanzi Danso who's known for his action-adventure movies. He was scheduled for a segment on the live late show because one of his blockbusters was just released. He brought your mother with him as his guest."

"Okay, well, that's not horrible," I replied, relieved. I looked at Tara. She shrugged before leaning back in to listen to the rest of the story.

"He also announced his lifelong dream to quit acting and lead a one-way expedition into space. He dropped the name of an American billionaire and invited him to call."

"It wouldn't be my dream, but again, not so bad," I told Blackstone. "Maybe he was done with making movies."

"He credits your mother as the person who inspired him to chase his dream," said Blackstone. "He's under contract for several more movies, but he told the audience he's breaking with the studio."

"I'm sure it's a big deal for some people," I said. "But this isn't the same as when she was with *Rhino Vomit* and blocking traffic in a pop-up concert. She's not breaking any laws by supporting people who want to change their careers."

"That's true," he said. "My concern is this will be all over the news before the day is over. Because your mother was on the show and introduced as Lydia Swift, the Fringe will know she's now in Matar."

"Damn," I swore. Blackstone was right. This was not good at all. Tara and I would need to get to Matar as fast as we could.

"Is your plumber through?" Blackstone interrupted my thoughts. "Maybe you can come back to Northgate and we can strategize where she might be heading next. I'll see what else I can find out."

"The plumber?" I was still thinking about my mother.

"Didn't you say a plumber was coming to your house this morning?" Blackstone questioned.

Right, the plumber! "He was delayed. I'll see if I can come over later." I made big eyes at Tara. She shook her head and mouthed 'time to hang up.' I turned my attention back to the call. "I'll do my best. I'll get back to you."

After ending the connection, I put my hand to my forehead. What in the world was my mother doing? I knew she was generally oblivious to danger, but it was as if her zaniness had amped up.

I still needed to text Jack. I sighed as I looked at my phone and thumbed to my favorites. Tara offered a token of support by giving my arm a squeeze.

I knew Jack was busy teaching the last class of the morning, so I decided it was a good time to send the text. It would never be a good time for what I was about to type.

Hey Jack, I wrote. *Mom is in MATAR. I'm going to catch up with her. Jo's escorting me into the Empire. Once I'm with Mom, I'll send you a message through the Empire's service. I won't be long. We'll come back by train. I'm leaving now but wanted to text you before I didn't have any phone coverage. I love you.*

I stared at the message. There was so much I wanted to say but couldn't. Jack would be furious. Even if by some crazy, one-in-a-million stroke of good luck I found my mother today and returned home right away, he wasn't going to let me off the hook for this one.

I reread the message one more time before sending it. Once the message had flown off into the ether, my gaze lingered on the sent confirmation. Jack would see it after class. I could just imagine his –

The phone started to vibrate, making me jump. Jack's photo appeared on the screen showing him as the caller. Shocked, I lifted my hand and stared at his smiling face as the buzzing continued.

Tara reached over and removed the phone from my grasp. She calmly declined the call before powering the phone down. She handed it back to me. "There aren't any phone towers in the Empire, right? The call would not have gone through."

"Yeah, right," I sighed. I felt horrible and knew I was really letting Jack down this time. I pushed the silent phone into my bag and leaned my head against the window. There was nothing to do except wait until the train pulled into Anwat. Then we'd have to race to catch my mother in Matar.

"Hey," my best friend said softly. "It'll be okay. Once we get our bearings, you can send Jack a message through the Empire's service."

"It's just…" I shook my head.

"Let's look at The Book," Tara suggested. "Sometimes it helps."

I dug inside my shoulder bag past my top hat and pulled out The Book. I released the lock with the hat pin. Maybe Tara was right. The Book might give me some guidance. I let it fall open and was again presented with the message about communication.

COMMUNICATION
News will travel
Through many mediums
Sent by both
Friend and foe
Learning the difference
Makes all the difference.

"Communication seems to be the big deal this time around." Tara pointed her chin at my father's writing.

"I hear you," I replied. "I'm worried about the foe part."

"Who wouldn't be?" Tara said. "What else do you have?"

I turned the pages. "Did I show you this one

yet?"

Don't miss
The loudest Whis-
...per.

Tara shook her head. "I wonder if that's literal or metaphorical."

"What do you mean?"

"Well, is it really a loud whisper, or is it a gut feeling? You know, that little voice telling you something's up."

"That's quite insightful," I said to my friend. "Duly noted."

"Anything else?"

I traced the words on the page with a finger as I thought about my father. What could've he foreseen when he wrote in this journal? What memories did he record? I let my fingers glide to the page's corner and lifted the paper. I wondered if he knew my mother might someday be in danger.

I slowly turned to the next page. There, a sketch of two figures appeared, intertwined in an embrace as if spinning in a dance. One wore a top hat; the other, a flowing dress swirling around her legs. The faces held no defining features. Underneath the spare drawing my father's handwriting scrawled across the page:

That first night
the View
was only you

*filling my eyes
with stars.*

Tara read the passage silently. When she finally spoke, her voice was quiet. "I hope someday I find someone like your father."

❉ ❉ ❉

Shortly after the train bound for Anwat picked us up from the offside railroad track, Tara leaned into my seat to watch out the window with me. The train car exchange happened somewhere deep in the woods. We watched for a recognizable landmark as the scenery flew past, but there was nothing we could identify. We assumed at some point we entered the Empire. The weather was definitely sunnier. Eventually, the trees and fields gave way to small towns and little houses before changing again to a cityscape with buildings and more traffic. A few minutes before two, we pulled into the station in Anwat. We grabbed our bags from the overhead and joined the others exiting the train.

I gave Tara the cash I brought along and pointed to the currency exchange. "Go ahead and swap all of this for Empire dollars. I'll see what I can find out about traveling to Matar. If we rent a car, it might be faster."

Tara ignored me and was turning slowly, taking in the sights and sounds of the busy station.

"Weird," she said.

"What?" I looked around. "What's wrong?"

"It looks exactly like any train station back home," she answered.

"What were you expecting?"

She cocked her head to the side, her eyes still wandering. "I thought everything would be sepia toned or something."

"Sorry to disappoint," I responded.

"Meh." She took my cash and headed for the exchange counter. I went off to locate a board showing the inter-Empire train schedule. Maybe something for Matar would be leaving soon. If not, we'd have to see about a car rental.

I walked in the opposite direction of Tara toward the wall of arrival and departure boards. Now that I was back in the Empire, I paid closer attention to my surroundings. The Empire was the Fringe's home turf, not mine.

The departure board revealed a train bound for Matar had left shortly before we arrived in Anwat. Another wouldn't be leaving right away, so I started to look for directions to a car rental section. Tara was still in line at the exchange counter.

Off to the right of my friend, I noted a young man in dark, fitted jeans and a denim jacket slouching against the station wall. He was of average height, with black hair. In his hand he held a cell phone. He appeared to be texting. A

Rabbit?

I quickly crossed the room. "Hey," I began. "Sorry to bother you, but I'm hoping you can help."

Dark eyes flicked up from his phone before looking me up and down. "Yeah, what do you want?"

"Um," I faltered. I was so used to my Rabbit's affability I was momentarily confused. Maybe this wasn't a Rabbit? "Oh, I'm sorry. I'm looking for my friend, Rabbit. I was going to ask if you'd be able to help. I thought you, ah, were one."

Awkward.

"I'm a Rabbit," he sneered. "But I'm not a delivery boy."

"Okay, sorry." Maybe not all Rabbits were nice. I only met two the last time I was in the Empire. I supposed there were jerky Rabbits just like there were jerky Salesmen.

Before I could retreat Tara stepped up to join us, having completed her transaction at the exchange counter. She glanced at the surly Rabbit and offered a polite nod before turning to me. "Alright, Emily, we're all set. Are we taking a train or renting a car? How expensive is it?"

"We need to rent a car," I said to Tara. "The train for Matar already left. Driving might be faster anyway. We can ask at the counter," I told her.

"That's fine. I'll put it in my name. Which way

do we go?" Tara asked, her eyes scanning for a sign.

The man had perked up at the sound of my name. He leaned closer, squinting. "What did she say your name was?"

I hesitated for a beat before realizing I'd have to explain who I was anyway if I hoped to get a message to my Rabbit. "Emily."

He studied me more closely. "Emily who?"

"Emily Swift," I answered.

"Really?" he replied, his eyes lighting up. "The Emily Swift the Fringe is chasing?"

I didn't care for his choice of words. "Was chasing. Look, we're trying to get to Matar and not make a big deal about it. You understand, right?"

He smiled then, but his face lacked warmth. "Oh, I understand. Car rental isn't cheap, you know. Why don't I drive you there? I'm heading in that direction. I'll even charge you less than the rental agency would."

Tara's little nose wrinkled. "I think we're good."

"How much would you charge?" I asked against my better judgement.

The man examined my face. "Two hundred," he said.

"Way too much," Tara cut in. She was growing impatient and was ready to ditch this guy. "Em?"

She was right, it was too much, but I was hoping to get more out of him. Plus, I really needed to send a message to Rabbit – *my Rabbit*.

"That's a bit steep," I told him. "How about one hundred?"

"One-fifty."

"Sold," I said.

"What?" Tara's voice rose. She held up a finger. "Wait a minute. If you'll excuse us." She pulled me to the side. "What are you doing? Getting into a car with some strange man?"

"It's not a strange man," I told her. "It's a Rabbit."

She frowned as she checked over her shoulder. He smirked at us. "That's Rabbit?"

"No, that's a Rabbit. It's not Rabbit," I explained.

"Should I understand this?" she asked.

"You will eventually," I said. "Look, he's a Rabbit. He can pass a message through his network to let my Rabbit know what's going on. And, if we hire him to drive us to Matar, we might get some more information out of him on the way. Win-win."

"This is so not win-win." She sighed, shaking her head. "We're going to trust him?"

"Yeah, I'm sure it'll be okay." I retraced my steps back to the Rabbit. Tara reluctantly followed. "How long will it take to drive to Matar?"

"I can get you there in an hour and a half if we go now. It's pretty much a straight shot. The train takes a lot longer," he finished.

Leaving right now would mean we'd get to Matar much sooner. I'd have a better chance of catching up with my mother. "Tara?"

"Fine, Emily." Tara slung her bag back over her shoulder. She glared at the Rabbit. "Well, where's this fast car of yours?"

"Relax," he rolled his eyes. "This way." He turned and began to weave through the throng of travelers. Tara and I followed.

"This can't be good," my best friend grumbled.

"Don't worry," I said. "You'll see. My Rabbit might even be able to meet us in Matar." We headed for the station's exit and out into a surprisingly warm spring day.

❃ ❃ ❃

"Your weather is certainly better than ours," Tara noted from the back seat. She had no desire to sit up front alongside our driver even though I'd offered. This Rabbit drove a newer model Chevy SS. When she saw our ride, Tara snorted and mumbled something about trying to look sporty in a Chevy.

His brown eyes flashed up to the rearview mirror. "It's been like this since the beginning of the week. It's not usually this nice this time of year."

"It looks more like early summer," I noted. It was true. Trees were greening and there were flowers everywhere. A real color riot. Our winter coats were too heavy.

"What are you going to Matar for?" he asked. Now that we were trapped in his car rocketing down the road, I knew I wouldn't be able to brush off his questions.

"I'm meeting up with someone," I said. "Showing Tara around."

"That so? Who are you meeting up with?"

I figured after my mother's guest appearance on *Good Night, Matar* it wasn't exactly a secret. He was a Rabbit, after all. "My Mom is there. She's, um, catching up with friends."

"Is she now?" The Rabbit turned his head and shot me a curious look.

"Hey," Tara called from the back, snapping her fingers. "Eyes on the road, Speedy."

"Do you want to walk to Matar?" he snarled back, his gaze moving once again to the rearview mirror.

"Okay, guys," I began. "Let's all play nice."

Tara made a sound from the back seat. I flipped the visor down and peered into the mirror. She threw up her hands and blew out a breath so hard her bangs fluttered. She turned her face toward the window.

"Anyhow," I started again. "It's a long story. We're not staying in the area long."

"Then where?" he asked.

I didn't know if he was being nosy because he was a Rabbit, but I thought it might be a good time to ask him if he could get a message to my Rabbit. "Depends. Hey, it would be great if I could have Rabbit meet me there if he's in the region. I was hoping you could, you know, text him."

While there were no phone towers in the Empire, rendering my phone useless, Rabbits seemed to be able to text from phones without issue. That was one way they passed information.

"And what Rabbit is this?" He sounded annoyed.

Now, I don't quite understand how it works, but Rabbits always seem to know which Rabbit you're referring to. Every Rabbit is called... well, Rabbit. But maybe this one needed a bit more guidance. That was fair. "Rabbit was with me in Vue last December. He, ah, helped me find some things I needed. For work."

Well, sort of.

"Oh, *that* Rabbit." The greasy smile was back. "The one who helped you find the Crimson Stone?"

Startled, I turned in my seat. Tara's reaction was similar. "You know about that?"

"Of course," he answered smugly. "I'm a Rabbit."

"Okay," I said. Tara's eyebrows were raised. "I guess that makes sense. It's been a while, but I thought it was still a secret. I don't have it, by the way."

"Then what did you do with it?" he asked. He pulled a pair of aviators out of his jacket pocket and put them on.

"Turned it into the Empire," I lied. It was strange this Rabbit knew we'd found the Stone and yet didn't know what happened next. I wanted to find out why but that would have to wait. "Anyhow, now that you know who I'm talking about, can you send him a message through the network? Let him know I'm going to Matar?"

"Yeah," he answered. "Sure. I'll do it when we arrive. You don't want me texting and driving, do you?"

"No, of course not," I said, eyeballing his jacket. His phone was in the pocket. I hadn't heard it buzz once. Odd for a Rabbit. Maybe no one liked him.

"Where do you want to be dropped off in Matar?" He fiddled with the radio. Something obnoxious blasted out of the dashboard.

I thought for a moment. "Do you know where *Zenith* is? It's a restaurant."

"You want me to drop you there?"

"That would be perfect." I raised my voice to be heard over the noise.

He nodded. With the music blaring, we rode in silence the rest of the way to Matar.

❊ ❊ ❊

Speedy, as I knew Tara would come to call him, dropped us in front of *Zenith*. As I leaned in through the window to fork over the one hundred and fifty Empire dollars, I reminded him he agreed to text my Rabbit. He made an exasperated noise in the back of his throat and pulled out his phone. His fingers worked across the screen.

"Done," he said.

"What did you tell him?" I'd expected him to ask me what I wanted to say.

"That Emily Swift is in Matar and she wants the Rabbit from Vue to catch up with her. I'm sure that's enough."

Tara managed to wriggle in beside me, shoving me to the left. "Did you tell him where we were? How will he find us?"

Speedy scowled at her. "I said you were dropped in front of *Zenith*. He'll find you."

I pushed Tara back. "Okay, well, thanks. It's been... fun." I stepped away from the car and gave a little wave. He watched us for a moment before merging back into traffic.

"What. A. Jerk." Tara said.

"Yeah," I replied. "That was unexpected. But, hey, we got to Matar safe and sound. And we got a message sent to Rabbit. I want to know what he's heard about the Fringe. If we haven't found my mother by the time he catches up with us, we'll get his help."

"If he's anything like Speedy..." Tara began. I grinned. I so called that one. She smiled back. "Anyhow, what I was saying is I hope your Rabbit is much nicer."

"Oh, he is. He's such a good guy. You'll like him," I promised.

"Good," she said. She paused to look around at the busy street. "Okay, Sherlock, what now?"

"We start here." I pointed to the restaurant sign on the building behind us. "My Mom dined at *Zenith* last night. Let's see what we can find out."

❈ ❈ ❈

It was too early for dinner. I doubted *Zenith* catered to the early bird diner, so it was quiet when we entered the restaurant. The waiting area leading past the coat check to the hostess stand was lush, with large green plants and colorful artwork on the walls. Tara nodded her approval as we walked through the space.

"We're probably underdressed, but I'd love to see the menu," she said.

My stomach growled as I caught the scent of something wonderful wafting out from a hidden kitchen. "We should probably watch our

THROUGH THE DOOR

budget, but let's get something to eat when we leave here."

We approached the hostess stand as an attractive, middle-aged woman came around the corner from the dining room. "Oh," she said when she saw us. "I'm sorry. Have you been waiting long? Would you like to make a reservation? I'm afraid we're booked for two weeks out."

That was more than I needed to know, but the woman was pleasant. She hurried to her day planner and flipped through a few pages.

"Thank you, but no," I answered. "Actually, I'm here to ask about the woman you saw leaving the restaurant last night in a cab. She has strawberry-blondish hair that's usually pulled up, slender, about five-foot-two." I pantomimed my mother's height.

"We're asking about the woman the Empire guards were already here about," Tara interrupted.

"Right," I said, pointing to my friend before continuing with the hostess. "Sorry. That's probably more helpful."

"Why are you asking about the lady?" the hostess questioned. "You're not with the guards."

"I'm her daughter," I explained. "We're trying to find her."

The hostess tapped her manicured nails on the stand. "Well, I don't have much to tell you. I wouldn't have even seen her leaving, but I checked outside when I heard the commotion."

"Commotion?" Tara and I spoke at the same time. *What now?*

"We were quite busy last night, but at one point when the restaurant door was being held open, I could hear a bunch of people clapping and cheering. A few of our patrons waiting to be seated remarked on the 'circus' outside." The hostess shook her head. "It's not unusual to have street performers in this neighborhood, but I wanted to make sure no one was blocking our door."

"What was going on?" I asked.

"It seems like there was a small troupe of contortionists. They put on a little impromptu show. When I stepped outside, I saw one of the members walk on his hands through the crowd carrying a rose between his teeth. He walked over to a woman," the hostess paused. "Well, you know what I mean. He walked on his hands."

"We got it. Go on," Tara prompted.

"Anyhow, he walked over to this woman and bends like –" We watched as the hostess started to lean over and lift her foot. "I can't do it."

"That's okay," I said. Good grief. "Tell us what happened. Was the woman my mother?"

The hostess nodded. "I think so. I mean, if your mother is the same woman the Empire guards were asking about. The contortionist bent his back so that his feet were in front of his face. Wait, did I tell you he was barefoot?"

"You didn't, but that doesn't matter." My patience was stretching thin.

"But it does! He grabbed the rose from his mouth with his toes." The hostess grimaced. "But at least he didn't seem to touch his lips with his feet. Yuck!"

"Some people like that," Tara shrugged.

"Not. Now." I shot her a dark look.

"Once the rose is between his toes, he lifts his leg and holds it out to the lady – I mean, your mother. She took it," the hostess finished with a final leg lift. Maybe she had dreams of becoming a Rockette. "Then she sort of squatted down and said something to him before patting him on the head. A cab arrived behind her and she got into it. She blew the contortionist a kiss through the window and waved as the car pulled away. Everyone clapped like it was part of the show."

I rubbed my hand on my cheek. If there were any doubt the woman was my mother, I let go of it. It was, as Tara would say, classic Lydia.

"Do you know where the cab went?" Tara asked.

"I don't. But I told the guards it was one of the city's black livery cars. It stood out because they have a small number of these vintage vehicles they use. It's sort of a gimmick, but people like it. They're more expensive. Usually, they're reserved for celebrity types."

That was helpful. "And you don't know where the taxi was going?"

"No, I'm sorry. Everyone was in such a happy mood, though. It must be this crazy warm weather we're having. I've never seen anything like it, but I'll take it." The hostess gave us a big smile. We thanked her for her help and left the restaurant.

Once outside, I turned to Tara. "This gives us someplace to go. We know it was a city-owned cab."

My friend twisted her lips to the side. I could tell something was percolating in her brain. She held up a finger. "I don't know. Maybe we should skip to the talk show. If the livery vehicle is usually reserved for celebrities, that might explain how Lydia met what's-his-name."

"The actor? Lubanzi Danso," I said.

"That's an awesome name."

"It is a great name," I agreed. "You have a point though. If we could talk to someone on the show, then maybe we can figure out where she went next." I raised my hand to flag down a cab. It wasn't a fancy vintage car, but I was sure the driver would know the way to *Good Night, Matar's* studio.

As we tossed our bags into the back seat, I felt a little prickle run down the back of my neck. I froze, my eyes quickly roaming the street. The paranoia was familiar. I looked behind me but saw nothing out of the ordinary. I ducked into the car. Turning and looking out the back window as Tara directed our driver, I remembered the radio message received only a few days ago: Emily Swift, the Fringe is watching you.

CHAPTER 8

We arrived at *Good Night, Matar's* studio in no time. I had no idea how we'd find the right person to ask about my mother's appearance, but we had to start somewhere. Since the show was broadcast live, there was no taping going on in the afternoon. However, there was a bit of activity around the building. We explored, rounding the corner toward the back. It looked like some equipment was being moved from the studio. Workers were loading a big truck bearing the name *Ivanov Transport*. I took a closer look. Wait, could these be a bunch of Rabbits?

"Come on," I said as I pulled on Tara's arm. "I think this is a good sign."

The crew was busy moving what looked like large stage lights. Their dress was similar: jeans tucked into work boots, fitted tee shirts. Several of the guys had chains stretching from their wallets to belt loops. One male Rabbit paused for a moment to run his hand through his dark hair. When he lifted his arm, I saw a *Rhino Vomit* logo stretched across the front.

A few wore knit caps even though the day was warm. Black curls poked out from underneath their hats. Every few minutes, one would pull out a phone and text.

"Ah, excuse me?" I said by way of a greeting. Half a dozen pairs of curious eyes looked up and flicked their gaze from me to Tara and back again before returning to their task. One young woman – she looked barely seventeen – pulled a phone from her back pocket and thumbed a text. She tilted her head to the side and stepped away from the rest.

"What do you need?" she asked, looking up from the screen. Her dark brown eyes combed over my face. She looked so much like *my* Rabbit, my heart hurt.

"Sorry to bug you," I started. "But I had a question about the show held here last night. I was wondering who I could talk to about it."

"What's your question?" She gave Tara's face another quick scan. "Maybe I can help."

"There was a woman on the show, and I was hoping to find out where she went after the broadcast. Is that something you might know, or could you point me in the right direction?" I hoped she would be open to sharing with me.

The young Rabbit took a moment to consider my request. Suddenly, she grinned. "I can probably find out for you. She's caused a bit of a ruckus."

"I've heard," I said. "The whole movie star issue."

"That too." The Rabbit's eyes glittered. "So, who's asking?"

"Her daughter," I answered.

The Rabbit nodded. "I had a feeling you were going to say that."

"I figured you probably knew because of the Rabbit who drove us in from Anwat," I said.

"I hadn't heard about that yet," she cocked her head to the side as she looked at her phone. Her fingers flew over the screen. "But Emily Swift… It's nice to meet you. I heard you outsmarted the Fringe a time or two."

"I think I got lucky," I admitted. "Anyhow, we only arrived in the Empire today. I'd really like to get to my mother fast. I'm also hoping to catch up with Rabbit. The guy who brought us here said he sent a message to him. If we find out where my mother went, maybe Rabbit can meet us there."

"Message to Rabbit, huh? Interesting." She continued to study her phone. She shook her head. "Well, sure. We can send an update. Hang on."

Tara focused on another Rabbit who pulled off his shirt before leaning against the side of the truck. He was lean, but all hard muscle. He noticed her shameless stare and winked before tipping his head back and drinking from a water bottle. Tara's lips curved up in a saucy smile. "And that's the opposite of Speedy."

The female Rabbit glanced up, raising a dark eyebrow.

"Please ignore her," I said, elbowing Tara.

The phone in the Rabbit's hand buzzed. She reviewed the message and nodded. "Here we go. Lydia Swift. Last seen boarding the ferry in the Port of North. Looks like she's heading for Vue."

I smacked my forehead and groaned. "Vue?"

"What's the matter?" Tara asked. She'd returned her wandering attention to the conversation.

"Vue is on the other side of Anwat! We came up to Matar on a wild goose chase." My head dropped back and I stared up at the sky. "What did I do to deserve this?"

The young-looking Rabbit reached over and put her hand on my shoulder. "Mothers, huh?"

I nodded.

"Look, tell you what, Emily Swift. All's not lost. We're moving this equipment, but then we're on our way to a meet-up south of here for the night. We're having a big bonfire – tents are already set up. There's plenty of room. The location is private, and it's on the way to the Port of North. Tomorrow someone can help you get to the ferry and then you can cross over to Vue." She nodded as if I'd already agreed. "Rabbit?" she called over her shoulder.

"Yeah?" A man who appeared to be in his mid-twenties looked up. Rabbits aged incredibly slowly. He was probably about fifty-five years old.

"We have two guests joining us on our road

trip."

* * *

We agreed to return to the studio to meet back up with our new friends after grabbing a fast bite to eat. I was thrilled with our good fortune. THIS was the Rabbit experience I knew. We located a nearby food truck dishing out a simple fare of burgers and fries. We sat on a bench off to the side and started to wolf down our meal.

"Why did we wait so long to eat?" I complained, wiping my hand on my jeans.

"Hyper focus," Tara replied.

"I guess so. Look here. I want to show you a map so you can see where the Port of North sits in relation to Matar and Vue." I pulled The Book from my shoulder bag and opened the lock. I turned to the map that guided me when Anne and I traveled through the Empire last year. Matar was located the farthest north. Vue would be all the way to the south. Port of North sat at the top of Sight Sea. My father had written a small note between Matar and Port of North: *Hidden cluster? Is Rabbit there?*

I pointed to the note. "I wonder if this is where we're going tonight."

"It seems about right. That girl said the bonfire was south of Matar."

"That 'girl' is probably in her early forties," I replied. "Remember, Rabbits only look young."

"I forgot about that. So strange." Tara bit into a French fry. Mid-chew she stopped and rolled her eyes. "Oh, wonderful."

I looked up to see what caught her attention. There was Speedy, leaning against the back of his car, watching us. Damn. I hoped he wasn't a part of the group heading to the bonfire tonight. I shoved The Book back into the bag.

He crossed the road when the traffic grew lighter and stood over us. He sniffed before helping himself to one of Tara's fries. She smacked at his hand.

"Hey, Rabbit," I said. My voice was strained. I couldn't fake any enthusiasm for this man.

"Any luck in finding your mother? She made quite the splash on late night television," he finished. His upper lip curled.

"Yeah, I know." I balled up the wrapper from my burger and started to put the trash into our empty food bag. "We're heading down south tonight toward the Port of North with some of your fellow Rabbits. We'll stop for the night along the way. My mother is on the move again."

"How'd you know we were here?" Tara interjected.

"Because I'm a Rabbit," Speedy snapped.

"The Rabbits' network," I told Tara. "It's pretty quick." I looked back up at him. "Are you traveling with us?"

Speedy jerked a thumb over his shoulder toward his car. "Driving down later. You're stopping on the way to the Port?"

I nodded. "We might as well rest before picking up the trail again. She's probably already in Vue. We were invited to stay in a tent at the bonfire."

Speedy stroked his chin. "Bonfire. Yeah, bedding down there for the night is a good idea. I'll catch up with you later."

"Great." *Not great.* Well, maybe with other Rabbits around, Speedy would be less of a pain.

Tara took advantage of the conversational lull. She nudged me in the side. "Let's get going."

"I suppose we should." I stood up, gathering my shoulder bag and the additional overnight bag I'd been hauling around. I'd ended up tying my coat around my waist. Who could've predicted the nice weather?

"See ya," Tara said as she abruptly walked away from the bench.

"Okay, so we're going. Uh, drive safely," I added in an effort to be polite.

Speedy's smile didn't quite reach his eyes. "Looking forward to seeing you again."

Making my exit, I hurried to catch up with Tara. I looked back once before rounding the corner. Speedy stood there watching, the spooky smile still on his face. Creepy.

* * *

The friendly female Rabbit who took us under her wing showed us to a bathroom at the back of the studio before we embarked on our road trip. I didn't relish the idea of an outhouse, but apparently that would be our only choice other than the great outdoors once we reached our destination. Glamping this would not be, but the Rabbit assured us that things were kept clean. I'd have to trust her.

Our ride to the bonfire was in a vintage Volkswagen microbus retrofitted with an electric motor. It was orange and white.

Tara literally squealed when she saw what we'd be riding in. The previously bare-chested Rabbit from earlier raised his thick eyebrows before inviting her to sit next to him.

I sat next to the female Rabbit and pulled the seatbelt across my lap. She made room at our feet for my overnight bag. Another Rabbit swung into the driver's seat and started the vehicle. I looked around. There were nine of us, including Tara and me.

"Hey, I've got some info for you," my new Rabbit friend said low as she leaned closer. "It's not very good."

I felt a pit open immediately in my stomach. "My Mom?"

"No, that's not it," she assured me. "You're connected to a man called Rene Blackstone, aren't you?"

"Yes." Oh, no. He knows I'm in the Empire. I groaned. "What about him?"

Her nose wrinkled as if she smelled something rotten. "Does the name Patricia Pickelsimer mean anything to you?"

"It does," I answered. I had a familiar, bad feeling.

"Apparently she was killed this afternoon."

"What?" My reaction was noisy. Tara turned around in her seat, a worried expression creasing her forehead.

The Rabbit nodded. "The information is coming through informal channels right now, but the network is buzzing about it since she worked for the Warden of the North Door."

Blackstone was the Warden she referred to. "What happened?"

"She was run off the road while driving. The accident killed her."

"How do they – I mean, you – know she was run off the road?" I immediately thought of Jack and his frightening experience with the car following him.

"Other drivers saw it happen. It was a large SUV. It looked like she was being chased because she was weaving in and out of traffic on a highway and the SUV stayed right on her bumper. She lost control of the car and slammed into a cement divider on the roadside. She was going so fast the impact spun the car off the road and over an embankment. It tipped end over end and landed on its roof." She put her hand on my knee. "The woman died before an ambulance could get there."

I closed my eyes. "Did they catch the person who did this?"

"No. They located the SUV right away in a shopping plaza lot at the next exit. Witnesses there told your police the SUV roared into the lot and slammed to a stop at the curb. A man jumped out and ran along the sidewalk before darting through a door into one of the stores."

"Let me guess," I said as Tara wedged into the small space in front of me. She leaned into my lap, listening. "No one saw him in the store because he must've found the 'right' door."

The Rabbit nodded. "Salesman. It was probably the Fringe."

"Was he wearing a top hat?"

"No one reported one. It'd be something people would notice."

"What's going on?" Tara asked, her voice hushed. The Rabbit next to me filled her in.

"It's like Elsa," I said, referring to Blackstone's previous housekeeper. The woman was killed in a home invasion. Someone hit her over the head at Blackstone's last year.

"Except Elsa was a victim of being in the wrong place at the wrong time," Tara pointed out. "Patricia wasn't at Blackstone's."

"But she was driving Blackstone's car," I said. "The windows are a little tinted. The last time I saw her, she had her hood pulled up."

"You're thinking the SUV driver didn't know it was the housekeeper." The Rabbit furrowed her brow. "The driver thought it was Blackstone."

"That's what I'm thinking," I replied. My gaze met Tara's.

"Interesting." The Rabbit began tapping out a message into her phone. She had new information to share.

"I'm worried," I said to Tara.

She nodded. "Jack."

The Rabbit stopped her texting. "Do you need me to make sure someone gets a message?"

"My boyfriend, Jack. Let him know I'm heading to Vue to get my Mom. And let him know I'm worried the Fringe is in Kincaid. Please tell him he must be aware of what's going on around him at all times."

"I can do that." Her eyes dropped back to her phone. "Tell him that you love him?"

I swallowed the lump in my throat. "Please."

* * *

The rest of the ride to the bonfire was uneventful. Most of the others dozed – even Tara rested her head against the male Rabbit she befriended. I stared out into the fading light, worried about everyone I loved: Jack, my mother, and even Tara, who jumped in feet-first to help me.

It was clear to me it made no difference if I removed myself from the equation. The people I cared about could be in danger even if I wasn't around. Getting to them was one of the ways the Fringe was getting to me. It made me feel helpless.

As the shadows swam over the landscape, we traveled farther out into the countryside. My own eyes grew tired. I let my mind wander as the setting sun flicked its last beams of light at the van. The last time I was in Vue, I was searching for the Crimson Stone. This time my journey into the Empire was to find my mother. In both trips, I was seeking something. In both trips, I was being chased. This time, I couldn't see who was pursuing me. I simply felt their presence.

My head bobbed as I flirted with sleep's pull. I drifted off, my chin slowly lowering to my chest. Memories of my last visit to the Empire flitted along the corners of my mind. Always running, feeling overwhelmed. My eyelids fluttered. Men in top hats chasing me, a man in a top hat taunting me. *Templeton,* I mused dreamily. *Do you know what's happening out there this time? Where are you now?*

Emily, I heard a low voice slide into my thoughts. *You just can't stay out of trouble, can you? The Fringe knows you're here.*

Templeton? I wondered.

Beep beep! The van's horn blasted, jerking me from my slumber. I shuddered, shaking off the dream as I realized I was still in the vehicle. The others around me stirred, too. We slowed to a stop and a face appeared at our driver's window. A few words were exchanged, and we pulled away.

The female Rabbit read my puzzled look. "Checkpoint," she explained. "It's good to know who's in the area. The Fringe is trying to establish a foothold here. We're working to keep them out."

I nodded and peered back out the window, trying to let go of the troubling thoughts swirling in my brain. The driver's window remained down, and fresh air felt good. I also smelled smoke.

We'd arrived at the bonfire.

❉ ❉ ❉

If we'd been in the Empire under happier circumstances, I would've thoroughly enjoyed the party-like atmosphere of the Rabbits' bonfire under the night's blue-black sky. There were thirty or so Rabbits milling around in the firelight reaching out into the surrounding darkness. Tara sat with a noisy group – probably asking a million inappropriate questions. Frequent laughter bubbled up over mysterious music played by two Rabbits sitting on the ground near the fire. The glow cast dancing shadows over their faces. Hands moved swiftly over round, saucer-shaped instruments, pulling a soft, haunting sound from the metal.

"You like it?" asked the female Rabbit as she appeared at my side. She gestured to the musicians.

"I've never heard anything like it," I told her. "It's beautiful."

"They're hang drums," she explained.

The melody shimmered around us. Some Rabbits began to sway to the sound, gathering closer to the bonfire. More joined in and the female Rabbit took my hand, pulling me along.

"Oh, I'm not so sure –" I protested, but she cut me off.

"You need to do this," she smiled. "It'll help chase the dark thoughts away. You need a break. Dance with us."

With that, she flowed away from me, her slim body blending in with the others as the hang drums sang. Another Rabbit squeezed my shoulder gently as he passed. His eyes sparkled in the firelight and he motioned for me to follow.

The music swept over me so sweetly, I couldn't help but surrender to it. I danced with the Rabbits, swaying and spinning as we circled the flames. From a distance, I imagined the act seemed primitive, but I felt like I belonged here. An ancient comfort enveloped me. The rhythm increased and we moved faster around the fire. I lifted my arms high above my head, rotating my wrists as my fingers fluttered to the music. Tara joined in. Rocking her hips side-to-side, she danced with her Rabbit.

I twirled, laughing as my fingertips touched others while the sound swelled. I felt as if something was getting ready to happen, but I wasn't afraid. I felt safe.

Dancing closer to the musicians and their drums, the music seemed to fade. A rushing wind filled my ears and a slight dizziness made me step to the side. I put out a hand to steady myself. My gaze traveled over the dancers winding in and out of the blackness, along the flames in the middle of our circle, and to the other side of the bonfire. There, a man moved slowly, walking through the dancers, his eyes locked to mine. He wore a top hat. I sucked in a breath, shaking my head to clear the loud noise from my ears. I searched again through the smoke and the flames. He was gone.

Regaining my footing, I hurried around the ring of dancers. I saw no one in a top hat. The man was nowhere to be seen. Tara appeared at my side, concerned.

"Em, what's wrong? Are you okay?" she questioned.

"Yeah. I think so." I scanned the crowd and tried to see into the darkness beyond the light. "But I swear, I just saw Templeton."

❊ ❊ ❊

Tara and I walked the perimeter of the Rabbit gathering, but Templeton was not to be found. Asking some of the Rabbits if they'd seen a tall Salesman stalking the edge of the bonfire only earned us bewildered looks. They assured us we were the only non-Rabbits present.

"Em, I hate to say it, but..." Tara's voice trailed off. She shrugged, lifting her hands. "It's a magical place here under the stars. I know I was feeling pretty euphoric. Between the fire and music, I'd say the night was ripe for imaginations running wild."

Tara wasn't wrong about that. It did seem like we were in a special space. And well, we were in the Empire. Magic existed here.

"You're right," I agreed. "I think I was overcome or something. Listen, you don't have to come with me, but I think I'm going to turn in for the night. A good night's sleep is what I really need."

"I won't be late," Tara said. "But yeah, I'd like to spend more time out here."

"With the guy," I said looking past her at the

Rabbit who'd won my best friend's attention.

She laughed. "I like him. He's so nice. I did tell him I couldn't figure out the whole Rabbit-name thing and I'd need to call him something else."

I grimaced. "You didn't offend anyone, did you?"

"I told him from now on I would call him Handsome. He preferred that to Hottie."

"Who wouldn't?" I rubbed the back of my neck. Tara could take care of herself. And frankly, she was in good hands with the Rabbits.

"I think nicknames are okay. They can be terms of endearment." Her face split into a wicked grin. "Or not. I noticed Speedy didn't make an appearance tonight."

"Shh! He might be like Beetlejuice," I warned.

"That would be our luck." Tara waved at Handsome as he danced by and mouthed 'be right there.'

"Go on." I nudged her with my hip. "Don't be too late, and…"

Tara fixed me with a stern look before walking toward the throng of cavorting Rabbits. "We'll all be sleeping alone tonight. I'll be quiet when I come in later."

I watched her blend back in with the dark-haired dancers before seeking the shelter of our tent.

❋ ❋ ❋

On my way, I made a pit stop at the outhouse – which was not at all what I expected. It was more like the bathrooms I'd used at the State Park when I was a child. There were even showers, but no hot water.

The Rabbits were generous, providing us with a sizable walk-in tent. The walls and ceiling consisted of a thick, tarp-like fabric. The windows were zipped tightly shut. I imagined it could withstand some inclement weather. The tent was fastened to the ground with thick rope and stakes. Inside, two cots were placed against the walls. Between them, a raised wire rack sat opposite the tent 'door' and held my bags. A short, wooden trunk rested at the foot of Tara's cot.

A string of hanging LED lights softly lit the space. I unpacked a nightshirt from my overnight bag. I would've loved a shower, but the cold water was a deterrent. Maybe tomorrow I'd get a chance in Vue. Or maybe I'd be lucky enough to be on my way home. A shower in my own bathroom sounded divine.

I pulled off my shirt and shimmied out of my jeans before folding and sliding them back into the bag. If being in the Empire taught me anything, it's to always keep a bag packed in case you need to take off in a hurry. I put my hand to my chest, hesitating and letting my fingertips touch the top of the fabric covering my heart. I decided it would be smart to keep my underclothes on. Socks, too. It wouldn't be comfortable, but I'd deal with it. I pulled the thigh-length nightshirt from my overnight bag and slipped on it over my head.

The Book laid on the foot of the cot. I planned to look through it before going to sleep. Turning to retrieve it, I saw I wasn't alone. Startled, I shuffled backward and knocked into the wire rack – which pushed into the side of the tent and caused the string of lights to swing back and forth violently, forcing the shadows and the light to play together. I stifled a shriek by slapping my hand over my mouth.

Templeton stood scowling, his arms crossed and his head tilted slightly in an attempt to avoid contact with the tent's ceiling. His top hat, finely made, dangled from the fingers of his right hand.

"What are you doing here?" I hissed. "How long have you been standing there?"

An evil smile played across his lips. "Long enough to witness the last bit of your dancing."

My face burned as I realized what he meant. I pointed a shaking finger at him. "Get. Out."

"No."

"Get out or I'll scream."

"No, you won't," he replied. He eyed the space around us, which suddenly seemed very small. "No chair?"

"Templeton, get out." I glanced to The Book

sitting on the end of the cot. It was closer to him. His eyes tracked my gaze. I stepped forward to recover my Dad's journal, but he was quicker. Templeton swept The Book up with his left hand. Slipping his top hat under his right arm, he turned the book on its side and gingerly fingered the lock. His cold eyes narrowed.

Anger boiled inside me. "Give it back," I growled, stepping toward him.

He blinked slowly before fixing me with an amused stare. "You shouldn't leave a Salesman's journal sitting out." He tossed The Book back onto the cot. I was so relieved that he didn't take off with it, I dropped my threatening act and grabbed The Book. I shoved it into my shoulder bag on the rack behind me.

"What are you doing here, Templeton?" I demanded. If he wasn't going to leave immediately, I might as well find out why he was there.

"You're heading to Vue." It wasn't a question.

There was no reason to deny it. If he knew I was here, he probably knew where I was going. "Yes. My mother is there. And by the way, you could've saved me some time and told me she was in the Empire. I might've already caught up to her."

"Doubtful," he brushed off my comments. He considered the trunk at the end of Tara's cot. Bending and turning it onto its side, he used it as a chair. His top hat was gently placed beside him on the cot. Templeton rolled his shoulders and stretched out his legs. He paused, flicking a piece of lint from his sleeve.

"Aren't you warm?" Annoyed, I motioned to his dress coat. Templeton always seemed overdressed to me.

"Are you inviting me to take it off and stay?"

"No! Dammit, Templeton, why are you here? Let's get a move on this." I huffed and sat down on my cot. I realized my mistake too late. I now sat much lower and had to look up. My knees stuck up in the air.

Templeton's shrewd eyes evaluated me. I pressed my knees together, pulling my nightshirt tight around my legs. He rolled his eyes before continuing. "You might want to hurry on to Vue. There's quite a bit of chaos there. It appears your mother met up with some others this evening. Others, like her."

"What do you mean, like her?" I made a face.

Templeton dropped his head back and stared at the ceiling. "I grow so weary of your ignorance," he sighed.

"Excuse me?" I would've jumped to my feet in protest, but I couldn't have done it without a clumsy struggle from the cot.

Templeton looked back down at me. "How well do you know your mother's family?"

"Just stop," I said, lifting a hand. "Please don't insult me by talking about my mother and her family like you somehow know them."

"I'm guessing you haven't met the cousins she's meeting in Vue this weekend." He smirked.

Crap. I so hated this. "Which cousins?"

"I'm sorry, but I don't know your mother's family well enough to know people's names." Templeton was enjoying this. "I do know one cousin made the journey from California. I believe the other was last in Europe. Diplomacy is her specialty."

"Why are they there?" I forced myself to be civil.

He shrugged. "Family reunion? Anyhow, Ms. Swift, I recommend you catch up to your mother tomorrow. You might even consider risking the wrath of the Salesman Court and door traveling to Vue."

I studied Templeton while I chewed my bottom lip. "Is the Fringe close?"

"They've been close for a long time." He didn't look away. "Their reach is growing. You are aware of what happened to Blackstone's housekeeper?"

"I heard. But I can't leave Tara behind," I said, shaking my head. "The Rabbits will get me to the Port of North in the morning. I'll find my Mom tomorrow."

"Very well." Templeton stood. "Be prepared when you get to Vue. Lydia and her cousins have made quite the impact." He retrieved his top hat and turned to exit the tent.

Tara chose that moment to step in through the tent's flap, stopping short when she saw Templeton. "Whoa! You are here!"

"I am," he replied, gracing her with a rare smile.

"Why? What are you doing here?" Tara looked at me, then back to Templeton. She edged around him and moved closer to me. "What are you doing *in* here?"

Templeton shot a wicked smile my way. "I'd hoped to catch a last dance with Ms. Swift, but alas, she's ready for bed. I do like this nightshirt better than the pajamas she wore the last time."

"Goodbye, Templeton," I said through gritted teeth. It was hard to look tough sitting on a cot that was only a foot and a half off the ground.

"Ms. Parker-Jones." He inclined his head toward my friend – albeit awkwardly because of the low ceiling – and slipped out through the front of the tent.

I pointed to the flap. "Is there a way to sort of lock that?"

"No, it just zips." She made sure the zipper was all the way to the ground. "Oh, wait. There's a snap, too."

"Great." I shook my head. Just a zipper and a snap between us and whoever else was out there in the night.

"Should I ask what all that was about?" Tara

said as she began to change into her pajamas.

"Yes," I answered. "Tomorrow."

CHAPTER 9

Breakfast was cooked by our hosts over an open fire. We carried our plates off to the side and snagged a couple of folding chairs, pulling them up to a wobbly card table. Over black coffee and omelets filled with veggies, I filled Tara in on my conversation with Templeton the night before.

"How did he get here?" Tara wondered as she shook ketchup on her eggs. "Hey, did you see any bacon? I'd kill for some bacon."

Two Rabbits sitting on a felled log next to us raised their heads in our direction.

"What?" she asked, looking back and forth between the two. "What?"

"Vegetarians," I responded.

"Oh," Tara sighed. "Damn."

"Focus," I said. "Templeton probably door traveled."

"Through where?"

"Outhouse." I pointed to the building across the way. "There are doors right there."

"But how did he know to come here? Or even how to get here?"

"That I can't tell you," I said.

A Rabbit walked by with a frying pan. "Home fries?"

"Yes!" Tara answered. The Rabbit scooped

some potatoes onto both of our plates. "Hey, have you seen Handsome this morning?"

The Rabbit's nose twitched, and he cocked his head to the side. "You could call me Handsome."

"No, I'd call you Super Cute. Now, where's Handsome?" Tara teased.

The Rabbit actually blushed – *adorable!* – and pointed toward the van we traveled in the day before. "I think he was looking for you earlier. We're going to be leaving soon. Check over there."

"Thanks!" Tara wiped her mouth with a paper napkin. "I'll be back."

We watched her go. "I'm sorry," I apologized. "She's a flirt."

The Rabbit chuckled. "It's fine. Everyone likes her. We can see what a loyal friend she is."

"She is," I agreed. I loved how Tara fit in so easily with the Rabbits. They were one of the best things about the Empire.

I finished my breakfast, wrapping Tara's plate in a brown sandwich bag yet another Rabbit handed to me. I'd make sure she finished her breakfast at some point.

Rabbits who'd driven in from Anwat would deliver us straight to the Port of North where we'd then catch the ferry to Vue. They waved off any suggestion of returning us to the train station. This would be faster. We promised to buy them lunch.

Before I left, I found the female Rabbit who'd so readily helped us in Matar. She and her crew were heading back to the city. They'd picked up an odd job at another studio.

She gave me a hug as we said goodbye. "Well, Emily Swift, I'm glad we met."

"Me, too," I said. "We owe you a lot. Thank you."

"No worries," she said. "I hope our paths cross again soon."

I nodded. "It's not always easy to find a Rabbit."

"Unless they want to be found," she grinned.

"Hey, Rabbit!" The man Tara dubbed Super Cute yelled from the van. "Move your tail!"

As she turned to leave, I reached out one more time, catching her arm. "Wait, a second."

I dug through my shoulder bag and pulled out The Book, releasing the lock with the hat pin. She watched closely, missing nothing. I turned through the pages until I found the handwritten note from my father.

If a Rabbit has no tale, can he still tell a story?

I slid my fingertip to the bottom of the page. My father had included a string of numbers: 4.23.67.7.78.

"Are we here?" I asked.

"Well, in a way, yes. We are at the destination of these numbers."

"What do you mean?"

She tapped the numbers with her own finger.

"I mean, these are directions to get here."

"But I don't know how to read them."

The Rabbit nodded. "But a Rabbit will."

"Rabbit!" yelled Super Cute. "We're leaving you here!"

"I've got to go," she laughed. "See you around, Emily Swift."

I watched her leave, waving as the microbus whirred out of sight. You had to appreciate the irony of no running hot water in the showers, but an electric charging station for their vehicles.

❊ ❊ ❊

One of the Rabbits taking us to the Port of North was a news junkie – even by a Rabbit's standard. He filled us in on everything he'd heard about recent Fringe activity in the Empire. I was glad to learn the Fringe didn't seem to have a strong presence in Vue. Hopefully, my mother was keeping out of the spotlight there.

Yes, my wish was a tall order.

"What about in Kincaid?" I asked him from the back seat.

"Definitely activity going on there. It's the whole North Door thing," he waved a hand. "Hey, can you try to not hit *all* the potholes?"

Our driver, another young-looking female Rabbit, wrestled the wheel as we bounced over another crater in the road. "You'd think the Empire would keep these roads in better condition," she grumbled.

We were flying along a byway in an older, hard-top Jeep. Like the microbus, it'd been converted to electric power. The Rabbits assured us there'd be an on-ramp to a highway a few miles down the road. Hopefully, the highway would be smoother.

"As I was saying," the man continued. "Kincaid's somewhat of a hot spot. Having the North Door there makes it all the more attractive."

"Wait," Tara interrupted. "It's not as if the Fringe is using it to go back and forth. It's in Blackstone's house."

"That's true," he answered. "But the North Door is a portal that can go both ways."

"But only on the Winter Solstice," I argued.

He raised an eyebrow. "You don't think it can be altered?"

"Rabbit," the driver warned. "Don't you think that's enough?" She squinted at her rearview mirror and our eyes met. "No offense."

"None taken," I replied.

Tara, however, was chewing on a thought. "Altered, huh? Like, with magic?"

"Exactly like that," he said, his eyes glittering through thick lashes. "And then, anyone at any time could easily go back and forth from the Empire to Kincaid."

"Anyone?"

"You think only Salesmen can go through the North Door?"

The idea was alarming. "Anyone at any time, and if the Fringe controlled it…"

"Yup. Bad news for the good guys," he said. "And there are three other directional doors in and out of the Empire. If one falls, the others will weaken."

"It would have to be powerful magic," I said.

"It would," he agreed.

"Like the Crimson Stone?" Tara suggested. I fired off a warning look in her direction.

The Rabbit's eyes shone brightly as he leaned farther between the front seats toward us. "Exactly like the Crimson Stone. What do you know about it?"

"Nothing," I cut in.

"Not nothing," Tara said. She offered an innocent smile. "Last I heard, Templeton had it."

"Oh, brother," I mumbled. I gave my head a shake. "We don't know who has it."

He leaned his head against the side of his seat and considered my words. "We've heard rumors about that, but I don't think they're true."

"You'd know better than we would," I said. I was eager to shut this conversation down.

"We heard Templeton was at the bonfire last night," the Rabbit said suddenly. "I was hoping to meet him. I hear he's hot."

"He is," Tara nodded. "Hey, are you seeing anyone? My assistant Marley might be interested in meeting you – although he's a bit of a hot mess right now."

I put both of my hands over my face and groaned. This was torture. The Rabbit laughed before turning to our driver and scolding her again for slamming through potholes.

"That's the least of our worries," she informed us. Her eyes were riveted to the rearview mirror. "Someone is starting to ride on our tails, hard."

Tara and I both turned in our seat just in time to see a large, dark SUV race up to the back of the Jeep.

"Why do the bad guys always drive black SUVs?" Tara asked.

"Hang on," the female Rabbit warned. She sped up.

"He's staying right with us," Tara said.

She was right. The SUV windows were tinted, and we couldn't see the driver. I wondered how many Fringe members were in the vehicle.

The male Rabbit had grown silent. His face was still as stone as his fingers flew over the text screen. He was reaching out to the network.

The SUV finally made contact with our bumper. The Jeep shook and our driver swore a blue streak. "We need to go off-road," she said.

With that announcement, she jerked the wheel, and we went spinning off the byway into a field, bouncing hard across the terrain. I couldn't believe she didn't roll the Jeep. Everyone but the driver yelled in surprise – the male Rabbit the loudest.

"What in the name of the Empire?" he shouted.

"Shut up!" she yelled back. "Get us some help!"

The SUV swerved off the road and followed us. They had dropped behind, but they'd catch up. I immediately pictured Blackstone's housekeeper, Patricia. This must've been the fear she felt before she was killed. I was sick to my stomach.

"They're catching up!" Tara grabbed hold of me, her fingernails digging in through my shirtsleeve.

"We need to find the right way out of here," I said. "The right path!"

Something clicked.

I had to help us find the right path.

I sucked in a breath. Tara's face was pale; she was terrified. She was yelling but my mind could not pick out the words. I closed my eyes. Reach, I thought. Reach.

The energy built in my chest and I pushed it as hard and as fast as I could out of my body. I forced it out, out from the Jeep and listened for the corresponding path. Where was the 'door' I needed? Where was the right path to help us escape?

A buzzing sound filled my head, not unlike the noise I heard when the right door rattled for me.

I opened my eyes and leaned forward between the seats, staring through the windshield. We were moving away from the tree line at the edge of the field. Our driver was trying to get to the byway. But we needed to head back toward the trees. The right path would be there. It would open for us.

"Go back," I directed. "Go back to the tree line!"

"There's no way to go," the driver said. "We've got to get back on the road."

"No, trust me. Please! I can feel the door there," I begged.

This time the female Rabbit didn't look in the rearview mirror. She twisted her neck, looking over her shoulder. Dark eyes met mine. Something unsaid passed between us. She faced forward again and spun the wheel back toward the tree line.

"What are you doing?" cried the other Rabbit.

"Listening to the Salesman," she said.

The Jeep raced across the field. I could see a flicker of light, then a shimmer as we got closer to the trees. I pointed through the windshield. "There!"

On the edge of the field, I could barely make out an opening to a narrow dirt road. The Rabbit slammed her foot down on the Jeep's accelerator and we shot into the woods. The SUV was larger and could not navigate the opening. The driver didn't stop in time. He – or she – crashed the front of the SUV into a large oak. It stopped the vehicle in its tracks. We kept on going.

"Get us a map," the female Rabbit ordered. "Let's find out where this goes."

I sat back in my seat, exhausted as the adrenaline high started to rollback. Tara squeezed my hand.

"Let's not do that again," she said.

❆ ❆ ❆

Before we could find a map to figure out where the road led, it stopped. It just abruptly stopped.

"Huh," said Tara as the four of us sat staring out the windshield. "It doesn't go anywhere."

None of us moved. This, we did not expect.

"Well, let's get moving," our driver finally said as she climbed out of the Jeep. She retrieved a backpack from the rear cargo hold. She pointed. "That way."

Since I had no idea which way to go, I didn't argue. We gathered our bags and started to pick our way through the woods.

"Dammit," Tara said, slapping at her neck. "Mosquitoes."

"I bet you wish it was Handsome," I muttered. Apparently, an adrenaline crash also put me in a lousy mood.

"Oh, stop it," Tara scowled.

"Both of you stop it," said the female Rabbit.

She batted a sapling back after it whacked her in the face. We continued on in silence.

After about thirty minutes of hiking over fallen logs and trying to avoid twisted ankles, we could see a brightly colored sign in the distance. I was out of breath and my water bottle was empty.

"What's that?" I asked, squinting as the sun made an appearance through the tree leaves above. You would've thought it was the middle of summer, it was so green and lush.

"That," said the male Rabbit, "is a snowmobile trail sign. We can follow it and eventually we'll come out to a road. It'll be easier to walk it than fight with this underbrush." He pushed a branch out of our way, and we trudged onward.

The sign indicated we were on the Red Trail and provided mileage to points in opposite directions. We were only a couple of miles from a place called Becket. We all turned in the same direction as one unit, Becket-bound.

Now that the trek was easier to navigate, my attention turned to the Rabbits. I noted their phones were suspiciously quiet. I didn't hear the almost constant buzz of text alerts.

"Why aren't your phones going off?" I asked. The two glanced at one another. Something was up. "What?"

"We're kind of on radio-silence right now," the male Rabbit admitted. "We're in Fringe country.

That SUV was a reminder. We sent a message out to the network, but we're not transmitting anything – just in case."

"Just in case?" Tara repeated.

"Yeah, in case the wrong people are listening in. We don't want them to find us," he said.

I knew we weren't out of danger, but the thought of being on foot and having the Fringe find us was sobering.

We walked without talking for some time, with only the occasional sound of slapping at mosquitoes and the rustling of squirrels and chipmunks in the underbrush. At least, I hoped the noise was caused by cute furry animals.

How did I zone in on the path at the edge of the field? I wondered, stepping over a small branch that had fallen across the trail. It was so much like door travel. I could hear the path. I could see the energy surrounding the entrance. I'd have to talk to Blackstone about this.

No, maybe Jo would be the better person to talk to. In fact, I would send her a message as soon as we reached my mother in Vue. I needed to get another message to Jack, too. I wondered if he was trying to get one to me? I missed him terribly. I was scared for him.

A high whine in the distance caught my attention, and I realized the two Rabbits had frozen in place, noses twitching and eyes shining as they listened intently.

"Rabbit," the male said softly. "Do you hear that?"

"Of course, I do." Her voice came out as a harsh whisper. We all listened as the noise got stronger and seemed to multiply. Something was racing through the leaves and twigs along the trail. Every few seconds there was a significant thud. The din grew stronger and morphed into the sound of whirring motors racing in our direction.

"Behind us, bikes! Move!"

The four of us broke into a run as a motocross bike came into view – *in front of us* – the rider and bike jumping through the air. We slid to a stop, turning to run the other way as a swarm of bikes appeared over the short rise behind us. They rushed us from both sides.

"Scatter!" ordered the female Rabbit, turning into the brush.

I grabbed Tara and pulled her onto a narrow footpath, probably created by animals over time. "Hurry!"

But the footpath only slowed us down, and we turned to get back to the trail where we could move more swiftly. The bikes zoomed and zipped by; helmeted riders trapping us. The sound of the motors hummed in my ears. Yet another bike raced up behind us as one appeared in front, sliding to a stop, rider and bike presenting themselves sideways. I swung my shoulder bag with the intention of knocking him over – *really, for the record, I knew this was hopeless* – and he blocked the blow with his forearm. He held up his right hand in submission, while the fingers of his left moved fast to release the strap under his chin. He yanked off his full-face helmet.

A grinning face with friendly, brown eyes appeared. On his head, a wild mop of dark curls.

"Rabbit!" I threw myself into his arms.

* * *

After tackling my dear friend, I explained to Tara that this man, this rough and tumble man in a dirty, white motocross uniform, was Rabbit. *My Rabbit.* My white knight on a bike in synthetic armor.

"I can't believe you're here," I said. I was overjoyed. The two Rabbits who'd been our travel companions in the Jeep joined us.

"About time," said the female Rabbit. She looked around at the other riders. "Should we get a move on?"

She was right. There was still the risk of being found by the Fringe. The four of us each climbed on the back of a bike. I wrapped my arms around Rabbit's waist. He'd insisted on making me wear his helmet. The Rabbit carting Tara along did the same.

"Hold on," Rabbit said, as we took off down the

trail. "We're heading somewhere safe."

※ ※ ※

When we reached our destination, I had a headache. Even without the fancy jumps and loud motors, the ride out of the woods on the electric motocross bikes left a throbbing pain behind my right eye.

Rabbit and his crew brought us to a small cabin on the outskirts of Becket. After freshening up in the bathroom, Tara and I sat on the front porch stairs and filled Rabbit in on the few details he didn't know. I popped an aspirin and followed it with a gulp of water. Nearby, a group of four Rabbits played Euchre at an old, wooden table.

"What I want to know," I began after I swallowed, "is how did you know we were out there? How did you know where to find us?"

"I was already here in Becket," he explained. "I started to hear chatter you were in the Empire, so I stayed put. I kept listening."

"You heard from the Rabbit who drove us to Matar?" I asked.

"Speedy," Tara quipped from the top step.

Rabbit shook his head. "No, I knew once the train crossed into the Empire you were back. One of the passengers witnessed you door traveling. Or rather, they witnessed a female Salesman door traveling on the train. I knew it was you."

"Seriously? I tried so hard not to make a scene," I groused.

"She so made a scene," Tara told Rabbit.

"I sent a Rabbit to Anwat to meet up with you at the train station," he said.

"Yeah, we met him. He's the one who drove us to Matar," I told him.

"No," Rabbit said. "I sent a woman, not a guy." He shrugged. "Anyhow, we knew we missed you and were waiting for you to pop back up on the radar. Then I got a message from the late show's studio crew in Matar."

"From the crew?"

"Yeah, about five Rabbits reported you were hitching a ride with them to the bonfire," he laughed. "I couldn't make it last night, so I figured I'd catch up with you at the Port of North and we'd go to Vue together."

"You should've messaged me," I said. "I've been looking for you."

"We've had some issues with keeping certain communications private," he admitted. "I've been watching what I'm putting out there in the way of information."

"We heard the Fringe was around here," I said.

"They are. We got the distress signal from the Rabbits who were driving you to the Port. They referenced where they went off the road before they powered down." Rabbit took a drink from his water bottle. His dark eyes flashed with anger. "The Fringe is becoming more violent. A couple of Rabbits were attacked in Matar last week."

"I'm sorry," I said. The memory of Justice Tahl Petrovich spouting off his hatred for the Rabbits before he was arrested for murder popped into my head. What did he say? He wanted the Rabbits exterminated. I shuddered. If he felt that way, so did the Fringe.

"We have trail cams throughout the woods. Once we pinpointed the area you were stranded in, you were easy to find," he told us.

"I can't thank you enough," Tara said. "I was scared out of my mind."

"No worries," Rabbit said. He raised his water bottle and pointed it toward me. "I was afraid the Fringe would get to you in Kincaid. The traffic heading into your city isn't a secret."

"It was a secret until Blackstone finally told me," I replied. "Hey, that reminds me. Did you somehow break into my car radio with a warning message about the Fringe? I mean, through the weather band radio?"

Rabbit grinned as he took a swig from the water bottle, his attention turning toward the four Rabbits playing cards. "Hacking into government weather band radio transmissions is illegal."

I studied the side of his face. Not a trace of guilt. "Thank you."

He tossed a wink in my direction.

Tara pointed toward the card game. "I thought Euchre was a Western New York thing?"

"He has a girlfriend in Buffalo," Rabbit answered, gesturing to a Rabbit wearing thick-framed glasses. The man looked up and smiled.

"Hmm," Tara said, lifting an eyebrow. I assumed she was thinking about Handsome.

I stood up and stretched. My headache was lessening. "We should probably get going. When can we leave for the Port?"

Rabbit capped his water bottle and joined me. "Give me five minutes and we'll hit the road."

❊ ❊ ❊

I was getting a little sick of road trips. I thought about Templeton's suggestion to just door travel down to Vue. In fact, I knew a destination I could focus my energy on: Tuesday's bakery, *The Sweet Spot*. Tuesday was one of Anne's friends, a plump little woman with a knack for scrumptious pastries. She was sort of goofy, but a welcoming hostess. I planned to stop in to see her once in Vue.

But even though my door traveling on the train hadn't stayed a secret, I still was hoping to operate under the radar. Rabbit's admission about the Fringe worried me.

After we were dropped off at the ferry, Rabbit produced three tickets so we could board immediately without waiting in line at the counter. The ferry only carried pedestrians. It wasn't big enough for vehicles, but it had three decks. We moved to the top one where lounge chairs were set out in the sunshine. Tara bought a floppy hat from a vendor by the beverage bar. She picked a chair in the center of the deck and lowered herself into it. Bags at her side, hat low on her face, she settled in for a nap. Rabbit and I walked to the railing to talk.

The sunlight bounced off the water of Sight Sea and we stood in comfortable silence watching the passengers board. As the ferry pulled away from the dock, I paused to dig into my shoulder bag for a hair tie. I couldn't find one. I lifted my hair off the back of my neck, hoping for a cooler breeze.

"The weather is so different from ours," I told him. "What is it, eighty degrees?"

Rabbit gave me a sideways look before returning his attention back to the water. He sighed. "It's your mother."

"What about her?" I contemplated going for another bottle of water.

"The weather. It's because of Lydia." He kept staring across the water.

"What's the weather got to do with my

mother?"

"She's the reason it's so nice here, Emily. Lydia's inspiring spring to come early. By the looks of it, summer's not far behind."

"Rabbit, that's crazy talk." I pulled on his shirtsleeve so he would look at me. "My mother doesn't control the weather."

Rabbit's eyes held mine for a moment. He took a deep breath and shook his head. He was struggling with something. "No, Emily she doesn't."

"She's an artist, that's how she 'inspires' people." I was annoyed but felt a flutter in my stomach. "Oh. There's something else, isn't there?"

"It's not my story to tell," he replied. His nose twitched.

I paused, considering his choice of words. I thought of the passage my father had written in The Book:

If a Rabbit has no tale, can he still tell a story?

"I think I need to hear this," I told him. "I need to know my mother's story."

Rabbit ran both hands over his head and through his hair. He looked into the blue sky above.

"Please," I said.

He nodded, placing his hands on my shoulders. He gave them a gentle squeeze. "Your mother is an artist, Emily. She's many different artists, in a way."

"Because she's creative in all kinds of mediums," I said. "I get it."

"No, that's not exactly what I mean." He slid his hands down my arms to my hands. "Emily, your mother is a Muse."

"I don't understand." I searched Rabbit's face for clarity. "What do you mean?"

"Your mother is a very special being," he said, his voice soft and kind. "The inspiration she brings to your world helps keep the darkness at bay. Her energy – her power – is like a warm glow filling people up. Artists in particular are highly sensitive to the vibrations she puts out there. And that's what she does. She's a transmitter, Emily, constantly sending out inspiration into your world. Her creativity is what fuels imagination in others. Sometimes, if she comes in contact with the right person, especially a highly creative person, the inspiration they receive is more potent. Next thing you know, you have the next Vincent van Gogh."

"I don't... I don't." I pressed my lips together. All those paintings, and sculptures, and poems. "So, it's my mother painting? Or composing the music? Not the painter or singer?"

"Not quite," Rabbit said. "Those artists are still creating their own unique work. Your mother is simply filling the creative well they tap into with her own art."

And that made me want to cry. I pictured the

beautiful work my mother engaged in over the years. We had none of it. She had none of it. My eyes grew wet.

"Hey, hey," Rabbit shushed, putting his arm around me. "It's not the same for her. She loves what she's doing. It's her purpose. She embraces it. From what your father described to me, she's the happiest when she's helping people drink from the well."

I remembered all of the times my mother became excited: when she was asking Tara about her writing, or when she was singing along with the radio, or when she was joining in a standing ovation after a musical, calling out bravo. In those moments, my mother seemed to shine.

"Why didn't she tell me?" I asked. I walked to the nearest lounge chair and sat down. I bowed my head, staring at my hands folded in my lap. Rabbit followed, sitting on the seat across from me.

"Emily, it's different with people like your mother, like your father," Rabbit said. "Part of them assumes you already know things like they do, that they don't need to explain because you have 'abilities,' too. Another part is afraid to talk about this other world that's right beside the one you know. They don't want to alarm you as much as they don't want to tempt you. They want to keep you safe."

"But in the end, they can't," I replied, looking

back up.

"No, they can't. They can only help." He reached across and patted my knee.

"So…" I looked around the deck as if I could find the answers tucked in between the people laughing and walking around me. "If she creates all this inspiration back home, what happens when she's here in the Empire?"

Rabbit took a breath before he finally spoke. "She creates chaos."

❦ ❦ ❦

This is why it was so important for me to catch up with my mother and return her to home. This is why Blackstone wanted her out of the Empire immediately.

My mother's energy swirled harder, faster, and higher when she was in the Empire. This world fueled my mother. My mother didn't need fueling. Not only did people tap into my mother's energy, so did nature. Everything wanted to wake up and thrive in her presence. Rabbit warned that nature, although beautiful in many ways, could also be destructive. He was worried. As Lydia's energy increased, we could be in for some rough storms – literally.

"It wouldn't be the first time," he sighed.

Vue was a magnet for my mother because of the artist community thriving there. Rabbit said there'd been reports of massive artistic explosions – a Renaissance of sorts in Vue. In short, artistic chaos.

As if all this wasn't troubling enough, it was overshadowed by the Fringe. They knew exactly who Lydia Swift was. Her travels through the Empire were impossible to miss.

"Can we get a message to her in Vue?" I asked. "Why don't we see if we can get her to meet us somewhere when we arrive?"

"Because she's about as slippery as they come," Rabbit grinned. "We've been a step behind her all week."

I blew out a breath. That wasn't surprising. She was hard enough to nail down back home. If the Empire amplified her energy, it was probably worse here. "That figures. Well, we'll just deal with it when we get there."

Rabbit checked his phone. "Why don't you join Tara and I'll see what I can find out. Let me see what's going on in Vue right now."

My friend was still dozing on the lounge chair. "I think I need a break from the heat. I'm going down to the next deck. Rabbit, can you watch my overnight bag?" I asked. The shoulder bag I kept, pulling the strap over my head so that it crossed my chest, the bag itself resting against my hip.

I took the steps down to the deck below. It was cooler and I strolled along the railing on the shadier side of the ferry. My head was full of so many questions, about my mother and who she was – about who I was in light of this revelation.

At the end of the second deck, I was met with another set of stairs leading to the first level of the ferry. A sign indicated there was a café below. I continued. The bottom deck was fairly empty of passengers. A portion of it was enclosed to protect the small café. I skirted the edge to the front of the ferry. The space was narrow, but the breeze was refreshing. Every now and then, I felt a misty spray of water.

I continued my exploration and came face-to-face with a man blocking my passage. His cool gaze traveled from my feet to my face.

"Excuse me," I said, intending to pass on by. When he didn't move, I hesitated. My first thought was he couldn't be the Fringe, because I didn't see a top hat. My next thought was a rogue Salesman wouldn't necessarily be using a top hat.

"Never mind," I said, backing up. I turned and hurried back the way I came, rounding the small building housing the café. I retraced my steps until another intimidating figure came into view. I stopped short. He was large, filling the small space between the railing and the enclosure. This man smiled, and it was evil.

I spun again and started to move faster as my heart thumped harder in my chest. Why did I come all the way down here? I lamented. The first man appeared in front of me again. I was trapped. What would they do? Throw me over the side? Kidnap me? Fear washed over me, my knees buckling as I stopped, gripping the railing behind me. I needed to get out of there. I needed to get to my mother!

A metal door stamped 'Utility' was only a few steps away. As the second man came closer, I heard him growl I wasn't going anywhere. I stared hard at the utility door. Yes, I was. I was going through *that* door. I made a dash and only heard the hum of door travel after my fingers turned the doorknob. The first image I conjured inside my head was of Tuesday's bakery. I smelled her delicious pastry. I was heading for *The Sweet Spot*.

CHAPTER 10

When I first learned of door travel, I was told traveling off something moving – like a train – wasn't possible. Then I proved it was. Well, supposedly Templeton accomplished that little feat before me, but no one could really be sure he pulled it off. It was a rumor.

Doors, like those on a train, or in this case a ferry, were moving targets. Your destination would be affected. You might end up in a place you didn't want to be.

I'd also been coached that door travel involved finding the 'right' door. And it seemed it was still true. But what if you could force a door to be the 'right' door? What if you could choose a door and travel to where you needed to go with your intention alone?

As I whipped through the door of *The Sweet Spot*, staying on my feet but rushing in like the devil was at my back, this was the thought flitting through my mind. What if I could make any door the 'right' door?

And how else had I been misled?

I skittered to a halt before knocking into any displays. The India bells hanging from the bakery's door were still swinging when tubby little Tuesday popped up from behind the counter.

"Oh!" she startled. "That's quite an entrance!" Her round cheeks were flushed from the heat in her kitchen. White flour powdered her white hair. She blinked rapidly.

"Sorry, Tuesday," I said, straightening my shoulder bag and running a hand through my hair. The door travel hadn't been particularly violent this time, but I still felt the need to rearrange myself. I took a moment to check my top hat. It remained safely inside my bag.

Tuesday pulled on a pair of glasses; her eyes enlarged by the lenses. "Emily! Oh, my goodness, it's you! It's you!" She scurried around the edge of her counter and tossed herself into my embrace. I was short, but Tuesday was shorter. She was also very cushy. I loved that.

"It's me, Tuesday," I laughed. "You don't know how happy I am to see you."

"I've missed you! How is Anne? Is she with you, too?" Tuesday straightened her glasses and peeked around me to the door.

"I'm here by myself for now," I told her. I explained how Rabbit and my friend Tara were not far behind me on the ferry bound for Vue. "I had to door travel off the ferry. I think a couple of Fringe members tried to grab me."

"But you escaped!" she observed. She wagged a finger at me. "The Fringe are bolder these days. They don't know who they're up against."

"Well, I don't believe I'm much of a match for

them, but I'm glad to be at *The Sweet Spot*," I said. "I planned on coming by after we arrived. Once I meet up with Rabbit and Tara at the dock, we'll come straight back."

"How wonderful!" She clapped her hands together and a puff of flour appeared. I checked my shirtsleeves for Tuesday's handprints, but noted nothing.

"Um, Tuesday?" I began.

"Let me make sure I have a vegetarian lunch puff for your Rabbit." She danced back behind the counter and through the swinging door into her kitchen.

I shook my head and chuckled. Tuesday was just as entertaining as I remembered. Now that I knew about my mother's status as a Muse, I put the pieces together on Tuesday. Anne had once remarked Tuesday was like my Mom. I'd have to learn more at some point.

"Yes!" she announced, returning. "We'll have delicious treats for everyone. Now, Emily, what are you doing in Vue? Are you here for the festival?"

"The festival?" I repeated.

"Yes, there's a big art festival happening all over the city. Quite the spontaneous event! Nothing was planned until this summer. The park leading to the ferry dock is packed. You'll want to give yourself some extra time to get there and meet your friends," she told me.

Oh boy, an impromptu art festival. I wondered how much of a role my mother played in this surprise event. "I'm actually in Vue to catch up with my mother, Tuesday. She's been leading me on a real wild goose chase."

Tuesday tilted her head to the side. "Is she meeting her cousins?"

Damn, Templeton. I hated it when he was right. "I think so. I heard that from, ah, another person. You don't know my Mom's cousins, do you?"

"I've known Aster for years. She stopped in yesterday with Minerva."

"Aster and Minerva?"

"Your mother's cousins. They didn't mention meeting up with your mother, but I'm sure that's the plan if she's in Vue, too." Noise rose outside Tuesday's bakery and she moved to the front of the shop to peek out a window. "A parade!"

"Really?" I joined Tuesday and watched as a band of uniformed musicians marched by playing their brass instruments. Acrobatic clowns danced in front of them.

"I wasn't expecting a parade today," Tuesday tapped her pursed lips with a finger. "And I do love a parade."

"Well, you have a prime spot to watch," I said.

"Watch? Oh, Emily, no! We're going to join!" Tuesday scampered to the back of the bakery.

A moment later she returned with two bags of candy. She handed me one. "Let's go!"

Shaking my head, I followed Tuesday out of the shop. She locked her door before we blended into the growing crowd of people. We moved closer to the street, Tuesday grabbing my hand and giving me a pull. We popped out right as a group of costumed performers strolled by, waving to onlookers on the sidewalk.

"Tuesday, I don't think –" I began.

"Look! There's Suzette Mira. She's the star of my favorite musical!" Tuesday pointed to a small float and wiggled her fingers at an actress wearing a dazzling gown. The woman blew Tuesday a kiss. Smiling, Tuesday filed in lockstep behind the troop of actors, tossing candy to the spectators.

I guess when in Vue, if you can't beat 'em, join 'em. I walked beside Tuesday, following her lead. As we rounded the corner, I hollered over the din. "Where are we going?"

"To the park," she called back. She motioned vaguely in the direction we were pointed. We weaved through the street flipping candy to the parade watchers. I recognized a few of the storefronts I'd passed during my first visit to Vue.

The throng of people continued to swell, and we were swept forward. The street widened and we spilled out into the park. People parted to the left and right as the parade marched forward and up a large sidewalk leading to one of the many performance platforms forming the festival grounds.

I spun around, my eyes roaming over the dizzying display of color. Flowers bloomed everywhere. Tents were set up displaying artists and their work – from paintings, to sculpture, and everything in between. Music genres bumped into each other as we wandered farther into the park.

I noted an audience filing into rows of wooden chairs in front of a small stage set under a banner proclaiming *Sustainability, Plastics & Culture: A Debate*.

"That's unexpected," I said, pointing at a raised panel. Two groups of four each sat on opposite sides of a podium. A moderator cleared his throat into the microphone.

"The art of debate, my dear," Tuesday said, looking around. "Minerva would enjoy this. I wonder if she's here?"

"It's like nothing is being left out," I observed. I wiped a hand across my month. The air felt thick to me – all the sounds, colors, and smells. "Is this because of my mother?"

Tuesday turned her little round face toward me and looked up. Her eyes twinkled behind her glasses. "I'd say Aster and Minerva are adding a little something. It's what they do."

"They?"

"Three Muses in Vue – two Major Muses and one Meta. This has been a glorious week." Tuesday's dimples deepened.

I felt lightheaded. "Tuesday, Anne said you were like my mother, once. Are you one, too? A Muse?"

"I'm a Minor Muse," she nodded with a smile. She suddenly looked around. "We should get something sweet."

Before I had a chance to tackle this latest revelation about my mother and Muses, a loud clatter pulled both of our attentions to a nearby display tent. A short man stood with his arms crossed, an easel and canvas on the ground at his feet. Sunlight bounced off his blond head as he sneered at a man waving paint-splattered hands.

"How dare you?" raged the painter. "You cannot pull me from the show at the last minute! Everyone is coming tonight. They expect to see my work. You cannot do this to me!"

"It's my gallery and I can remove your… work, if that's what this fingerpainting is supposed to be." He sniffed as he surveyed the pieces displayed on the tent walls. "I have no idea how you were approved to participate. Someone clearly made a dreadful error. This isn't up to par with my standards. It's trash."

"Trash?" the artist sputtered, clenching his fists. "You wouldn't know art if it shot out of your –"

"Who is that?" I asked Tuesday. "What's going on?"

Tuesday wrinkled her nose, peering through her lenses. "Ugh. The man with the crossed arms is Peti Kis," she said. "He's a horrible person with a lot of money and power here in Vue. He owns one of the most popular galleries in the city, but I find some of the art he endorses lacking in spirit. Still, if you want to skyrocket to success as an artist, Peti's gallery has made some of the biggest names in the Empire. But he's a ruthless gatekeeper, approving artists on a whim – or tossing them off with a devastating review. He's a mean, little man."

We watched as Peti snapped his fingers and a woman stepped forward to remove a sign indicating the uninvited artist was appearing at the *Peti Kis Gallery*. The smug smile Peti wore remained on his face as he turned and pranced his way through the gathered crowd, leaving the angry artist alone with his frustration.

"What a jerk," I said. While I was no art critic, the artist's landscape paintings were charming. Even if they weren't the finest art, there was no reason to stomp on someone's heart and soul like that. The gallery owner could've been discreet.

"That's pretty typical of Peti," Tuesday said, looking at her wristwatch. "I'd better get back to the bakery. Listen, once your friends get here, bring them to *The Sweet Spot*. I'll make sure everyone's well-fed!" Tuesday did a little jig.

I laughed, thankful I was with someone who could lighten the mood. "Sounds good. I'm going down to the dock now. Better to get there a little early."

We split off in separate directions. As I walked along one of the many paved park paths, I allowed my route to bring me closer to the statue of my father erected in his honor following his death. He supported the artist community in Vue, and they loved him back.

Before I reached the small clearing housing his statue, I bumped into an old friend: Speedy.

He stood to the side, his thumbs in his front jean pockets. A scowl sat on his face as he watched the flow of people stream by. Before I could turn in the opposite direction, we made eye contact.

"Hey, Swift!" he called. "Over here!"

Great. "Hey… you," I answered as I walked toward him. I felt a little awkward having my last name called out like that. I supposed there were other Swifts in the Empire, but I was reluctant to draw any attention to myself.

"You got here fast." He raised an eyebrow. "Where's your friend?"

"I'm meeting her at the ferry," I said.

"I'll walk you down to the dock." He motioned

for us to continue down the path. "So, what did you do? Door travel?"

"Yeah. I did." Now that I was connected with Rabbit, I had even less of a desire to spend time with Speedy. "What are you doing here?"

"Thought I'd check out the festival. Everyone's an artist, huh?" He pointed at a sculptor working clay in front of his tent and laughed. "Except for that guy."

"I don't think I'm qualified to judge," I replied. "Look, you don't need to escort me down to the dock. In fact, I already connected with –"

"Emily Swift?" A slim woman asked as she approached me from the side. Dressed in a fitted black tee shirt with ripped jeans tucked into work boots, the Rabbit leaned forward as she examined my face. Her skin was fair, and she wore a gold nose ring. Her dark hair was pulled back into a long, thick braid.

"That's me," I answered.

The woman's gaze flicked toward Speedy. She paused for a beat before bringing her attention back to me. "Rabbit sent a message from the ferry. He couldn't find you and took a chance you were in Vue. He said if we saw you, to tell you to go to Tuesday's." The woman scanned Speedy a second time before continuing. "He wants you to stay there and wait for him. It's safer."

Speedy frowned at me. "I thought you said you

were meeting your friend Tara."

"I am. And Rabbit's with her. We finally caught up with him. Or, he caught up with us," I said.

"Do I know you?" the female Rabbit interrupted. Her brown eyes zeroed in on Speedy. "I don't think I know you."

"Yeah, I'm not from around here," he shrugged. He backed away and tossed me a final look. "I gotta run. I'll catch up to you later, Emily."

"Okay," I replied, relieved he was leaving. I really didn't need to spend any more time with him.

The female Rabbit watched Speedy's departure with sharp eyes. I felt her hand rest on my upper arm. "C'mon. I'll walk you back to *The Sweet Spot*."

"Thanks," I said. I pointed my chin in the direction Speedy disappeared. "He's not the friendliest Rabbit, is he?"

"I don't know him," she said.

❊ ❊ ❊

After the female Rabbit returned me to *The Sweet Spot*, Tuesday insisted the woman take a bag packed with all sorts of treats before she left. Tuesday thought the woman was 'a bit thin,' and wanted to make sure she 'put some meat on those pretty bones.' If anyone else said something like that, it would've sounded insulting. Coming from Tuesday, it wasn't. She simply wanted to make sure the Rabbit was well-fed. She told her to come back anytime for more 'samples.'

"I love Rabbits," Tuesday sighed as she watched her go. "They're so much fun."

"I was at a Rabbit bonfire last night," I told her. "A lot of good energy."

She nodded. "They bring good things to the Empire. We need them."

Tuesday's observation was interesting, and I agreed. I helped her bring a selection of lunch puffs and other edible delights upstairs to her apartment. While we were at the festival, a young kitchen assistant reopened the bakery. When I asked the girl if she wondered where Tuesday disappeared to, she just laughed as she waved her shop key at me. She said Tuesday was often gone with the wind.

"There. That looks good." Tuesday placed her hands on her ample hips and surveyed the table. She'd piled the food high: lunch puffs – both vegetarian and with chicken, beignets, a king cake with cream cheese filling, pecan tart, anise sugar cookies, lemon bars, and carrot cake cupcakes with thick frosting and marzipan carrots for decoration. A bright yellow teapot sat to the side wrapped in a heated cozy. Four delicate cups in four shades of blue surrounded it.

"I think that's quite a spread, Tuesday," I said.

"I have a strawberry-rhubarb pie downstairs."

"There will only be four of us, including you."

"Right! Then I better get it!" She scurried back downstairs.

I shook my head. It would be impossible to starve around Tuesday. I walked to the front of the apartment, pulling the lace curtains aside so I could see out the window and down onto the street. Happy people strolled along laughing and enjoying the sunshine.

Somewhere in Vue, my mother could be out doing the same.

My mother. My mother the Muse. What did Tuesday say? She was a Minor Muse, and the others – my mother and her cousins – were Major and Meta Muses. Was Mom the Meta Muse? If she was making the impact on the Empire that Rabbit alluded to, then she must be. I needed to find out more.

I left the window and swiped a lemon bar from the table. It was heavenly. Maybe Tuesday's baking was so amazing because she was a Muse. Food tasted brighter when it came from her kitchen. The lemon bar made me feel good.

"Okay," Tuesday huffed as she cleared the last couple of stairs into her apartment. She balanced a pie in her hand. "This ought to do it."

"And then some," I said. "I just ate a lemon bar. It could be the best dessert I've ever eaten."

Tuesday pressed her palms together and

bounced on the balls of her feet. "Don't they taste like sweet sunshine? With the weather being so bright and breezy, I'm planning a nice selection of citrus treats."

"Well, I'm a fan," I grinned. I sat down at the table, folding my arms and resting my elbows on the tablecloth. "Tuesday, can I ask you some questions about what's going on in Vue? Can I ask you about my mother and her cousins? And you?"

Tuesday smiled warmly and took a chair across from me. "Of course, you can."

"I only found out today my mother is a Muse," I told her.

Tuesday sat back in her chair, surprised. "You didn't know?"

"No. She never said anything about it." I shook my head. "Rabbit is the one who told me. I don't think he wanted to, but he did. On the ferry."

"Well, hmm." Tuesday's brow dipped in thought. "Are you sure she never said anything?"

"Oh, I'm sure."

"Maybe she thought you knew?" Tuesday put her hands together and leaned forward. "Didn't you notice?"

I took a deep breath. "Tuesday, where I come from, people aren't Muses."

"But that's not true!"

"How so?"

"Your mother is one." Tuesday looked a bit confused.

I couldn't help but laugh. This was like talking to my mother. Tuesday was definitely a Muse if my mother was one.

"Fill me in on a couple of things. You said there are major and minor ones, and you also said something about meta. What does that all mean? Is my mother the Meta Muse?" I asked.

"Yes, she's the Meta. Aster and Minerva are Major Muses. I'm a Minor Muse."

"Go on," I prodded.

"My realm is baking – mostly pastries and sweets. If you enjoy my dishes, you'll be inspired to feel good, to look for happiness. If you're a baker like me, you'll be inspired to be more creative in the kitchen. You'll develop your own recipes. Baking will help you put goodies and good things out into the world." Tuesday placed her elbows on the table, lowering her chin into her intertwined fingers. She smiled dreamily. "The world tastes better because of bakers."

I believed everything she said. "And what about the others? My mother and her cousins?"

"Well, like I said, Minerva and Aster are Major Muses. Aster is behind the flower power here in Vue this week," Tuesday explained. "With Aster around, you'll find all kinds of plants and flowers that don't usually grow in our region – outside of a greenhouse. She inspires plants to grow, to be hardy and produce a lot of food. But she also lends strength to flowers and blooms, bathing the world in color and scents. She can inspire many things involving flowers. Romance, for example, or even comfort at a bedside when someone is sick. She can even encourage peace for mourners at a funeral."

Tuesday paused to pull two teacups closer. She lifted the pot and glanced up at me. "Tea?"

"Please," I said. "And how does all of that make her a Major Muse? How is that different from you?"

"Aster inspires a wider variety of people and scenarios because her domain is broader." Tuesday finished pouring the tea and handed me a light blue teacup. I smelled berries when I took a sip. "Trees, too. You've heard of activists who climb all the way up in those incredibly old redwoods and camp out to keep them from being cut down?"

"Out in California? I have. I think they call it tree-sitting."

"That's Aster at work," she nodded. "Aster's inspiration is deeply felt by activists and ecologists, gardeners, florists, all kinds of growers and farmers. Oh! Even seaweed farming. It's not only inspiration for plants grown on land."

"So, she's a Major Muse because the scope of her impact is bigger?" I was beginning to understand.

"Yes," Tuesday said. "Now Minerva inspires diplomacy. Her domain might seem narrow at first, but it's extensive as well. Her power is felt by peacemakers, negotiators, delegates. She inspires them to listen and to understand other points of view."

I thought about the debate being held at the art festival. "You said Minerva would enjoy it. I'm not entirely sure why. I mean, it's essentially an argument."

"Debaters need to be good listeners, too," answered Tuesday. "Those drawing from Minerva's inspiration tend to be drawn toward peaceful pursuits. They're looking for a common good, a well-being between different groups of people. A passion drives them. Politicians, for better or worse, drink deeply from Minerva's well. The wiser ones become statesmen."

"And the others?"

"Remain politicians," she winked.

I laughed. Tuesday was not known for her wit, but she nailed it. "I think I can see why Minerva is a Major Muse, then. That just leaves my Mom."

Tuesday ran a fingertip around the rim of her teacup, eyes big and round on the other side of her glasses. "Meta Muse."

"Who does she inspire?"

"Everyone."

✣ ✣ ✣

Lydia, Tuesday explained, was the purest vein of inspiration in human form. It didn't matter who you were, if there was something you yearned to do, if you were open to a nudge, my mother could inspire you to act. Artists in particular felt her impact the most. Creation served as a ritual calling upon my mother's power.

"But wait," I interrupted. "She doesn't affect me. Is it because I'm her daughter? Or maybe because I'm a Salesman?"

"What makes you think she doesn't affect you?" Tuesday smiled into her teacup as she sipped.

"Well, I don't see how she has. I mean, I'm not an artist in any way. I don't think I'm inspired to… to have a passion. I don't think it works on me," I said.

"Adventurers can be inspired," Tuesday said.

"You think I'm an adventurer?"

"Well, aren't you?"

"I…" An adventurer? I hesitated. "Tuesday, even if that were true, I've only been 'an adventurer' since I turned thirty and became a Salesman."

"And that, my dear, is when you went to the well." Tuesday stood up. "Hear that? The India bells just announced a Rabbit. I bet your friends are finally here!"

CHAPTER 11

Tuesday's prediction was true: Tara and Rabbit finally arrived. Tara hugged me for a long time while she scolded me for wandering off by myself. Rabbit guessed I'd fled the ferry because of trouble. He was glad to learn the Rabbit with the braid walked me back to *The Sweet Spot*. We dug into the feast Tuesday laid out for us. Our hostess excused herself back downstairs to the bakery leaving us to plan our next steps.

"Things are ramping up. This art festival has everyone's attention," Rabbit said.

"Like the Fringe," I replied.

"And Empire leadership. They don't like the instability of things."

"It's not just my mother," I told him. "Her cousins are Muses, too."

"But your mother increases their influence. They're not immune. I saw a Naupaka shrub flowering at one entrance of the park when we left the dock. They're native to Hawaii," Rabbit added.

I ran my hands through my hair, lifting it off my neck. The windows were open, but it was terribly hot in Tuesday's apartment. Tara dug into her shoulder bag and retrieved a hair tie.

"Thanks," I said, taking it and pulling my hair

up into a ponytail.

"So, now that we're in Vue," Tara began. "What next? How do we find Lydia?"

"Rabbits are watching for her, but even though she's causing bits of commotion as she goes, it's like we only hear about it after the fact." He grinned. "She's driving the network nuts."

"Again, that sounds about right." I finished my egg and artichoke lunch puff and helped myself to another lemon bar. "We need to figure out where she'll go next."

"Like an event," Tara nodded. "There's got to be a bunch going on because of the festival, right?"

"That's a good idea, but which one? Can we get a list? If this festival was unplanned, it's not like there's a bunch of advertisements," I said.

Rabbit's fingers flew across the screen on his phone. "Let me find out what big events are going on tonight. Maybe one will attract your mother."

"Should we split up?" Tara asked. "Not that I'm saying you should be alone, Emily. But maybe we could check out events that are close to one another."

"That could work," I answered.

"I'm not for it," Rabbit said, dark eyes still on his phone. "Emily's been chased by the Fringe twice now. It's too risky." He paused, scrolling. "Bunch of messages. Huh. *Rhino Vomit* is here tomorrow. Cool."

"Should we try there?" Tara asked, chuckling. "Afterall, Lydia was their groupie."

"My mother was not their groupie," I said. "I'd say let's pass on *Rhino Vomit*."

Rabbit looked up. "You don't know what you're missing."

"I'll live with it," I said. "What else you got?"

"Here's something," he said. "Tonight, there's a big art exhibition at a place called the *Peti Kis Gallery*. He's listing some big names."

"I know who that is," I grimaced. "I saw him at the art festival ripping some poor painter a new one. He's a real piece of work."

"But if this art show is a big deal, I think it's worth checking out. I'll get us some tickets." Rabbit tapped a message into his phone.

"Will we be underdressed?" Tara asked. "We packed light and all I have are jeans and heavier shirts. And the winter coat I've been dragging around."

"At least we can leave our coats here," I said. "I also asked Tuesday if we could spend the night and she said absolutely. Granted, she only has one bedroom, so we're going to have to flip for the couch."

"I have a place to stay in Vue," Rabbit said. "You and Tara can work out the sleeping arrangements here. If we're lucky tonight and find Lydia, you'll probably want to let your mother have the couch."

He continued. "I wouldn't worry about what to wear tonight, though. Some people will be dressed up, some won't. You'll fit in fine."

"What time does it start?" I asked.

"Doors open at seven. There's a reception in the attached garden." Rabbit reviewed the message on his phone. "It's a pretty big place."

"We've got time then." I looked at Tara. "There are shops on this street. Let's duck into one and get a couple of lighter tops."

❋ ❋ ❋

Rabbit insisted on going with us. He waited outside while we browsed the racks in a small boutique.

"He's pretty protective," Tara said. She looked out the window. We could see him texting. Every so often he'd look up and around, then it was back to his phone.

I paused and watched him for a moment. "You know, it's easy to forget how old he is because Rabbits age so slowly. I asked Anne and she guessed he was about fifty-five. Maybe older. He looks like he's twenty-five, but if you really think about it, he could be our father."

Tara held up a black silk blouse below her chin and checked her reflection in the full-length mirror. Her eyes caught mine. "I never thought of it. That makes sense. Plus, he knew your Dad.

I wonder if he feels sort of, well, fatherly around you. How old would your Dad be if he were still alive?"

"Sixty. He didn't marry my Mom until he was thirty." I pulled a bright blue blouse from the rack. It was a little on the boho side, with three-quarter length sleeves. The blouse dipped into points in the front and back with an asymmetric hem. Paired with my jeans and some brown flats from a nearby display, the chiffon top would create a casual but pretty outfit for the art exhibition.

Tara nodded her approval. "I like it. They have some jewelry at the counter."

We paid for our new clothes with the Empire dollars we'd picked up in Anwat. Rabbit met us at the door. "Anywhere else?"

"What are you wearing?" Tara asked.

He looked down at his concert tee. "This, why?"

"Really?"

Rabbit turned to me. "Is she serious?"

I laughed. "You're on your own."

"I think we should get back to Tuesday's," he said. "Tickets are waiting for us at *The Sweet Spot*."

❋ ❋ ❋

It felt good to shower and change into clean

clothes at Tuesday's. Hopefully, we'd catch my mother tonight and be on our way home in the morning.

Rabbit left to run an errand after giving us strict orders to wait for him before heading to the *Peti Kis Gallery*. While Tara was showering, I pulled out The Book from my shoulder bag. I turned the pages until I found the words my father wrote about communication. Now that Rabbit confirmed – well, somewhat admitted – he'd busted into the weather radio's transmission, it would seem the message had served its purpose.

COMMUNICATION

News will travel
Through many mediums
Sent by both
Friend and foe
Learning the difference
Makes all the difference.

But I couldn't shake the feeling the warning was still relevant. Rabbit was clearly my friend. Who was the foe? Well, the Fringe. Templeton? No. He lived to taunt me, sure, but he really didn't fall into the category of foe. Not really.

I turned to the back of The Book to check the last page. A message appeared there shortly after I returned home following my last trip to Vue. It simply said:

It's not about reaching the end.

I never shared the page with Jack or Tara. Maybe they'd seen it when looking through The Book, but they never said.

It was a curious last line. While it seemed some of my father's messages moved from page to page, this one remained in place.

"What is it all about, Dad?" I asked The Book. I thought about the statue of my father in the park. I wanted to visit it before I left, but I couldn't see how we'd have the time. Unless I hurried down and back before Tara was done getting ready. I shoved The Book back into my shoulder bag. I left a note on the table for Tara letting her know where I'd gone.

There was a nice breeze blowing through the street as I walked to the park. The festival grounds remained busy. They probably would until late into the night. I moved forward in the flow of happy attendees, not pausing at any of the tents.

I passed the gazebo near the clearing where my father's statue stood. The bronze likeness was raised on a pedestal, larger than life. I approached from the side, my heart tightening as I drank in the profile of the Empire's hero. My Dad. I placed my hands on the pedestal and looked up.

The coat the figure wore billowed out behind him. I stretched out a hand to touch the solid hem, to make a connection with who he once was in this strange world. Before my fingers made contact, a shadow crossed over the statue. It vanished just as fast as it appeared. I pulled my hand back and turned, my eyes roaming the faces behind me. Nothing seemed out of the ordinary, and no one stood near me.

But I had the very distinct feeling I was being watched.

I stepped away from the statue toward the passing crowd, my gaze searching between couples and groups. Nothing. Was the shadow a bird? I wondered. No, that didn't wash. It was a large shadow. No bird here was that big. I thought about Rabbit's warning to stay at Tuesday's. I'd make my visit quick.

When I turned back to the statue, a woman stood directly behind me, blocking the path to my father. Startled, I stopped short.

She wore a thin, silver dress over her shapely figure. Sleeveless, it clung to her curves, flowing softly over her hips, and swirling around her ankles. She was barefoot, with several silver rings adorning her toes. Her skin was the color of polished onyx, and a large dark pendant sat in a thick necklace at her throat. The color of midnight, her long, straight hair cascaded over her shoulders, reaching her waist. Her eyes were framed by thick eyelashes, guarding pitch-black pools. Full lips were painted a red so deep it was almost black. The woman towered over me.

"Excuse me," I blurted out. "I didn't see you there."

She raised a winged eyebrow.

"Because you weren't there a second ago," I finished.

The woman still did not answer, but casually appraised me from head to toe.

"Should I know you?" I asked. The air was charged with an energy I recognized, but I couldn't put my finger on it.

She lifted her gaze. "I planned to meet you in Matar, Emily Swift, but you left so quickly."

In Matar? Anne's magical contact flitted through my brain. "Are you Lucie Bellerose?"

"I am not."

I looked around. No one took notice of us. No one was alarmed by the sudden appearance of this being before me. Maybe I was the only one who could see her. I could certainly feel her. Little knocks of energy pressed up against mine.

"How do you know me?" I wasn't sure I wanted the answer. Stop that, I thought. I batted away an invisible touch on the exposed skin of my arm.

"I have been watching you for a while," she answered, her eyes once again roaming over me. A ghost of a smile floated on her lips. "You surprised many with your abilities, Emily. We are, curious."

With so many people watching me, you'd

think I'd get used to it. But I was not. I didn't like how this woman made me feel. I didn't like how she kept looking at me. And I definitely did not like this energy she was pushing around me.

"Who are you?" I asked. Damn, she felt so familiar, but I knew we'd never met. Her probing left me feeling exposed. I wanted to concentrate and pull up my door-travel energy to push back at her. But I couldn't concentrate with her standing so close.

"She is Nisha," came the answer from my right. I turned my head as Rabbit appeared at my side. His own dark eyes glittered, unblinking as he met the women's stare. His hand moved in front of me, and he gently began to push me behind him.

"Rabbit," her voice eased slowly into the air around us. "Fánaí, it has been a long time."

"It has," Rabbit answered, low. I didn't miss the slight jerk of his shoulder when Nisha spoke to him. "Emily has nothing to offer you."

"That is not true. She has hidden the Crimson Stone nearby." Nisha's voice no longer mixed into the breeze but slid directly into my mind. "Haven't you? I can sense it."

I bit my tongue, feeling the slight squeeze of Rabbit's hand against me. While I didn't know what was happening, I understood Nisha was dangerous. He wanted me to remain silent.

"The Crimson Stone is no longer here in Vue,"

Rabbit said. "I can assure you. There is nothing for you here, Nisha."

The woman coolly looked up into the bright sky above. "A storm will visit tonight."

Rabbit nudged me. "Let's go back to Tuesday's," he murmured.

The woman's eyes lowered once again to mine. "I will see you in Matar, Emily," she said. Her attention drifted back to my friend. "And Fánaí, be wary of becoming too protective of this Salesman. Her enemies will not hesitate to harm anyone who surrounds her. They will punish those who protect her. Even you."

Rabbit flinched as she walked her gaze over his body. "Goodbye, Nisha."

The mysterious woman cast one last look in my direction before her entire being collapsed into a shadow at her feet. Nisha's silhouette slid up the statue of my father and disappeared into the air above.

"Ho-ly hell," I breathed, staring at the empty space she left behind. "Who was that, Rabbit?"

Rabbit placed his hand on my shoulder and coaxed me away from the statue. "I want us back at Tuesday's. Now."

"Okay, sure," I said. We moved away from my father's figure and back onto the paved path. Rabbit took my hand and pulled me through the crowd to the other side.

"It'll be faster if we cut across the grass. This

way," he said.

We hurried through the park and back onto the side street that would eventually lead us to Tuesday's bakery and apartment. The air was becoming even more oppressive. The humidity felt high.

"Are you going to tell me who that was?" I asked again, sneaking a look at him as we walked. By the tense line of his jaw, I knew he was upset. "Rabbit, she knew who I was and said some pretty scary things. I think I should be told who she is."

"She's a Priestess. It's... hard to explain." He shook his head. "She's very powerful, Emily. You should avoid her."

"She's like a... She's magical, right? Like a..." I looked for a word to describe what I had seen. "Like a witch?"

"She's not a witch, but she practices magic."

"Obviously," I said, picturing her dramatic departure.

"Nisha comes from an old line of magic, Emily. Even by Empire standards she's otherworldly. There are devotees who worship her, who serve her in any way she requires. Desperate people seek her out for help. Those who go to her pay a high price."

"But you know her? I mean, she knew you."

"I know her." Again with the jaw twitch. Rabbit's phone buzzed and he answered a text. "As soon as we're back at Tuesday's, we'll grab Tara and go straight to the art gallery."

"How do you know her, Rabbit?" It was unlike him to be so evasive with me.

"Our paths crossed before."

"And she called you something," I said. "It sounded like Fawny. What does that mean?"

"Fánaí. It's my name."

* * *

I held my tongue for the rest of our walk to Tuesday's – which was short under our hurrying feet. My thoughts rocketed through my brain. Rabbit had a name? And this scary Priestess woman knew it? And she was dangerous. It felt like a weight sat on my chest.

We offered an extra ticket to Tuesday, but she said she'd rather eat pickle encrusted pumpkin pie than step foot in Peti's gallery. That said, Rabbit, Tara, and I hoofed our way over to a busier street where Rabbit flagged down a cab. We piled in and he gave the driver our destination. He avoided looking me in the eye. As curious as I was, I decided to let it go. For now.

"What's up with you two?" Tara asked. She sat between us in the back seat. Rabbit continued to stare straight ahead.

"I'm not supposed to take off on my own," I offered. "I'm sure he's not happy."

Tara twisted her lips to the side, eyeballing me. "Huh. Well, whatever. We've got a job to do."

We arrived at the art show shortly after the doors opened. The gallery was huge, consisting of two stories of rooms and a large, walled garden outside. People milled in and out of the building, enjoying the lush garden and the artwork displayed there.

"Should we split up?" Tara asked.

"Maybe," I said. I watched as a striking couple strolled in front of me. The man wore a tux while his date sparkled in a red gown adorned with what looked like diamonds. "Are you sure we're not underdressed?"

Tara gave Rabbit the side-eye. He wore black skinny jeans tucked into work boots. His black tee shirt bore an intricate logo I didn't recognize, but I assumed it belonged to a band. "Oh, no," she said dryly. "We're dressed completely appropriately."

We began to make our way through the rooms with the rest of the noisy crowd. A server passed by with a tray of champagne flutes. Tara lifted her hand, but he resolutely ignored us. Rabbit stepped forward and said something to the man. The server sighed and turned back toward us. "Ladies?" he said, sniffing as he reviewed our outfits.

"Thanks," I said, embarrassed, but taking a flute. I didn't plan on drinking it but wanted to do something with my hands.

Tara's eyes narrowed. Oh, boy. "I don't suppose you have any beer?" she asked.

The server frowned. "Beer? No. We are not serving beer."

"Too bad," she said. "I was hoping for some *Rooster Broo*."

"Tara," I warned.

"Because I like their slogan," she continued.

"Tara!" I grabbed at her arm.

"Do you know what it is?" She leaned toward the server – who was looking particularly uncomfortable.

Tara's next words were drowned out by a commotion erupting across the room. Angry voices lifted and people backed away from an argument. I recognized the men: Peti Kis and the painter he'd belittled earlier in the park.

"I'm here for my paintings!" The artist shouted. He swayed on his feet. "Now. I want them now. If you're not going to honor the agreement we had, I want them back tonight!"

"I think he's drunk," Rabbit said, pointing his chin at the yelling man.

"This is not the time for you to pick up your trash," Peti barked. "Get out! Someone call security and remove this loser."

The man pushed Peti, drawing a few gasps from the crowd. "You're the loser – you're the biggest loser here because you're a joke. Everyone hates you."

Peti shoved the man's hands away. "Security!"

Rabbit started to move forward to intervene when out of nowhere my mother, in a flowing spring green dress, glided in between the two men, placing one delicate hand on the furious painter's shoulder, the other against Peti's chest. Her lips moved as she leaned in closer to the artist's ear, whispering. The man took a step back as if zapped, the anger washing out of his face. Peti removed my mother's hand from his chest, grimacing as if it were a rotten piece of fruit.

"Mom!" I yelled as I started across the room, spilling my champagne. I pressed my glass into the hand of the man in the tux. "Take this. Mom!"

I tried to weave my way through the onlookers. The late appearance of the gallery's security guards blocked my path. Several of them guided the onlookers backward, their beefy arms spread wide. Two others apprehended the painter. As soon as they grabbed him, he lurched forward at Peti, surprising and knocking the gallery owner into a narrow display stand. A glass sculpture of a knife toppled toward the floor.

In an instant, my mother swept down and caught the piece of art by the handle before it shattered. The whole room held its collective breath as she carefully placed it back on its stand, the glass blade catching a beam of light and sending a rainbow up a nearby wall. She smiled kindly at Peti.

Peti's face was on fire. His eyes bugged out of his head. "Look what you did!" He roared at my mother and the painter. "Get out, both of you! Get out! You!" He jabbed a finger at the restrained man. "You're a hack! You're a loser! You will never sell another painting again in the Empire. I will see to it! You should do art a favor and DIE!"

The room fell silent as the painter's body sagged, held up only by the two security guards detaining him. Tears spewed from his eyes and a keening so deep erupted from what could only be described as his very soul.

My mother stood stunned; her eyes wide. Her mouth popped open, and she raised both of her arms toward the crying man as if she would embrace him. Her hands slowly balled into fists. She whirled around, facing Peti, her arms now stiff at her sides. Wisps of strawberry and gold slipped from the combs in her hair.

My mother's voice was very soft, but everyone in the room heard her as she leaned toward Peti:

"You kill art, Peti Kis. You have much to answer for. I will see to it."

✼ ✼ ✼

The security guards dragged the poor artist from the room and Peti shouted for his assistants. The crowd flooded back into the center of the room – many a sycophant stepped forward to soothe Peti's ego. I pointed in the direction of my mother. I could see her strawberry-blond curls fluttering between the gaps in the crowd. I called to Rabbit. "Over there!"

Tara hopped up and down trying to see through the mob. People flowed in from other rooms, late for the drama but still hoping for excitement. "Where is she?"

"There!" I pointed again. I tried to yell over the din. "Mom!"

"Lydia!" Tara called. She pressed between several couples, driving herself in the last known direction of my mother.

Rabbit disappeared into the throng, a talent I envied. I followed, trying to keep up. We burrowed through to the other side. Nothing.

Tara joined us. "Where'd she go?"

"I don't know!" I felt frantic. "She's got to be here. Find the security guards! Maybe they grabbed her. We need to split up."

Rabbit jerked a thumb toward a room to the right. "I'll go this way. Tara, check the garden. Emily, see if you can find the security guards. See if they have her."

I nodded. "Go! I don't want to lose her!"

Tara and Rabbit split up and I began my hunt

for the guards. I watched for my mother as I edged through each room. Nothing. A man in a security uniform crossed through the door in front of me. I reached out for him, pulling my hand back quickly when his hand moved to the truncheon dangling from his belt.

"I'm sorry! I need your help," I said. I held up my palms. "Please."

He frowned. "What do you need?"

"I'm looking for my mother," I told him, lowering my hands. "She was the woman in the other room. The one with the incident."

"The lady in the green dress?" he asked.

"Yes, that's her. She was trying to break up the fight," I explained. "Do you know which way she went?"

The security guard shook his head. "We were going to ask her to leave because that's what Mr. Kis wanted, but before we could, she was gone. People said they saw her leaving through the front doors."

I dropped my head back and stared at the ceiling. We missed her. Again.

❖ ❖ ❖

I found Tara and Rabbit circling back into the original room. I explained what the security guard reported. My eyes filled with tears. We were so close. Tara hugged me and told me we'd find her. She asked Rabbit to hail a cab.

As we rode back to Tuesday's apartment, all of us were silent.

Outside, a streak of lightning raced across the sky and thunder smacked into the city.

A storm had come to Vue.

CHAPTER 12

The rain came down in sheets. We were soaked by the time we dashed from the cab to Tuesday's apartment. She welcomed us with hot chocolate and peanut butter cookies. Rabbit said his goodnight – he would bed down somewhere else. My friend didn't meet my eyes. I would need to talk to him when we had some time alone.

Tara and I toweled off and slipped into our pajamas. After visiting with Tuesday and filling her in on the evening's excitement – and ultimate failure – all three of us turned in. Tuesday was an early riser because of the bakery. Tara and I were just plain tired. Two out of three wins in rock-paper-scissors landed Tara on the couch. Tuesday gave me a bunch of pillows and blankets for the floor. It wasn't great, but I felt safe for the night.

The storm raged outside. Lightning lit up the sky and thunder rocked Vue until midnight. We closed the windows to keep out the rain, so the air in the apartment felt thick. I laid awake until after twelve worrying about everything. Not only did my mother keep slipping through my fingers, Rabbit hadn't mentioned a message from Jack. Rabbit might be acting a little strange because of the interaction with Nisha, but he would never hold back on telling me if Jack sent a message.

I was now on my second night in the Empire. Tomorrow morning would mark two days since I'd seen Jack. Two days since I'd misled him.

I realized the sound of rain had stopped. In the distance, I heard a deep rumble of leftover thunder. Sitting up, I grabbed a blanket and wrapped it around my shoulders, before slipping on my sneakers. Taking care to not wake Tara, I crept to the back of the apartment past Tuesday's bedroom door. A small window faced out onto the alley behind the building. Beside it, a narrow door leading to a little balcony.

Holding my breath as I unlocked the door, I eased out onto the welcoming terrace. Tuesday kept several potted plants and containers of herbs pushed up against the railing. Little sparkling lights weaved in and around the bars, casting enough light for me to see my way to a small metal table and chair tucked into a corner. Although the air was still humid from the storm, I wrapped the blanket around me so I could sit sideways on the chair and stay dry.

Below, the space was less of an alley and more of a long courtyard between buildings. While a narrow road for delivery vehicles was available, there was a huge swath of green running down the center. People planted flowers and gardens. It was wide enough, and the buildings lining the alley short enough, to let the sun in.

I closed my eyes and leaned against the building, the back of my head making contact with the damp brick. The smell of soil from the potted plants reminded me of the florist shop back in Kincaid. I was homesick.

If I could only see Jack, to talk to him and tell him I was okay – that I was worried about him and wanted to make sure he was okay, too. I was so tired of everything. The chasing, the running, the truth I hid from Jack. It was exhausting. If I could talk to him and touch him, I could explain what was going on. If I could just have his arms around me.

"Emily?" I heard a voice ask.

I opened my eyes and blinked. "Jack?"

Jack knelt beside me in pajama bottoms, his chest bare, his arms covered in goosebumps. I reached out and touched his shoulder. His skin was cool under my fingertips.

"Emily," he said again. "Where are you?"

"I'm right here," I said, sitting up straighter and looking around. We were still on the balcony at Tuesday's. "We're right here in Vue. Together."

My boyfriend slowly climbed to his feet. They were bare. "Am I dreaming?"

"I... I'm not sure." I stood, pulling the blanket off my shoulders and wrapping the dry side around his. "But you're here."

Jack accepted the blanket, but confusion filled his eyes. He turned and looked past the balcony, across the alley. "I must be dreaming, because I'm not here," he said. "I'm home. I'm home, Emily."

"I think you're..." I faltered. It had been such a long time since I pulled Templeton into my dream, but this was different. I knew then I was dreaming and worked to call Templeton to me. He wasn't happy, of course. Then again, I didn't like it when Templeton pulled me into his dreams. You felt powerless when it happened. It was like having someone run their hands over your body when you didn't want to be touched.

"I know I was on the couch," Jack frowned. He was still trying to put it together. "I must've fallen asleep. But why doesn't this feel like a dream?"

"Jack," I began. "You're not dreaming. I am."

"I don't understand."

"I'm dreaming. I called to you – to your subconscious. Remember how I told you that happened to me last year? That's what's going on now. I must've reached out and pulled you to me." I pressed against him, my arms wrapping around his body. How I missed being with him! My heart ached. "I miss you so much, Jack."

He didn't speak right away. When he did, his voice was quiet. "So, you... reached into my head or whatever and brought me here?"

I leaned back and looked up. My fingers dug into the blanket covering his arms. "I just wanted to see you."

Jack's body stiffened. "Emily, do you really believe I'm okay with you walking around my head and 'pulling' my thoughts into yours?"

"But I'm not doing that," I argued. "I'm bringing you into my dream so I can see you."

Jack's hands appeared from under the blanket. They wrapped around my upper arms and he pushed me back a step. "I didn't invite you into my head."

"It's not like that." My eyes felt hot. I blinked several times to clear my vision. It wasn't supposed to happen like this.

"It's exactly like that." Jack let go of my arms and turned his back to me. He crossed the short distance to the other end of the balcony before spinning to face me again. "You manipulated my subconscious in some way. Do you know how invasive this is? Do you know how wrong this is?"

"But, Jack, I miss you. Things are out of control. I am so –"

"You should've thought of that before you ran off!" Jack's voice rose. "You should've told me what was going on!"

"I wanted to! I really did, Jack. I wanted to tell you everything, but I thought you would try to stop me. Even if I asked you to go with me, I knew you would say no!"

"You never even gave me a chance to say no!" Jack hissed at me. "You just took off. I knew something was going on. I knew you weren't telling me everything."

"I was scared. I had to go." I took a step and reached for him.

"No." He put up a palm to stop me. His other hand was balled into a fist, clutching the blanket to his chest. "We are done here."

"Jack... Jack! Don't!" I pleaded. I held out my hand again. "Please."

His eyes dropped to my open palm and he snorted, shaking his head. I watched as the love of my life turned away from me, leaving the balcony through the door into Tuesday's apartment.

"But I'm so scared," I whispered into the empty space. Pain spread across my chest as I covered my face with my hands and wept.

Thunder cracked in the sky above, shaking me awake. I sat on Tuesday's metal chair on the balcony. My backside felt wet. I shivered as the wind picked up announcing the storm's return. I stood, searching the balcony floor for the blanket. The sky opened above me and the rain burst down. Abandoning my search, I scurried off the balcony and through the door into the apartment.

In the bathroom, I ran a towel over my body for

a second time that night. I looked in the mirror at my red face and wet hair. I'd never felt so ugly.

Tiptoeing, I slunk back into the living room to my bed of blankets and pillows on the floor. There in the dim light, I found the blanket I'd taken with me to the balcony. I sank to my knees and touched it. It was damp. I hugged it to me, breathing in the smell of Jack's skin as I rolled into my pillow and cried silently.

✳ ✳ ✳

At five in the morning, Tuesday began making tea in the kitchen. She'd closed the door, but since I hadn't slept well, my ears caught the sound of her activities. Tara snored lightly from the couch. She was still out. I climbed to my feet and padded into the kitchen.

"Good morning," I said, pushing the door open and speaking quietly.

"Oh, Emily. I'm sorry I woke you," Tuesday said. "But I need to get down to the kitchen before six."

"Trust me, I was barely sleeping," I assured her. I rubbed an eye and yawned. "I'd love a cup of tea. Actually, do you have coffee instead? I'm going to need it today."

"Of course. Let me brew a pot."

I perched on a stool and leaned on the counter. "That storm was pretty wild last night."

Tuesday measured the grounds into the coffee basket. She nodded. "It was a particularly strong one. With the weather we've had, I'm not too surprised. All that pent up energy, it had to be released."

"Or maybe it has something to do with warm and cold air coming together?" I smiled. "Either way, it was wicked."

Tuesday kept busy putting together a few odds and ends. I realized in addition to the bagels and pastries she set out for us, she was making lunches: three brown paper bags, three sandwiches. "These are for you and your friends in case I can't get away today. Bacon, lettuce, and tomato sandwiches, with avocado instead of mayonnaise. In honor of Rabbit, the bacon isn't real meat, it's 'eggplant bacon.' You bake it with Worcestershire sauce, paprika, and maple syrup, among other things. Completely vegetarian for all three of you today. It's very good."

"I have no doubt, Tuesday. Thanks. You're so good to all of us," I told her.

"I love having you here, even though I know it's not under the best of circumstances," Tuesday replied. She glanced at the coffee pot. "Go ahead and help yourself. I'm going to get ready to head downstairs to the bakery."

"Awesome." I retrieved a cup from the cupboard and poured my coffee. Yesterday it was black coffee over breakfast with the Rabbits. I preferred milk in mine. Tuesday kept a bottle in the refrigerator, and I added some to my cup.

The storm wasn't the worst part of the night. I worked over the visions in my head, running through the events on the balcony. What I experienced in my dream was not imagined. Jack was pulled into my dream because I wanted him there. I reached out and brought him to me. I was unsure of how I did it because previously when I pulled Templeton in, I'd entered the dream first and then made a conscious decision to bring him to me. It was not the same with Jack last night. I was tired and missing him terribly. It just happened.

And he was furious.

I stared into my coffee cup and heard his words again. He said I manipulated him. He said what I'd done was invasive. My throat tightened. He said we were done. I was afraid to think about what he meant.

I had to find my mother today. I couldn't afford to fail again. I had to get back home.

And I had to make things right with Jack.

❊ ❊ ❊

Tara rolled off the couch a little before six. Her hair was snarled on one side. "Better than the cot, nowhere near as good as my bed."

I handed her a cup of coffee. "Drink and live

again."

"How'd you sleep? I admit it, I'm feeling guilty you were on the floor," she said before taking a sip.

"Guilty enough to let me have the couch the next time around?" I asked.

"Yeah, no. Rock-paper-scissors. It's a dog-eat-dog world." She set her cup down on the coffee table, before executing a full-on downward dog yoga pose. "When's Rabbit getting here?" she asked from beneath a curtain of fair hair.

"I'd guess by seven," I said. "We should be ready to go."

Tara moved back into a standing position and headed for the kitchen. "I'll be ready, but I'm starved. Do I smell bacon? What's for breakfast?"

She disappeared through the kitchen door. I began to pick-up and fold our blankets. Hopefully, we wouldn't have to use them tonight.

Before I could finish, one knock sounded on Tuesday's apartment door before a grim-faced Rabbit entered. I opened my mouth to say good morning, but he cut me off. "We got a problem. Peti Kis is dead and your mother's going to be arrested for murder."

"What?" My shout brought Tara back from the kitchen.

"What's going on?" she asked, holding a bagel in her hand. "Why are you yelling?"

"Peti Kis is dead, and Rabbit says my mother did it!"

"No," Rabbit frowned at me. "I said she's going to be arrested for murder. I didn't say she did it." He ran his hand through his thick hair. "I need coffee and I want both of you to be quiet while I talk." He marched into the kitchen.

Tara turned toward me, her brown eyes wide. We hurried after Rabbit.

He poured a cup of coffee and faced us as we entered. "You might want to go back out into the other room and sit down."

"No. Just tell me what's going on," I said. I steadied myself by gripping the edge of the counter. Rabbit noticed but continued.

"Peti Kis was found stabbed in the chest in his art gallery late last night. Empire guards found him after they were called to a disturbance in the alley behind the building." Rabbit's eyes grew dark. "People reported a scream sometime before midnight. Guards found a female victim in the alley. She was also stabbed. The weapon was still sticking out of her body."

"Oh, no," whispered Tara. She covered her mouth with both hands.

Rabbit paused, his jaw working. "The guards on the scene noticed an open door at the back of the art gallery. It had blood smeared on it. They went in to investigate and found Peti dead in one of the exhibition rooms."

"Stabbed?" I squeaked out.

"Stabbed." Rabbit took a swallow of coffee and stared at the floor. "There's more, Emily."

"Is my mother okay?" I was shaking. Tara moved to my side and put her arm around me.

He met my eyes and shook his head. "I don't know where she is right now. But we hacked into a security camera facing the back of the art gallery's building. There's footage of Lydia going into the building shortly after eleven."

"What? My mother went into the back of the building?" I gently pushed Tara away. "I don't believe it. It must've been someone else. Why in the world would she go back? Wait, just… Seriously. My mother is not the type to go sneaking around buildings, breaking into them. She's not a murderer!" My voice rose.

"Of course, she's not," Tara said sharply. "Rabbit, I'm sorry. You're wrong. This is bull crap. Lydia didn't do this."

Rabbit took a deep breath, his eyes once again on the floor. "The network chatter is also saying the weapon was the glass knife Lydia saved from hitting the floor at the gallery last night. Both victims were likely killed with the same weapon."

I turned to Tara shaking my head. "What are we going to do? We've got to find her. This is bad."

Tara reached for me again. "We'll find her. We

will." She abruptly stopped and directed her attention back to Rabbit. "Wait, there's footage of her going into the gallery, but not leaving it?"

"That's right," Rabbit answered. "The storm caused an electrical surge. It blew out the camera after Lydia went in. There's no footage of her coming out."

I threw my hands up in the air and stormed out of the kitchen. "That's just great!"

Tara was on my heels. "Okay, Em, we'll get this figured out. First, we've got to find Lydia. We'll find her and get everything straightened out. I promise."

"Her prints are going to be on that knife," I shouted, staring at my friend. My meltdown had finally arrived. This was the moment. "A room full of people heard her threaten Peti last night. We haven't been able to find her – until last night. This is so bad, so bad, Tara. It can't get any worse!"

"It can," Rabbit said quietly. He walked to the couch and sat down. He leaned forward, his forearms resting against his knees. His hands were loosely clasped together. His head dropped.

"What is it?" I sat down on the end of the coffee table, my chest tightening in anticipation of more bad news.

"The victim in the alley," he began, lifting his gaze to mine. He cleared his throat. "She was a Rabbit."

* * *

She was the Rabbit with the braid, the woman who walked me from the art festival, away from Speedy, and safely back to Tuesday's bakery. She was the Rabbit who Tuesday wanted to feed, to help 'put some meat on those pretty bones.'

And now, she was dead.

People believed my mother was the murderer.

"My mother would never, ever do this," I told Rabbit, my voice quivering.

He took another deep breath. "I know she wouldn't. But the guards are looking for her. So are the Rabbits."

"Okay, that's good," I said, rising to my feet and starting to pace. "This is good, if anyone can find my mother, it'll be the Rabbits."

"Emily –" Rabbit said.

"No, I'm okay, Rabbit. Your network will find her, right?" I stopped and knelt in front of him. "The Rabbits will find her."

Rabbit put both hands on my shoulders. He was very still, and his dark eyes shone. He spoke softly to me. "Emily, the Rabbits don't know she's innocent."

"What do you mean?" I searched my friend's face. "You know she would never do this."

"I don't believe your mother killed anyone," he said. "But I don't speak for the network. I'm telling you what you need to know."

Rabbit's hands slipped from my shoulders as I sat back on my ankles, defeated. I shook my head. "What do we do?"

He sighed. "We listen."

✽ ✽ ✽

Tara and I still needed to get ready to head out to look for my mother. I wasn't in the mood to eat, but she insisted I take a bagel with me in addition to our bagged lunches when we finally left Tuesday's apartment. Tara stopped into *The Sweet Spot* to give Tuesday an update.

I stood on the sidewalk next to Rabbit while we waited for Tara. The awkwardness between us continued. I wasn't sure how to fix any of it. I stole a glance at him. He was texting.

"Has the news spread about all of this, or is it just the Rabbits?" I asked.

He looked up. "It was only the network until about thirty minutes ago. Peti was a well-known figure in the art world, even if he wasn't liked. It's now officially part of the Empire news."

"And have they said anything about my mother?"

"They have. They've posted a photo from the security footage. It's not the best image, but it's clear it's Lydia. They've identified her. They're asking for anyone with information on her whereabouts to come forward," he finished.

"And now Spell knows. And Blackstone." I blew out a breath. He nodded. Jack will know soon enough, too, I thought. Even if he's not making contact with Blackstone, Anne will surely hear about this and reach out to him. "Hey, Rabbit?"

"Yeah?" He stopped his texting.

"Did you... I mean, I sent a message to Jack before the bonfire through one of the Rabbits working on the studio crew. I don't suppose anyone in the network mentioned there was a message sent back to me in some way?" I was hopeful, but I knew what the answer would be.

"None I know of," he answered. "But I can ask. Do you want me to make sure he gets a new message?"

I worried my bottom lip with my teeth, considering his offer. I had no idea where to start. I shook my head no. "Not now. I don't have anything to say."

Rabbit gave me a curious look but didn't press. "I'll let you know if I hear anything out of Kincaid," he said.

Tara joined us on the sidewalk. "Alright, where to?"

We decided our best chance of finding my mother again was back at the festival. Rabbit would monitor the network, and Tara and I would keep our eyes peeled. If we learned of any event that might draw in someone like my mother, we'd look there, too. Our search was less of a targeted plan, and more of a stab in the dark. But I couldn't sit still even though I knew locating my mother would be next to impossible.

The next several hours saw us sweating in the humidity as we combed the festival for signs of my Mom. We ate our bagged lunches early – Tuesday's sandwiches were awesome – and by eleven, we still had nothing. Rabbit reported a quiet network.

"That's it," Tara announced. "I'm hot and sweaty, but there's no man involved."

Rabbit raised an eyebrow.

"I know," I said. "It feels useless to be doing this."

"We need a beer." Tara pointed to a beverage tent in a roped off area.

"It's not even noon," I said.

"It's a festival, it doesn't count."

"You want a beer?" I asked Rabbit.

"I could use one," he admitted.

"I guess we might as well add alcohol to the mix," I shrugged. "What could possibly go wrong?"

"Exactly," Tara said, pulling me along. "Come on."

The three of us ordered at the beverage counter before snagging a small table. Tara and I set our shoulder bags down and collapsed onto the chairs. I took a gulp of my beer. "I guess it hits the spot."

"To *Rooster Broo*," Tara toasted, lifting her plastic cup.

"I hear the slogan is based on an intoxicated Australian heckler," Rabbit added, touching his cup to hers. All morning he'd remained silent, but I understood. He was mourning the loss of the Rabbit found in the art gallery's alley.

Tara smirked. "No way! Someone made that up."

My two friends continued as I sipped from my cup and watched the crowd. I knew it was impossible, but I fantasized my mother would walk on by and we could grab her.

Before the guards did. Or the Rabbits. Or the Fringe. I closed my eyes. How could one woman cause such trouble?

"Ah, Emily?" I opened my eyes. Tara sat upright, staring past Rabbit toward the beer counter.

For a brief second, I entertained the hope my mother had magically appeared. I leaned to the side so I could see around Rabbit. Nothing was out of the ordinary. "What?"

"There's a screen behind the counter."

"So? I think it's a large computer screen. They're streaming something." I squinted. Images of art flashed across the display. "Probably some event."

"No, look at the bottom of the screen, Emily. I

think it's the news." Tara stared, unblinking. She pointed. Rabbit turned in his seat to get a better view. On the screen, a group of people walked in a huddle behind a man with a microphone – Empire guards surrounding a woman with strawberry-blond hair, their hands firmly wrapped around her upper arms. Tara gasped. "And that's Lydia in handcuffs!"

CHAPTER 13

"Holy hell!" I jumped up from the table and rushed the counter. Rabbit steadied my cup before it tipped over. I leaned across the serving area and waved at the man filling plastic cups. "Can you turn it up? Is there sound?"

The beer-tender looked over his shoulder at the screen. He shook his head. "Sorry. I don't have any speakers hooked up."

My eyes stayed glued to the screen. Across the bottom read a headline: Arrest Made in the Peti Kis Murder. I groaned, finally turning away from the news when my mother and the guards disappeared into a building.

"Where are they taking her?" I asked, looking from Tara to Rabbit. They joined me at the counter. "And, how come we're just hearing about this? Why didn't you hear anything, Rabbit?"

Rabbit was texting furiously, his lips pressed together tight.

"Maybe they're keeping him out of the loop," Tara said softly. "Because, you know." She gestured to me.

"Rabbit, is that true?" I asked. "Would they do that?"

He kept texting, his eyes never leaving his phone. "I don't know. But I'm going to find out."

"We need to learn where they're keeping her. We need to get to her," I said.

"No," Tara shook her head. "We need to call for help."

"Help? What are you talking about? We need to get to my mother!"

"No," Tara repeated, pulling me back to the table to retrieve our bags. "We need to go back to Tuesday's and Rabbit needs to get a message to Jo."

* * *

"What in the name of the Empire have you gotten yourself into now, Emily?" Jo burst through Tuesday's door and into the living room, briefcase in hand. This was no graceful entrance. This was a full-on storming in. Her shrewd eyes flitted to Tuesday. "Apologies for the rude interruption."

"Jo," I began. "How did you get here so fast?"

Everyone turned and looked at me.

"I mean, yeah, I know how, but you know what I mean," I said. My hand fluttered pointlessly. "I thought we'd hear from you first or something."

"Oh no, you're not asking any questions, Emily! You're listening to me and answering mine. What were you thinking sneaking into the Empire? And then door traveling without a Senior Salesman? Oh, yes. I know. Everyone knows. Blackstone knows. The Court knows! You're on Spell's list. You've really done it this time."

Jo didn't stop. She turned on Tara next. "And what are you doing here? How could you encourage her to do this? You're her best friend – you know this is not good for her! She is in real trouble. And you!" She spun around and faced Rabbit. "And you! I don't know you!"

"Rabbit," he answered.

"Right. Rabbit." Jo took a deep breath. Her attention swung back to me. She opened her mouth to unleash another tirade.

"Cookie?" Tuesday held out a plate to my mentor. "They're marble chocolate chip. I just baked them."

Jo scowled at the plate. "I love marble chocolate chip cookies. They're my favorite."

"Please have one?" Tuesday offered sweetly.

"Well, I shouldn't because I'm limiting my sugar, but one couldn't hurt. I mean, it's just one cookie." Jo chose one and took a bite. She chewed thoughtfully. Her gaze drifted in my direction. She swallowed and pointed the rest of the cookie at me. "Tell me what's going on."

"My mother's been arrested for murder," I said. I snuck a look at Tuesday. She was humming while she arranged plates and other goodies on the table.

"I have a hard time believing she actually killed

someone," Jo answered. She swiped a second cookie from the plate and sat down, placing her briefcase on the floor at her feet. "What do you know?"

I sat across from Jo and filled her in on what had happened, from the evening at the art gallery to the morning news. She listened without interrupting. I finished by saying, "And we didn't know who else to contact for help."

"You did the right thing," Jo said. "However, criminal law is not what I practice. I can reach out to a couple of attorneys here in the Empire who might help. I'll meet them where your mother is being held and we'll get in to see Lydia."

"Can I come with you?" I asked.

"No. I want you to stay here and wait until I return," Jo instructed. She softened. "They won't let you in to see her anyway, Emily."

I nodded. Jo was right. But I hated waiting around and not being able to help. "What will happen?"

"Well," Jo sighed. "She'll be processed and arraigned – that's where the charges will be announced. She'll be held in jail unless we can get her released on bail. She's Daniel Swift's widow, that will count for something. But, because of the severity of the crime and the evidence, they might want to hold her. There's no shortage of witnesses to what went down. All of you heard her threaten him."

"That can't happen, Jo. My mother can't be held in jail – and she didn't do it!" I felt dizzy. Tara came up behind me and placed her hands on my shoulders.

"Jo, Lydia wouldn't hurt anyone. She's good and kind. What happened last night was a bad man behaving horribly. Lydia only said what she did because of what Peti was doing to that artist," Tara stated. "No one believed for a minute she would kill him!"

"And yet, he's been murdered," Jo shifted her gaze to Rabbit. "And so has a woman."

Rabbit stood motionless, listening. Finally, he spoke. "Peti's death will overshadow the murder in the alley."

"Her murderer is Peti's," Jo said. "Justice will be served."

Something was left unsaid between the Salesman and the Rabbit. I was about to ask what was going on but then it hit me. No one was talking about the Rabbit killed in the alley. The news never reported on it – at least as far as we knew. The only murder being discussed was Peti's. "Rabbit?"

"Some things never change, Emily," he said, his voice dull. "Your father was a friend to the Rabbit community, but our history with the Empire is not one that often works in our favor."

"I see," I said. He was telling the truth. There

were Empire leaders who hated Rabbits.

"I'll send an emergency message through the Empire service to the attorneys I mentioned," Jo said, standing. She glanced at Rabbit briefly. "Then I'm off to find out if I can get in to see Lydia while we wait. If she hasn't been arraigned – and that's possible – I can delay it until the criminal lawyers arrive. Tuesday, do you have a phone up here?"

"In the kitchen," Tuesday replied. "I'll show you." The two women disappeared into the other room.

"She has a phone? I need to get a message to Marley." Tara stopped rubbing my shoulders and followed, leaving me with Rabbit.

"I'm really sorry," I told him. "I was so caught up with my mother missing, then being arrested. I know you lost a friend."

"I didn't know her well," he said. He sat in the chair Jo vacated. "But yeah, it sucks. Whoever killed Peti killed her. Wrong place at the wrong time. But I don't understand what she was doing there. No one seems to know."

"Are they holding back from you?" I thought about what Tara suggested at the festival.

"Maybe some are, but I've plenty of friends keeping me updated."

"And what are you telling them?" I fidgeted with a napkin, watching my fingers.

"I've told them I don't believe Lydia would kill

anyone, and that they need to keep listening. Something doesn't smell right," he said. He put his large hand over mine. "I'm not mad at you, Emily."

A shuddering sob rocked through me. I pulled my hand away and covered my mouth. "I'm so sorry," I whimpered through my fingers. I lowered my hand. "This is nothing like last time, Rabbit. Last time was horrible, but I felt like we would win. I felt like we had something on our side. Something good. Good was on our side. And now, it seems like everything is out of control and I can't help anyone. I can't win this battle."

He ignored my teary ramble. "It is different this time, Emily. Your family is involved. Things went from bad to worse."

"They can't get any worse," I said, wiping my eyes with the napkin.

"Don't say that," Rabbit shook his head. "Don't tempt fate."

I barked out a laugh. "Yeah, right."

"Hey," Tara began as she returned from the kitchen. "Jo sent a message to her attorney friends and took off. Before she did, she checked her messages. Lydia is being held in a downtown Empire guard base. Jo said stay here and she'd give us an update as soon as possible."

Rabbit's phone buzzed and we all jumped. It was the first text in a while. Tara raised her eyebrows at me. Rabbit reviewed the message and thumbed in a reply.

"Well? Anything?" I asked.

Rabbit finished his text. "It looks like Lydia turned herself in as soon as word got out about the security feed. That's how the guards 'found' her. She went to them."

"What?" I was back on my feet. "What are you saying?"

He held up a hand. "Just because she turned herself in doesn't mean she's admitting she did anything. She probably came forward to prevent being chased down and arrested."

"But she was arrested?"

"Yeah, but it's better she went to them instead of appearing to be running from the Empire guards. That would look worse," he finished.

"He's right," Tara agreed. "This is a step in getting her name cleared."

I scuffed my shoe against Tuesday's rug, mulling over Tara's words. She was right.

Tuesday returned from the kitchen and stayed silent during our exchange, a thoughtful expression resting on her round face. She sat down at the table, her hands loosely wrapped around a teacup. She spun it in a slow circle between her fingertips.

"Maybe we should see if we can find Aster and Minerva. If Lydia was with them at the time of the murder, she would have an alibi," Tuesday said.

"Who are Aster and Minerva?" Tara asked. Her eyes flicked to Rabbit. He shrugged.

"My mother's cousins." A wave of relief wanted to roll over me. I held my breath. "Tuesday, do you know where they might be now? You said you saw them a couple of days ago, right? And you know Aster?"

Tuesday's head bobbed up and down. "They were in the bakery on Friday. I don't know where they're staying, though. They're not from here."

"Rabbit, could you –" I started.

"Got it," he interrupted, then grinned. "*Bedrest Inn.*"

For the first time in several days, I let loose with a genuine laugh. "Perfect."

"What am I missing?" Tara's nose wrinkled. "What? What's so funny?"

"Emily's visited the hotel before," Rabbit told her. "I believe she executed a door travel landing into a bathtub."

"Even better, that's where I got the best of Templeton when I pulled him into my dream." My smile faded as I thought of my experience with pulling Jack into my dream the night before. I pushed aside the image of him turning away from me. There was no time to feel sorry for myself. "Shall we go?"

"What about Jo? She said to wait here," Tara reminded us. "Oh, wait. What am I thinking? Let's go!"

"Tuesday, will you be here to fill Jo in on where we're going and why?" I asked.

"Let's also leave a note," Tara said, lifting her eyebrows. "You know, just in case Tuesday has to go to the bakery."

"She's worried I'll forget," Tuesday winked.

Tara's cheeks grew pink, but she scribbled out a message on a notepad she'd pulled from her bag. "There. I told Jo what we're doing."

"Alright," I said to my little crew. "Let's get back to it."

❃ ❃ ❃

Bedrest Inn was within walking distance. The first time I was in Vue, I ended up spending the night there. In the morning, I'd walked to the ferry dock to meet up with Rabbit and Anne. There were many memories from that first trip. Some were horrible; others were good. We'd triumphed over evil and won the battle. This time, things felt different. But somehow, hopefully, we'd be able to repeat our past success.

On the way to the hotel, Rabbit told us he put out a message to his network asking if any Rabbit was near the *Bedrest Inn*. If there was one in the vicinity, they'd watch to make sure the two Major Muses, Minerva and Aster, did not leave before we got there.

"How will they know who they are though?" I asked. "How will they recognize them?"

Rabbit grinned. "We have ways of knowing."

"Do I want to know?"

"Not really."

"I do," Tara chimed in. I rolled my eyes. Rabbit shook his head and went back to texting.

It was eight blocks to the hotel and the sky was beginning to darken in the western corner. I gestured toward the clouds. "I hope it doesn't rain again."

"We'll get a cab if we have to," Tara answered. "In the meantime, move it."

We picked up the pace and by the time we reached the *Bedrest Inn*, big raindrops began to splatter on the sidewalk. We hustled into the lobby. Rabbit made a beeline for a young male Rabbit leaning against one of the floor-to-ceiling columns. They put their heads together in a private conversation.

"Let's ask at the desk if these cousins are still staying here." Tara pulled on my shirtsleeve.

"I'm not sure if they'll give any info out," I said. We crossed to the check-in desk where a blond woman tapped away on a keyboard with polished nails, her unblinking eyes glued to her screen.

"Welcome to the *Bedrest Inn*," she automatically said without looking up. "May I help you?"

I paused. It was the same woman who checked

me into the hotel last year. I didn't remember her as being particularly helpful, but she was our only choice. "Hi," I began. "I think my mother Ly –"

"Not her mother," Tara interrupted. She shot me a pointed look. I frowned. "I'm looking for my aunt. I'm hoping she's still staying here."

The woman lifted her head. She still didn't blink. "The name?"

"Minerva," Tara answered.

The blonde finally blinked. "The full name?"

"Uh," Tara turned to me for help.

I went with the first thing that came to my mind. "We're not sure about her last name. She gets married a lot."

Tara's mouth popped open.

The woman's expression didn't change, but her eyes returned to the screen in front of her hands. She began to type. "Date of check-in?"

"Last week?" I guessed.

The woman's perfectly painted lips thinned. She typed for a moment longer. "Minerva Mirta checked in last Monday. She has not checked out."

Relieved, I slumped against the counter. "Thank goodness. May I have her room number?"

The fingernails continued their clacking on the keyboard. "We're not allowed to give out the room numbers of our guests. You may leave a message."

"That's not helpful." Tara snarled at the blonde.

The woman's eyes narrowed, and she glared at my friend. "Will you need a room for this evening, ma'am?"

"Did she just call me ma'am?" Tara's question was directed at me, but she scowled at the hotel employee.

"Ladies?" Rabbit interjected. He gave a nod to the hotel employee. "I think we got what we came for."

"We did?" I asked.

"Yeah, let's go." He cocked his head to the exit. He also flashed me a hotel key card.

"Okay," I said. Tara and the blonde were still giving each other the eye. I poked her in the side. "Come on, tough guy."

❈ ❈ ❈

We left the *Bedrest Inn* on Rabbit's heels. Hurrying between the raindrops, he led us around the side of the building toward a separate guest entrance – which required a key card to get in. Rabbit swiped the reader. The light flashed green, and we snuck into a ground floor hall and out of the rain.

"And the plan is?" I rubbed my arms. The rain was cold even though the weather was still warm.

"Minerva Mirta, second floor, room 229." Rabbit pushed open the door to the stairwell and we climbed up a level. The hallway was empty. The cousins' room was located at the other end.

"If they're in there, they probably won't open the door. They don't know us," Tara pointed out.

"I'll explain who I am," I told her. We stood in front of the door and I knocked. We waited.

Nobody answered. No one called through the door to learn who was in the hall. I knocked a second time.

Still nothing.

"Let me try," Tara said. She rapped on the door several times. "Hello? Minerva? Aster? Anyone home?"

"I don't think anyone's in there. Or they've checked through the peephole and decided to ignore us." Down the hall the elevator bell dinged. The doors slid open and two women, presumably in their fifties, stepped out. They carried wet umbrellas and their raincoats were slick with the afternoon shower.

"I really wish I would've brought my wellies," one of the women complained as they marched down the hall. She was tanned, with short, brown hair worn in a pixie cut. Sunshine had added highlights over time.

"Or at least some rubber mocs," the other woman replied. "My pants are damp. The wind drove the rain sideways." She was taller than her companion by at least six inches. Her hair was a mix of silver and black, cut in a trendy layered bob. As they approached, I noted her eyes were a striking shade of green. They gazed directly into mine. "Well, what have we here?"

"You wouldn't be Minerva and Aster, would you?" I asked.

"We would." She leaned in, studying my face. "I've seen your picture. You're Emily, aren't you?"

Relief washed over me. "I am. And these are my friends, Tara and Rabbit."

"You don't know how happy we are to see you," Tara added.

The taller woman offered a wan smile. "You're here because of Lydia. Let's go inside the room. Aster and I need to change clothes."

❊ ❊ ❊

Last time I was in a room at the *Bedrest Inn*, I was surrounded in various shades of beige: walls, curtains, and carpet.

Not much had changed. However, throughout the room there were bouquets of colorful flowers. Bunches of blooms overflowed several ice buckets, coffee mugs, and a couple of empty wine bottles.

We stood awkwardly waiting while the two

cousins took turns changing into dry clothing in the bathroom. The shorter of the two, Aster, directed us to sit in the available chairs and on the end of one of the beds.

"This is a serious situation Lydia is in," said Minerva as she joined Aster on the other bed. The ladies sat side-by-side. "I've made some calls to a few elected officials here in Vue – actually, Aster and I just met with one – but I'm afraid because of who your mother is, each is reluctant to be the first one to help."

"I don't understand." I shifted on the bed. "Why won't they help? What's the problem?"

Aster spoke first. "We may have made an error in judgment when we told Lydia we were coming to Vue." She looked briefly to Minerva. "The three of us haven't seen each other in many, many years. We were eager to get together."

Minerva waved her hand. "We knew there'd be an uptick in activity here, but we didn't expect this level of disruption. Lydia's grown stronger over the years. Soon after she arrived in the Empire, we felt it."

"She's always been powerful," Aster picked up the conversation. "But what we didn't realize is that while she was putting out a high level of inspiration, she was being fed by the energy here in the Empire."

"Too many magical people in one place," added Minerva. "Still, we were glad to see each other again. We didn't plan on staying for long."

"Where are you from?" Tara asked. "You don't live in the Empire?"

"No, we don't live here." Aster got up and began to rearrange a group of flowers in one of the ice buckets. "I live on the central coast of California. I'm originally from a small town in Pennsylvania. My family operated a large greenhouse. We had two florist shops." She paused and smiled at the blooms at her fingertips – or maybe her memories. "I moved to California soon after I turned twenty. And now, after thirty years, I'm getting ready to retire. We specialize in orchids. My son is taking over."

Minerva waited patiently for Aster to finish. "I recently came back from an extended-stay in Europe. I'm living in New York for now, but I've considered making the move to Matar. My presence there won't be disruptive, though."

"Like my mother's presence here in the Empire." I snuck a look at Rabbit, wondering what information he'd relay to his network. He'd left his chair and leaned against a desk. His arms were crossed, and his phone was buried in a pocket.

"Unfortunately, Lydia's week in the Empire made an impact. That's why some officials are unwilling to step forward to help. I thought because of your father's history in the Empire she might have a champion… But politics." She rolled her eyes. "We'll need to find legal representation to extricate her from this mess."

"One of my friends, Jo, is a Senior Salesman." I hesitated. "You do know what a Salesman is, right?"

Minerva's eyes twinkled. "We do. And yes, we know you are one. But tell me about this Jo."

"Jo is also a lawyer in New York. She contacted a couple of criminal lawyers here in Vue to meet her at the Empire guard base. They're going to see what they can do. In the meantime, we realized you and Aster might be able to help by providing an alibi for my Mom." Optimism faded quickly when I saw the grim look on Minerva's face. "She wasn't with you, was she?"

"No, dear," Minerva said. "Aster?"

"Well, she was with us earlier in the day, then we split up in the evening. She went to that art gallery. Minerva attended a feminist performance at the theater, and I agreed to lead a tour of flowers at a botanical garden. Some only bloom at night." Aster sat beside me.

"And you didn't see Lydia at all last night?" Tara interrupted.

"She came in late," Minerva answered. "The storm was in full swing. We were in bed already. Lydia slipped in and I believe I heard the bath running. I was drifting in and out of sleep."

"We shared a bed. I'm a pretty solid sleeper, but it was after midnight when she climbed in."

Aster cocked her head to the side. "I think."

My hope of securing a believable alibi for my mother was dwindling. "And then what happened? Rabbit said she turned herself in."

Minerva nodded. "When the morning news reported the guards were looking for her in connection to the murder, she agreed she needed to meet with them at their base."

"And they arrested her?" Tightness built in my chest.

"Shortly after we arrived at the base," Minerva confirmed. She rubbed her chin with her fingertips. "One guard was quite reasonable, but he had to follow a process."

"Did she tell you where she was when the murder happened?" Tara asked.

"No, nowhere specific," Aster answered. "She said she'd attended the event at the gallery but the man who was murdered humiliated an artist, so she left. She told us she went for a walk. Eventually, she visited some smaller art galleries where people were friendlier, and art was more heartfelt."

"If we can find out where she went, then maybe we can establish an alibi." Okay, so maybe hope was returning.

"Your friend Jo and the other attorneys will want to work with your mother to establish a timeline of events," Minerva said. "Once that is in place, they'll release her. She still might need to stay in the Empire while they completely absolve her of any involvement, but they won't keep her jailed."

Rabbit's phone began to buzz furiously in his pocket. He retrieved it and scrolled through the messages with his thumb. He froze before slowly lifting his head. "There's been an attack," he said, his jaw clenching.

I stood up, my heart jumping in my chest. "Where Rabbit?"

His eyes dropped to the screen on his phone. The next words were snapped out. "Downtown. Outside the Empire guard base. The Fringe. Jo was hurt."

"My Mom?" I stepped toward him as Tara clung to my arm.

Rabbit looked up, his dark eyes now black and glittering with anger.

"Rabbit?" My voice rose.

"They took her."

CHAPTER 14

"Keep waving it under her nose," a voice said. "Just don't touch her face with it."

"I think she's coming to," another voice sounded above me. Was it Tara? "Emily? Emily, can you hear me?"

The light of the room seemed brighter, and I blinked against it. The fragrance of lavender and rosemary filled my nostrils. My hand flailed in front of my face.

"There she is," a third voice observed as someone gently pulled my hand into theirs. "Take it easy, Emily. You passed out. Don't try to sit up yet. Just take a moment. I think we can stop with the oils, Aster."

I took another deep breath as the scents lessened, clearing my throat. My eyes finally started to focus. Three worried faces peered back down. "What happened?" I croaked.

"You fainted." Tara smoothed my forehead with her hand. "You scared me."

"Help me sit up." I was on the bed and the three of them pulled me into a sitting position.

"Don't stand yet," warned Minerva.

"What happened?" I asked again. Tara's grave expression triggered my memory. "Oh, no. My Mom!"

"Shh." Aster sat down beside me, putting an arm around my shoulders.

"Where's Rabbit?" I eased away, swinging my feet over the side of the bed. The world rocked for a second, but I remained upright. "Rabbit?"

"He left to find out more," Tara explained.

"He left?" My mouth popped open. "He tells me the Fringe has my mother and then he leaves?"

Tara lifted her hands, palms facing me. "Listen to me. He left to find out if we can get downtown. He said he'd be right back."

I started to stand. "We need to go with him."

"Emily, knock it off and listen to me!" Tara shoved me back onto the bed. "The Fringe is in Vue – we knew they were here, but the game just changed. They attacked in broad daylight. They attacked Empire guards, Emily. They know you're here, too. It's not safe to run out there on the street. Rabbit knows this. You know this. He's going to find out what he can, then he's coming back here with a car. We're going back to Tuesday's apartment. And then we can go after Lydia once Rabbit gets a bead on where they're taking her."

Determination lined Tara's fine-featured face. I ran both of my hands over my head and through my hair before placing them palms down on the bed at my sides. I dropped my head back and stared at the ceiling. "You're right. We need to think this through."

"I think maybe some water?" Minerva offered me a plastic bottle. I accepted it and took a swig.

"Thanks." I wiped my lips with the back of my hand. "I'm sorry."

Aster reached out and touched my hair. Her smile was kind. "I know you're terribly afraid right now, and I know you won't believe me, but we've known Lydia a long time. We grew up together. She has survived some pretty trying times."

"How come I've never met you before? Or you?" I gestured toward Minerva.

The cousins shared a knowing look before Minerva spoke. "That's for your mother to tell you. But I think you can see from what's happening in Vue that when the three of us get together, there's a little bit of a stir. But it's not usually at this level."

"Except for that time in the eighties," Aster began.

Minerva shook her head, cutting the other woman off. "Not now, Aster."

I looked at the boring beige carpet trying to wrap my head around what was going on. A Fringe attack. When my father was alive, the Fringe grew bolder up until they killed him. Then they went underground. Now they resurfaced in more frequent strikes. Today's attack proved they weren't afraid of the Empire or its authority. My head snapped up. "Wait, what about Jo? Is she alright?"

"Rabbit's going to find out. He didn't know when he left," Tara shook her head.

A knock at the door made the four of us jump. Minerva held up a hand to keep us quiet. She walked to the door and looked out through the peephole. Her shoulders relaxed and she turned the handle, allowing Rabbit to enter.

"Everything okay here?" he asked as he crossed the room. "I have a car waiting downstairs to take us back to Tuesday's. There's no way we're getting anywhere near downtown."

"We're better," Tara answered for me. "What'd you find out?"

"I don't know which way they went with Lydia yet. Jo's still on the scene downtown. She's banged up. She'll be okay, though. She fought back." His eyes flicked to the cousins. "Are you staying here?"

Minerva nodded. "Yes. We're not leaving until Lydia's safe. Please keep us informed. I'm going to start reaching out again to officials I know. Maybe now they'll be inspired to act."

"I'll make sure you get updates," he said. He handed Tara her shoulder bag before picking up mine and holding it out to me. "Ready, Emily?"

I accepted the bag and finally rose to my feet without a wobble. "Lead the way, Rabbit."

❋ ❋ ❋

We made a fast escape to the car Rabbit had waiting for us at the curb. It was an old Subaru Justy, painted matte black. The Rabbit sitting behind the wheel glanced up as Tara and I climbed into the back. Rabbit rode shotgun.

"I hope this thing makes it back to Tuesday's," Tara muttered. The driver tossed her a grin from the rearview mirror.

"Can we talk?" I leaned between the front seats.

Rabbit nodded, motioning to the driver. "He knows everything I know."

"And?" I prompted.

"It sounds like the attack came when Empire guards were escorting Lydia across the street to the courthouse. She was going to be arraigned. Jo and the attorneys were with her, so they clearly got in to talk to her," Rabbit said.

"Okay, good, good. Then what happened?" I was gripping the seat. I felt Tara trying to wedge in next to me, so I shifted to give her room.

"They attacked when everyone was in the middle of the street. There was a lot of confusion because the press was also there. A couple of Rabbits were keeping their eyes on the base ever since Lydia was arrested." Rabbit paused to twist his head back and forth. I heard his neck crack.

"So, they saw it happen," Tara said.

"Yeah. It was fast. Men swarmed in and shots were fired. It was chaos, but one Rabbit saw a guy carrying your mother over his shoulder and out of the crowd." Rabbit stopped. He leaned close and peered into my face. "I don't want you to faint again."

"I won't," I promised. I hoped I could keep it. "Just tell me."

"They threw her into a black SUV and took off."

"Again with the stupid SUV," Tara snorted. "Not much for being original, are they?"

"And no one followed them?" I was incredulous.

"Someone might've if the bomb didn't go off," he told us. "A van on the street was rigged with explosives."

I sat back into my seat. I wasn't surprised. They bombed my father's train when they killed him.

Rabbit pointed out the windshield and told our driver to turn into an alley behind Tuesday's building. "Park here. Can you wait for a few minutes? I might need you for another lift."

The driver said waiting wouldn't be a problem. Rabbit, Tara, and I rounded the building warily before entering *The Sweet Spot*. Tuesday's kitchen assistant directed us to head upstairs.

"Emily!" Tuesday met us at the apartment door. "Your mother!"

The sweet woman pulled me into a hug. I sank into the scent of warm cookies. "It's bad, Tuesday."

She sniffed. "They are bad men."

"Yeah, Tuesday, they are." I looked over her shoulder at Tara. She offered a weak smile. "It's a bad situation."

Tuesday released me and put her hands on the sides of my face, her eyes searching. "You'll get her back."

It wasn't a question. I swallowed the lump in my throat. "I know."

The baker turned and checked on Tara next. My eyes tracked back to Rabbit. "You said Jo was still at the scene?"

"Yeah. She wasn't shot, but she got knocked around. She managed to slam one guy in the face. Some sort of ferocious palm strike to the nose. Rabbits reported she must've broken it because there was blood everywhere. She really did some damage."

"Don't mess with Jo," I said. "Did they at least get that guy? Any of the Fringe?"

"Not a one," he replied. His phone buzzed and he looked at his hand. "Great. The SUV was found. Empty."

"What does that mean?"

"It means they switched vehicles. Now we wait and see where they show up next," he said.

"No, I can't keep waiting." I threw my hands up.

"I agree, and I have some ideas. We all need to talk." Rabbit inclined his head toward Tara. "First, she needs to go home. It's not safe for her here."

Tara was telling Tuesday everything we knew. I nodded. "I know. Hey Tara?"

Tuesday disappeared into the kitchen and Tara joined us as Rabbit and I sat down at the table.

"Next steps?" she asked.

Before I could say anything, Rabbit spoke up. "You need to go home, Tara. The driver downstairs is going to drive you straight to Anwat. It's a long drive, but this will be faster than waiting for the morning ferry and then taking a train from the Port to Anwat. There's a late train bound for Kincaid you can catch tonight if you leave right now." Rabbit leaned forward, resting his folded arms on the table. "You're a good friend. You understand Emily can't be slowed down once we get a lead on Lydia. The Fringe is going to come at Emily from every direction now. You're a target here, too."

Tara opened her mouth to protest, then abruptly shut it. Her wide, brown eyes grew wet. She nodded. "I wish I could help you."

"You've helped so much already," I told my best friend, reaching for her hand. "You can help me now by going back to Kincaid." I hesitated. "You can tell Jack I'm doing my best to get everyone home."

Tara blinked several times and nodded again, squeezing my hand. "I think it's time you started to break the rules more, Emily. You need to start door traveling. It's the only way you're going to catch up."

I glanced at Rabbit and he agreed with Tara. "When the time comes, you'll go ahead of me, wherever that is. I'll make sure some Rabbits are there to meet up with you."

"I guess I'd better be going then," Tara said, pushing her chair back and standing. She rolled her shoulders. "You sure that car's going to make it to Anwat?"

❊ ❊ ❊

Rabbit asked me to stay in the apartment while he walked Tara down to the car in the alleyway. I hugged her and promised we'd send as much information as we could through the Rabbits' network. She asked if we could send 'Handsome' to Kincaid to update her.

Good grief.

Tuesday followed my friends downstairs to pack a sack of goodies for Tara's road trip. Tara left with my winter coat after I emptied its pockets and also took my travel bag after I moved a few items into my bulging shoulder bag. I tried to pack light and not crush my top hat. As soon as we had a clue as to where my mother was being held, I'd be on my way. Rabbit believed they kidnapped her to lure me in. We'd find a way to get her back.

I decided to go out onto the balcony to wave to Tara as she left. The rain had stopped, and the fresh air would help clear my head. The temperature dropped a bit, so even though it was humid, the air didn't feel oppressive.

Opening the narrow door, I stepped out onto the terrace. Templeton stood at the other end facing away from the building. He leaned against the railing as he gazed down into the alley. I viewed his profile with frustration.

"And I never got to take her up on the Friday night takeout invitation," he tsked. "Well, maybe another day."

"You're here because the universe hates me and wants to punish me," I said. What in the world did I do in a former life? I was surely paying for something.

Templeton turned to face me. He was dressed in a pair of grey summer trousers and a black button-down shirt. The sleeves were rolled up to just below his elbows. The top button of the shirt was undone. He held his top hat by the brim in his left hand. A sly smile played about his lips. He raised an eyebrow. "Do you need to be punished, Emily? What have you done now?"

"Give it a rest," I spat. "What are you doing here?"

"I'm here because, between you and your mother, the Empire is in an uproar."

I pointed a finger at him. "Don't you dare even

speak of my mother."

Amusement gone, his mouth flattened into a thin line. We glared at each other. He finally spoke. "They took her because they want the Crimson Stone."

"I don't have the Crimson Stone," I shot back.

"You have a piece of it, Emily. That gets them one step closer to the whole gemstone."

"I'm not giving them anything," I stated evenly. Gritting my teeth, I stepped closer to him, my hands balled into fists at my side. "Do you know where she is? Do you know where they took her? If you hold back, Templeton, I will make you pay if anything – *anything* – happens to her."

"Are you threatening me?" he asked softly. He leaned closer. The translucent blue of his eyes flashed. Power rolled off him in waves, his energy intermingling with mine.

I held my ground. "Yes."

His eyebrows raised and he straightened. "Well, nice to see you still have a backbone, even though you're full of foolish confidence."

"Stop it. Where is she?"

"I don't know – yet. What does Rabbit say?" Templeton fiddled with the sleeve on his right arm, pushing it up further. His fingers lingered as he searched for a piece of lint to pluck.

"He doesn't know. The SUV was abandoned," I said.

"Matar would be my guess," he answered, finally removing an imaginary thread from his shirtsleeve. "That's where I would head."

"Emily?" I heard Rabbit call from inside Tuesday's apartment.

Templeton cocked his head to the side. "Your protector is back. Time to go." He shooed me away with an impatient hand.

"We're not done, Templeton," I said. "If I find out you're holding back on me –"

"Yes, yes," he interrupted. "You'll make me pay. Now go. I'll be using that door."

I fired one last hostile look at him before spinning on my heel and opening the door back into Tuesday's apartment.

"See you in Matar, Emily," his voice taunted behind me.

※ ※ ※

Even though Rabbit monitored the network for any blip pointing in the direction of where the Fringe might be holding my mother, we hadn't learned anything. Pacing the apartment wasn't helping, but Rabbit wouldn't let me leave. I knew he was right. We didn't know which way to go. Still, Templeton made his remark about Matar. His instincts could be right.

"I should go to Matar," I said to Rabbit. I told him about Templeton's visit and what was said.

Rabbit admitted the Fringe might return there because they had such a strong presence. There were also Salesmen in the Empire's leadership who secretly lent them support.

Rabbit stood at the front of Tuesday's apartment, the curtain pulled aside as he stared down at the street below. His phone remained in his hand and his eyes flitted to it every thirty seconds. The device remained oddly quiet.

He let the curtain drop. "Matar's an option if you door travel. I think you're strong enough to come back to Tuesday's if you need to. The problem I have is catching up with you. I don't want to be halfway there and find out we're going in the wrong direction."

He had a point. I rubbed my finger over my lower lip as I pondered our options. "Is there no way you can come with me when I door travel?"

"I don't understand." His dark brows dipped down.

"Well, Jo and I door traveled together at the same time – until she got sick of my energy jerking her arm out of its socket. And I door traveled last year with poor Mr. Havers. We went from Blackstone's to Matar." Alfred Havers was a Senior Salesman who'd traveled with my father. While escorting me to the Salesman Court, we were attacked by the Fringe. Havers was killed. It was because of me he died.

"You're all Salesmen, Emily," Rabbit replied.

"Rabbits don't have the ability to door travel."

"But what if I just, I don't know, carried you with me." A vision of piggybacking Rabbit through time and space flipped through my mind. A nervous giggle escaped my lips. I was having a hard time holding it together.

"Yeah, I'm gonna take a pass on that," Rabbit said, lifting his chin and tilting his head to the side. "You okay?"

"No. I can't stay still anymore. I think I should go." Before I could finish, Tuesday poked her head out of her bedroom.

"I heard the India bells downstairs," she said. "The bakery door is locked, but I think a Salesman just arrived."

A knock on the apartment door followed. Rabbit raised his hand, motioning for us to be still. He walked to the door. "Who is it?" he asked, his voice gruff.

"It's Jo Carter," my mentor answered from the other side. Rabbit unlocked the door and held it open for her. She nodded her thanks and caught sight of Tuesday. "I figured after my last entrance, I should exercise some more courtesy," she said dryly.

Jo had a horrible black eye, and her lower lip was swollen and split on the right side. Her clothes were dirty, and the sleeve of her blouse was ripped. In her hand, she held a battered top hat. She caught me in a hug when I lunged for her.

"I hear the other guy looks worse," Rabbit said. He reached between us when Jo released me and gently turned her chin toward him. His eyes narrowed as he examined her face. "Did you go to the hospital? Are any of your teeth loose?"

"I'm fine," she assured him. "I didn't need to go to the hospital, but I had to give several statements. You know everything that happened today?"

"And then some. The SUV was abandoned," he said.

"I heard," she said. "Emily, I am so sorry about your mother. They swarmed in out of nowhere. No one was expecting it. The Empire guards were caught off… well, guard." Frustrated, Jo shook her head and rolled her eyes up. "It was fast. They knew exactly what they were doing. They ripped her away."

"Jo, there was nothing you could do," I told her. "Nothing. You were just trying to help."

"I did get to talk to your mother beforehand," Jo said. "She was pretty rattled, but okay. I was able to get a timeline of her travels the night before. I passed the information to the attorneys I contacted earlier. They'll work jointly for your mother. However, once they establish her alibi – and they will – she won't be charged. She was arrested, but that's it."

"She wasn't arraigned?" I asked.

"No. We were on our way to the courthouse when the attack happened. She was not formally charged."

"That's one piece of good news in this whole freaking mess," I sighed.

"I wish I could change what happened," Jo said, rubbing her arms. "I need to go home to my family, Emily. And the guards want me to escort you out of the Empire. They're concerned you're the next target. There's no safe place for you here. While I haven't heard from Blackstone or the Salesman Court, I can assure you they want you back in Kincaid as well."

My eyes shifted to Rabbit. He inclined his head slightly toward the closest door. Jo missed the movement. "I don't know, Jo. I get what you're saying, and I know I'm in trouble, but I can't leave until my mother's safe."

"There's nothing you can do," Jo said gently. "It's dangerous and you don't even know where she is. The guards will do their job. They'll find her."

"The Fringe killed my father, Jo."

Jo's shoulders dropped and she nodded. "I know. Please Emily, let's get you home. I promise I will do everything in my power to be there for you and to help you. But you need to come with me. Get your things."

Rabbit was silent during the conversation. When our eyes met, I knew he understood what

I was about to do.

"Alright, Jo. I get it. You're right." I crossed the room to Rabbit and gave him a big hug. "Keep monitoring the network, okay? You'll be in contact, right? Send a message and all that?"

Rabbit's eyes shimmered and his nose twitched. "You know it."

"Tuesday?" I held out my arms to the little, round woman. Her embrace was warm.

"You're always welcome here, Emily Swift," she said, her sweet face shining with kindness. "I hope your mother comes home to you soon. I know she will."

"She will," I repeated. I retrieved my shoulder bag from the couch, pulling my top hat out. I smoothed the purple feather before placing it on my head.

"Thank you, Tuesday, Rabbit, for taking care of her," Jo said. "I know she's been in good hands." She gave me an encouraging smile. "Okay, Emily. Let's go back to Kincaid by way of Blackstone's library. I know it's getting late, but he'll certainly be waiting. Which one of these doors can you tune into? Which one is the right door to take you back home?"

I nodded at my mentor before turning away and reviewing the several doors within view. My eyes bounced to Rabbit one last time. He didn't look up. He was already busy texting.

I didn't need to find the 'right' door to go back

to Kincaid. I'd learned I could make any door the right one. And in fact, I could hear the buzzing starting already. The door leading out of the apartment began to vibrate.

"I got it," I smiled.

"Great," Jo answered. "I'll be right behind you."

Hiking my shoulder bag up a little higher, I moved toward the door. As my fingers grazed the doorknob, flecks of energy snapped around my hand. I glanced over my shoulder at Rabbit, catching his grin as the door swung open and sucked me through to Matar.

CHAPTER 15

Jo was going to kill me when we reconnected, I had no doubt. I didn't blame her. I probably gave her an ulcer.

When door traveling, you need to focus on a destination. You need to raise your own energy and feel your way to where you want to land. It helps if you can tie an emotion or a prior experience to it. I did just that as I left Tuesday's apartment in Vue and stepped through the door leading into *Zenith's* lobby. It seemed like the safest place to land.

I stumbled in through the double doors but managed to avoid making a scene. I caught my top hat as it slipped off my head and carefully put it into my shoulder bag. There were several patrons at the coat check, and a woman was on the phone at the hostess stand. No one paid me any attention. Being Sunday, the restaurant wasn't busy. Still, it was one of Matar's hot spots, so they were serving dinner until eleven.

Getting to Matar was the easy part. Now I had to figure out where to go. I thought about returning to the studio where *Good Night, Matar* was being recorded in hopes of finding the same crew of Rabbits who helped before. They could get a message to my Rabbit back in Vue. I nixed the idea. There was no guarantee they'd be there.

I tapped a finger against my lips while considering my options. Anne provided me with the name and address of a woman in Matar who she believed could help me with any magical abilities I might have. I had the name and address with me. I dug the paper Anne gave me out of my bag and unfolded it.

Lucie Bellerose, 1106 Autumn Avenue, Matar.

Stepping outside onto the sidewalk, I raised my hand to flag down a cab. One pulled up and I climbed into the back seat, instructing the driver where to go. As she reported the destination to her dispatch, I noticed a smartly dressed Speedy stepping out of *Zenith*, an unknown man by his side. The two stood talking, unaware I was only a few yards away.

Speedy's companion didn't appear to be a Rabbit, although his wavy hair was dark and thick, longish even. But he wasn't fair skinned like the other Rabbits; he had more of an olive skin tone. He was taller than Speedy – probably just over six foot – and sported a Van Dyke beard. The tailored suit he wore was black. He was attractive. In fact, if Tara would've been with me, she would've climbed back out of the car to give him her number.

The men said a few more words before parting and walking in opposite directions. I turned my head so Speedy wouldn't recognize me if he looked toward the cab. The moment I witnessed left me confused. I guessed there'd be occasions when a Rabbit would dress up, but something about the scene felt off. It left me feeling troubled.

As we pulled out into traffic, I craned my neck to see if I could spot the man Speedy left behind, but he was already gone. I settled back into my seat and considered what I should do next. The drive would take about twenty minutes. I hoped this Lucie would be home.

The cab driver dropped me at the curb in front of a charming brownstone with window boxes overflowing with lush green plants – a result of the unseasonably warm weather. Several sets of stairs led to the building's different doors. Each staircase was lined with a wrought iron railing winding up from a brick sidewalk or traveling down toward a basement residence. The railings were different at every entrance. Some entertained playful silhouettes woven into the iron; others displayed more ominous characters, with horns hovering over grimacing faces.

The door to Lucie Bellerose's home was painted a glossy black, emphasized by the spotless white of the transom and side windows. A faint light shone through, touching the stairs. A polished mail slot sat level with the doorknob, while an ornate brass door knocker, in the shape of a crescent moon embracing a full sun, served as the door's centerpiece. I ascended slowly, considering the best way to explain my unannounced visit.

The last stair was slightly wider than the rest, allowing me a moment to pause and take a breath. Since I didn't see a doorbell, I reached out and lifted the door knocker, gently rapping it three times against its plate. A minute later, a brighter light shone through a side window and a woman's face appeared. Before I could pantomime who I was and why I was there, she opened the door.

"Hello," she smiled. "Are you Emily?"

"Ah, yeah. Lucie, right" I replied, surprised. "Did you know who I am because of, um, magic or something?"

The woman laughed. "No, nothing that mysterious. Anne sent a message a couple of days ago saying you might be coming through Matar this weekend. She also told me to expect you to show up unexpectedly."

I had the good graces to look embarrassed. "I'm really sorry," I said, wincing. "I wanted to reach out ahead of time, maybe even invite you to coffee."

"Oh, don't worry about it," Lucie said, opening the door fully and gesturing. "Please, come in. You look pretty drained. No offense."

"None taken. It's the truth." I stepped inside. The brownstone apartment was even more charming on the inside, with a blend of new vintage-styled light fixtures alongside original gumwood and leaded glass. The entryway boasted a tiled floor in two-inch black and white hexagons arranged in a spiral. Straight ahead I could see brighter lights and what looked like the entrance to a kitchen. Barstools were lined up in front of a counter. To my right, a pocket door with twelve glass panes closed off a small sitting room. A mantle sat opposite the door. A squat lamp had been left on, casting its light over an unlit fireplace.

"This way. Leave your shoes on," she instructed. I followed Lucie toward the kitchen. "Would you like something to drink? Are you hungry?"

I considered saying no, but I realized I was famished. Tuesday kept everyone well-fed, but I lost my appetite after the attack that morning. "I'd love something to eat. Thanks. Again, I'm sorry."

"You," Lucie said as she stopped and waved a finger at me, "have got to stop that. Anne's message said you were coming to the Empire to find your mother. I heard the news about what happened in Vue. I can't imagine the hell you're going through."

I climbed onto a leather barstool. "It's a bit surreal at this point. You were the only person I knew to look up when I got back to Matar."

Lucie nodded. "I'm glad you did. Do you like lasagna?" She didn't wait for an answer, pulling out a casserole from her refrigerator before clicking on her oven. "Big piece or little?" She pointed a knife at the pasta.

"Medium."

"It won't take long to heat up," she said, cutting and transferring a slice to a small baking dish. She slipped it into the oven. Next, she retrieved a paper-wrapped loaf from the counter bread box. Sliding the bread from the bag, Lucie cut off a piece. "Bread? I'll warm it."

I watched my hostess work. Lucie appeared to be about ten years older than I was. We were about the same height, but she probably had an inch on me. She was fit, with auburn hair pulled into a messy knot at the nape of her neck. Her bangs were brushed to the side over bright, blue eyes. Small, silver hoops hung from her ears. She wore jeans and a plain heather grey tee shirt. On her feet, navy slip-on sneakers.

"Okay," she said, pouring and handing me a glass of red wine. "Let's give the lasagna some time to heat up, then I'll toss the bread in toward the end. In the meantime, catch me up on what's going on. How can I help?"

"I'm not sure how anyone can help," I began. "I have to find my mother and get her back."

"How are you going to do that?" Lucie asked.

She leaned against the counter, her eyes searching my face. "Not the finding part, the getting."

"I..." I blinked. "I guess I'll find out where she is first, and then I'll decide."

"Hmm. Well, wherever she is, you'll be able to get in because you're a Salesman. It's getting her out that's the problem," she said.

"Yeah," I sipped my wine. "In a way, I was kind of hoping that's where you might be able to help."

"Oh?" She lifted an eyebrow. "How so?"

"I know Anne told you I might have some 'magical abilities,' and I thought if you could help me understand how I could use them, that might be an option." Even as I said the words, I felt my confidence lowering.

"Magical abilities," Lucie repeated. She tilted her head back, twisting her lips to the side and looking up at the ceiling. She stroked the hollow of her neck with an index finger. She dropped her gaze back to me. "Even if you're able to tap into some sort of ability, learning to master it will take time. It's my understanding you don't really know what you can do."

Lucie was not doing much for the faith I wanted to have in myself. "I get what you're saying, but I don't have much choice here and I don't have a lot of time."

"And you don't want to bring in the Empire guards? Even if you can locate your mother?"

She frowned.

"The Empire guards didn't do such a good job protecting her from the Fringe," I replied.

"Point taken. Well, let's think about this. Let's talk about what you know, and we'll see if we can craft a spell to help us locate your mother. That's going to be the first step. But before you go in, magic blazing, you'll need a good plan. And backup," she added.

"I don't know much at all," I said, shaking my head. "But I've noticed I'm getting better with door travel. I've also used some of the same energy to help in different ways." I explained to Lucie about finding the path in the woods when we were in the Jeep being chased by the black SUV. I also told her about the person hiding in the shadows across the street from my house and how I reached out with my energy to try to learn who was there. That got Lucie's attention.

"Did you determine who it was?" she asked.

"No. In fact, it felt like I got slapped just as I was getting close enough to see more," I said.

"Another magical being, I assume." The oven dinged and Lucie put together a plate for me. She wedged the toasted bread alongside the lasagna. She passed me a napkin and a fork.

"Maybe," I said, using the side of my fork to cut into my dinner. "That was the last I saw of her."

"Her? You knew it was a woman? Interesting. Well, we won't focus on the other person right now, but let's talk about using energy in magic."

I ate while Lucie explained how personal energy was used to empower certain items for magical purposes. She also described using energy to block another's probing, or like in the case of my prior experience, to reach out to learn more about someone.

"What about something like a magical gemstone?" I wondered if I could use the Crimson Stone to my advantage. I would need to bring all three pieces together, which meant getting Rabbit's and Justice Spell's pieces, but it was the only magical object I knew I could use successfully.

"Sure, some items you can bond with more closely. It also depends on what kind of power the gemstone owns. If it's a protective one, you can use it for that. What did you have in mind?"

"What about a Stone that dishes out justice?" I'd been told the Crimson Stone gave absolute power, but I wasn't sure I fully understood the extent. Still, it helped me bring Petrovich to justice, so that was the experience I focused on.

Lucie cocked her head to the side and nodded. "That might work. But magic can be a tough teacher, Emily. If you're not precise, the ramifications can be terrible. I will tell you if you're planning to work a 'bring someone to justice' type of spell, you better have all your own deeds in line. What you put out there you will get back," she finished. "The advice 'make sure your own slate is clean' comes into play here."

It made sense. Lucie and I seemed to be feeling each other out. I decided to go for it. Anne trusted this woman. I would, too. "What about using the Crimson Stone?"

Lucie's eyebrows shot up. "You're not telling me you have the Crimson Stone, are you?"

"Well, yes and no," I said. "I had it in Vue last year, but it was too dangerous to keep in one piece, so I separated it into three. I might be able to get all the pieces together and reform the gemstone."

Lucie frowned. "Did you break it?"

"No. The Crimson Stone itself is in three pieces you connect to form one gemstone. It was part of a necklace we found hidden in an antique shop last December. I separated the pieces from each other and sent them off with different people," I said.

"So now they're in different places." Lucie tapped her fingers on the counter. "I wouldn't let that information get out, Emily – certainly not where they're hidden. But if you've used the Crimson Stone before, you might be able to use it to get your mother back. The Stone will likely recognize you and respond to your energy."

"My friend Rabbit is in Vue. He's one of the people who took a piece of the Stone. He knows I door traveled to Matar, but he doesn't know where I am. Maybe we can try to get him a message." I waved my fork. "I don't dare use the Empire service right now, but could you send a message for me?"

"Absolutely," Lucie replied. She grabbed a notepad and pencil from a drawer. "What's the message? Where should it be sent?"

I explained if Rabbit was still in Vue, he'd probably be in an apartment over a bakery called *The Sweet Spot*. I told her the message could be relayed to Tuesday if Rabbit wasn't there, just in case he circled back. I did worry a little about Tuesday's flightiness, but she certainly understood the gravity of the situation.

"The message should say his friend is here at your house, but we need to give him a hint about bringing his piece of the Stone. Add that he needs to bring the 'thing' his friend gave him in Vue last December," I said. "I think that's cryptic enough, but he'll still understand."

"Got it. I'll also send one off to Anne letting her know you're here." Lucie opened a cupboard door and revealed what looked like an old rotary wall phone. I had an aunt in Pennsylvania who owned one. I was fascinated with it when I was little. This phone, however, did not have a dial – or buttons of any kind for that matter. There was only a cradle for the tan handset. Lucie placed it to her ear and popped the cradle down once.

"Hello. Yes, I need to send a message to an

apartment over *The Sweet Spot* bakery in Vue. The recipients are either the bakery owner or the Rabbit staying with her. What?" Lucie rolled her eyes. "Yes, I know finding a Rabbit is impossible unless they want to be found. Trust me. This one wants this message to find him."

Lucie provided the Empire service with the message we discussed. I finished my late dinner as Lucie relayed a second message to be sent to Anne in Kincaid. She was told it might be delayed because the Salesman leadership was monitoring messages being sent into and out of the Empire. Lucie kept the message brief, sharing only that 'Anne's friend' had arrived safely at her house.

"So, what next?" I was mindful of the late hour, but it was hard to stop for the night. I was also afraid if I stopped doing something, my mind would go to bad places. I didn't want to think of what the Fringe might do to my mother.

"What about the other pieces of the Crimson Stone?" Lucie asked.

"I gave one piece to a justice on the Salesman Court," I said. "I need to get in contact with her. I'm guessing she's at home now."

"But would she keep it at her house? If she's part of the Empire leadership, it must be under lock and key somewhere safe."

I nodded. "Maybe that's where I go first thing in the morning."

"What about the third piece?" Lucie put my dinner plate into the sink before holding up the bottle of wine. "Another glass?"

"Just a little bit." I held my glass out and she poured in a small amount. My hostess pulled a second glass from her cupboard and poured wine for herself. I was reluctant to tell Lucie I kept the third piece of the Crimson Stone. I also didn't want to tell her where it was hidden. I hadn't told anyone. "I can get my hands on the third piece."

"Hmm," she said, eyeballing me before moving around to my side of the counter and climbing onto a barstool. "Next we need to figure out what kind of finding spell we can do to locate your mother. What other magical items do you have?"

"I don't have any," I said. "Well, I have a book."

"What type of book?" Lucie sipped her wine as her gaze slid to my bulging shoulder bag. "Do you have it with you?"

I set my wine down and pulled the bag closer. Reaching around my top hat, I let my fingers touch the cover of The Book. "This was my father's Salesman journal. It's sort of magic in that sometimes his old notes guide me to what to do next."

Lucie's big eyes sparkled, her glass halfway to her lips. "Really? Would you show it to me?"

I finally pulled The Book, with its worn blue

cover and its gold 'S' imprinted on the front, out from my bag. Retrieving the hat pin key from the tiny wooden box I kept it in, I opened the lock holding the covers together. I laid my hand on the cover. "I don't show this to everyone, Lucie. Only a few people have seen it."

"I understand," she said. "I wouldn't let many look at it if it were mine. Can I feel around it a bit? You don't have to open it."

I wasn't sure what she meant but nodded. "Sure. What do you want to do?"

"It's fine there on the countertop." Lucie hovered her right hand over The Book's cover. Her eyes closed and she took a deep breath. She let it out slowly and stilled, her lips parted. Her chin lifted slightly, and I could see her eyes moving under closed lids. A small smile crept across her lips. "There it is." Her voice was soft.

"What? What is it?" I asked.

"The spell attached to your father's journal."

* * *

The Book was magic – or at least someone placed a spell on it at some point. Lucie said it had all the signs of a protection spell, but there was something else there, too. She couldn't identify it, but believed its intentions were good.

"It's definitely an old spell," she said. "The language powering it is no longer used, but it's strong. My sense is it never weakened as the years passed."

"As far as I know, my father didn't practice magic," I told her.

"The signature on the spell doesn't feel male to me," Lucie replied. "It seems like the work of a female practitioner. But I can't be positive."

"And you don't think it's there for nefarious reasons?" My fingers stroked The Book's cover.

"No. And if what you say is true, that it's served as a guide for you, then maybe the spell was placed with the intention of helping you. Maybe your father had someone spell his journal on purpose." Lucie rubbed her hands together. "I can still feel the energy from it. Show me how you use it."

"Sometimes, I simply look through it until I find new messages or sketches."

"And other times?"

"Well, you might think it's silly," I smiled shyly. "But do you know what a Magic Eight Ball is?"

Lucie laughed. "I love those. My favorite message is 'ask again later.' As if it's tired and just can't make the effort."

"I kind of hold it up in the air and ask it a question," I winced. "Then I open it."

Lucie gestured toward The Book. "Give it a whirl. Let's see what it tells you now."

I eyeballed The Book before looking back up to

Lucie. This was awkward. She rolled her hand in a circle, motioning for me to get on with it. Picking it up with both hands, I held it up in front of me, my eyes closed. Taking a breath, I opened one eye. "Are you watching me?"

"Of course. I want to see how you do this," she said. "Relax. Reach out with your energy to The Book. Let it happen."

Breathing deep through my nose, I kept both eyes closed and remembered Jo's advice to ground and center myself before raising my energy for door travel. I did that now, rolling my shoulders before raising The Book again.

I felt the breath glide in and out of my body as I centered my thoughts on my chest. I pictured a ball of energy forming, growing as I brought my focus to the space directly in front of me. In my mind's eye, I saw it as a rolling ball of white light. I pushed it toward The Book, keeping my eyes closed.

There was another energy reaching from The Book toward me. I didn't realize it at first, but as it blended with mine, I sensed it circling the ball I pushed forward. It was seeking, testing. It vibrated alongside my energy, before flashing brightly, startling me.

"Oh!" My eyes popped open as I dropped The Book on the counter. It smacked the surface with a crack and fell open. Pages rustled back and forth furiously while the air around us swirled. The lights flickered and as I reached out to stop the pages from turning, everything slammed to a halt.

One last page slowly fluttered before floating back down to lie flat. On the page was my father's note:

Don't miss
The loudest Whis-
...per.

Lucie leaned forward, her eyes running over the short message. "Don't miss the loudest whisper. Do you know what this means?"

"No," I answered, shaking my head. "But I first noticed it last week."

"Then it must be relevant," she said.

"My friend Tara wondered if it meant to go with my gut instinct."

"Maybe. What do you think?"

I shrugged. "I really don't know. But The Book always seems to steer me in the right direction."

Lucie bobbed her head toward my shoulder bag. "Anything else in that behemoth?"

"It does hold a lot," I agreed. "My top hat never gets crushed." I dug back into my bag. "Outside of The Book and the top hat, I don't have anything. Oh, wait…" A small, white envelope was tucked deep into the bag. I'd grabbed it from my pocket before Tara left Tuesday's with my winter coat in tow. I didn't give it a second thought – until now.

"What did you find?"

I pulled the packet from my bag. "I'm not sure, but a florist in Kincaid gave me these. She and her husband deal in magical botanicals."

Lucie's face lit up. "This might be helpful. Open it."

I ran my fingertip under the envelope's tiny flap. We could hear a small rattle as I tore it open. I peeked inside. Seeds. Little, brown seeds. I showed Lucie the contents. "They're seeds."

"Do you know what kind?"

My eyes drifted from the seed packet to the words in The Book.

Don't miss
The loudest Whis-
...per.

"I'm pretty sure these are Whispering Flowers," I said. "When I visited *Petaling* last week they showed me a flat of flowers that looked like Daffodils. But they weren't. They called them Whispering Flowers."

Lucie rested her chin in her palm as she leaned on the counter. "They must be fairly rare. I use a lot of plants in my spell work, but I'm not familiar with them. Do you know how they're used?"

"The florist told me if you whisper your question to them, they'll listen for an answer and bring one back to you."

"Really?" Lucie replied. "That's what you need right now. Except you need the flowers, not the seeds."

"Exactly. But I was told they grow fast."

"How fast?"

"Overnight."

Lucie jumped off the barstool, startling me. "Perfect. Let's get to it, then. Tomorrow is a Full Moon. It's the Pink Moon – a perfect time to get these flowers into some soil. I'll grab a little trowel and a watering can."

I followed Lucie around the counter and into a small pantry off the kitchen. There, she pulled a basket of gardening tools off a shelf. A plastic watering can sat on the floor.

"There's water in the can. Grab it and follow me," she instructed, inclining her head toward a second door at the back of the pantry.

"Where are we going?" I asked, picking up the can.

"To my kitchen garden." Lucie flicked on a small outside light and led me into a narrow garden surrounded by stone walls. Raised beds and planters filled the space. A workbench sat near the door. "I get just enough sun back here to grow what I need."

"It's really pretty," I said, peering past her toward the back of the garden.

Lucie rummaged around under the workbench. She retrieved a small planter and a bag of potting soil. "I'm not sure how big of a planter they'll need, but let's use something we can set between us."

I watched as she filled the planter with potting soil, mixing in peat moss and vermiculite. "Do you know how we should do this?"

She looked up from her preparations. "This is your show, Emily."

"But I don't know if there's a right way to plant the seeds," I argued. "I don't know if I'm supposed to do something... you know, magical."

Lucie finished mixing the soil and extra ingredients. She picked up the planter. "Tapping into magic is not difficult for those who know how to do it. Let's keep this simple. We'll sit on the ground facing each other with the pot between us. You hold onto the seeds. Take some time to ground and center. When you feel relaxed, I want you to plant as many seeds as you think you should in a spiral starting from the center of the planter. Gently press them into the soil. They're small, so maybe only about a quarter of an inch deep at max. Focus your energy as you go, see the seeds sprouting and taking root. Shut out all other thoughts. Keep pouring in the energy and when you're ready, gently dribble some of the water over them. When you're finished, continue to focus on putting your personal energy into the soil. Hold your hands over the surface and picture the seeds producing lovely, healthy flowers. Push your energy down over them and pull their energy up."

I nodded, although I wasn't sure I agreed tapping into the magic would be easy. We sat cross-legged on the ground, the planter between us. My hands rested in my lap and I held the seed packet in my right hand. Again, I practiced the same breathing technique I applied in the kitchen. In. Out. Roll shoulders. Deep breath in through my nose, out through my mouth.

As I concentrated on focusing my energy, I felt Lucie's hands on my knees. They were warm through my jeans. I heard her murmur about lending strength to my energy. I felt it welling up again, the power seeming to form in my chest. I imagined it flowing down both of my arms and into my hands.

I opened my eyes and poured a small number of seeds into the palm of my left hand. My eyes flicked up to Lucie only once. She sat leaning forward, her hands still on my knees. Her bowed head was slightly turned to her left. Her bangs swept forward, and her eyes remained closed. I could sense the energy she was using to support mine.

Bringing my attention back to the planter, I began poking the Whispering Flower seeds into the earthy mix, starting in the center. My fingers moved to the right, the spiral forming as my hand traveled in a clockwise motion. I envisioned the brown seeds sprouting, pushing up green shoots from their protective shells, while roots webbed out from the bottom of each seed, seeking nutrients from the soil. After pressing in thirteen seeds, I used the watering can to dampen the surface. When finished, I held my hands low over the planter, my palms facing the dirt. I imagined the warm sun heating the soil and the Whispering Flowers growing swiftly, strong and full. I pushed as much positive energy as I could into the planter. I could feel a trickle of energy flowing up against the skin of my palms. The seeds seemed... *activated*.

"I think I'm done," I said to Lucie in a quiet voice. "Now what?"

A slight smile floated over her lips. Her eyes remained closed. "Go ahead and relax. Put your palms together and let the energy subside."

I did as she told me, closing my eyes and letting the energy fade away. I felt Lucie's hands slip from my knees. I opened my eyes. "Do you think we helped?"

Lucie grinned. "I'm betting we'll find a pot full of healthy flowers first thing in the morning. Emily, I was going to boost your energy with some of mine. I could sense right away I didn't need to. Instead, I simply formed a foundation to make it easier for you to concentrate since you're still new to all of this."

"Oh," I said, nodding. I didn't understand, but I had a lot to learn. "Okay, good."

Lucie climbed to her feet, picking up the

planter and moving it closer to the door leading into her home. "The sun will reach it here. In the meantime, it's late. I have a spare bedroom with the most comfortable bed. I bet you'd like to call it a night."

The work we did in the garden drained me even more. "Yeah, I'm ready for bed. Thanks."

"Of course," she said. We passed back through the pantry and into the kitchen just as a knock came from the front door. Lucie raised an eyebrow. "Now who's here?"

We trekked out of the kitchen and down the hall to the front door. A push-button light switch controlled a soft light over the front stoop. Lucie paused at the door and peeked out the side window.

"Is someone there?" I asked. It was late and I worried who might be on the other side of the door.

Lucie looked back over her shoulder. "I think it's a Rabbit."

CHAPTER 16

The Rabbit was a girl dressed in a well-worn jean jacket, a short denim skirt, and large Doc Martens. Her wavy black hair was pulled tight into a high ponytail. A bright pink stripe dyed a swath of hair starting at her right temple, running up and back before disappearing into the thick mane piled on top of her head. Her right eyebrow sported several piercings. If she weren't a Rabbit, I'd bet she wasn't a day over thirteen.

"Emily Swift?" She grinned. "Rabbit got the message. He said he's gotta go find the Tortoise, then he'll catch up with you."

"Find the Tortoise?" I repeated. *Tortoise?*

The female Rabbit nodded. "Yeah, then he'll come to Matar. He wants you to stay put and not go anywhere, okay? He said he really means it this time."

"When's he going to get here?" I asked.

"Dunno. The Tortoise is hard to find, but if Rabbit is looking for him, it's gotta be important." She shrugged. "That's all I've got."

"Okay, thanks. I'll wait for him here," I answered.

The Rabbit bobbed her head and flashed me another smile. "Alright, gotta run."

"Wait," Lucie interrupted. She held up a finger.

"You want to take a veggie-hummus wrap for the road?"

The Rabbit's friendly face lit up. "I could eat."

"Come on," Lucie said, leaving the front door open and leading the Rabbit back toward the kitchen. I smiled to myself as I closed the door. I thought about what Tuesday said about the Rabbits back in Vue.

They bring good things to the Empire. We need them.

Lucie made sure I was comfortable in the spare bedroom before turning in for the night. Even though my stress levels were probably at an all-time high, I slept – not even a dream disturbed my rest. The morning's bright sunshine woke me early the next day. I was eager to check on the Whispering Flowers, so I washed up in the bathroom and got dressed. Lucie was already making coffee when I descended the stairs.

"I was worried about waking you," I said as I entered the kitchen.

"Me?" She shook her head. "I'm an early riser."

"Did you check the flowers yet? Did they grow?" I asked, passing her on the way to the pantry.

"Go see for yourself. I think you'll be very happy," she called after me.

I opened the door leading from the pantry into Lucie's kitchen garden. The planter we used last night held a beautiful bunch of yellow flowers, their flutes turning up toward me as I stepped outside. I was so happy, I laughed out loud.

"Incredible, right?" Lucie said, wiping her hands on a kitchen towel as she joined me. "I didn't do anything with them. I only peeked out and checked to see what we'd have. Pretty little things, aren't they?"

"They're awesome," I said, kneeling beside the planter. I gently put a fingertip to one flower's buttery trumpet. It fluttered under my touch. "This is better than I expected."

"And now you ask them a question?"

"That's what the florist said. I ask my question and the flowers bring an answer back to me when they hear it – or find it. This is the part I don't really know."

Lucie wiggled a finger at the flowers. "I'd get a move on it."

"Right." I continued to run my fingertips over the flowers while I thought of how to word my question. Being specific was important. I considered my options. I could ask where the Fringe was hiding my mother – that was certainly straightforward. But even as I mulled over the question, I realized it still was a little risky. She could be moved before I reached her.

No, I wanted to phrase the question in a way that it encompassed the future, too. I wanted to know where I'd *find* her. That's what I needed to ask. I leaned closer to the blooms.

"Where will I find my mother?" I whispered into one flower's flute. The bloom quivered. Amazed, Lucie and I watched as the flower turned toward the one beside it and brushed its petals against it. The second flower turned to a third and repeated the action. Then another joined in. All the blooms began to dance against each other in a rustling of tender waves. Their flutes turned up toward the sky and they swayed back and forth before suddenly stilling.

I looked up at Lucie. She shrugged. "What do you think they're doing?" I asked.

She paused for a moment, then answered. "Listening."

❋ ❋ ❋

The Pink Moon is not really pink. It's named for the wild growing Phlox blooming during this time of year. Lucie explained the name as she placed items into a basket she was taking to a special meeting. I watched as she added a couple of small bottles of dried herbs and a smudge stick.

"What kind of meeting?" I asked, peering into the basket.

"A meeting of like-minded people," she said, raising an eyebrow.

"Anne works with herbs," I remarked, thinking of my friend back in Kincaid.

"Anne's the one who told me about this group," she said. Lucie didn't seem eager to offer more, so I let it go.

"I'm going to try to see Justice Spell this morning," I said, changing the subject. "If I can get her piece of the Crimson Stone, I'll be one step closer to getting my mother back."

"Do you believe she'll give it to you?" Lucie laid a pink cloth over the top of the basket.

"I don't know," I said. I knew it was a longshot, but I hoped to convince the justice to at least let me borrow her piece. I'd remind her I was the one who made sure she got it when we separated the pieces in Vue.

"You don't know unless you ask," Lucie said. "I like to have a fallback plan whenever possible. I'm going to ask some of the members at today's meeting what they think about working magic with a piece of a magical gemstone versus the whole thing."

"You're not going to tell them about the Crimson Stone?" I asked, worried.

Lucie shook her head as she waved her hands at me. "Oh, no. No. Don't worry about that. But it's a good idea to learn what you can from others. They might have a perspective we wouldn't consider." She picked up her basket. "I'm not convinced you couldn't use a piece of the Crimson Stone for magical purposes. It might be weaker than the whole deal, but I'd like to know what's possible."

She had a point. Many of the rules and beliefs I'd had since learning about being a Salesman and the Empire seemed to have exceptions. I sucked in my lower lip, considering. "If that's true, even one piece would give the Fringe an edge."

"It would." Lucie grabbed a set of keys from the counter. "I'm off, are you?"

"I am. Wish me luck," I said.

"Door traveling?"

"Yup. I'm going to show up with a hat in my hand." I placed my top hat on my head. "Pun intended."

✸ ✸ ✸

I door traveled from Lucie's kitchen straight through the front doors of the Salesman Courthouse in downtown Matar. This was the seat of power in the Empire. This is where I appeared before the Court to request recognition as a Salesman. This is also where Templeton blocked that request. It worked out – eventually the Court approved me. However, I was certainly not one of Justice Spell's favorite Salesmen at the moment.

The door travel was seamless. Maybe it was a boost from the energy work I did with Lucie. I might not have the grace and poise of Jo, but

I stepped into the Courthouse without even a wobble.

I stood in the wide lobby watching Salesmen, Empire guards, and others as they hurried past. Security had certainly beefed up. A row of metal detectors stood in a row with armed guards monitoring traffic in and out. A guard at each screening gate held a wand to run over anyone who triggered the gate's alarm.

I passed through without incident. My shoulder bag traveled a conveyor belt through a screening machine. I snagged it before making my way to the information booth.

"Hello," I began as the jowly man behind the counter ran his eyes over my face. I removed my hat. "I was hoping you could point me to Justice Spell's chambers."

Bushy eyebrows lifted. "Justice Spell does not accept visitors unless there is a special appointment." He eyed at my casual outfit. "You have one?"

"I don't, no." I offered my best smile. "But I think she'd make an exception for me. If you could tell me where her offices were located, maybe there's an assistant I could talk to?"

"Justice chambers are off limits to the public," he replied.

"Is there someone you could call? It's really important."

"Emily Swift?" A voice to my right asked.

I turned to see who'd recognized me. A balding man with a mustache stood beside me wearing a quizzical expression. I frowned. Why did he look familiar?

"Good morning, Justice Smith," the man behind the information counter addressed him.

Justice Smith? That's right! Norford Smith sat on the bench with Justice Spell. He also knew my father when he was alive. "Hello, Your Honor."

"Emily, what are you doing here?" He put a hand on my elbow and gently led me off to the side.

"I'm trying to reach Justice Spell, sir. It's really important. I'm not going to lie to you, she's going to be very unhappy to see me, but I promise – it's a matter of life or death." The last word caught in my throat as I spoke.

The aging Justice nodded. His voice was soft when he spoke. "I know about your mother, Emily."

"I think there might be a way to get her back," I told him. "But I need to see Justice Spell first."

Justice Smith's eyes roamed the lobby. He was considering how to proceed. He finally nodded. "Come with me. I'll take you to her chambers."

"Thank you," I said as he led me to the elevators.

❖ ❖ ❖

Justice Spell did indeed have an assistant staffing the desk outside of her offices. Smith paused to ask if the other justice was alone before he stepped forward and tapped on a door.

"Come in," came a woman's voice.

He inclined his head toward the door and gave me an encouraging smile. "Go on in, Emily."

"Thank you," I said, turning the handle and stepping into Justice Spell's realm.

She sat behind her large desk writing. She glanced up once, then went back to her work. If she was surprised to see me – and I thought she would be – she hid it well. "Ms. Swift, you're supposed to be in Kincaid."

"I know, Your Honor," I said. "And for the record, Jo Carter tried to get me to go back home."

Spell looked up. "Ms. Carter is not pleased with you."

"Not many people are right now," I said. "But I couldn't abandon my mother, Your Honor. There was no way I could go home."

"Emily," Spell removed her glasses and set them on her desk. "You cannot beat the Fringe. I'm shocked you think you can rescue your mother. I promise you the Empire guards are doing everything in their power to find her. This is an extremely dangerous and difficult situation for trained guards. The Fringe is a violent, strong terrorist organization. You are… one person."

"I can use the Crimson Stone," I told her. I looked down at my hat. Huh. I really was standing before the Justice with my hat in my hand.

"You cannot," Spell answered. "The Stone is not for your use, Emily. The Empire is disappointed you did not turn in all the pieces."

"But I did give you one, Justice Spell. I did want the Empire to hold a piece of that power. It's just…" My voice trailed off. I cleared my throat. "Tahl Petrovich was a justice for the Empire. Look what he did."

"No one denies the Fringe has influenced some leaders in the Empire," Spell said.

"And that's why I couldn't risk giving the whole Crimson Stone to you," I said. Spell knew all of this. We were wasting time. "Please, Your Honor. I will return the piece to you. I promise."

Justice Spell gazed at me. The pity rolled off her in waves. When she spoke, her voice was gentle, but the words still cut into me. "Ms. Swift, your promises mean nothing to this Court. You haven't done what we've asked of you. You are reckless. I can't support your foolishness, no matter how fervently I hope for your mother's safe return to you."

"So, you won't let me borrow your piece of the Stone," I said quietly.

"I will not. Go home and wait, Emily. Go home to your friends. Go home to your… what was his name?"

"Jack," I answered softly. I blinked rapidly, fighting tears.

"Jack, that's right. I'm sure he's very worried about you." Spell sighed, picking up her glasses and putting them back on. She looked down at her desk. She shook her head refusing to look back up. "Go home, Emily Swift."

* * *

I excused myself from Justice Spell's office. The tears started to spill before I crossed the threshold into the assistant's office. I moved quickly, slipping into the hall. It was empty, this part of the building being much quieter than the rest of the Courthouse. I leaned against the wall, my head tilted back, and my eyes shut.

I'd admitted to Lucie it was a longshot. Maybe Lucie learned something from the others attending her morning meeting. Maybe Rabbit was in Matar now. If he had his piece of the Stone, there must be something we could do.

Pushing off the wall, I walked down the corridor, my footsteps echoing. I placed my hat on my head and picked a door on my right. I'd go back to Lucie's to see if the Whispering Flowers had heard anything yet.

* * *

Lucie wasn't back from her morning meeting. I checked on the flowers, but they were in the same still position, flutes pointed toward the sky. Every now and then one would quiver, but other than that, they had little to say.

I didn't know what to do with myself. I had nowhere to go, and everything was at a standstill. The Book was as silent as the Whispering Flowers. No new passages appeared.

The sunny day became mostly cloudy. I took a glass of water into Lucie's garden and sat at the small table next to the wall. Staring at the pot of flowers and willing them to answer my question, I contemplated what to do next.

I considered going home. Not for good, but to see Jack – to assure him I was okay. To assure myself we were okay. Since I turned thirty, we'd been through so much. He was a good person, and I didn't doubt for a moment he loved me.

But he hated this chaos. I knew he believed the Empire's demands would overshadow our lives. I'd promised him they wouldn't. I meant it when I made the promise. I didn't know it was one I wouldn't be able to keep.

It was Monday and Jack would be at the college. He wouldn't be home. Suddenly showing up at his office didn't seem wise. I was afraid to use the Empire service to send a message. If it was being monitored, I didn't want to risk tipping anyone off to my whereabouts. I didn't want to reveal I was at Lucie's. I worried Justice Spell might decide to order the guards to escort me out of the Empire. Still, she didn't shout for them when I appeared in her chambers. She simply appeared to be… weary of me.

I closed my eyes and leaned back into the comfortable cushion of the lawn chair. The sun played peek-a-boo through the clouds and every so often it warmed my face. My mind wandered, images from the past several days floating through my thoughts. So much had happened. It was only Monday.

Rabbit would come through for me, he always did. *He had to.* He would be here soon – he knew where I was. I would wait for him. This time I meant it. I would wait and once he was here, maybe the Whispering Flowers would tell us where we'd find my mother. He'd have a piece of the Stone. My hand drifted up and lay against my chest. I allowed myself a hopeful moment. We'd have two pieces. Maybe Lucie was right and a piece of Stone by itself would have some power. Two would be even better.

Drowsy, I wondered if I should risk a visit to Anne. Maybe she would have some insight. I could see Tara, too. I could ask her if she talked to Jack – if he was still angry. Maybe she could tell me if I'd really broken everything this time.

The sunshine was soothing. My body was exhausted from the worry my mind inflicted upon it. A shaky sigh escaped through my lips and I dozed on and off. Maybe I remained mostly awake because I could still feel the sun on my skin. But my mind roamed without discipline and I remembered my last exchange with Templeton on the balcony at Tuesday's. Our meetings were never pleasant, but I was almost relieved to see him. He knew things, so many things. But he never told me exactly what I needed to know when I really needed it. He barely pointed me in a direction. Why did he keep playing these cat and mouse games? Was the Crimson Stone worth that much?

Our relationship troubled me. *Relationship?* Why had my thoughts conjured that word? We didn't have a relationship. We had an opposition. If Templeton hadn't made himself known to me, I still would've turned thirty last December. I still would've become a Salesman. The Fringe would still be fighting the Empire. My father would only be there for me in old memories.

But what about Anne and Rabbit? Would I have met them, racing with them to find the Crimson Stone? I didn't know. There must've been many paths to my becoming a Salesman. The one unchanging element putting me on the path I ultimately took was Templeton.

Why? I didn't quite believe Anne when she said he was curious about me. But then, even

Templeton admitted it, didn't he? When was that? He'd said something about being curious about me on some level. Why? Because I was Daniel Swift's daughter?

Or, because I was Emily Swift?

A shadow moved over my eyelids, blocking the sun. It was too dark to be a cloud. I opened my eyes, squinting against the intense light surrounding the person who leaned over me. I blinked several times trying to focus through the colored streaks caused by the brightness. A firm hand landed on my shoulder and the shadow said my name.

"Emily."

CHAPTER 17

"Emily," the voice repeated as the hand dropped away. "Wake up. Your friend Rabbit is here."

I sat up straighter in the lawn chair, shaking my head to clear my rambling thoughts. After several more blinks, I could see clearly. Lucie squatted by the Whispering Flowers, peering into the planter.

"Still no answer?" she asked.

I stood and stretched, my fingers wiggling as I reached for the sky. "They haven't told me anything."

"I bet they're listening, though." Lucie stuck her index finger into the soil to check if they needed to be watered before she rose from her crouched position.

"Where's Rabbit?"

"In the kitchen. I'm feeding him." She led the way back into her home through the pantry. "I told him about the flowers and how we're waiting to hear what they have to say."

Rabbit sat in the kitchen on a barstool eating one of Lucie's hummus and veggie wraps. I hurried around the counter and gave him a hug. "I'm so glad to see you," I said when I finally released him. "I was worried you'd leave Tuesday's before I could get a message to you."

"You almost missed me," he admitted. "I was on my way when Tuesday came chasing after me down the street."

"Really?"

"Really." His eyes twinkled as he grinned. "She's pretty light on her feet, that one."

"Thank goodness for Tuesday," I said. "I'm going to find a way to repay her someday. She takes good care of us." I checked out Rabbit's lunch. In addition to a wrap, a big bowl of some sort of salad with feta cheese sat beside his plate.

"Vegetarian bulgur salad with feta and carrots." Lucie nodded toward the food.

"Are you a vegetarian?" I asked, mainly out of curiosity.

"Nope." She bared her teeth and tapped a pointed tooth with her fingertip. "Canines. I'm a meat eater. I just like Mediterranean food."

"Well, Rabbits have canines," I said, pointing my thumb at my friend as he ate. "At least the human Rabbits do. I think."

Rabbit looked up, swallowing. His eyes bounced from me to Lucie and back to me again. "I'm not showing anyone my teeth."

"Oh, sure they do. I was just being cheeky." Lucie handed me a bowl of the bulgur salad. She leaned against the counter and dug through her own bowl with a fork. Fishing out a piece of feta, she continued. "Besides, ever read *Watership Down*? Or see the original cartoon from the seventies?"

"I know I saw the cartoon a long time ago. Kind of intense, right?" I asked. "There was some surprising violence. Not all rabbits are cute, cuddly, and harmless."

"Remember that," Lucie said, pointing an empty fork at me. Her gaze met Rabbit's briefly. She changed the subject. "Anyhow, what are your next steps? The flowers haven't talked yet, but maybe you've heard something?" She directed the last question to Rabbit.

My friend watched Lucie with a thoughtful expression following her comment about *Watership Down*. His nose twitched once, and he cleared his throat before speaking. "We still haven't heard anything specific. We think Lydia is in Matar, though. Or, at least close to the city. The Fringe has a real stronghold here."

"And what about the Stone?" Lucie continued.

Rabbit looked to me, surprised. "You told her?"

His reaction made me uneasy, but I pushed the feeling aside. "Anne trusts her, and we need all the help we can get."

Rabbit frowned but didn't argue. "I don't have it, yet."

I was disappointed. "But you know where it is, right?"

"I gave it to the Tortoise."

There was that reference again – *Tortoise*. "Who is the Tortoise?"

Rabbit wiped his mouth on a napkin before balling it up and tossing it onto the counter. He folded his arms and leaned forward. "The Tortoise is a Rabbit, a very old one."

"How old?" I asked.

"He's the oldest Rabbit. He's not always easy to track down."

"But he has your piece of the Stone?"

"I gave it to him right after I left Vue last December," Rabbit said. "I knew if anyone could keep it safely hidden, it would be the Tortoise."

"And now you can't find him." I set my bowl on the counter. "I talked to Spell this morning. I asked her if I could borrow her piece of the Stone. She said no."

"You thought she'd say different?" Rabbit cocked his head to the side. "Well, don't give up hope. I've got one more place I'm going to look for the Tortoise. Outside of Matar toward the Walled Zone. There's time if the flowers and the network haven't given up a location yet."

"But my mother doesn't have time," I stressed. "It's been twenty-four hours now. I don't even want to think about it." I put up my hand to stop any comments. "Not thinking about it is the only way I'm keeping it together while we search."

"I know, Emily," Rabbit said. A big glass of water sat by his plate. He took a long drink. "And that's why I'm going back out. As soon as I find the Tortoise, I'll get my hands on the piece of Stone. Then I'll be back."

"And we'll figure out what we can do with pieces of the Stone," Lucie added. "There must be magic in each bit. Listen, at my morning meeting I asked a couple of practitioners about gemstone magic." She waved a hand. "I've used stones before to lend energies to my workings, but I've never owned a piece of spelled jewelry like the Crimson Stone. They couldn't agree if a piece of a magical gemstone would retain any power. One said yes, the other said no – but then another said if the broken piece still had some power, it would be risky to use it. Broken, unreliable magic. Never one definitive answer at these shindigs."

"That sort of makes sense," I said. "But the Crimson Stone is already in three pieces. You combine them to form one Stone."

"Then the question is this: are the pieces of the Crimson Stone magical by themselves, or do they only come alive when they are joined together?" Lucie asked.

Rabbit shrugged. "It could be either."

"There has to be someone we can talk to specifically about the Crimson Stone who might know," Lucie said.

Rabbit and I looked at each other. I rolled my eyes. "Yeah, there's one person who probably knows."

"Who?"

I sighed. "His name is Templeton."

❉ ❉ ❉

Rabbit was off to continue his search for the Tortoise. He reluctantly added there might be one other place in Matar we could go to for answers – but only as a last resort. The network offered no updates on Fringe activity or where my mother could be. It was quiet. The Whispering Flowers still seemed activated but gave us nothing. After Rabbit was gone, I explained Templeton to Lucie.

"I don't know him," she said. Lucie was drying the lunch dishes. I noticed she never seemed to use her dishwasher. "Then again, I'm not a Salesman."

"Anne knows him," I told her.

"Maybe through different circles, but I don't know many Salesmen. Including you, I might know three."

"I always feel like here in the Empire, there are Salesmen everywhere."

"And maybe they are," Lucie said. "I only knew you were one because Anne told me about you before you arrived. But it seems like you're more than that if you have magical tendencies. Interesting that this Templeton uses magic, too. I wonder what's different about you both?"

"My mother is a Meta Muse," I said. "Maybe that has something to do with it?"

"Could be. Honestly, I don't know. Once you have your mother back and things settle down, I'll help you dig into it. I love to do research. Maybe this Templeton could be a resource for us?"

I snorted. "Trust me on this one. No."

Lucie raised an eyebrow. "Gets to you, huh?"

"Yeah, you could say that." I wanted to change the subject. I pulled The Book out of my shoulder bag. "I'm still not finding anything new in here."

"I'm inclined to believe it's also waiting on the flowers," Lucie replied as she finished drying a glass. She placed it in a cupboard. "Tonight, I'm attending a sacred circle to celebrate the Full Moon. I was thinking, I've used a gemstone called beryl to aid in finding something I've lost. It worked well. I don't have any now, but I know of a specialty shop in a corner of Matar that might have what we need. I'll look for goshenite. That's clear beryl. I'll pick up any extra supplies we'll need, too. Then tonight during the circle, I'll complete a cleansing and charging of the beryl. Ideally, you'd be a part of it, but with your emotions running high with worry, I don't think it's a good idea. I'll be your proxy. When I return home, we can work on a finding spell. I'll be all keyed up after the circle, so if you're up for it, we can do that."

I stared at Lucie. "Is this what people mean by having a 'new normal?'"

The woman laughed. "Yup."

"I'd love it if you helped me with a finding spell and this beryl," I nodded. "But maybe the Whispering Flowers will come through for us by then."

"That's what I'm hoping, but I'm always one for having a backup plan."

※ ※ ※

Lucie left early to gather supplies for the finding spell. She explained we'd use the beryl as a pendulum to try and pinpoint where my mother was being kept. She also needed to pick up a map of Matar. Because there was little for me to do but wait – *again* – she also gave me a stack of books explaining various forms of magic and spell ingredients. Maybe as I looked through them something would resonate with me.

Any other time, browsing through Lucie's books would be interesting. Unfortunately, my attention span was that of a fruit fly. Several times I returned to the potted Whispering Flowers to see if anything had changed. Each time I was disappointed.

"I can't just sit here," I complained to the empty kitchen. Even if I only went out for a latte, at least it wouldn't be sitting and waiting on everyone else. I grabbed my shoulder bag. Before I could step outside, it started to rain.

"Oh, you've got to be kidding me," I whined, standing inside as the rain splashed up off the stoop. I shut the door. I no longer had a coat of my own, but I remembered a long-sleeved blue jacket hanging on a chair in the spare bedroom I'd slept in. Maybe Lucie wouldn't mind if I borrowed it.

I hurried upstairs to retrieve it. I crossed the bedroom, snagging the light coat from the chair. Turning to set my shoulder bag on the bed, I about jumped out of my skin when I saw Templeton. He stood with his arms crossed as he leaned against the doorframe, his eyebrows drawn together in a frown.

"Dammit, Templeton! Stop doing that!" I said, as I threw my bag down. "And you know what? This isn't my house. You can't just go walking into other people's houses like this. I know I read that somewhere."

He sneered. "I'm sure you've branded all of the Empire's rules and regulations into your brain. You obey them so well."

"I'm serious," I said, glad that the bed was between us. "You shouldn't be here. Tuesday's balcony was one thing. Door traveling into Lucie's home is a violation."

Templeton ignored me. Instead, he stepped

into the room and began to explore. He nosed through a couple of books left on a table. "At least she has taste." He sniffed. "Actually, the witch would probably appreciate my appearance. I could enlighten her about a crack forming in one of the wards she put up."

I knew wards were used by some magical practitioners to keep people out or to make sure something was protected. I folded my arms. "I'm sure she'd appreciate that. Maybe you should leave and call her someday to make an appointment."

"I don't have time to play teacher to your little friends," Templeton huffed as he moved closer to me. He stood at the end of the bed.

I was determined to keep him from rattling me. "And you're here because?"

"Because I believe there's someone who could tell you where the Fringe is hiding your mother," he answered, removing his top hat and gently placing it on the bottom of the bed.

My mouth popped open. "Who? Where is she, Templeton?" Without thinking I closed the space between us and seized the front of his grey dress shirt with both fists.

Templeton's hands wrapped firmly around my wrists as he pulled me off. Anger flashed in his eyes. "Don't do that again," he warned. He held my wrists.

"Where is she?" I repeated, twisting my hands

as I struggled to make him let go.

"Listen to me!" He gave me a shake. "I said I might know someone who can help you. I don't know where your mother is at this point." He suddenly released his grip, pushing me away at the same time.

I glowered at him, catching myself as I stumbled backward. "Who. Is. It?"

"No one you want to do business with, I assure you," he said, looking down and straightening his tailored shirt. Annoyed, he pressed his lips together before continuing. "I will speak with her. But it'll cost you."

"Cost me? What do you mean?" I asked, rubbing my forehead with my hand. I eyed my nemesis. "How much will this 'help' cost?"

After tending to the front of his dress shirt, he checked the buttons at his wrists on both sleeves. He didn't bother to look up. "Your piece of the Crimson Stone."

I threw up my hands, spinning around and stepping away. "You have got to be kidding me! You've gone on and on about how the Crimson Stone needs to be in capable hands and now you're telling me to give it up to some extortionist who wants my piece in exchange for what is essentially my mother's life? This is – no! No!" I whirled back around, furious at Templeton for his part in all of this. I stabbed my index finger at him. "You are going to take me to your 'friend' and I'm going to rip off their arm and beat them with it until they tell me where my mother is!"

My outburst earned me an amused smirk and a wicked light flickering in Templeton's cold blue eyes. "That won't be necessary, Emily. The Stone *will* remain in capable hands."

I sucked in a breath. "No... The piece of the Stone is for you, not the other person," I realized.

His smile didn't reach his icy stare. "She'll require payment as well, but I'll cover it as part of our deal."

"There is no deal," I gritted. "You can't have it."

"Then I can't help you." He swept his top hat off the bed, pivoting on a heel before heading for the bedroom door.

He only made it a few steps. "Wait!" I blurted out.

Templeton paused, turning slowly. Anticipation danced in his eyes. "Are you going to give up your piece of the Stone?"

"This is my mother's life, Templeton." I heard the pleading in my voice.

"And time is running out for her," he said evenly. "Everything has a price, Emily."

Giving Templeton my piece of the Stone would leave me with nothing, unless Rabbit came through. There was no guarantee Templeton would help me – or that this friend of his would have the information either. "How do I know if this person actually knows where my mother is?

Even if they're willing to tell me anything, how do I know it's correct?"

"It will be."

"But how do I know? You're asking me to trust someone I've never met who charges for information that could save a person's life!" And you're asking me to trust you, I thought. And I don't.

"Deals can be gambles," he replied. His gaze slid over me, landing at my feet before moving back up to meet my eyes. "I never make a bad bet, Emily. You will get the information you need."

"When do you need the Stone?" I asked, frustrated. My jaw clenched. I couldn't believe what I was about to do.

"Now. Do you need to retrieve it, or can I?" He was growing impatient.

"There's nothing else I can give you instead? No other way?" I felt lightheaded and there was a ringing in my ears. There would be no going back once I did this.

"I told you what I want."

I swallowed, gripping the front hem of my shirt, slowly lifting it. "So, you're giving me no choice?"

Templeton was horrified, lifting his hand. "What are you doing?" he sputtered.

"Giving you what you've been after for months," I answered. I pulled my shirt up, exposing the lacy material of my bra. The white garment formed a small pocket of fabric between my breasts. I held my shirt up with my left hand while I used the fingers of my right to reach into the pocket. Motionless, Templeton watched me.

I managed to flip out a lumpy, cloth packet. It hung from a safety pin over the front of my bra. Tucking the shirt's hem under my chin, I used both hands to pop the pin open and pulled the packet free. I removed the pin from my bra before pulling my shirt back down.

Templeton let out a breath. He gave his head a shake before clearing his throat. "What is that?"

I placed the safety pin on the nightstand. The cloth packet, sewn in a rough square shape, was made of plain, white cotton. I rubbed the hard item hidden inside between my thumbs and fingers. The cloth was warm from resting against my chest.

After returning home from my quest last year, I spent a week wondering what I should do with my piece of the Crimson Stone. In the end, I was too afraid to let it out of my sight. I stitched together a small, fabric envelope and kept it pinned to the inside of my bra. The only time it wasn't on me was at night when I unpinned it from my underclothes and placed it in my nightstand drawer in my bedroom. In the morning, I reattached it to my clothing.

Now I circled the end of the bed and approached Templeton. Standing in front of the arrogant Salesman, I tilted my head up and glared into his face.

"Your piece of the Stone, you've had it on you the entire time," he stated. His nostrils flared.

"Yes."

"This is why you shouldn't have it, Emily. You take such stupid risks." Templeton shook his head in disbelief.

"Shut up," I said. "Hold out your left hand."

I felt rather than saw Templeton's hand as he raised it between us. Never breaking my gaze, I dropped the cloth packet into the palm of his hand. He closed his fingers around it. Victory flashed in his eyes. Before I lost my chance, I covered his fist with my right hand.

"This piece will always be mine," I asserted. "It'll never be yours."

He answered me with a scowl, pulling his hand away. "I see it differently."

I had to know. "Does one piece retain any magic of the whole Crimson Stone, Templeton?"

Templeton held up the little cloth packet to the light, squinting. "Yes."

"How much?"

"Enough." He lowered his hand. "I can already sense the energy rolling off it."

Annoyed, I stepped away and gathered the coat and my shoulder bag from the bed. "You got what you wanted, Templeton. Now it's your turn to make good. Take me to this friend of yours. I'm guessing we're door traveling, so you better be pretty specific about where I need to land."

"Don't be ridiculous," he snapped at me. "You're not going with me." With that, he turned and strode out of the spare bedroom and into Lucie's hallway. I rushed after him.

"Oh, no you don't!" I grabbed at the back of his arm.

"Stop it, Emily!" He paused only to bat away my hand. "Stop being a nuisance!" He zeroed in on the bathroom door. Still holding the piece of the Crimson Stone in his hand, he zipped on through.

"Damn you, Templeton!" I lunged for him, but it was too late. I grabbed the door handle hoping I could pick up some sort of travel trail and find him. I sensed the familiar tendrils of his leftover energy, but the door wouldn't open. It was locked.

"I hate you!" I yelled at the door.

* * *

The rain stopped before I stepped outside to resume my search for a coffee shop. I felt dazed after my encounter with Templeton. I handed over my piece of the Crimson Stone – *to Templeton!* Oh, hell, what had I done?

My only hope was Rabbit. When he returned, we'd figure out how to use his piece to get my mother back. Templeton admitted a piece would still have some magic in it.

The brick sidewalk was slick after the rain. I trudged along, picking a direction at random. I would duck into the first coffee shop I found. My head swam with images from the clash with Templeton. His thrill over getting my piece of the Stone drove me mad.

I didn't let it go without a fight, however. Earlier, when reading through Lucie's books on magic, I learned about projective and receptive hands. Frequently, your projective hand is the one you use to write. Your receptive hand is the other. Templeton might think he's special, but he's a 'righty' like most of us.

When I gave him the cloth packet, I made sure he accepted it with his receptive hand – the left one. I passed it to him with my projective hand before telling him the piece would always be mine. It was my form of a spell. It was speculation on my part, but I took a chance my gut feeling would be stronger than Templeton's intentions.

After walking two blocks, I noted a coffee shop nestled between a real estate office and a little bookstore. I'd reached the beginning of the commercial district bordering Lucie's neighborhood. I climbed the two stairs leading into *Coffee*

Cove.

CHAPTER 18

I placed my order at the counter for a latte, plain, two percent milk, with light whipped cream. The barista took my first name and I moved to the side to wait. In a nearby rack, I noticed a stack of newspapers. My stomach churned when I read the headline: Fringe Attacks Guards, Kidnaps Murder Suspect.

"Bad business," said an older man on my left. He dipped his head toward the newspaper. Somewhere in his mid-sixties, he wore a corduroy blazer with patches on his sleeves. His hair was a thinning mix of salt and pepper. On his nose perched a pair of thin-framed glasses. Brown eyes bookended by smile lines regarded me through the lenses. I blinked. This was Jack in thirty years.

"Yeah," I replied uneasily. I looked away.

"I remember when the Fringe attacked all those Salesmen and their families fifteen years ago," he continued.

"Seventeen," I said, my gaze moving up to study the chalkboard behind the counter.

"Seventeen?"

"It was over seventeen years ago," I said. I leaned forward and checked on the employee who took my order. I wanted her to hurry up.

"You were pretty young," the man observed. "It must've left quite the impression."

I refused to face the curious man. "I knew someone. I'm in a hurry. Is it always so slow here?"

"They're pretty good," came a woman's voice from my right. "They look short-handed to me today." She picked up the conversation I tried to drop. "That poor woman they took, the one accused of murder, you know she was that Salesman's widow, right? The famous one who was killed? David something."

I gritted my teeth and refused to look in her direction. "Daniel. Daniel Swift," I said low.

"That's what I read," the man confirmed. "There was a smaller report a few pages in with her lawyers saying they're verifying her alibi and that charges will be dropped."

"Oh, that's good. I hope she's innocent. I'd hate to think she was guilty. It must be so difficult being married to a Salesman, especially one in the Empire leadership. And then to have him die in that train wreck. Tragic."

I closed my eyes and breathed in through my nose and out through my mouth.

"It was reported as an accident," the man said, "but I never believed it. There was too much evidence of the Fringe. Someone brushed a lot under the rug. They knew it was an inside job."

"That's what they do," the woman agreed.

I opened my eyes. I stared straight ahead. "That's what who does?"

"The Empire – the Salesmen leadership. They're quick to circle the wagons when something is shaking things up in the ranks. Look, I haven't anything personal against Salesmen. I like living in the Empire. But overall, I don't trust the leadership." Out of the corner of my eye, I saw the woman gesture toward the newspaper rack.

"Latte for Emily!" A cup appeared on the counter.

I lurched forward and snagged the hot drink. I'd planned on parking my behind in a chair while I drank my coffee, but there was no way I was staying now. I needed some air.

✼ ✼ ✼

I prowled Lucie's neighborhood and the surrounding streets for the next hour. It was a comfortable area, a bit on the too-trendy side, but welcoming. I bought a banana at a farmer's market and ate it while sitting on a bench. I felt a little safer in this part of Matar. Mostly I felt like I blended in.

I dreaded telling Rabbit about giving my piece of the Crimson Stone to Templeton, but I'd have to come clean. Lucie would probably think I was an idiot. I thought I was an idiot – and a desperate one at that.

The conversation at the *Coffee Cove* haunted me. I knew they were only commenting on the news, but the woman's words made me uncomfortable. *It must be so difficult being married to a Salesman.* Jack and I weren't married, but it wasn't off the table. We just simply weren't 'there' yet. My new life as a Salesman unexpectedly rocked our easy world. I wouldn't call us boring, but neither one of us had much of a wild side. The Salesman Empire introduced me to the supernatural while Jack served as a reluctant witness.

And yet, months after turning thirty, I'd been called an adventurer. Me, Emily Swift. I could magically travel through doors. I could handle magical items – although we didn't know what other kinds of magical abilities I possessed. I seemed to be able to do things other Salesmen could not. Through it all, the Fringe's shadow followed me. My family was targeted. My mother stolen. Jack, the love of my life, now pulling away from me.

The woman was right. At best, it was difficult having a Salesman in your life.

Tossing my empty cup and banana peel in the trash bin, I pointed myself in the direction of Lucie's. The return trip wouldn't take me long. Maybe I'd be rewarded for my patience and the Whispering Flowers would finally talk.

❖ ❖ ❖

I wasn't kidding: the universe hated me and wanted to punish me. As I neared the stairs leading up to Lucie's front door, I saw a Rabbit looking into her home through the side window. At first, I was excited, thinking my Rabbit had sent a message to me. Then the man on Lucie's stoop turned. I groaned. *Bleeping Speedy.*

He broke into a broad grin as I approached. "Emily, where've you been? Out getting coffee? Sightseeing? Didn't you hear? Your mother was kidnapped."

"Yeah, I'm aware." Jerk.

"She's also up against a murder rap." He descended the stairs and joined me on the sidewalk.

"Again, aware. What do you want?" Any politeness I'd shown before was gone. I was so over Speedy.

"Relax, Emily." He brandished a dazzling smile. "I'm here to help you."

"I have plenty of help, thanks." I gave him a wide berth and started up the stairs.

"Oh, so you know where she's being held?" Speedy sneered.

I stopped and dropped my chin to my chest, sighing. Apparently, we needed to play this conversation out. I finally turned. "No, I don't. Are you telling me you do?"

"I do." His thumbs slid into the front pockets of his jeans and he rocked back and forth on the balls of his feet. His tone mocked me. "But if you're not interested…"

He had to be lying. "You're telling me you know where the Fringe is keeping her, but Rabbit doesn't know?"

"You think he's being kept in the loop now?" Speedy rolled his eyes. "Look, a lot of information is being passed back and forth. Some of it's bogus. An elite group of Rabbits is holding onto the real information. For the right price, you can have it."

"Are you seriously saying the Rabbit network would charge to tell me where my kidnapped mother is being held by the Fringe?" My voice rose and I took a step toward the vile man. My hand holding onto the strap of my shoulder bag balled into a fist.

He put his hands up. "Hey, calm down. That's not exactly what I'm saying. Not that you should be surprised Rabbits are extortionists, by the way. How do you think we make a living?"

"Then what are you saying?"

"I'm saying they'll probably want you to fill them in on some things, too. But they'll tell you about your mother, don't worry. Just come with me." His hand landed on my upper arm. I bristled.

"Why can't you just tell me here?" I asked.

"Because they want to tell you." He let go of my arm and backed off. "If you want to go find her on your own…"

I ran a hand through my hair, frustrated. "Send Rabbit a message. Tell him where we're going and ask him to meet us there. He's in Matar. I want him with me."

"Sure," Speedy pulled out a phone. I watched as he thumbed a fast text.

"Well? What did you tell him?"

"I said we're going downtown and to meet us there." He started to walk away, requiring me to follow if I wanted to continue the conversation.

"Yeah, downtown is vague," I said. "Be specific."

"*Zenith*."

"You told him to meet us at the restaurant? Why there?" This didn't make any sense.

"We'll just meet in front of *Zenith*," he sighed. He picked up the pace. "Hurry up. I had to park a few blocks away. No freaking decent parking in this neighborhood."

All the bells and whistles were sounding. Something was off – way off. But if there was any chance Speedy could help me find out where my mother was being kept, I had to take it. *Zenith* was at least a public place.

"I saw you there last night, you know," I said. "At *Zenith*. You were with some other guy. It wasn't a Rabbit."

"I'm allowed to hang out with people other than Rabbits," he grumped.

"I know, I'm just saying I saw you." I caught a glimpse of a shadow flowing swiftly across the side of the building on our right. I looked up but it was gone. "You got to Matar pretty quickly from Vue."

"I drive fast."

"Yeah, I know." My gaze dropped to the sidewalk. Another shadow scooted in front of us and disappeared into the cracks between the bricks. "Did you see that?"

"What?" Speedy's voice pulsed with exasperation. "See what?"

The shadow was gone. "Nothing. Forget it."

"My car's up ahead," he said. "Move it."

"So, who were you with? You were all dressed up, too." I reverted to my earlier line of questioning.

"When?"

"Last night at *Zenith*?"

"Give it up, Emily," he barked. "It's none of your business!"

I flinched at his outburst. At the same time, a car alarm sounded behind us. We both checked over our shoulders, our attention diverted by the commotion. When I turned back, Nisha stood before us.

She looked largely the same as before: Tall, exotic, dangerous. She wore a similar silver dress. Maybe it was the same one. Her feet remained bare. She cast a look at Speedy, dismissing him before focusing on me.

"Emily Swift," she began, her deep voice resonating in the air. "You are in Matar."

I remembered Rabbit's warning. I nudged Speedy to the side. I planned on crossing the street. He scowled and moved out of my range. "I am. But I'm not staying long. In fact, my friend and I have to be going."

Nisha paused to appraise Speedy a second time. "He doesn't appear to be a friend."

"Well, we're not close," I answered.

"That is true," Nisha said. Her black eyes strayed back to me. "But a friend of Emily Swift's came to me and asked for a favor."

Speedy interrupted. "What kind of favor?"

Nisha switched her focus to Speedy. I feared for the despicable Rabbit. Her lips formed a pernicious smile. "You do not want my attention. You would do well to cross the street. Alone."

Speedy paled and his hand moved to his throat. He coughed. A small trickle of blood appeared at the corner of his mouth. His hand rose higher, and he touched his lips. He looked down at the red wetness painting his shaking fingers.

"Stop it!" I moved in front of Speedy, placing myself between him and Nisha. "Don't hurt him!"

Nisha turned her dark gaze to me. My insides

fluttered, but I held my ground. "He said you are brave."

"Who?" I asked. "Who said that?"

"Your friend." Nisha raised her hand, palm up. She motioned to the other side of the street. "I am only warning this twit once."

I understood. I turned to Speedy. "Please, just go. I'll meet you in front of *Zenith* as soon as I can. It's not safe for you here."

Speedy managed to wipe blood across his cheek. Both hands were smeared as well. He was still visibly shaking. I dug into my bag and pulled out a tee shirt. "Here. Just… just use this." I pressed the clothing into his hands.

The man put my shirt to his face and stumbled away, tripping as he stepped off the curb. He caught himself on a parked car, leaving a bloody handprint on the hood. I watched as he crossed the street. When he was safely on the other side, I faced the frightening being who'd refocused her attention on me.

"What favor did my friend ask?" I licked my lips. My mouth was dry.

"You seek your mother," she replied.

I nodded. "The Fringe kidnapped her. I have to find her."

Grey mist swirled briefly in Nisha's large, unblinking eyes. "Tonight, the Full Moon will shine its glow on a symbol. You will find your mother under this sign."

"What... what is the symbol?" I stammered.

"Hold out your hand," she commanded.

I hesitated. "Which one?"

A thin smile flickered over her wide mouth. "Your choice. Palm up."

I swallowed and held out my right hand. I looked down at my palm and took a deep breath. Imagine you are totally wrapped in door energy, I thought. Push it out of every pore. Nothing can get inside you.

Nisha placed her fingertip against the skin of my palm. "Emily Swift, you can drop this Salesman energy away. The debt was already paid by your friend."

I didn't follow her instructions to let down my guard, but I did watch as her fingertip drew a symbol on the palm of my hand. The symbol she traced was black – a capital I with a capital T crossing over it. The T was slightly lower than the I. The black lines shimmered for a moment, before they pulsed and faded.

"Did you show this to him, too?" I realized the 'friend' she referred to had to be Rabbit. This was the other Matar resource he mentioned before setting out to look again for the Tortoise. My heart twisted. He must've been desperate.

"You are the only one who needed to see this symbol," Nisha answered. She stepped away. "Return to the new witch's home and wait. Do not follow that other man."

I opened my mouth to ask why, but like that day in the park, Nisha's towering figure abruptly cascaded to the ground in a pool of shimmering black before her shadow slid over the sidewalk and up the side of the building. She disappeared into thin air.

I looked at my hand. The symbol was long gone, but I still could feel the itchiness of Nisha's energy hovering over my palm.

※ ※ ※

I trusted Speedy got the help he needed. I wondered if he'd wait for me at *Zenith*. When I returned to Lucie's, I let myself in through the front door.

"In here!" I heard Lucie call from the kitchen.

I joined her. "Has Rabbit returned?"

"Not yet." She worked a sandstone mortar and pestle, grinding up herbs. I smelled parsley.

"And the flowers?"

Lucie looked up from her task. She shook her head. "I looked about ten minutes ago. No change."

"Damn." I climbed up onto the barstool and slumped forward. Elbows on the counter, I dropped my head to my hands. "This has not been a good afternoon."

She set the mortar and pestle aside. "What happened?"

Lucie's eyes grew wider as I filled her in on everything, from Templeton's sudden arrival upstairs, to Speedy showing up in front of her home, to Nisha, appearing out of nowhere on the street.

"Good grief," Lucie said. "What are you going to do?"

"I have no idea." I resisted the urge to bang my head on the countertop. "Wait for Rabbit? Wait on the flowers? Wait on freaking Templeton?"

"Well, let's start with this," Lucie said. She pulled a notepad and pencil from a kitchen drawer. "Draw the symbol. Let's see it."

"It's like a capital I with a capital T over it, but lower." I drew the same symbol as Nisha traced in my palm earlier. "Does it look familiar to you?"

Lucie shook her head. "No, but it also looks like two capital E's back to back."

I frowned at the paper. "Yeah, maybe. With a tail."

"With a tail," she repeated. "Or it's a capital I and capital T."

"Maybe Rabbit will know," I said.

"He'll probably be able to find out through the network."

"Right. Ugh, that reminds me. Speedy told me there's an 'elite group' of Rabbits who are holding onto information. Those are the ones who supposedly know where my mother is being held."

Lucie wrinkled her nose. "Do you believe that?"

"Maybe," I shrugged. "We think the network was holding back from Rabbit in Vue."

Lucie's attention shifted back to the paper and the symbol I'd drawn. "Emily, I have an idea. Where's your father's journal? Now that we know it's spelled, let's find a blank page and you can draw the symbol on it. Let's see what happens."

"That's a great idea," I said, excited. I dug through my shoulder bag. "It never even occurred to me."

"I'm brilliant like that."

I looked up and we both laughed. It felt really good.

"Okay, let me see." I turned to a blank page.

"Ground and center your energy first," Lucie reminded me. "Relax, and then when you're ready, reach out to The Book. Connect with The Book's energy and draw your symbol."

Taking a deep breath, I did as Lucie directed. I felt a calm roll over my shoulders and the familiar energy building in my chest. I formed it into a ball of light and pressed it toward The Book. The moment The Book responded, I sensed it. It was warm, comforting. Before I picked up my pencil, I touched the page with my finger, tracing the symbol as Nisha had done to my palm.

What does this mean? Where will I find this symbol?

A soft glow appeared on the page under my fingertip. The symbol emerged as I wrote. I gasped.

"Nicely done, Emily," Lucie said. "Now hold that image in your mind, where will you find it?"

The Book's pages quivered under the energy I pushed into it. We watched as more writing appeared. A line. A string of numbers:

4.36.59.12.84.

Lucie read the numbers out loud. "Do you know what this means?"

I grinned, remembering what I learned from the female Rabbit after the bonfire. "No, but Rabbit will."

❋ ❋ ❋

The Whispering Flowers held their rigid pose, the blooming trumpets pointing soundlessly toward the sky.

"Nothing?" Lucie said as she poked her head from the doorway.

"Not a word," I answered, standing and brushing my hands off on the front of my jeans. "Seriously, do you think they're broken?"

"Nope, I think they haven't heard the answer yet. The florist said they grew overnight, right?

He didn't say they coughed up an answer overnight."

"I know," I said. "But my mother's been gone for almost two days now. I've been thinking. If Templeton was right and they took her to get my piece of the Crimson Stone, why didn't they contact me? You know, for the ransom?"

"Interesting." Lucie cocked her head to the side. "That's a good question. Then again, maybe they don't know where you are right now."

"I suppose," I said. I looked down at the planter. "Any day now, guys."

"Listen," Lucie began. "I've got to get going soon for tonight's Full Moon ritual. I'm taking the beryl. Gorgeous piece. The gemstone was already set in a divining pendant, so after it's cleaned and charged, it'll be ready for us to use when I get back tonight. I spread the map of Matar out on the countertop by the barstools. We can work there."

I smiled. "Great. Thanks, Lucie."

"Don't mention it. Hang in there," she added. "We'll find her one way or the other."

Lucie disappeared back into the pantry and I was left alone. I wished Rabbit would hurry back. I was eager to show him the numbers that appeared in The Book. We might not even need the Whispering Flowers. A piece of the Crimson Stone was another subject. Damn Templeton!

Still, if Rabbit did find the Tortoise and got

the other piece, I'd at least be back to where I started. Templeton confirmed there was magic in the pieces. I still had hope.

I sat at the little table in Lucie's backyard and sipped my water. The garden was pretty, and other plants and flowers were starting to pop up. I wondered if the warm weather would stay once I took my mother home. I couldn't wait to find out.

A rustling not unlike the flutter of a bird's wings caught my attention. The Whispering Flowers began to move, their flutes quivering as if a breeze worked through them. I jumped from my chair and knelt by the planter. The yellow flowers swayed, and they turned their soft-petaled faces toward me. I leaned in closer. "What is it?" I asked, my breath blowing over them.

I listened.

And listened.

Then I heard it, the loudest whispers.

"Warehouses. Find her... warehouses."

CHAPTER 19

Warehouses. The Whispering Flowers kept repeating the same few words. Warehouses... find her... warehouses.

I was beside myself. Warehouses? Where? In Matar? Some other city?

I hovered over the flowers. "Please," I begged. "Where is the warehouse? Is it here in Matar?"

The flowers continued their constant chant. Warehouses... Find her... Find her... Warehouses. I rubbed my hands over my face. I didn't expect the answer to be so vague. Warehouses?

I climbed to my feet. Okay, think. Think, think, think. Let's go on the assumption the warehouses are in Matar. Let's start there. I took a deep breath. Let's be calm, Emily.

The sky was beginning to get darker, and the Full Moon started to rise in the sky. One more deep breath in. Ground and center. Let it out.

Abandoning the murmuring chorus, I passed through the pantry back to Lucie's kitchen. I paced back and forth. The flowers clearly said warehouses. My eyes tracked to the cupboard where Lucie's wall phone was hidden. I'd call the Empire's service for help. I was desperate.

I opened the cupboard door and reached for the phone's handset. I placed it to my ear, the cord stretching from the phone to me. I clicked the cradle once.

A crackle of static, then: "Hello, this is the Empire service. May I help you?"

"Yes. I think maybe. I'm actually looking for information."

"What is the question? Do remember most Empire offices are closed at this time of night and I will not be able to transfer you."

Well, that was a new one. "Actually, I'm trying to determine where the warehouses are located in Matar."

I was met with a long silence.

"Is there a warehouse district or something like that?"

"There are warehouses throughout Matar. Please provide more information."

I twisted the phone cord around my finger and leaned against the kitchen counter. "That's the problem," I said. "I don't have more information. Just, warehouses."

"Without more detail I cannot be of assistance to you," the clipped voice said. "I do suggest, however, that you consider consulting a map of the city."

My lips formed a little 'oh' and my eyes cut to the map Lucie left on the counter. "Right, a map. I'll start there."

"Very good. Will that be all?"

"Yeah, that's all." I moved toward the cupboard.

"Very good," the voice replied. "Goodbye."

After hanging up the phone, I smoothed the creases of the map. Matar was fairly big. The map, without Lucie's piece of beryl, wouldn't necessarily tell me where to go, but maybe I'd get some ideas. I wouldn't find warehouses in downtown Matar, and my bet was on the outskirts of the city. I knew Anwat was a big travel hub for the Empire, and it was southwest of Matar – actually, mostly west. The Walled Zone, where the Fringe was rumored to have a strong presence, was northwest of Matar. My assumption, then, was they'd hang in the western part of the city.

My fingers slid over the surface of the map to the western side of Matar. The map only listed street names and some landmarks, but it did show a bunch of lines that didn't appear to be roads. I checked the key and confirmed my suspicion. Train tracks. Warehouses store items prior to shipping. I tapped the map. If I had to make a guess, I'd say that part of Matar would be good a place to start.

There was a decision to make. Everyone ordered me to wait here. Rabbit, Templeton, and even Lucie expected me to sit still until she returned. Justice Spell – the Empire – expected me to wait at home.

I drummed my fingers on the counter. Tuesday called me an adventurer. I didn't choose this one, but I was not going to sit and wait any longer. Each hour that passed without saving my mother would make it even harder to get her back, I was sure of it.

The Book sat by the map. I opened it to the page where I'd drawn the symbol with my fingertip. It remained on the page. I grabbed Lucie's notepad and pencil and drew the symbol on the paper, adding the string of numbers: 4.36.59.12.84.

Then I wrote:

Rabbit, these numbers appeared in The Book when we drew Nisha's symbol in it. According to her, my mother is being held somewhere under this sign. The Whispering Flowers finally spoke, too, but the only thing they keep saying is 'Warehouses, find her.' Lucie is at her Full Moon ritual. Templeton was here and I gave him my piece of the Stone. It's a long story, and I hope I didn't make a huge mistake. I hope you found the Tortoise. I'm leaving to look for a 'warehouse district' here in Matar. I can't keep waiting. It's torture. Come find me.

– Emily

PS: Lucie, if you read this note before Rabbit, please make sure he gets it.

No one was going to be happy with me. I'd flag down a taxi and ask if there was a warehouse district in the western part of Matar. That's where I'd start. I could always door travel right back if I got into trouble.

I shoved The Book into my shoulder bag, double-checked on my top hat, and grabbed the jacket I borrowed from Lucie.

❋ ❋ ❋

Not even a block from Lucie's home I saw a cab. The driver responded to my upraised hand and pulled to the curb.

"Is there a warehouse district or something like that in Matar? Maybe over to the west?" I leaned toward his window.

"What are you looking for?" he replied. His arm rested on the wheel.

"I don't know. Maybe a whole block of warehouses or something? You don't have any docks or canals in Matar, do you?" Great. Now I was brainstorming with the cab driver.

"No water here in Matar," he answered. He squinted up at me. "What are you trying to do?"

"I'm meeting a friend," I lied. "He said he'd be in the warehouse district, or something like that. I think a bunch of train tracks are to the west. I was thinking, maybe near them?"

The driver looked straight ahead out through the windshield. He sucked on his teeth, making a wet squeaking sound. After a moment, he stopped. He peered back up at me. "Get in. There's an industrial section your friend might mean. It's a good twenty-five minute drive. Don't know where I can tell you to go without an address, but it's your dollar."

"That's fine," I said, loading myself into the back seat. "I can pay. Maybe it'll be obvious where to go once we get there."

It wasn't.

In fact, this section of Matar was dark and mostly deserted. Almost every lot was behind a chain link fence. A couple of buildings the size of city blocks housed factories. They appeared to be active, but only a skeleton crew of vehicles dotted their lots behind security guard checkpoints. The sidewalks were empty. We kept driving.

"This friend you're meeting," the driver spoke over his shoulder. "Are you meeting up to go to a party or something? Sometimes kids squat in these warehouses for a night with a DJ. They dance, hook up, probably do drugs. I'm not really seeing any signs of that, but we can pull down into some of these alleys."

"I'm not really looking for that kind of party," I said. "Just my friend. But yeah, maybe try an alley."

My driver pulled into the next one he found and drove in about twenty feet. He turned in his seat and looked past me to the back window. The car began to back up. "Dead end. Hang on."

As the back of the car re-emerged from the

alley, I looked out the back passenger window. I caught a glimpse of two men rounding a corner. They walked in the light of the streetlamp long enough for me to guess they might be Rabbits. At least they were dressed like Rabbits.

"Hang on," I told the driver. "I think I see someone. Here." I passed a small wad of bills over the seat.

He bent his head and peered in the direction of the disappearing men. "Are you sure? I mean, are you really sure?"

I was wasting time. I scooted across the seat to the door. "I am. Thanks."

"I'm going to wait here five minutes," he said. "If it's not what you think, come back."

I gave him a weak smile. "I'll be okay."

"Be careful," he called as I shut the door behind me and darted toward the corner. My heart was thumping, and I hoped like hell I wasn't chasing a bunch of trouble. Well, any more trouble. I rounded the corner and found an empty street. No men, no one I could see. They probably went into one of the buildings.

A couple of streetlights lit up random sections of the sidewalk, and a few entryways had a lightbulb over the door. One flickered noisily as I passed under it. The electricity buzzed behind the fixture.

If the Rabbits ducked into a nearby building, finding them would be next to impossible. I let go of the idea.

The plan? Keep walking. Yes, I know. It was a poor one, but it was all I had.

I comforted myself with the fact I was a Salesman. If I sensed trouble, I'd pick a door and go. I crossed the empty street and kept walking. Turning right, I stopped short. The Full Moon rose huge in the sky over Matar. It seemed so close to the city. Everything was bathed in its cool light. I paused, letting my eyes roam the one-way street, deciding on where to go. A sign bearing names of companies along with directions for trucks to follow arched over the road, glowing arrows pointing to the left and right. I scanned the sign, sucking in a breath when I realized what I'd found.

Ivanov Transport. Its logo? A capital I with a capital T crossed over it. It was the exact symbol Nisha drew in my hand.

The arrow for *Ivanov Transport* pointed to the left. I sprinted across the street and began to jog on the uneven sidewalk. I searched as I hurried. A few more signs indicated *Ivanov Transport* was ahead. Others signaled train tracks were in the same direction. As I got closer, the last sign announced truck docking past the gate to my left. The bar at the guard shack gate was down; the shack left unattended. I looked up and down the sidewalk. No one. I stood in front of the gate and squinted into the poorly lit lot. Again, nothing.

It looked empty.

"Well, here I go," I breathed, ducking under the gate's arm and moving into the shadows. I had a fleeting vision of hungry guard dogs appearing out of nowhere and tearing me to shreds. My hand pressed against my chest and I strained to listen for charging animals. Nothing. Wait a minute, I thought, there was no fence to keep animals in. I'd take that as a sign no beasts with vicious jaws watched me from the darkness. At least none of the canine kind.

The Full Moon's light helped when nothing blocked its glow. I crossed the open space as quickly as I could and moved closer to the buildings at the edge of the lot. Truck trailers lined one side, and several were backed up against loading docks. I cut between two and skirted the outside of the building. I was looking for a door.

Once or twice, I heard noises, but they were far enough away that I couldn't determine exactly what I was hearing. A door shutting? A heavy box dropping? Several times the distant sound reverberated like metal against metal. Another buzzing bulb appeared over two side-by-side doors about halfway down the building. Between the light and the top of the doorframes, *Ivanov Transport* and its logo – the symbol – appeared. One door was marked office; the other, warehouse.

Please be unlocked. Please don't sound an

alarm, I prayed as I gently turned the doorknob and pushed. I cringed. Silence. A puff of air passed my lips when I released a breath. Things were finally going my way! The absurdity of the thought did not escape me. I snuck inside the building.

I let my eyes adjust in the darkness. After a moment, I could see more clearly. Faint lights lined a few of the catwalks I could make out along the walls. The space was huge, perhaps a good three or four stories high. Emergency lights appeared over fire extinguishers and alarms at various points along the wall. Nothing was well lit, but it was enough to guide me.

If my mother truly were being held in this space, I'd have to search every floor. The building, even only the warehouse portion, was massive. I needed a lot of help.

A tall desk stood near the loading doors of the warehouse. It was dirty, covered with coffee-stained paper cups, logbooks, and receipts. I parked my shoulder bag on top of the mess and pulled out The Book. I needed a little 'Eight Ball' magic. I rested my butt against the hard metal of the desk's stool.

"Here we go again," I muttered. I lifted the journal. "Book, please help me find my Mom. She's here somewhere. She's in danger. Please tell me what to do."

My energy took its familiar journey from my

chest toward The Book. My father's journal responded, this time pulling my energy deeper between its covers. The energy drew my hands down, and I placed The Book on top of my bag. I rested my palms on its cover, closing my eyes.

I could see into The Book, the various pages I'd puzzled over, the sketches and notes my father left behind. I saw the symbol I'd traced onto the page, the one that brought me to this place. In my mind's eye, I read my father's warning:

COMMUNICATION
News will travel
Through many mediums
Sent by both
Friend and foe
Learning the difference
Makes all the difference.

Messages from the Rabbits, from Nisha, and even from Templeton. Who was the foe?

I envisioned the pages turning. Then a pause. A new sketch, a Daffodil. No, not a Daffodil, a Whispering Flower. The penciled petals fluttered on the page. Letter by letter, words began to appear under the drawing:

Warehouses... Find her...
Look up.

My head was lifting before my eyes opened. Several loading docks over, a set of metal stairs climbed to the first catwalk secured against the warehouse wall. Three doors appeared, each separated by about fifteen feet. A window high above the docking area let in the moon's glow. Somewhere, outside, *Ivanov Transport's* logo must've sat between the moon and warehouse. It cast its shadow above the first door on the catwalk.

Hurriedly, I shoved The Book back into my shoulder bag. My mother was hidden somewhere behind that door. I scurried as silently as I could across the concrete to the metal stairs. I unhooked the chain which draped between the railings over the first step, wincing as it jangled when lowered against the wall. The rubber soles of my shoes made no noise as I ascended, but the metal made an occasional squeak under my weight. I moved swiftly, hoping my presence was still a secret.

The marked door was unlocked, and I passed through into an empty hall. There was less light without windows and the Full Moon. At the end of the hallway, I could see another dull light over a fire extinguisher. I headed toward it, wincing when the floor creaked as I walked. Halfway down the hall, I heard a soft sound. I paused in the darkness, my heart pounding in my ears. Swallowing, I willed myself to calm down and listen. It was a voice. Someone was singing.

I crept forward. I couldn't hear the words, but I recognized the melody. It grew louder as I approached the end of the hall. Yes, I knew this song. Which way to turn? Right or left? I began to hum softly with the singer.

I love the bumblebees, I love the stars above, when night turns into day…

My feet turned left, and I padded forward about ten steps. I sang the song's chorus in my head. The singer's voice faded. No, this was the wrong way! I whirled back around and headed in the opposite direction. I passed the extinguisher and pressed into the darkness. A light flickered under one of the closed doors. The singing rose again.

I love the sunshine, I love the butterflies, I love the windblow, I love the river flow, I love the city lights, when the moon is high…

"Mom?" I called softly through the door. I tried the doorknob. Locked. "Mom?"

The singing stopped. I heard a rustling and a shadow appeared with the light under the door. My mother called back. "Emily? Emily? Is that you? Are you there?"

"Shh," I warned. "It's me. But we need to be quiet. Hold on."

I wiggled the doorknob again. It was definitely locked. I felt around the door jam. In my fantasy, the key would be hanging from a hook right about… *there*. My fingers flexed.

And… we got nothing.

"Damn," I said. "Mom, give me a few minutes, okay? I need to think. Is there a place you can sit down and wait?"

"Yes," came the hushed reply. The shadow under the door slipped out of sight.

I pressed my forehead against the door and closed my eyes. What to do, what to do? This is where the superhero breaks the door down. Not going to happen. What about door travel? I could travel in to see her – my hand twisted pointlessly against the doorknob – but I couldn't door travel my mother back out. She wasn't a Salesman.

I'd have to find a set of keys. It's possible there'd be more than one set for the doors in these hallways. I'd go back down to the loading dock desk and check there. Maybe one of the offices on the other side of the warehouse had a set.

"I'll be right back. I'm going to see if I can find a key," I said to the door. I heard her soft acknowledgement.

If the loading dock desk didn't pan out, I'd try the offices. I felt my way back down the dark halls until I was back at the door leading to the catwalk. I opened it slowly and peeked out. No one waited for me. I tiptoed back across the catwalk and down the metal stairs, grimacing every time the metal made its small, screaky noise. Back on the concrete, I skittered across the warehouse floor to the loading dock desk. Fumbling under papers and books, I felt for a set of keys. Nothing. I pulled open the top drawer.

SCREECH! Holy hell! I jerked my hand back from the handle. The shrill sound echoed through the warehouse. I crouched and listened, breathing through my mouth until I was sure no one had come running to investigate. I swallowed and stood back up. Nothing I could see had changed. I wedged my hand into the drawer's opening and felt around. No keys.

There were three more drawers to open. I ruled the bottom one out because it looked like a large file drawer. Painstakingly, I inched open the other two. Neither of them contained a set of keys.

I squinted back at the warehouse's entrance. By it, there was a second set of stairs leading to another catwalk. I could make out a door at the top. It must go into the office building next to the warehouse.

Leaving the loading dock desk and the open drawers, I made a beeline for the second catwalk. These metal stairs were just as noisy as the first. I hustled up to the catwalk and through the door marked 'offices.'

The door led into a shabby lobby with a closed reception window facing an elevator. One fluorescent light lit the room; the other bulb had blown. I crossed the lobby to yet another door, this one presumedly leading to the *Ivanov Transport* offices. It did. Upon entering the hall, I realized I could get into the receptionist's room sitting behind the window. I would start there. I flipped the switch on the wall so I'd have more light as I surveyed the space.

No keyrings hung from an under counter hook, no set of keys had been tossed on the desk. I sat down in the rolling desk chair and continued my search. These drawers didn't make any noise when opened, but they didn't deliver the goods either. I stared into the last drawer I'd combed through, my hand rubbing over my mouth. I'd have to start working my way through the other offices.

A tap-tap-tap against the reception window jerked me from my reverie. Speedy stood on the other side, grinning.

❋ ❋ ❋

"Hello, Emily." Speedy met me in the hall as I exited the receptionist's room.

"What are you doing here?" I whispered, looking around. I was afraid we'd be caught.

"I told you, some Rabbits knew where the Fringe took your mother." He looked past me into the receptionist's room. "What were you doing in there?"

"I was looking for keys." I eyeballed his clothing. He'd changed. Of course, after the experience with Nisha, he'd had blood on his shirt. "Are you okay?"

Speedy frowned at me. "Yeah, no thanks to that monster. You need better friends."

"She's not my friend. Listen, I found my mother. She's in a locked room on the other side of the warehouse, but we need to find keys to get her out." I motioned to the other doors. "You look in the offices on the left, I'll look in these on the right."

"Why don't you just grab a crowbar or something? Pop it open? Some sort of sledgehammer?" Speedy reached for my arm. "Come on."

I sidestepped his grab. "I'd like to avoid making noise. I don't think I'm lucky enough to have the warehouse to myself for long. The Fringe could show up at any time."

"I don't think this is the place to look," he replied. "I doubt they'd just leave keys lying around."

"This is not helping," I told him. "I don't suppose you've texted the network? Rallied the troops to help? Or are you still running with your 'elite' Rabbit group? Still not sharing information with everyone unless they can pay?" I spit out the last sentence.

He shrugged. "Some people are better than others, Emily."

"Yeah, you're a freaking peach." I pointed to a door. "Just... Just start in there." I moved toward an office on my right, opening the door.

I glanced back at Speedy. He stood scowling. I waved my hand at the office door nearest him, mouthing *Go!*

Instead, he spun on his heel and bailed out through the door leading into the lobby, shutting it behind him. My mouth popped open. *Why that little...* I followed. Dammit! This was not helpful. The lobby was empty. I opened the door leading out onto the catwalk, checking the stairs and the warehouse floor below. Speedy was nowhere to be found.

"Son of a..." I pressed my lips together and turned back to the lobby. The elevator appeared unused. I checked another door, but as suspected, it was only a maintenance closet. "Such a jerk."

There was nothing to do but return to my search for keys to free my mother. I tried to ignore the feeling time was running out.

❊ ❊ ❊

After ransacking three offices, I started to think Speedy was right. No one had keys. No one even bothered to lock their office doors. Huh. I stopped my rummaging. Why were none of the doors here locked? Well, none except for the door leading to my mother.

Returning to the lonely hall, I decided I'd take a page from Speedy's playbook and go find a tool to pry open the door. Or smash it. Or something.

Out of the office building of *Ivanov Transport* and back into the warehouse side I went. I didn't see any tools by the loading docks, so I resigned myself to exploring deeper into the warehouse. I'd stick to the side of the wall and try to remain out of sight. Speedy had to be somewhere. What was he doing here? I didn't like him, I certainly didn't fully trust him, but he might be strong enough to help get the door open so I could free my mother.

Then I'd beat him over the head with a crowbar. A giddy titter escaped my lips. Oh, good grief, I thought. Hold it together, Emily. Just hold it together.

The farther I wandered, the more pallets and heavy equipment I passed. Row after row of pallets towering with shrink-wrapped goods lined the floor. Sleeping forklifts waited at the end of many of them.

Just past the rows, I discovered another open space. I could see massive rolling tool chests on a far wall. Jackpot! I hiked my bag up on my shoulder and diverted my course across the middle of the warehouse.

Halfway to the toolboxes, all the lights came on.

CHAPTER 20

It's just like in the movies.

All the lights suddenly come on, blinding you. You raise an arm to block the bright light. You squint, your stomach rolls, and depending on your story, you're saved – or things get oh so much worse.

Guess what story I'm in?

I could make out multiple people moving toward me as I worked to refocus. I turned and was met with another set of bodies barring an escape. There were probably ten to twelve Fringe members around me. A couple wore top hats, but most of them did not.

No one moved toward me. It was as if they were waiting.

"Okay, then," I began. "I'll just be going." I took a step to my right. A man stepped forward and lifted his hand. He had a gun. He shook his head no.

"I guess I'll wait right here," I said. He smirked.

"You can put the gun away for now," a deep voice came from behind. "I doubt she's armed."

Purposeful footsteps sounded behind me and I looked over my right shoulder as the owner of the voice came into view. Oh, crap.

"Emily Swift," he said, stopping in front of me.

He held out a hand. "Sebastian St. Michel."

I stared at the extended hand, trying to get my bearings. I gave my head a shake and lifted my gaze. A brilliant smile flashed across his handsome face.

"You're the man Speedy was with," I stated. I didn't take his hand.

"Speedy?" he replied, puzzled. "I'm not sure who you mean."

"Dinner, at *Zenith* last night. You were with Speedy."

"Last night?" Realization dawned. "Simon is Speedy?" He laughed, joined by the other Fringe members. "Well, I guess if anyone were going to be 'speedy,' it would be him." More laughter. He wagged a long finger at me. "Emily, I didn't anticipate such a naughty girl."

I frowned. "What? Ew, no!" I blanched. "It's his driving. He speeds. Speedy."

Sebastian put his hand to his cheek. "I'm so relieved. I would hope you'd have better taste." He winked before turning and walking in the opposite direction. He lifted his hand as he strolled, motioning for me to follow with two fingers. "Come, come!"

When I hesitated, Mr. Gunman pointed his gun at me again. I complied.

We didn't go far. Sebastian led me to a table and chairs. A bottle of red wine and several glasses sat amid stacks of boxes and folders. He poured two glasses before offering me one. I looked away.

"Hmm," he said, his lips pursing as he shook his head and set it back on the table. He sat down in one of the chairs and picked up the other glass. He crossed his legs, his left ankle balanced on his right knee. He sipped his wine, thoughtfully.

I studied him. My original instinct was right. He wasn't a Rabbit. Now I knew he was a Salesman and a member of the Fringe. Speedy – or Simon, whatever his name was – had been working with the Fringe.

Sebastian was disturbingly attractive, with wavy brown hair so dark it was almost black. It hung down a breath below his collar. Thick eyelashes framed heavy-lidded, brown eyes. The devilish smile hadn't left his lips. A wicked, yet perfectly groomed, mustache and goatee accented the olive skin of his face. The Van Dyke didn't make him look like a ridiculous hipster. Instead, he looked like a rock star.

"I want you to let my mother go," I told him.

He nodded, uncrossing his legs while he set the glass down on the table. He leaned forward, feet flat on the floor, his hands on his knees. "I can do that."

"Now would be good."

Another burst of laughter. "I like you," he said. "I wish you'd share some wine with me, Emily."

"No, thank you."

He lifted his hands in mock surrender. "Okay, we'll do it your way. I, for one, like things to be nice. But we can get down to business."

"What kind of business?" I asked. I would make him say it.

Sebastian waved off the others. They retreated. "I will personally arrange for your mother to be safely returned to her home immediately after you give me the Crimson Stone. No harm will come to her."

"See," I said, swallowing my anger in an effort to remain calm. "That's the problem. You've kidnapped an innocent woman to try to get your grubby little hands on the Crimson Stone – and I don't have it."

"Grubby little hands?" He examined them as he held them up. "I wouldn't call these little, would you? In fact, I wouldn't call anything about me 'little.'"

"Certainly not your ego," I blurted out.

Sebastian rose to his feet. "You are so much better than I imagined," he said, shooting another playful smile in my direction. "This banter is exciting, isn't it? I'm enjoying it. But we both have objectives we need to meet tonight, so let's take care of that first. Now, the Stone. I suppose it's too much for me to hope you have it with you? I assume you'll need to go get it. The problem with that is I cannot let you leave unchaperoned. I'm going to require you to travel with some of my associates." He nodded toward two men who'd moved in behind me without me noticing.

"Sebastian," I said through clenched teeth. "I do not have the Stone – at all."

"Oh," he taunted. "I like how you say my name. Say it again."

"I said I don't have the Crimson Stone. I would not give it to you if I did." I turned away. I pretended Mr. Gunman was not pointing his weapon at me.

"I can't believe you're going to make me do this the hard way," Sebastian sighed. He stepped closer. "One last time. Where is the Crimson Stone? I know you found it in Vue. I know you took it away from Tahl Petrovich. He couldn't get the job done, so now we're forced to do this unpleasant work."

I looked up. Sebastian was awfully close. "If you know all that, then you also know Templeton was there."

The corners of Sebastian's mouth quirked up, but he said nothing.

"Why don't you ask Templeton for the Stone? He's the Salesman who can handle magical items."

"Are you saying he has it?" Sebastian dropped the smile.

"Yes." Well, a piece of it.

"You see, Emily," Sebastian began. "That might be a believable story, except I know Templeton doesn't have it. How? If he did, he wouldn't be trailing after you, obsessed."

I snorted. "He's hardly that. Templeton and I have other... stuff. That's all. He has the Stone. Go find him. Good luck."

"Other stuff?" Sebastian frowned. He cocked his head to the side. "Do you like it when Templeton sniffs around? Do you like it when he saves you, Emily?"

"He doesn't save me!" I protested. Sebastian lifted an eyebrow. I narrowed my eyes at him. "I don't need saving."

"Isn't that what happened in Vue?"

"There were others in Vue. We all worked together." Good grief. I needed to shut up.

"Interesting." Sebastian said, stroking his chin. "All of you, hmm?" He shrugged. "No matter. This was just a side exercise. I never thought Templeton wanted a pet, but here we are."

I bristled. "I am not his pet."

He ignored me. "The Crimson Stone. Where is it?"

❋ ❋ ❋

This went on for another twenty minutes. Sebastian asked me for the Crimson Stone, I told him I didn't have it. What I did realize from all of this was that Sebastian didn't know the Stone was currently in three pieces. That secret seemed to remain intact.

"Enough!" Sebastian finally slammed his glass of wine down on the table. Some splashed over the rim. "Get her out of here. Stick her in one of the rooms reserved for us. Do not put her in with her mother. In fact, skip taking her up front. Find something back here. I don't want them close to each other."

Sebastian faced me. "I'm extremely disappointed in you, Emily. But you'll come around. I'm confident." He directed his next words to one of the men standing by Mr. Gunman. "Tie her to a chair. I don't want her door traveling out of here." He waved his hand, and two men took me by the arms and began to march me away.

In my mind, I ran through all the self-defense and escape moves I'd ever heard of, both believable and not. I came up short. I was so screwed.

But I decided to at least put up a little fight – not enough to get me killed, but enough to make these despicable Salesmen work for it. I tried to pull backward, bracing my feet against the floor.

"Knock it off," the taller of the two said, giving me a yank. "No one's in the mood."

I squirmed and wriggled, forcing them to constantly reshuffle their grasps. My rubber soles gave me some traction, and I bucked between them, causing the other man to lose hold. He recovered quickly, thick fingers pressing into the flesh on the back of my arm. I'd have bruises.

"Can we hit her?" he growled.

"St. Michel would have our heads," the first replied. I tried to leverage an elbow into his side. "Stop that!"

We'd trekked away from the others as I kicked at them. That proved ineffectual, so I decided to use the same trick every two-year-old having a meltdown in public knows: I went completely limp, forcing them to drag me up off the cold floor.

"Lift her," the first man grunted. They hauled me to my feet, hands under my arms, lifting me just a bit higher than necessary as they propelled me forward on my tiptoes. We slogged along.

I heard a loud *ZZZZeeet!* and the three of us were immediately plunged into darkness. Whereas before all the lights blasted on, this time, they all flashed out.

"What the –?"

The one opportunity I'd been waiting for arrived – kind of. I was as dumbfounded as the men were. But as their grips loosened in surprise, my feet hit the floor and I lurched forward, wresting myself away.

❈ ❈ ❈

I ran as fast as I could through the sudden darkness, my shoulder bag slapping into my body. There was no way I was door traveling out of there and abandoning my mother. But I needed help. Where was Rabbit? Why hadn't he come?

The men chased behind me, and I heard one very frightening yell to 'go around and cut her off.' The only thing I could do was hide and delay being caught until help arrived. If help arrived.

I darted between towering pallets, winding through them like a maze. Another yell: 'I think she went this way!' Men's voices rang through the warehouse. I needed to find a place to hide, but I also needed to make sure I was running away from the Fringe and not toward them.

Ducking around the corner of one of the stocked pallets, I stopped to catch my breath, my chest heaving while I took silent gulps of air. I leaned with my back against the side of the pallet, the palms of my hands flat against the shrink-wrap. I pressed my fingers into it and pulled. I rolled my body along the thick plastic, now pressing my chest against it. I reached over my head, staring up into the darkness, gripping the plastic. The pallet's goods were piled high. What if I climbed on top and laid flat?

A hard body pressed against my back at the same time a hand firmly covered my mouth, blocking the yelp wanting to escape my lips. "It's me, be quiet!" Templeton hissed into my ear. "Do not make a sound."

I stilled. We stood mutely as footsteps came closer. I held my breath under Templeton's hand. I felt his energy edging around us. One of Sebastian's men stopped at the end of the pallet row. Backlit by an emergency light, his shadow reached into the darkness that hid us.

"We need flashlights," he called to the others. "Until we get all the lights back on, I can't see squat!" He moved on from our row.

The tension drained out of my body. I slumped against Templeton. He pulled his hand away from my mouth.

"Listen to me closely, Emily. Find a door and go," Templeton breathed into my ear.

"I can't leave my mother," I shot back as quietly as I could.

"I will get her," he replied, his voice sharpening. "For once, do what you're told." He pulled away, releasing me.

I cautiously turned to face him, barely making out his features through the darkness. "Is anyone else here to help? Is Rabbit here?"

"I don't know where Rabbit is," he answered. He pulled on my shoulder and guided me farther into the blackness. "It doesn't matter. There is no fight to be won here, only escape." His fingers flexed against my shoulder when we heard footsteps drawing near. We stepped back from one another, pressing ourselves against opposite pallets. I was sure my thumping heart would give us away. It beat loud in my ears.

The footsteps retreated.

"Emily," Templeton's voice drifted softly from the other side of the aisle. "Keep following this row to the end. There are doors along the wall you can use. I don't care where you go, just get out of here."

"Templeton –"

"You are wasting time! Go!" I heard a rustle and could vaguely make out Templeton's tall form slipping back the way we came and away from me.

"Dammit!" I turned in the opposite direction, keeping one hand out in front of me and the other gliding along the wall of stacked pallets. I navigated my way to the other end of the row.

Templeton was right, there were a couple of doors along the wall under weak, emergency lighting. The warehouse was even darker after the bright overhead lights were zapped out. I didn't know if the dousing of the lights was an accident or Templeton's doing, but I was grateful.

I crept along the ends of the pallet rows, moving closer to the first door. I was still a good two rows away when it popped open and one of my captors stepped through. I dodged back between the stacked pallets. A flashlight beam waved past the end of my row and I recognized the voice of the man who asked if he'd be allowed to hit me. I shrunk back even farther into the shadows.

"I hope St. Michel knows what he's doing," the voice said.

"I wouldn't say that to him if I were you." Another voice – his tall friend.

"And this is the famous Emily Swift, huh? I expected more."

"She managed to get a hold of the Crimson Stone," his partner replied. "She took Petrovich down." The flashlight beam stopped wobbling. "Did you hear something?"

I held my breath.

"I can't tell," the other man complained. "Personally, I'm about done with this. If she's right and Templeton has the Stone, I'm not messing with that."

"St. Michel can handle him."

"Maybe. Let's go this way." The flashlight beam swung around and disappeared.

I put my hand to my chest and took a long, quiet breath. After calming myself, I peeked around the end pallet. The coast was clear. I resumed inching forward, focused again on the first door.

Templeton's plan for me to leave and for him to 'get my mother' really didn't work for me. But he was right; we were outnumbered. I'd take a page from Lucie's handbook: I needed a backup plan. I would door travel right back to the offices I'd ransacked earlier looking for keys. Now that I'd found my mother, I was going to call the Empire guards – honestly, I didn't know who else to call. Then I'd door travel into my mother's locked room and wait. I'd fight tooth and nail if anyone came through the door to harm her.

I'd seen two phones on the reception desk. One probably dialed the other offices. That meant the second phone had to be connected to the Empire's service. I was going to tell them where we all were.

"I can't believe he's making us go back!" The men with the flashlight returned.

"Oh, good grief," I muttered, diving once again into a row. "Freaking Laurel and Hardy."

"He's going to have Simon's hide for all of this," said the other. "He told him to grab the mother. We're moving out of here."

I startled. I couldn't let that happen. If they took her somewhere else, she'd be lost to us. I didn't trust they wouldn't hurt her. Sebastian's patience was running out. My mother would become a liability instead of leverage.

Sneaking to the edge of the pallet, I crouched and waited until the men passed by. They weren't even pretending to search for me. I focused on the closest door. It was going to be my 'right' door. My emotions were certainly high enough to propel my door travel right into the *Ivanov Transport* offices.

"One, two...three!" I mouthed the words, bursting into the open space from between the rows of pallets on three. My sprint toward the door didn't go unnoticed as my shoulder bag jostled the contents inside, causing enough noise to catch the men's attention.

"Hey!" The yell followed me. I reached the door quickly and grabbed the doorknob. I didn't have any time to think about raising my energy for door travel. Instead, I simply pictured the surface of the desk in the receptionist's room. I saw the phone in my mind's eye and whisked through the door.

I ran into the receptionist's room and halted to a stop. "Good job, Emily," I breathed. "You didn't knock into a single thing."

The overhead lights in the offices were out, too. Everything was probably connected. A dim emergency light in the lobby cast a small glow into the room. The two phones sat side-by-side on the desk, black and tan. The black phone had buttons – it was probably the one used to ring the other offices. The tan one, buttonless, must be the one for the Empire's service.

I picked the receiver up and put it to my ear as I bopped the cradle with my other hand to activate the call. No static. I pressed on the cradle deliberately, depressing it fully before letting it raise back up on its own. Still nothing.

"Oh, come on," I moaned. I bounced the cradle up and down a few more times. It was useless. The phone didn't work. Maybe it was affected by the same circumstances as the lights. Ugh.

I sat down in the receptionist's chair, leaning on the desktop. I dropped my head into my hands, closing my eyes. Now what? Okay, I got this. I'll just door travel back to Lucie's, make the call, then come straight back here. Right. That's a good plan.

Tap-tap-tap.

Well, it *was* a good plan.

CHAPTER 21

Sebastian stood on the other side of the reception window tapping a knuckle against it. He did not look happy.

I glanced toward the door on my right.

"Don't even think about it, Emily," Sebastian warned through the glass. A moment later the door opened, and the same ol' Mr. Gunman stood in the doorway.

"Let's go," he said wearily, motioning with the gun. I obeyed, standing and moving back out into the hall. Sebastian waited for us in the lobby with two other Fringe members.

"Emily," he sighed. "I really want to believe you're brave instead of stupid."

"Yeah, a little bit of both," I answered. I wondered if Templeton had made his presence known. I prayed they didn't catch him, too.

Sebastian nodded. "With the scales tipping toward stupid. Take her downstairs to the loading docks. Keep the gun on her."

Our little party filed out onto the catwalk and down the metal stairs leading to the warehouse floor. I was led past the wall of loading docks to the other side of the building. We stopped about thirty feet from the stairs leading up to the floor where my mother was kept. Someone had located an emergency blackout lantern and it cast a sinister glow across the space.

"Alright," Sebastian called toward the catwalk, shining his flashlight upward. "Bring her out."

The door opened and Simon appeared, pulling my frightened mother with him. He roughly shoved her in front, pinning her against the metal railing.

Her face glowed under the flashlight's beam. Her wavy hair was loose, a wild mane falling around her shoulders. Her head swiveled back and forth as she frantically searched the group of people assembled below. She spotted me. "Emily!"

"Mom! Simon, let her go!" I made a move toward the stairwell and was blocked by a wall of Fringe. My eyes cut back to the dirty Salesman above. "I swear on everything holy, Simon. If you do anything to her, I'll rip your beating heart out of your chest and force it down your throat."

"Emily," Sebastian began, "you don't want to see your mother hurt, do you? Simon has a lot to make up for. He's been almost useless this whole time. Still, with two killings under his belt, I'm guessing one more won't matter as much... If it comes to that." I froze as Sebastian walked in a circle around me.

"What do you mean?" My eyes tracked him. Long gone was the blinding smile, the 'let's be friends' façade. In its place, a dangerous, hungry animal.

"Simon had one job – just one. Find Emily Swift's mother and keep her in one place until we could arrange for her detainment. One job, that's it." Sebastian glanced up at the catwalk. The fake Rabbit named Simon rolled his eyes.

Sebastian continued, addressing him. "And you were so close, weren't you, Simon? Oh, sure, your methods for tracking the old woman were stupid – no one told you to try and be Emily's new buddy, to parade around like some damned Rabbit – but ultimately, despite your incompetence, you caught up to Lydia. You found her and almost had her that night." Sebastian sneered as he held up his thumb and forefinger, keeping them a half inch apart. "So close."

I swallowed. "What night, Sebastian?"

Sebastian abruptly turned away from Simon and faced me, the flashlight beam crossing my face. "He followed your mother Saturday night in Vue after the scene with Peti Kis. She kept slipping away from him, getting lost in gallery after gallery in the crowds. At the last minute, he thought he got lucky. She went back to Peti's gallery, knocking on the front door. She'd left her purse behind in the earlier commotion. Apparently, she didn't notice until after the gallery had closed. Kind of flighty."

"She's not flighty." He didn't get to call my

mother names. My face was hot. I defended her. "She's a caring person who focuses more on the happiness of others."

"Is that so?" He looked back up at his hostage. "Simon followed her around the building to the back door. Whoever used it last didn't shut it all the way when they left. She just slipped right in."

I lifted my gaze. One of Sebastian's men kept his flashlight focused on the evil Salesman and my mother. Simon held onto her from behind, his hands clamped tightly around both upper arms. A terrified expression covered her face. "Simon went into the art gallery after her, didn't he?"

"He saw an opportunity," Sebastian said. "Unfortunately, Lydia wasn't alone. Peti was still there. He confronted your mother and they argued. He threatened to call the guards. She left and Peti made to go as well. Simon didn't want to get stuck in the gallery – especially if Peti was going to set an alarm – so he made a break for it."

"I don't understand," I said. "He killed Peti to get out of the gallery?"

"In a way, yes. Killing Peti wasn't part of the plan. It was the byproduct of a poorly executed abduction." Sebastian frowned at the floor. "I'm still extremely disappointed in you, Simon. You've drawn a lot of attention to our objectives."

"It's not my fault," Simon protested from above. "I was trying to get out of there, but I bumped into one of the tall cocktail tables and a champagne glass tipped off. The gallery owner heard it break on the floor."

"And that's when – what do you call him again? Speedy?" Sebastian picked up the story. "That's when 'Speedy' made the split decision to muscle his way past Peti. They wrestled, and in the chaos, he grabbed that glass knife sculpture and stabbed Peti. Bloody mess, wasn't it Simon?"

Simon shrugged. "Bystanders get killed in battles."

I swallowed the bile threatening to invade my mouth. Peti wasn't Simon's only victim. "And what about the female Rabbit in the alley? What was that, sport?"

Simon snorted. "That one was hardly an innocent bystander. She'd been following me. She came at me in the alley. Told me she knew I wasn't a Rabbit. She saw the blood and the stupid glass knife in my hand. She threatened me, said she'd tell the Empire guards."

"So, you killed her, too." I cut my eyes to my mother. Her eyes shut and she turned her head to the side as if she could shut out Simon's story.

"She put up more of a struggle than Peti," Simon grinned. "Filthy Rabbits know how to fight. It felt good to watch her drop, like a little gutted animal."

The image overwhelmed me, and I bowed my head. I felt the rage building inside. "You'll pay for all of this."

"Well, now that we've enjoyed a bedtime story," Sebastian interrupted. "Let's get back to it, shall we? I have a new idea. Did I promise not to hurt your mother?"

My head shot up, horrified. "Don't touch her, Sebastian."

"Please," he held up a hand. "I'm more creative than that. What I am going to do is bring your mother down here and we're going to play a little game."

Whatever Sebastian planned it was going to be very bad. His face remained unsmiling. He snapped his fingers. "Let's get a move on it, Speedy Simon."

Just as Simon gave my mother a little push toward the stairs, the glowering face of Templeton emerged from the shadows beside him. I gasped, drawing everyone's attention back to the catwalk. Before Simon knew what danger lurked a hair's breadth away, Templeton slapped him up the side of his head. He jumped in surprise, letting go of my mother and spinning around toward his attacker. My mother gripped the railing as she stumbled.

"Mom!" I yelled, my chest seizing in fear. And then, we all watched Templeton shove Simon backward over the railing, his body falling a story and a half headfirst into a bunch of boxes. He crashed into them, disappearing. I winced at the muffled thud.

"Emily, Emily!" my mother cried from above as she cringed, one hand held up to keep an advancing Templeton back. Her other hand still clung to the railing. He slowly reached for her. I could see his lips moving.

"Do NOT let him take her!" Sebastian roared. Men charged for the stairs.

"No!" I shouted as I started after them. "Templeton! Templeton! Get her out of here!"

Templeton finally snagged my mother by the wrist, yanking her delicate frame toward him. The catwalk shook under the pounding feet of the Fringe as they clamored up the stairs. My pursuit was thwarted when I was jerked backward as Sebastian caught me by the hair.

"You're not going anywhere," he snarled, wrapping my hair in his fist.

My eyes never left my struggling mother and Templeton. She continued to cry for me, holding her hands out. Templeton's eyes darted from the approaching Fringe to me, gnashing his teeth.

"Go!" I screamed, waving an arm and writhing as Sebastian savagely shook me. "Templeton, go!"

Templeton yelled something and reached for the door behind him – the same door I'd passed through earlier in the moonlight. My mother pulled free as his hand brushed the doorknob. Lightning fast, he snatched her back, his arm around her waist. The door swung open, and I watched as Templeton and my mother were sucked backward, the door slamming shut as they disappeared.

The first Fringe member to reach the spot where they once stood threw open the door and looked down the hall. He turned back around and looked down at Sebastian, shaking his head.

Templeton and my mother were gone.

Sebastian twisted my head toward him. His face was close to mine. Hot, wet breath touched my skin.

"This is very bad for you, Emily," he said softly.

❊ ❊ ❊

This was it; this was the moment I was going to die. No final goodbye to Jack, no last words to my friends. I wouldn't even get to tell Templeton I didn't hate him – *much*.

But my mother was safe, that I knew.

Sebastian paced a short tract back and forth, dragging me along by the hair. I stumbled as I worked to keep up with his strides.

"It didn't need to be so hard!" he thundered. "The mother walks right into the Empire, pretty much puts a damn spotlight on herself the whole time she's gallivanting back and forth, and no one can catch up with her! How many men are in this room? How many?"

"Thirteen?" A man to the right guessed. "Fourteen if you count Simon."

Sebastian slammed to a halt, shoving me forward toward the floor. I stumbled and fell hard, my palms slamming into the concrete and my shoulder bag swinging wildly from my shoulder. The snap popped open, and my top hat and The Book slid out across the floor. I chased after them on my hands and knees, losing my shoulder bag in the process. One of the men stepped in front of me, stopping me in my tracks.

I stared past the man's legs at The Book.

Sebastian stormed by, picking up my top hat. He shook it, the purple feather waving. He made a face. "What. Is. This?"

I blinked slowly and lifted my chin. Contempt filled my whole body. "It's a fish, genius."

The men around us snickered and Sebastian reacted by holding out my hat and kicking it like a football. It tumbled out of sight. "Everyone thinks she's funny? Who wants to join her on the floor?"

No one spoke.

"Now, where were we? Right. Simon had one job. One old lady to grab – an easy trade. The mother for the Crimson Stone. Right here, in our own backyard." Sebastian walked over and squatted beside me. "One easy job. No one even had to be hurt. We could've made a trade. I'm reasonable."

Past Sebastian, I saw one of the men pick up The Book. My heart dropped.

"Hey, Sebastian?"

"What?" he spat. He rose to his feet and pointed in the direction of where Simon had fallen. "Someone go and drag that failure's body over here. If he's not dead, I just might shoot him."

Two men scurried out of sight.

"Sebastian, look at this," the other man tried again.

"What?" Sebastian whirled around.

The man held up The Book. "It's her journal."

Sebastian swiped it out of the man's hands. The scowl on his face grew more curious as he examined The Book. He stroked the lock with a fingertip, shifting his gaze to me. "This isn't your journal, is it Emily?"

I wasn't going to kneel a moment longer. I climbed to my feet. "It's mine. Give it back to me, Sebastian."

He took in a deep breath through his nose, pressing his lips together. He shook his head before he spoke. "No. This is not your journal. It's too old. You've only been a Salesman for less than a year. This is Daniel Swift's."

The men around me began talk in hushed tones at the mention of my father. I clenched my fists. "There's nothing in it for you, Sebastian. It's only a memento leftover from my father."

Sebastian stroked the hair on his chin. "Interesting choice of words. I wasn't yet a Salesman when he was killed, but I heard there was not much leftover at all."

The words struck me in the chest, driving me back a step. "You're not even fit to be in the same room as his memory, you piece of crap."

"What would you give for this journal, Emily? Hmm? Maybe the Crimson Stone? Surely there are secrets in here you wouldn't want me to see." Sebastian waved The Book at me. "What's it worth to you?"

Even if I were willing to give Sebastian the Crimson Stone in trade, I wasn't that naïve. He'd keep both. "No deal."

He barked a laugh and tossed The Book back to the man who originally picked it off the floor. "Break the lock. Let's see what's in there while we're waiting on – *ah!* There he is. Simon. Speedy. Speedy Simon."

The Book went with the man into the shadows. My thoughts swirled as I focused in the same direction. Hide, disappear, hide it all. I closed my eyes, desperately driving my energy out into the darkness beyond the lantern light.

A man pushed a disheveled Simon toward Sebastian. He was limping and holding his left arm at a weird angle. He glared at me and blurted out: "Killing that Rabbit was easy. No loss to the Empire."

"What kind of a sick maniac are you?" I made it three steps toward him before I was pulled back by one of Sebastian's men. I twisted from the thug's grasp but didn't advance toward Simon a second time.

"You want to know what gets me the most?" Simon hissed, his face screwing up in ugliness. "You and your damned Rabbits. Rabbit-this, Rabbit-that. Where's Rabbit? Did you talk to Rabbit? We've been breaking into their network for months. Months! And I still can't figure out who is who! Rabbits are impossible to find, but they come through that station. I knew it was only a matter of time before I found some and I was going to infiltrate them for the Fringe! They have all this access to Empire information we need. But you showing up in Anwat when you did was a gift, you know that? My lucky day! Who walks up to me at the station? Emily-freaking-Swift herself! I couldn't believe it. It was a sign."

Simon's eyes were wild. "Sebastian didn't like my plans to go undercover – but access to you? Suddenly I was an important part of the Fringe's work. I got to keep tabs on you while I tracked your mother. Do you know how much power I'd get if I brought Sebastian your mother and ultimately the Crimson Stone?"

Simon's deranged diatribe was interrupted by a man handing The Book back to Sebastian. He shook his head grimly, sneaking a quick look at me before stepping away.

Sebastian opened The Book and strolled off to the side as he turned the pages, browsing. My stomach rolled. For once I was not going to think it couldn't get any worse.

Sebastian redirected his path until he stopped in front of me, The Book shut. The charismatic smile had returned. "The pages are all blank."

I dropped my head forward, blowing out a relieved breath.

"This book is spelled," Sebastian said, shaking his head. "I shouldn't have expected otherwise."

I met his gaze, failing to suppress a tiny smile. "Sorry, I can't help you with that."

He shrugged. "Oh, I'll find someone to remove it." He held The Book out toward his men. "Someone take this." The Book was carried off a second time. He clapped his hands together, the noise making everyone jump. "Now, where were we? Right, Simon's crazy, probably a liability, and you were going to tell me where you've hidden the Crimson Stone. We've moved past the point where I'm going to be nice, Emily. It's going to hurt you a lot now."

"Even if I had it and was willing to give it to you, you're not going to let me go so..." I lifted my hands and shrugged.

"That's not entirely true. What I might do is give you and Simon each a bat and let you fight it out. Winner walks." He lifted a finger. "After you give me the Crimson Stone."

"Let me have a go at her now," Simon said, coming closer, still favoring his arm. "I'll make her tell us."

I noticed several members of the Fringe behind Simon started to fidget, casting their eyes about the room. A few shifted and turned, peering into the darkness around them.

"You might get a turn," Sebastian answered. He reached out and stroked my cheek. I jerked back. "But I have some ideas on how to get the information I need. If Templeton also knows where the Crimson Stone is hidden like she claims, it might be fun to do something to his pet where he can witness the action. A little payback for his interference here today."

A sound of metal scraping metal reverberated from deeper in the warehouse. A chilling scurrying filtered out from the shadows. A couple of Sebastian's men started to back away. One coward turned abruptly and ran.

"What?" Sebastian asked, scowling. He dropped his hand. "What's going on with all of you? What's the matter?"

"Didn't you hear that?" asked one of the men who'd remained close. He was young. He pulled a small handgun from the inside of his coat. He swung it back and forth.

"Watch what you're doing!" shouted Sebastian. He jumped out of a possible line of fire. "What is wrong with you?"

"I think someone's here," said another man as he began to move toward a lit exit under the catwalk. "I don't like it, Sebastian."

Sebastian paused and listened. More scraping, swift shuffling beyond the glow from the lantern. His nostrils flared. Then, realization. He looked at Simon. "I wash my hands of you."

"What? What do you mean?" Simon was alarmed. Sebastian snapped his fingers, and the remaining men made a quick exit. They couldn't leave fast enough. "Wait? Where are you going? What's going on?"

Sebastian took one last look in my direction, his face a mask of frustration. He said nothing before turning away to seek a door to travel through.

I was just as bewildered as Simon, turning toward the confessed murderer. A moment later, I understood.

Have you ever glanced away from something, then back, and the picture had silently changed in a flash?

That is what happened next.

I blinked and realized we were surrounded by Rabbits. And they were terribly angry.

❊ ❊ ❊

"What the hell?" Simon yelped, spinning around and realizing an escape was no longer in the cards.

Men and women stood around us in a wide circle, Rabbit faces missing smiles. Hard lines and shadows replaced the friendliness I'd always found. One young man, he barely looked twenty, stood with a short two-by-four balanced on his shoulder. Another held a bat.

"What's happening?" Simon repeated, his voice squeaking.

"I think you're in a lot of trouble, Simon," I whispered. I was scared, too.

"Hold up." A familiar voice called out and my Rabbit stepped past his brethren and into the circle. He reached for me, touching my arm. "Are you okay?"

I nodded. My eyes roamed the space behind him and across the pale faces lit in the dim light. "Rabbit, what's going on?"

"Your mother, gone?"

"Templeton got her. She's not here. Rabbit..." I flinched as a couple of the Rabbits stepped closer. "What's going to happen?"

"You need to leave now," Rabbit said firmly, his eyes black, glittering as the clouds parted outside and the Full Moon cast one last beam through the window above the loading docks.

The female Rabbit who worked on the studio crew, the one who took Tara and me with her to that wonderful bonfire, appeared at Rabbit's side. Solemnly, she handed me my top hat.

Another man came forward with The Book in one hand, my shoulder bag in the other. My Rabbit took both, shoving The Book deep into the bag and rearranging contents so it sat snugly and safely at the bottom. Satisfied, he slid the strap up my arm and over my shoulder.

"Go home, Emily. You don't want to be here for this."

I backed away from the assembled Rabbits, my heart drumming wildly in my chest. The night air was suddenly thicker, angrier. I could smell it; this is what revenge tasted like. I bumped into a sawhorse as I moved, causing it to scrape against the concrete. A couple of young Rabbit faces turned in my direction, noses twitching. I risked a look at Simon. He stood in the center of the circle, gripping his arm and shaking.

"Don't leave me here, Emily!" He pleaded. "Don't leave me to them!"

I looked away, seeking my Rabbit one last time. He no longer paid me any attention; his focus on Simon – the fake Rabbit – in the middle of the circle. He pushed up his shirtsleeves, his upper lip curling back, threatening. He advanced on Simon.

Jolted, I spun and ran for the closest door – any door! Seconds before I reached one, I ventured a look back over my shoulder, my eyes drawn upward to the catwalk. I saw Templeton, leaning against the railing, watching the scene below.

❉ ❉ ❉

I didn't go straight home. Instead, I followed my gut instinct and door traveled straight into Anne Lace's apartment back in Kincaid. There, sitting on the living room couch with Anne's arm around her, was my mother.

She was safe.

When I entered, her tear-stained face turned up and a wailing cry burst out of her tiny frame. She flew into my arms and we hugged, rocking back and forth. I wrapped my arms tightly around her and begged her to never go wandering again. When I finally released her, I ran my hands over her arms looking for signs of injury. There were marks on her wrists, bruising from the Fringe or Templeton, I did not know. I explained we needed to take her to the hospital.

Mom refused to go, shaking her head adamantly. I could not force her, and she assured me she was fine. Mainly, she was left in the locked room by herself the whole time she was at the warehouse. Her captors gave her sandwiches and water, and she had a cot and a bathroom with a door. The worst part, she told us, was when she was first grabbed. They bound her hands and blindfolded her. She didn't know why she was taken. She was terrified. My stomach tied itself in knots the more I learned.

My mother also met Sebastian. When she was brought to the warehouse, he came to her room. He asked if I'd ever told her about a gemstone called the Crimson Stone, if she knew where he could find it. Since my mother knew nothing about the Stone, she couldn't tell him anything. She said he believed her and promised she'd be let go just as soon as I gave him what he wanted. And then he left.

Anne spent a long time examining my mother as she spoke, her fingers gently moving Mom's arms this way and that, before searching my mother's hands. She kneeled beside her and felt along her ankles. Back on the couch, she lifted my mother's fading strawberry-blond hair and checked her neck; her hand ran up and down her back. While Anne inspected her, she whispered little incantations, a low murmur under my mother's recounting. At one point, my mother stopped and looked up with her trusting blue eyes. She asked Anne if she was the tea lady Daniel knew. Anne just stroked my mother's hair and asked if she'd like a cup. My mother nodded. A lump grew in my throat and I turned away before she could see new tears on my face.

My phone battery was long dead, so Anne gave me hers to message Tara. I texted my friend, letting her know we were safe at Anne's. She replied immediately with a message of her own that she was on her way over.

I took Anne's phone into the bathroom and sat down on the side of the tub. Taking a deep, shuddering breath, I called Jack. He answered immediately. When I told him it was me and where I was, he told me to stay on the line, that he was coming to get me… To not hang up. To not leave Anne's.

To please stay.

CHAPTER 22

Why did I look for my mother at Anne's? Why not Tuesday's? Why not at my mother's home or even travel back to my home with Jack? Because I knew deep down Templeton would take my mother someplace safe, someplace outside the Empire and to someone he seemed to trust... To someone who admitted a 'true fondness' for Templeton.

Templeton door traveled with my mother wrapped in his arms and delivered her to Anne's. He stayed long enough to help my Mom to the couch, to make sure she was okay, and to rouse Anne from her bed. He told Anne I was still in Matar and that he needed to go back.

And just like that, he whipped out through Anne's apartment door. He was gone.

❖ ❖ ❖

After I left Lucie's to search for the warehouse district in Matar, Templeton was the first person to read the note I'd left behind for Rabbit. I know this because Lucie told me when she came to Kincaid a week after I'd brought my mother home. In fact, Lucie described how she found Templeton standing in her kitchen when she returned from the Full Moon ritual, my note in his hand.

Before she could react at the intrusion, Templeton yelled at her for leaving me 'unattended' and ranted on for a good minute or two about my foolishness before she slapped him down with a hiccupping spell.

That's right, Lucie gave Templeton the hiccups by casting a little witchy spell.

Templeton was furious, but he did tell her between spasms the symbol was a logo for *Ivanov Transport*. The Matar company owned a slew of warehouses in an industrial part of the city. Before he fled Lucie's kitchen, he ordered her to make sure Rabbit knew where to go – and then threatened he'd be back to discuss her 'playing around with spells' another time. I doubled over with laughter when Lucie imitated Templeton. I told her she could name her price if she taught me how to cast the same spell so I could see Templeton in action for myself.

After Tara arrived in Kincaid, she set up camp at Blackstone's using the resources the Record Keeper could access to try and track down my mother and me. Anne shared the message from Lucie explaining I was in Matar, and she agreed to escort Jack to the city to catch up with me if I wasn't back soon.

Since Tara returned, she's spent a lot of time in Blackstone's library, learning more about the

Empire. Now that she's seen this other world, it's a whole new set of books to care for and facts to learn. Handsome, her bonfire Rabbit, has enjoyed takeout with Tara in the back room of *Pages & Pens* on several Friday nights. As far as I know, Templeton has not.

Tara has also switched from *Rooster Broo* to *Rooster's Hard Cider*. She contends that slogan is much better.

My mother's cousins, Major Muses Minerva and Aster, came for a short visit before splitting off to California and New York City. We celebrated my mother's return with a big dinner at her home in Western New York. Minerva was curious if 'that local football team' ever won a Super Bowl. My mother smiled into the cup of tea she held and said next season might be their year.

Lydia McKay Swift, the Meta Muse, wasn't sharing all of her secrets.

In music news... *Rhino Vomit* shot up the charts with a new number one hit, a Death Metal ballad called *Lydia*. It's catchy.

My mentor, Jo Carter, won big. I'm happy to report it had less to do with her fighting prowess in the streets of Vue and everything to do with her big brain and high standards. This extraordinary Senior Salesman was tapped to join the Salesman Court as a Junior Justice. This was a big deal. In one year, she would be a full-fledged

Justice serving as one of the leaders of the Empire. She would fill Petrovich's empty seat on the bench.

And speaking of all that law-and-order stuff, the attorneys Jo brought in to help my mother produced a sound alibi for her on the night of Peti's murder. This, combined with the charges against Simon, meant my mother was a free woman. The Empire very clearly stated that she did not need to return to sign any final documents. Everything could be resolved at Blackstone's house. Justice Spell was happy to make the trip to Kincaid.

While Spell was at Blackstone's, she also suspended my door traveling permissions. There would be a review before I'd be allowed to door travel at all. I wasn't even allowed to travel with a Senior Salesman. I was officially grounded.

Pfft.

I learned from Blackstone that Simon, a/k/a Speedy, was delivered to the front steps of the Empire guard station in Matar the night we escaped. He was unconscious and savagely beaten. A note pinned to the front of his bloody shirt stated the disgraced Salesman was the Peti Kis murderer. The last line read: *He killed the Rabbit in the alley, too. Don't forget.*

The driver who ran Blackstone's housekeeper, Patricia Pickelsimer, off the highway remains at large.

I learned Sebastian St. Michel is from an old-moneyed family. They enjoyed a lot of prestige and power in the Empire, although none of the Salesmen from his family ever served on the Court. They 'influence' leaders rather than rule. Turns out Sebastian's never been linked to the Fringe. That is the Empire's official position. I asked Blackstone what Justice Spell thought about that, since now we knew the truth. He told me Spell's position was the Empire's position.

I haven't seen or heard from Rabbit since the night in the warehouse.

I was scared by what I saw, but I was more worried than anything. I remembered Rabbit's warning about the price paid by those going to Nisha for help. I feared for him, for what she'd take in return.

And then there's my mother... She recovered from the trauma a lot faster than most people would. Maybe this is part of her own power as a magical being. However, her pretty strawberry-blond hair finally faded fully to white. Despite it all, she was back to her shiny self in a matter of days. At first, I didn't want to let her out of my sight. In fact, I tried to convince her to move in with Jack and me and the Furious Furballs. That was not going to happen. Still, she said she'd consider moving to Kincaid, but reminded me she loved her home and that's where 'we all used to live.' I understood.

I asked her what happened that night when Templeton snatched her off the catwalk, when he pulled her through the door. I picked my words carefully. I knew now my mother knew about the Empire, but what did she know about Salesmen? About what we could – and supposedly couldn't – do? She seemed confused and could only say the man took her to Anne's, that it was very fast. She told me he was concerned about her and promised I would be okay, too. He wasn't like the others in the warehouse, she said. Was this man my friend?

I told her no, but when I saw him again, I'd thank him for helping her get back home.

So, what about the Crimson Stone?

We learned through Blackstone that Justice Spell's piece of the Crimson Stone went missing, but the Empire was keeping the information 'hush-hush.' I worried the Fringe's reach into the Empire's leadership was greater than I'd previously thought. And now it seemed they finally got a piece of the Stone. That meant they knew the Crimson Stone was in three pieces. I pictured Sebastian. Who in the Empire's leadership had he influenced or blackmailed into helping him? Blackstone had little information, of course. Spell only told him there was no evidence of a break-in and no security cameras showed the theft. I told Blackstone it had to be an inside job.

A missing Templeton kept my piece of the Crimson Stone. I knew from the beginning he wouldn't give it back to me, but I did entertain the fantasy.

And yet, the universe, which generally seems to hate me and seeks to punish me, finally took pity on the disobedient Salesman, Emily Swift. It came in the form of a surprise gift.

A couple of weeks after returning home, I finally cleaned out my bulging shoulder bag – wadded up dirty clothes shoved in a side pocket, a couple of food wrappers, some crumpled paper. I was just about to toss some of the garbage away when I realized one of the balled-up papers seemed to be wrapped around something hard.

I set my bag down and gently pulled the paper open. Inside was a small package, a lumpy packet of black tee-shirt material tied with twine. I set it aside and smoothed the crumpled paper. A note from Rabbit was scrawled in pencil. He'd written:

E. – The Tortoise is yet to be found. In the meantime, if Templeton has a piece of the Stone, so should you. – R.

Holding my breath, I untied the twine and unwrapped the soft cloth, revealing a piece of the Crimson Stone. I stroked the gem's surface with my fingertip and watched as a tiny tongue of crimson fire appeared inside. I shook my head, smiling.

Rabbits... They bring good things to the Empire.

And sometimes, they give them to me.

(Go to the Epilogue...)

EPILOGUE

Templeton stepped from the doorway and eased into the candlelit room. White candles, some tall, some wide and short, flickered around him. A thin, silver cloth hung over a large mirror to his right, the flames reflected eerily in the glass through the fabric. He removed his top hat, long fingers hovering over the brim as he searched for a piece of lint.

"You've returned earlier than I expected, Templeton." A deep female voice slid into the room from behind. "I'm pleased. The night is young."

He continued to examine his hat. He didn't look up as Nisha brushed by his arm. "I left the Rabbits to their work."

Nisha turned, facing him as she reached forward. Long fingernails grazed the bottom of Templeton's chin as she lifted, compelling him to meet her gaze. Dangerous black eyes stared into his faded blue ones. "Fánaí was there?"

"Yes," he answered. He flinched as she dragged a fingernail in a line from his chin down the center of his neck.

"I saw him in Vue," Nisha remembered, drawing away. A frightening smile played about her lips as they parted. Her tongue darted forward, tasting the upper one. She glided her fingers back and forth through a candle's flame, watching it sway. "I liked seeing him again. He spoke to me."

Templeton didn't reply.

Nisha continued. "I see he protects her, this Salesman."

"He was loyal to her father." Templeton watched the Priestess warily. She was his height in her bare feet. Her shapely figure was hidden under a shimmering, silken robe. It draped over her curves and skimmed her ankles. Her long, midnight black hair caught the candlelight's glow as she swayed.

"Hmm, yes." She continued to bat the flame back and forth with her fingers. "And she is gone now? She found her mother and they escaped? No more Emily Swift?" Her fingertips surrounded the candle's wick, snuffing the flame out.

The Salesman's nostrils flared. The acrid scent of the extinguished flame burned the air. "She's no longer in the Empire."

"You are here to pay your debt."

"I am." Templeton's jaw twitched.

Another small smile. "Then kneel," she commanded softly.

Gritting his teeth, John Templeton lowered to his knees. "One year."

"That was the agreement," Nisha answered.

She swept closer, the heady scent of her perfumed skin wafting around him in the night air. Her hands drifted to the sides of his face, cupping his cheeks and tilting his head so he was forced to look up at her. Her black eyes clouded with a milky mist. He felt the cold chill flowing from her palms and under his skin, crawling down his neck and through his body. He tensed.

"Don't resist me, Templeton," she warned.

"One year," he replied, feeling his power sink under the weight of Nisha's magic.

"One year." She threw back her head, her long neck bared as incantations from an old language poured from her lips calling to the Full Moon above Matar.

Templeton's body shook as the remaining energy drained from his body. He gripped the sides of Nisha's robe as his world came to a shuddering stop. He rested his damp cheek against her thigh and trembled.

Nisha stroked the top of his head, her fingers running possessively through his hair as he panted at her feet. After a moment, she pulled away, slipping across the room. Her figure blended into the dark as she moved out of the candlelight's reach. A rustle of silk puddled to the floor...

(*Doors Wide Open*, coming in 2021...)

ACKNOWLEDGEMENTS

I am incredibly fortunate to have a loving husband who encourages me daily to work my craft. To my Gordon, thank you for listening, dreaming, and cheering me on every step of the way. You are my greatest love.

My gratitude to Jill Arent Franclemont (website located at Jill-Elizabeth.com) is unending. When you're a writer and you find the reader/writer who totally gets your humor, understands your story, cares about your characters as much as you do, and also says, *Sure, I'll help!* when you ask – you know you've won the friendship lottery.

To my readers: YOU are making my dreams come true when you buy and read my books. As an independent, self-published author, reaching new audiences relies a lot on word-of-mouth. To those who tell others about my books, thank you. It means so much. To those who take the time review my book on Amazon and Goodreads - THANK YOU!

And finally, to my @WriterTracyBrown Instagram writing community friends... thank you for making me feel welcome. I am humbled!

FIND T.L. BROWN ONLINE

Website and Updates

Visit WriterTracyBrown.com to learn more about the Door to Door Paranormal Mystery series and to connect with the author in all of her social media channels.

Sign-up for the Door to Door Mystery Series Newsletter.

T.L. Brown Insiders Group (Facebook)

You are invited! If you like to have FUN when you read, this is the group for you! We talk about reading, new stories, and upcoming books. Get previews and enjoy author videos.

Join: Facebook.com/Groups/TLBrownInsiders

T.L. Brown on Goodreads and Instagram

Follow on: www.Goodreads.com/TLBrown and @WriterTracyBrown

BOOKS IN THIS SERIES

Door to Door (**Book One**)
First in series published in October 2020!

Seventeen years after Emily Swift's father died, a door is opened to a new world, an Empire led by peculiar men and women called Salesmen – transporters of magical items. These Salesmen have the unique ability to travel from place-to-place, and even world-to-world, simply by stepping through the "right" door. Now that Emily is thirty, it turns out that she can "door travel" too, stumbling unplanned into kitchens, bathrooms, and alleyways as her connection to the Salesman Empire is revealed.

Fueled by the cryptic notes and sketches in her father's journal, Emily discovers the real reason behind his death: he was targeted and assassinated by the Fringe, a terrorist group of rogue Salesmen.

Through the Door **(Book Two)**
*Relationships tested, friendships built,
secrets revealed, sacrifices made...*

Salesman Emily Swift is back – *and so is Templeton!* After learning about her supernatural abilities and finding the Crimson Stone, thirty-year-old Emily Swift returns home to Kincaid to rebuild a normal life with her boyfriend. As she struggles to get a handle on her "door traveling" energy, a strange warning squawks from her car radio: a rogue, terrorist group called the Fringe is still watching her.

Before she can figure out if the message is from a friend or foe, Emily's quirky mother, Lydia, goes missing – and resurfaces in the Empire! As Lydia travels from city to city in this peculiar world, a wake of chaos is created. Add the murder of a hated art critic and a kidnapping into the mix, and things go from bad to worse. The Fringe believes Emily knows where the magical Crimson Stone is hidden, and they'll stop at nothing to get their hands on it.

Friends Tara and Rabbit join Emily as they race against the Fringe to catch up with Emily's wandering mother. Will Emily's nemesis, the mysterious Templeton, join her in rescuing Lydia? What will it cost her? Is the price too high?

***Doors Wide Open* (Book Three)**
Coming in 2021!

Emily Swift faces her biggest challenges yet in this fast-paced third installment from T. L. Brown.

ABOUT THE AUTHOR

T. L. Brown is the pseudonym for the author who writes the Door to Door Paranormal Mystery Series. She was born in snowy Western New York where she developed a love of reading and writing. She holds a Bachelor of Arts from the University of Pittsburgh in History - Political Science.

After college, she moved to Rochester, New York and began to write a story about an average thirty-year-old woman who found herself caught between two worlds: the known one and a new, often dangerous place known as the Salesman Empire. That character became Emily Swift.

Ms. Brown now lives with her husband in the beautiful Finger Lakes of New York State dreaming up new stories and quirky characters that make life all the more interesting. She believes that magic exists; you just need to look in the right places.

Made in the USA
Columbia, SC
07 October 2021